Praise for

In Need of a Good Wife

"*In Need of a Good Wife* is as wonderfully candid as it is epic. Kelly O'Connor McNees creates unforgettable heroines (and anti-heroines), and infuses dreams of the American West with fresh spirit, humor, and yearning. I love this novel so much!"
—Wendy McClure, author of *The Wilder Life*

"Reading *In Need of a Good Wife* is like going on a great adventure into the past. As you turn the pages, you'll find love, imagination, and a kind of charm I didn't know existed anymore. It's a wonderful book—sturdy and delicate all at once."
—Rebecca Rasmussen, author of *The Bird Sisters*

"You will fall in love with the brave, resourceful women in this utterly captivating novel . . . Kelly O'Connor McNees writes with warmth, drama, humor, and tenderness, of love, loss, and hope, and how happiness can be found in the most unlikely situations if you open your heart."
—Stephanie Cowell, author of *Claude & Camille*

"*In Need of a Good Wife* is a beautifully wrought story, every page bursting with poetry and adventure . . . A simply gorgeous book that will stay with you long after you read the last word!"
—Susan Gregg Gilmore, author of *Looking for Salvation at the Dairy Queen*

continued . . .

"The three central, compelling women of *In Need of a Good Wife* are each, in turn, terribly lost and deeply brave. I adored them and rooted for them in their struggles, worrying about them when life forced me to set the book down to eat, work, and sleep. I found it deliciously satisfying that the redemption I wished for each of them arrived in completely unexpected ways, taking both me and the characters by surprise."

—Katrina Kittle, author of *The Blessings of Animals*

"With graceful prose and historical settings that shine with vitality, *In Need of a Good Wife* is unforgettable."

—Kristina Riggle, author of *Keepsake*

"Rare is the book these days that captures my undivided attention, but this story enchanted me, reminding me of a time in my life when reading was a comforting adventure, and my hope was to fall in love with a book and its characters . . . McNees weaves a hopeful, compelling story of love and resilience so engaging it is impossible to put down."

—Robin Oliveira, author of *My Name Is Mary Sutter*

"*In Need of a Good Wife* is a thoroughly charming novel, written with a gentle wry humor and an eye for detail I found delicious. Clara, the gutsy heroine, is delightful, as are a number of the other characters, the good and the bad alike. Beautifully imagined, beautifully crafted: I absolutely loved it."

—Sandra Gulland, author of *Mistress of the Sun*

"Anyone who grew up on *Little House on the Prairie* will instantly fall in love with this book. Kelly O'Connor McNees brilliantly captures the hope and hardships of the American West, and has created a story destined to be a classic."

—Tasha Alexander, author of *Death in the Floating City*

"Vivid, generous, funny, and often quite moving, *In Need of a Good Wife* casts light on a little-known corner of American history—and the women (and men) who struggled to make their way in an unforgiving world."

—Joseph Wallace, author of Diamond Ruby

"McNees has written a warm, generous story . . . She combines vivid historical detail with such emotional accuracy that I was convinced I, too, needed to escape grimy post–Civil War Manhattan and make the long train journey to Destination, Nebraska . . . *In Need of a Good Wife* is a richly drawn portrait of a uniquely American experience; this novel is an absolute treasure."

—Nancy Woodruff, author of My Wife's Affair

The Lost Summer of
Louisa May Alcott

"A charming novel, grounded in scholarship and fact but relying on imagination for the romance and fun."

—Minneapolis Star-Tribune

"McNees gets the period details just right . . . *The Lost Summer* is the kind of romantic tale to which Alcott herself was partial, one in which love is important but not a solution to life's difficulties. Devotees of *Little Women* will flock to this story with pleasure." —The Washington Post

"A bittersweet, stirring debut novel . . ." —BookPage

"So compelling and well written that I hated to see it end."

—Historical Novels Review

"I gladly followed Louisa down McNees's path, enjoying it so much I couldn't turn the pages fast enough. For those romantics among you, it's a real keeper." —*Lincoln Journal Star*

"*The Lost Summer of Louisa May Alcott* provides a tale of romantic fiction that will have fans of *Little Women* falling in love with Alcott in much the same way they fell in love with Jo March . . . a wonderfully creative and innocently sweet story." —*Express Milwaukee*

"McNees deftly combines historic figures and documented aspects of Louisa's life with speculations about what might have been. Fans of *Little Women* may be first in line to read the novel, but the book will also appeal to others who enjoy historical romance." —*Library Journal*

"The line between fiction and biography is tight and well-balanced. This book is a must-read for anyone who grew up with a dog-eared copy of *Little Women*." —*Fine Living Lancaster*

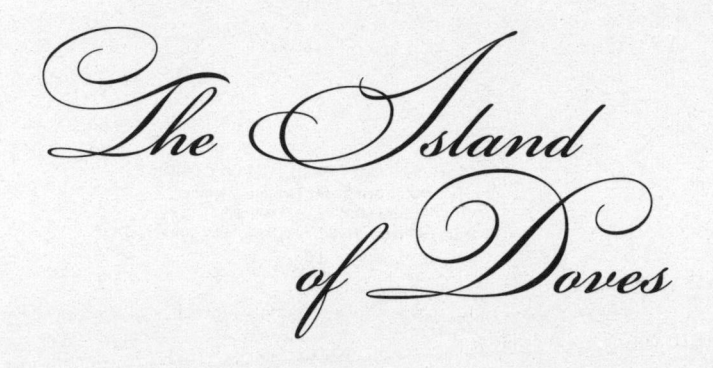

The Island
of Doves

Kelly O'Connor McNees

BERKLEY BOOKS, NEW YORK

THE BERKLEY PUBLISHING GROUP
Published by the Penguin Group
Penguin Group (USA) LLC
375 Hudson Street, New York, New York 10014, USA

USA • Canada • UK • Ireland • Australia • New Zealand • India • South Africa • China

penguin.com

A Penguin Random House Company

This book is an original publication of The Berkley Publishing Group.

Library of Congress Cataloging-in-Publication Data

McNees, Kelly O'Connor.
The island of doves / Kelly O'Connor McNees. — Berkley trade paperback edition.
pages cm
ISBN 978-0-425-26458-4
1. Kindness—Fiction.   2. Mackinac Island (Mich.)—Fiction.
PS3613.C58595I85 2013
813'.6—dc23
2013003492

PUBLISHING HISTORY
Berkley trade paperback edition / April 2014

PRINTED IN THE UNITED STATES OF AMERICA

10 9 8 7 6 5 4 3 2 1

Cover art by Trish Cramblet.
Cover design by Lesley Worrell.
Interior text design by Laura K. Corless.

For W. J., who turns the pages

. . . I love you as the plant that never blooms
but carries in itself the light of hidden flowers . . .

—Pablo Neruda, "Sonnet XVII"

Prologue

1816

When the warm spring air cracked the ice on Lake Huron, a sleepy fog began to curl across the water. Therese Savard was sitting beside the fire in her family's cabin on Mackinac Island, sewing the lining of a mitten, when she heard the knock. She stepped carefully around her nephew, Jean-Henri, who was stacking blocks on the floor, and put her finger to her lips to keep him quiet as she peeked out through the slight gap between the weathered door and the jamb, though she already knew who was knocking.

"Mademoiselle," Paul Pelletier called through the door. "Is Josette here?"

Therese winced. She had promised her sister Magdelaine that she would keep Paul away from their younger sister—*petit lapin*, they called Josette, their little rabbit—who was no longer little but a young woman, ready for marriage. The sisters were orphans now and had no one but each other to guard them from the world's dangers. Paul seemed determined to possess Josette. She had enjoyed the intensity of his attention at first, until she got a glimpse of his anger a time or two. Now she steered clear of him.

"Mademoiselle, I know you're in there," Paul said, his voice hardening. "I can hear you breathing."

Though the island was still blanketed in snow, the thaw had begun and spring would arrive in earnest in a few short weeks. Magdelaine would return and she would expect that Therese had kept her promise to keep the lovers separated. After all, Therese thought bitterly, Magdelaine was accustomed to giving orders. As a young widow with her late husband's money, Magdelaine enjoyed power and freedom as she carried on his work on the fur trade route, doing business with the Odawa hunters throughout the Michigan Territory, trading beaver and rabbit for guns and blankets and axes. Josette too had a kind of power: At seventeen she had beauty and a good many prospects for marriage. But because Therese had hesitated, had failed to commit to any of the few offers that had come her way years ago, the door to marriage was closed for her. Now, at twenty-seven, she found herself charged with the duties of a mere nursemaid. Magdelaine's husband had taught *her* to read and do figures, but no one had offered Therese the same instruction and now she felt too old to learn. The world had pushed her aside.

She sighed and opened the door. Paul stood with his arms crossed, his fur cap matted with dirt, and whiskers shadowing his jaw. He was a handsome man, Therese thought, despite being such a rough character. But why shouldn't he be rough? The fur trade was a dangerous business. A man could get rich on it, but he could get himself killed too. The strain of it must have weighed on Paul.

Therese smiled at him. "Welcome home." Perhaps he had chosen the wrong sister, Therese thought. After all, while Magdelaine and Josette shared their Odawa mother's tawny skin and thick black hair, Therese resembled their Quebecois father: pert nose, dark curls, and pale skin. No one could guess that she had Indian blood. Josette shied away from Paul's intensity, but it intrigued Therese. Maybe he needed a woman who was more French than Indian.

"You're looking well," she said to him, testing the waters. It was a lie, of course; he needed a bath and a good meal.

Paul sighed impatiently. "Josette—where is she?"

Therese's smile faded. She could see from his expression that she was a fool to think, even for a second, that he could see her as anything other than an obstacle in his path. Therese was invisible to him. So much had come easily to Magdelaine and Josette, but never to her. He would be angry when she told him where Josette was, but what of it? If her little sister was old enough for love, she was old enough for its consequences too. Josette had encouraged his affections, then changed her mind as a fickle young woman was wont to do. Why should Therese have to clean up her little sister's mess?

"She went with the Leveque boy to get firewood," Therese barked.

Paul's face darkened and without another word he stalked off toward the lane, leaving his packs on the ground in front of the cabin. Therese stood in the doorway and watched as he stepped onto his sled and shouted for the dogs to pull. The brief moment of satisfaction she felt was quickly replaced by a swell of panic when her gaze found the hunting knife that hung at Paul's hip.

"Paul—wait!"

He was out of sight by the time Therese shook off her paralysis and got her legs to work. She set out on foot through the snow in the wide tracks left by the sled's runners, and as each minute passed the terror clawed at her lungs, making it hard to breathe. Her heart pounded in her ears and all she could think was *faster, faster, faster.* But her feet were heavy—cold in her thin slippers—and she moved slowly, the way one moved in a nightmare.

When Therese finally made it to the other side of the island, what she saw brought her to her knees. Josette—her *petit lapin,* the one she had promised to protect—lay in the snow, a red cloud spreading out around her.

Part One

Flight

Chapter One

1835

Susannah Brownell Fraser, dressed only in her chemise and petticoats, stood before a three-paneled mirror in the morning light that filtered through the drapery. The dressmaker Madame Martineau held swatches of fabric to Susannah's bust and described the cuts and colors that would complement her fair complexion and red hair.

"The fashion this spring is a hem that goes all the way to the floor," Madame Martineau said as she draped a length of dark green gabardine from Susannah's waist. "It hides the shoes like this—very elegant."

Susannah sighed as she imagined wrestling with the impractical skirts. March still had the town in its chilly embrace. But when spring finally came to Buffalo, she would spend as many hours as she could walking in the woods to collect specimens for her herbarium, preparing the plants in her greenhouse, and recording their names and characteristics. The forest path was sometimes muddy and always narrow, and the rough-hewn worktable in the greenhouse likely to snag fine silk. But Edward had instructed his wife to order five new dresses in the latest styles, and Susannah had learned never to ignore Edward's instructions.

Madame Martineau measured out enough gabardine for a gown with gigot sleeves, the fabric ballooning out around Susannah's upper arms and tapering to tight cuffs at the wrist. Susannah said a silent thank-you that the bruise on her shoulder had lately yellowed to near invisibility. Next was sky-blue silk taffeta embroidered with nosegays for a dress with a high neckline that could be worn buttoned up or open with the collar turned back. After the taffeta came gauzy netting over red satin silk, then a soft cotton dress with piping and an elaborate lace tucker. The buttons would be mother-of-pearl or amber-colored glass; the hems would be wrapped in silk ribbon.

While Madame Martineau pinned and measured, Susannah's thoughts drifted over the horrors of the previous year, the way a bird might sail high enough above an acre of burning forest to avoid its smoke and heat. Had it been just twelve months since the March day when Edward first introduced himself to her father, Phillip Brownell? The simple handshake between two men who stood on the cobblestones of Amity Place in Manhattan City seemed to seal and hasten all of what would come next: Edward and Susannah's three-month courtship, their summer wedding, her parents' sudden death two weeks later when cholera surged through the city. Then, of course, Edward had discovered that her father had left nothing but debts for his new son-in-law. The Brownell money was gone.

By the fall Edward had sold her parents' row house and moved them to Buffalo, where his uncle helped him secure his first business loan. Soon Edward had established a brick-works and a construction company and was building houses at an astonishing pace. His ambition was matched—fueled, even—by his conviction that he had been robbed of what was rightfully his, the money his wife should have brought to their marriage. Though Susannah had had nothing to do with her father's financial woes, Edward needed someone to blame and she was the only Brownell left.

He had charmed her parents when he was seeking her hand, but now he revealed his true nature. Edward would tell anyone who asked that Susannah was merely clumsy. She fell down the stairs, put her hand too close to the fire, cut her lip on a chipped crystal goblet. She was careless and she was willful—the marriage was yet another trial for him to endure.

Only Susannah knew the terrible truth of it all, and there wasn't a soul on the earth to whom she could tell it. She had no family left, and Edward allowed her no friends of her own in Buffalo.

"My father *trusted* you," she said to him more than once, back when she still held out hope that he might come to his senses.

"Your father was weak," he had replied. "A fool."

But her father had never even struck her on the hand when she was a child to correct poor behavior. Susannah had not known this kind of violence. Sometimes, the morning after one of his episodes, Edward brought her a gift—a cluster of amaryllis bulbs with skins like parchment, a magnifying glass to use in her work with the plant specimens—though he never spoke of apology, never spoke at all, in fact, of what had taken place. And Susannah would wonder if she had misremembered. She felt betrayed by her own instincts, her own memories.

Madame Martineau was folding layers of fabric along Susannah's waist when she whispered, "These pleats are easily let out, should you find yourself with child." When she saw Susannah's expression change, she clucked her tongue. "You'd be amazed what one can hide under a well-constructed dress. You'll be out and about until quite close to your time."

Susannah stared at herself in the mirror and thought of the teaspoon of Queen Anne's lace seeds she chewed each morning to keep her womb barren. Edward, of course, had no knowledge that she was meddling with creation. She had learned the method from a pamphlet she found wedged between botany texts in a bookshop near Washington Square, just after Edward beat her for the first time, and she knew it would be her salvation. If she did not have a child, she thought, she had a better chance of escape. She had been hopeful then. Now she wondered whether she would spend the rest of her life in this hell. She was just twenty-three years old and Edward was just thirty—hell could last a long time.

After she and Edward first arrived in Buffalo, Susannah noticed the flowers—*wild carrot*, some called it—growing next to the roads into town. In the hottest part of the season the white flowers began to close, the long sepals pressing in on the spent blossoms from all sides like the ribs that held the fabric of a parasol in place. Susannah gathered as many clusters as she could in her apron each day, delivering them to a basket covered with a board in her greenhouse. Hiding them was unnecessary—Edward rarely came out to the greenhouse, and when he did, he merely scowled at her "collections."

Susannah wondered whether the method was an old wives' tale, but she was willing to try anything. She knew she understood anatomy better than Edward did. He viewed a woman's body as a mysterious vessel that did not operate according to reason or system. He would climb the stairs from his study where he worked into the late hours and nudge her awake, long after she had fallen into a deep sleep with a book splayed on her chest, and it never occurred to her to refuse him. Two flesh become one in marriage. As he heaved above her, rushing his seed to new places inside her he hoped to claim, he made the sounds of a laborer at his toil.

Once recently he had rolled off her and in a flash of vulnerability rested his cheek on her arm and asked, almost whimpering, "Do you think it will happen soon? For I should very much like to have a son."

And she smiled blandly and nodded, her heart so hard against him that even this show of tenderness couldn't make a difference. She saw in her mind a long line of the children they had never created, a row of cradles lined with fleece, a boy, then a girl, then two more boys, then three girls, stretching off into the distance like a road that no map had charted. She felt nothing for these babies, though it shocked her heart to admit it, and she knew she was flouting God himself.

"Are you all right, Mrs. Fraser? You look a little pale."

Susannah glanced at Madame Martineau, then took in

the peach frippery that encircled her own body. Beneath the soft layers of silk, the feminine rustle of the flounces cascading to the floor, Susannah could feel that her resolve remained lodged in her chest, as smooth and sure as a stone.

A large fire heated the room. "The room is a little too warm for me—that's all." Susannah felt herself sway on the platform.

"Indeed it is. But we are almost finished," Madame Martineau said as she handed the pieced peach silk to her seamstress, who hustled the bundle to the curtained back room where she and the other girls would work late into the night on the dresses. She gave Susannah the dress she had worn into the shop, then helped her lift it over her head and fastened the buttons at the back.

Susannah stepped down from the platform and Madame Martineau smiled at her. "We will send them to Hawkshill as soon as they are ready." Their house, a stately mansion Edward had purchased and renovated for them, was well known throughout Buffalo.

Outside the door of the shop, a paved footpath stretched along Pearl Street past the downtown shops. The chilly March air was a welcome relief and the sun shone brightly. The Saturday shoppers thronged about her, despite the cold. Two well-dressed women nodded to Susannah. "Good afternoon, Mrs. Fraser," they said in unison, stepping aside on the footpath to let her pass. The crowd seemed to part for her, each cluster of people deferring to her as the wife of one of the town's wealthiest men.

Since October had brought the frost, she had grown accustomed to work and solitude in her greenhouse, where winter never came. A woodstove boiled water that ran through pipes beneath the floor, and rows of steam-clouded glass panes captured and enhanced the weak light of the sun. Even now, in March, every surface was alive with the urgency of plants at work—climbing, rooting, stretching their petals. Grapevines crept like green insects up the glass walls, and the lavender fanned out in a muted purple cloud. On the highest shelf, orchid blossoms lolled, their leaves draping down like tongues. The most remarkable thing of all was that this life pulsed frenetically along in perfect silence. She heard only the occasional clank of the steam pipes.

Out on the street now with all the people coming and going, from the market to the theater to the saddle shop, the noise and motion were terrific. Carriage wheels crunched over snow-covered gravel in the road. A woman shouted after two cackling boys who had swiped a bun from her child's hand and taken off running; her little girl wailed. In front of a tavern, a tethered mare shied away from a terrier that nipped at its hooves. The horse's owner kicked at the little dog. "Get back, yeh!" he yelled.

Susannah stepped off the footpath and leaned against a brick wall, trying to breathe. Everything felt too loud, too bright. She smelled all at once coffee and smoked meat and manure and sugared almonds, and she tried not to gag as it all rushed in on her. She closed her eyes and inhaled, then willed herself to walk the last half mile back to Hawkshill. Edward wouldn't come home until the late evening; there were hours of peace to look forward to if she could make it the rest of the way home.

But just as she began walking again, determined to remain calm, she felt her breath catch in the bramble of her lungs. There *she* was again, the strange woman in the black gown and bonnet. Susannah had seen her three times in the last week alone: on the way home from church two Sundays in a row as she'd held Edward's elbow, and once as they walked to a party at the mayor's home. Always, the woman peered from behind a pillar or the side of a carriage, meeting Susannah's eyes but never revealing herself to Edward. She stood now on the opposite side of the street and watched Susannah, her hands clasped in front of her as if she were waiting. Two carriages shuddered by, then a wagon piled high with onions, translucent skins fluttering in the air as it passed. Finally the woman strode across the street to her.

"Good afternoon," Susannah said. "Is it more than a co-incidence that I seem to see you everywhere I go?"

"Mrs. Fraser," the woman said, her voice low. "Let us walk together for a bit."

She moved to touch Susannah's elbow, but Susannah moved it out of the path of her hand. "Who *are* you?"

"My name is Sister Mary Genevieve."

Susannah glanced at the simple woolen gown and white apron, the plain black bonnet tied beneath her chin. "You are . . . a Roman sister?"

The woman nodded. She seemed to be in her midforties and she had the long black lashes of a doe.

"I never knew there was a convent in Buffalo," Susannah said.

The sister nodded. "There is not, but I have been assigned at the rectory at the Lamb of God Church to assist Father

Adler." Susannah knew of the church—there was only one Catholic church in Buffalo, but one was more than enough, according to most people of her class.

People were stepping around them, each man tipping his hat, each woman bowing her head, all of them saying, "Good afternoon, Mrs. Fraser," then glancing curiously at the nun. Susannah could only imagine the explanations they were inventing, the rumors they might whisper about Susannah Fraser consorting with a Catholic woman in the street. The only thing Edward despised more than Papists was gossip, and what a woman might do to incite it.

"I see," Susannah said. She had walked past the church before, though she didn't know Father Adler or anyone associated with it. It was tucked away in the woods, little more than an old barn with a few colored-glass windows and a painted sign. "But what does that have to do with me?"

"I wanted only to make your acquaintance. Your hired girl, Marjorie, has often spoken of you." The nun held Susannah's gaze for a long moment. "And of your husband."

Susannah blinked at the nun, and the road seemed to lurch like a boat in a storm. *Oh, Marjorie*, Susannah thought. *What have you done?* If the girl had revealed anything about Edward, Susannah would pay the price.

"I have to go," Susannah said, still aware of the eyes of strangers.

Sister Mary Genevieve nodded. "Perhaps we will have the chance to meet again. If ever you find yourself in need of help, I hope you will remember me. My door is open to you."

Susannah turned away without responding, hurrying

down the road toward Hawkshill. Marjorie had each Saturday night off to spend with her husband in Black Rock, so for the few hours until Edward returned home, Susannah would be alone in the house. As she walked she tried to shake off the strange encounter and convince her rattled nerves that it would come to nothing. She decided to spend her evening doing the one thing that brought her peace: working in the greenhouse with her plants.

The greenhouse Edward had built for Susannah was to her both a heaven and a hell, a prison and an escape. At times she hated its stifling, fetid air and the clang of the steam in the pipes that kept it warm throughout the long winter. It was a mere *simulation* of the natural world, with the wildness edited out. For Edward it was a symbol of their wealth, a place for Susannah to host tea parties with the wives of prominent men. He had given her orchids and cloying over-blown lilies to tend because that was what a greenhouse was for: coaxing up temperamental plants designed for warmer climes, proving with each stretching stem, verdant tendril, and lush unfurling petal that nature was a pawn in man's ongoing game of dominance, that it could be tricked, cajoled, and compelled to bloom and flourish at the place and time of his choosing. A greenhouse was mind over matter, order over chaos, man over God. Susannah thought this false pride seemed dangerous in a place where enough snow could fall in twenty-four hours to bury a full-grown man.

But the greenhouse was, on the other hand, hers—the only place on the sprawling property where Edward seemed to let her alone. Perhaps he did so because he could watch her from a window in his study and confirm she was there inside the glass walls, potting and pruning and watering. Susannah was unsettled by the greenhouse's underlying purpose, by what Edward had intended it to do for—and *to*—her. But it allowed her to continue her work through the long winter. And there was nothing she treasured more than slipping her fingers into the mossy soil of her pots, collecting seeds from the surrounding woods and trying to understand by what mechanism or alchemy they transformed from a dry kernel to a sleek and thirsty living thing.

Susannah stood before the sturdy worktable inside the glass walls, her field notebook open to a blank page. A cluster of plumbago pencils in a chipped clay vase served as a bookend and held her collection of botanical guides upright where the corner of the table met the glass wall. As a girl of ten, Susannah had received Priscilla Wakefield's *An Introduction to Botany* for her birthday and read it until the pages were smudged and torn. From this book she learned how to build her herbarium, how to collect a complete botanical specimen: a plant's root, stem, leaves, flower, and fruit.

Back in New York Susannah had amassed a substantial collection of plants from the Hudson River Valley, but Buffalo was fresh terrain. It bordered fresh water instead of the sea, and its flora differed in interesting ways. She was counting the days until the first shoots emerged from the ground so that she might collect the spring flowers. First the anemone would appear, then the bloodroot, then the trillium.

* * *

On Sunday morning, Susannah sat at her dressing table brushing her hair. She saw Marjorie flit by in the hallway carrying a stack of folded linens, the starched strings of her apron trailing behind her.

Susannah's anxiety surged at the sight of her. Before, everything Edward had done to Susannah was sealed within the walls of Hawkshill, and at times she questioned her own mind, whether the things she remembered had actually taken place. It had never occurred to her that someone else saw these things too. The isolation of the last year had been nearly unbearable; to be seen, acknowledged, was a kindness that overwhelmed Susannah's heart. But she was also afraid and, because fear had controlled her for so long, furious at the thought of Marjorie's loose lips. Didn't she know what the consequences would be if Edward heard whispering about his private affairs?

Susannah held the silver hairbrush in midstroke, saw the curling letters of her monogram inverted in the mirror. "Marjorie," Susannah called to her.

The girl appeared in the doorway. She had a happy face, the round pink cheeks of a little girl's doll. "Yes, Mrs. Fraser?"

Susannah could think of no way to ask about the nun that didn't put her in league with Marjorie against her husband. "I was thinking of wearing the printed pink cotton tonight."

Marjorie hesitated and clasped her plump hands together. "Ah. Well, Mr. Fraser already has asked me to prepare the green silk for you to wear."

Susannah sighed. "I *abhor* that dress."

Marjorie bit her bottom lip, then giggled. "To be honest,

ma'am, I feel the same way about it. The fabric is so delicate! Every time I press it, I say the Ave Maria hoping not to scorch it."

"Oh, I wish you *would* scorch it." Perhaps, Susannah thought, she had misunderstood the nun, or perhaps the woman was merely a lunatic who had made up a wild tale she had no way of knowing was true. Marjorie had never been anything but kind and loyal since the day she came to Hawkshill.

The maid stepped behind her and took the brush, then began to sweep it through Susannah's hair with gentle strokes. "The green silk it will be, then," Susannah said. "For Mr. Fraser always has what he wants. And always will."

Marjorie paused her brushing and let her eyes rest on Susannah's in the mirror for a moment. She opened her mouth, then closed it, as if she reconsidered her words. She began to braid her mistress's hair.

"Perhaps," Marjorie said. "For now."

That night the Frasers hosted a Sunday dinner to celebrate the appointment of Nathaniel Root to the position of city attorney. When Wendell Beals, the chief manager of Edward's construction business, arrived, Marjorie led him into the parlor, where Edward and Susannah were waiting with Nathaniel. Edward poured champagne into four glasses and proposed a toast.

"To the future of the city of Buffalo," he said, his arm outstretched as he nodded to each of the men. He twisted his mouth into a sly grin. "To be created in our image."

As the men chuckled and drank, Marjorie nodded to Susannah from the doorway of the dining room.

"Why don't we take our places at the table," Susannah said. "The meal is nearly ready."

They made a quiet procession into the dining room and took their seats at the grand table.

"Beals," Edward said as they settled into their chairs. "How many houses did we build in the fall?"

"I believe the number is twelve, sir, not counting those begun in August." Susannah was fond of Wendell, a round man in his fifties with a fringe of hair encircling the bare dome of his scalp. He had been a midlevel clerk in a Buffalo bank before Edward met him and offered him a promotion. The sudden change in fortune seemed not to have changed Wendell. Susannah imagined that he had always walked with the same humble stoop, had always dabbed his brow with a crisp handkerchief. She supposed this gentleness was the very thing that drew Edward to him in the first place. Wendell made a solicitous subordinate and never questioned Edward's decisions.

Edward turned to Nathaniel. "Well. What do you think of that?"

Nathaniel seemed to choose his words carefully. As city attorney, he was the custodian of the laws of the county. He couldn't think only of profit but had to imagine its potential consequences too. "I think it is remarkable. I hope that you will be able to sell all those houses."

"We don't deal in hope, Root. Of course they will sell; we wouldn't have built them otherwise. Buffalo is teeming with Irish willing to pay an awful lot to borrow very little."

Nathaniel nodded. "Perhaps. But I am sure Mrs. Fraser does not want to hear talk of business at her table."

"I'll take that as a sign you are conceding the point," Edward said. "And of course we've broken ground on the city jail too, for those who fail to pay their mortgages."

"The design really is ingenious, Mr. Root," Wendell said. "The citizens of Buffalo can count on absolute protection from the criminal element."

Nathaniel set his jaw and took a sip of his wine. Susannah knew Edward had insisted they begin construction on the building even though the weather was freezing and the workers suffered in it.

Marjorie carried the platters from the sideboard and placed them in the center of the table. She lifted the lid on each and steam wafted toward the chandelier. As she prepared to serve the food, Edward looked at the enormous blue walleye and narrowed his eyes. Nathaniel looked down at his plate.

"Is something wrong?" Susannah asked. She glanced at Marjorie.

"Fish?" Edward said. "You're serving fish?"

Nathaniel held up his hand. "Please, Edward—it's fine. Don't trouble Mrs. Fraser."

"As I told you yesterday," Edward said, "Mr. Root does not eat fish."

Edward *had* told her, Susannah remembered now, yesterday morning before she had gone to the dressmaker. The unsettling encounter with the nun had shoved everything else from her mind. Now she turned to Nathaniel, mortified.

"Please do not worry," he said. "It is a peculiarity that

runs in my family. My father once swelled up like a soap bubble from a few bites of trout."

Susannah's hand flew to her mouth. "I am so sorry."

"Don't be," Nathaniel said. He gestured to a platter of potatoes with shaved ham and roasted pearl onions. "This looks marvelous. Truly." He turned to Wendell and aimed to change the subject. "I understand you will be traveling soon?"

Wendell nodded. "West to Green Bay. My cousin is homesteading there. This has been his first winter and I think he is eager for visitors."

Edward shook his head. Susannah could see from the way he held his jaw that he was still seething about her mistake with the meal. He restrained himself for now to answer Wendell. "Can you even imagine that life? A country full of savages? The Catholics in Buffalo are bad enough."

The conversation drifted unremarkably from travel to the weather, and soon the meal was over. Later, after the guests had gone home, Susannah moved quietly through the front hallway in the hopes of passing Edward's study unnoticed. She longed to close herself in the peace of her room to read a few pages of Mrs. Sedgwick's latest novel before drifting off to merciful sleep. But when her toe touched the first stair, she heard Edward clear his throat.

"Susannah," he said. "Come here."

She inhaled, closing her eyes in a silent prayer, then followed his voice through the study into the parlor.

He stood next to the piano and gestured to the embroidered cushion on the bench. "I am in the mood to hear some music."

She gave him a questioning glance, trying to discern his intention. "Edward," she said, "about dinner . . . I—"

"*I asked you,*" he barked, then softened his voice, "to play me a tune."

Susannah sat down on the bench and raised the fallboard, then placed her hands back in her lap. As she tried to think of what to play, her mind felt blank, slick as a sheet of ice. It mattered very much that she choose the right piece of music just now. She was weary with the number of times Edward had forced her into this dance—making her anticipate precisely what he wanted and how, tempering the tone of her voice and her posture so as not to provoke him. Susannah tried to think of something, anything, to play, but she was frozen in place.

Edward grabbed her wrists and mashed her open palms on the keys. The notes crashed through the silent room. A tear rolled down the bridge of Susannah's nose, and she felt it hang on the rim of her nostril. She didn't dare move her hand to brush it away.

Slowly, she began to plunk out the notes of an old Scottish tune. "See, O, see the breaking day," she sang, her voice a quavering whisper, "how the dewdrop decks the thorn. Hovering low, the skylarks lay, long preluding—"

One chord came out bent and Susannah's fingers froze above the keys. Edward flicked aside the latch with his index finger and slammed the fallboard down. When Susannah snatched her hands away, the left one was too slow and the heavy oak crashed onto her fingers. She heard the bones crack before she felt the pain. As Susannah cried out, a keening sound howling from her chest, Edward strode calmly into his study and closed the door.

"Mrs. Fraser," Marjorie cried, darting into the room. "What is the matter?" Susannah clutched her wrist with her right hand and stared at the broken fingers, her mouth stretched open in pain. The top joints were wrenched out of line. Already they were swelling.

"Jesus, Mary, and Joseph," Marjorie whispered, sinking down at Susannah's feet. "This can't go on."

At first light, Susannah set off running across the back of the property, then southwest through the woods that opened to Maple Street. Marjorie had wrapped the injured fingers of Susannah's left hand tightly together with strips of rag, and she held it gingerly at her hip. She darted among the bare trees and crossed a clearing created by a few fallen white pines. The dawn sun hung orange and lovely in the eastern sky.

Two log buildings came into view. The larger was a story and a half tall, a simple construction with the shape and pitched roof of a barn. Long narrow windows flanked the sides of the building, each a mosaic of colored glass. A door of carved oak marked the entrance and next to it hung a wooden sign that read, simply, *The Lamb of God*. Next to this sanctuary stood the rectory, a cabin with a shingled roof that sagged a little in the center, where a chimney emitted a broad plume of smoke.

Susannah pounded with the side of her fist on the door. There was a rustling inside, footsteps, then the creak of the iron latch lifting. Sister Mary Genevieve's face appeared, her long gray hair hanging loose on her shoulders.

"My dear girl," she said and opened the door. "I've been expecting you."

It was dark within the nun's cabin, despite the spreading dawn outside. Still breathless from running, Susannah glanced around at the humble furnishings—the stone hearth and iron pot, a table with two chairs, a long shelf that held cups and plates and one large bowl.

"Is Father Adler here now?"

"No. He travels often to the isolated villages that do not have priests." Sister Mary Genevieve caught Susannah's glance at the single narrow cot by the window. "And when he is here, I sleep in the church, of course. But I handle affairs in his absence, meeting with anyone looking for his . . . assistance."

"I don't know why I came here," Susannah said, almost to herself, and shook her head.

Sister Mary Genevieve settled Susannah in the worn armchair next to the fire, then pulled over a chair from the table and sat across from her.

"Why don't you just tell me what happened," she said, looking at the bandaged hand.

Susannah sighed. How simple just to say it, after all these months of explaining everything away with lies. She described the events of the previous day to the nun: the walleye, the broken ballad, her broken fingers.

Sister Mary Genevieve nodded. "May I ask, have you ever tried to leave?"

"Once."

The sister rose and went to the fire, stoking the banked coals to heat the water for tea. "What happened?"

"I waited until Edward was asleep, then slipped his coin purse from the desk in his study. I left the house, and ran." The words poured out now. Susannah no longer cared whether it was wrong to tell them. "I wanted to make it to Williams Mills by the morning and catch a stage from there to Rochester. But Edward had followed me the whole time, waited until I stopped to catch my breath, and dragged me back home. He locked me in a closet for a whole day and night without any food. After that, I stopped thinking about leaving."

"And you've no family who could help you?"

Susannah shook her head. "My parents are dead. Their parents are back in Ulster and for all I know, they are dead too. I am alone here."

"And no friends of your family? No one who knew your parents?"

"Everyone who knew my mother and father knows my husband too. I don't know where their loyalties lie."

The nun took two teacups down from the shelf and spooned tea leaves into each one. "You must be thankful that you have no children. God has protected you in that at least, I see."

Susannah stared at the woman's back, the black garment she wore even in sleep, and realized she was unafraid to tell the truth. "I do not rely on God for much anymore."

Sister Mary Genevieve ignored this comment and sat

back down in the chair. "What if I told you I could help you run away and he would never find you?"

"I would say that you do not know my husband very well."

"Perhaps. But Father Adler has known many, many men *like* your husband. And many women like you."

"He has?"

"Oh, yes. And just as he helped them, he can help you. The past can be lopped off like a head in a guillotine."

The image startled Susannah. "I'm sorry, Sister, but I do not believe anyone can help me."

The nun observed her a moment. "Do you believe that you are a daughter of God?"

Susannah looked down at her lap, her eyes pooling.

"Look at me, child." Susannah looked up, and the tears spilled down to her chin. "The Book of Matthew says that the very hairs on your head are numbered. Do you believe that is true?"

Susannah nodded. "I want to," she said, her voice breaking. "But I feel so very alone."

"Every particle of your body is sacred, each muscle, each bone." She touched Susannah's bandage. "But I must know if *you* believe that before Father Adler can help you. For the path will not be an easy one. One must want—need—to survive."

"I do believe it," Susannah said. She felt again in her chest, just as she had when she stood in the dress shop, the hardness of her resolve. No matter what happened, despite all of the ways in which she had suffered, that stone was always there, the weight that kept her from floating away.

"Then he and I will begin the arrangements. We are fortunate to have an early spring this year. The boats will start running soon."

"Where am I going by boat?"

The sister did not answer the question. "Still, I will need some time to prepare things. In the meantime, be patient and do not despair." She opened a small box on the table next to Susannah's chair and removed from it a pale gray feather. She placed it in Susannah's hand. "Keep this with you to remember: You can endure anything now, for this part of your life is nearly over."

The kettle had begun to boil. Sister Mary Genevieve dipped a tin pitcher into the water and filled their cups. The tea leaves hissed and expanded in the silence of the cabin.

"How will I know when to come to you?" Susannah asked, twirling the feather between her fingers.

"Don't worry. You'll know."

Chapter Two

Despite what Sister Mary Genevieve had said, Susannah did indeed begin to despair. As soon as she left the rectory cabin, in fact, fear and worry swarmed in. Wives just didn't disappear without their husbands coming to look for them. And Edward Fraser wasn't the sort of man who would merely shrug his shoulders and give up. He was as ruthless and unchanging as a man could be, and Susannah knew he would do anything, spend any sum, to bring her back under his control.

And if she doubted this fact as the days passed, Edward reminded her time and again. The worst night came three weeks later, after dinner in the cramped dining room at the Bealses'. Everything about the evening had seemed to irritate Edward. His soup was lukewarm. Eliza Beals's custard was too sweet, and the meddlesome woman had dared to ask about Susannah's injured hand, then didn't seem convinced by the explanation Edward gave.

They returned home and Susannah stood in her room pulling the pins out of her hair, her scalp tingling with relief. She unfastened her corset and marveled at just how many pins and hooks and laces it took to make her suitable for public display.

Exhaustion bore down on her and she slipped into bed without bothering to open her book. Images of the previous weeks tumbled over and over in her mind like leaves caught in a stream where two currents meet. She heard the whisper of Madame Martineau's peach silk, then felt the familiar heavy air of her greenhouse in her lungs. Susannah turned beneath the blankets. The piano keys flashed straight and white like Edward's front teeth, a smile masking his cruelty. And then there was the pain, throbbing in her fingers.

Thump.

The sound broke into the reverie and Susannah's eyes flew open. Edward's boots on the stairs, his hand on the doorknob. She sat up in bed, folding the blanket back neatly across her lap.

Edward entered and lit the lamp. His forehead shone and he walked to the window, throwing it open. "This room is stifling."

"I was trying to keep out the draft. Eliza was talking tonight about the fever again, and I suppose I let her worry me."

Edward took off his jacket and waistcoat, draping them over the chair in the corner. "Eliza Beals is a dim cow of a woman. Don't listen to a thing she says." His voice was distant, as if his mind weren't actually engaged with the words he spoke.

Susannah sighed. "All right, Edward," she whispered. "I won't."

He detected the exasperation in her voice and his mind snapped back into focus. "Dim she may be, but she *does* know her place. She had three children by the time she was your age. And she is a grandmother now."

Susannah eyed him carefully. Venturing to speak in any way on this subject—even an attempt to placate him, to apologize for her fruitless womb—was a dangerous business. Edward was sweating at the temples. A lock of his slick hair had fallen out of line with the rest and was hanging over his brow.

"The Bealses are blessed," she said.

Edward stood over her now, the lamp's light shining behind him, throwing his face into shadow. "And according to that line of thought, we are cursed. Is that what you believe?"

Susannah looked down at her lap.

"Would you like to know what I believe?" He was gaining steam and Susannah braced herself for the coming blow. She clutched her knees in closer to her body, wrapped her arms around her legs.

"I believe the divine has nothing to do with this childless home. I believe *you're* doing something to interfere."

Her head snapped up then, and she met his eyes. She tried to cover her surprise with the mien of the wrongly accused while her mind went instantly to the seeds in the greenhouse. Had he found them? How could he have discerned their purpose? "I can't imagine what you mean by that, Edward. Have I ever refused to lie with my husband?"

"You don't refuse me, but that doesn't mean you haven't meddled. You're doing *something*, I'm certain of it. We are young, I am healthy. My brothers have a dozen children between them and I *know* my seed is strong." His voice was hardening now. "The hindrance lies with you."

Susannah thought of the way the seeds stuck in her teeth as she chewed them. Perhaps they made no difference whatsoever and it was instead a flaw in her organs that kept her barren. She imagined her body was marshaling to save her, closing off the channel Edward was determined to travel. "We must be patient and accept the will of God."

Her words ignited his anger like a match, and he clamped a rough hand on her thigh. Nothing infuriated him more than a reminder that some things were beyond his control. He yanked back the blankets, trying to scare her, she knew, but Susannah felt absolutely calm. When he lowered himself on top of her, she tipped her head back and stared at the dark planks of the ceiling. Without warning he slammed himself against her. She wouldn't fight him, wouldn't cry out, because she felt sure now that there was no chance of escape.

And then, the very next afternoon, a feather appeared in her greenhouse, identical to the one Sister Mary Genevieve had given her at the cabin three weeks before. She noticed it where it lay on the worktable and plucked it up, holding it between her thumb and forefinger, and ran the soft fibers across the back of her hand. Anyone else who saw it might assume she kept it nostalgically, as a quill for her notations, but a careful eye would note that its tip hadn't been sharpened, didn't hold the stain of ink.

Susannah sank down on her stool and held her breath. She glanced up at the window of Edward's study out of habit, though she knew he was in Black Rock for a meeting about the railroad. The men planned to dine at the mayor's house, and Edward wouldn't be home until late in the evening. Susannah rose, her heart like a drumbeat, and walked across the greenhouse to the door. Her sleeves brushed the perfectly manicured globes of the orange trees, but she did not feel them. A spiderweb stretched taut in the doorway, its gossamer geometry a marvel, but Susannah did not see it. All she could feel, all she could see, were the years of misery and loneliness Hawkshill promised, and she moved as if they were chasing her.

She passed through the dining room to the door across from the kitchen and dashed out into the hallway. The oak stairs seemed never-ending and she took them two at a time, yanking herself along on the railing. In the bedroom she threw open the wardrobe door and scanned her dresses, realizing that she had no idea where she was going. Would it be cold there? Susannah selected a wool dress for its extra weight and warmth, laying it across the bed, and the boots she wore on her expeditions in the woods.

She closed the door and thought of her mother's velvet-lined jewelry box. Susannah hadn't opened it since her mother had died; the thought of it pierced her now and she went to the bureau. Cholera had taken her mother suddenly the previous year, but she had been ill for many years before that. Susannah's father had lost his fortune trying to care for her. She opened the lid of the jewelry box. There were several pairs of earrings: gold filigree with enamel pansies, coral roses hanging on a chain, two ivory half-moons. Susannah touched the rings perched on velvet pillows—one with a cluster of pearls, another with gold carved into vines. The tray beneath these held a necklace, a double strand of garnets the size of peas, set in gold. This piece had been her mother's pride and joy. Susannah had seen her wear it only once, but she let Susannah try it on many times at home when she was a girl. Her mother had explained that Noah himself had used the light from a garnet as a lantern to guide his ark.

The necklace glinted in her hand, catching the light from the window. She didn't know anything about where she was going or the person who had promised to take her there. How could she set out with nothing but trust? She laid the necklace back in its tray, then rose and closed the door to the room. Swiftly, she unhooked the buttons that secured her dress at the back of the neck and lifted it over her head. Standing barefoot in her chemise, she hung the dress in the wardrobe and closed the oak door. She glanced down at her legs, their outline visible through the translucent linen of her chemise. The last few months had wrung her out like a rag, and her silhouette showed it: thighs diminished, knees angular and unsoftened by flesh.

Susannah crossed the room to her sewing basket and retrieved a needle and a length of white thread. She pulled an embroidered handkerchief from the top drawer of the bureau and wrapped the necklace tightly in the cotton. Then she stitched it with quick strokes to her chemise at her thigh.

She broke the thread and plucked up the dress she'd selected, throwing it over her head. The dress draped well over the concealed necklace. No one would know it was there but Susannah. *Just in case*, she thought. *In case things aren't what they seem.*

She tried to pass quietly through the kitchen, but Marjorie

looked up from where she stood, chopping a head of red cabbage on the wooden block. Purple liquid trailed down her wrists and along the edge of the table. As Marjorie wiped her hands, Susannah gazed at them: fingers callused and knuckles rounded from work, a thin gold band on her ring finger.

Marjorie held Susannah's gaze, and something passed between them. "Going out for a walk?"

Susannah nodded, and her voice stuck in her throat like a husk. "Could you help me fasten this?" She pointed at the laces at the back of her dress, then held up her lame hand. Marjorie stepped behind her and pulled the laces tight, then tied one of her expert knots. Then she turned Susannah around by the shoulders to face her.

Susannah struggled to say the words. "Perhaps I will be gone a little longer than usual."

"Wait." Marjorie crossed the room to the back door, where the cloaks hung on a peg. She lifted a gray shawl and Susannah's cloak and carried them back to her. "Cover your hair. It stands out like a torchlight." Susannah stepped toward her, and Marjorie crossed the ends of the shawl beneath Susannah's chin, tucking them into the back collar of the cloak. Susannah leaned forward, pressing her cheek to Marjorie's for the length of one long breath.

"Good-bye," she whispered.

As she crossed the back of the property once again, the greenhouse loomed off to her left and reflected the afternoon sun. Susannah stepped inside and realized all at once that her cuttings and flowers and trees would desiccate in their clay pots, hostages behind the glass. All their striving for life would come to nothing without someone to bring them water. The herbarium too would remain incomplete. She felt the loss of it all but also a strange relief. Along with each specimen she flattened in the flower press, Susannah had preserved her anguish too. The herbarium was like a book of horrors, each page linked to a memory. The thought of abandoning it along with everything else thrilled her. She picked up her beloved Wakefield, its blue cover worn and soiled, and walked out.

Susannah made it nearly all the way to the rectory without seeing another soul. The frosted grass crunched beneath her feet. When she was almost to Pearl Street, a spaniel emerged from the trees, its mottled fur the color of coffee and milk. A man followed closely behind, a musket slung over his shoulder and swinging against his hip as he walked. When he stepped onto the road his eyes met hers. Perhaps he saw fear there, for he nodded and bowed a little. "Ma'am," he said, then kept on after the dog. When he had passed, Susannah craned her neck to see him once more, but he didn't turn back.

As the rectory came into view, Susannah wondered what would happen next. Sister Mary Genevieve hadn't left any instructions. Would she be waiting? It was nearly dark now and she could hear creatures flitting across the canopy. Her breathing quickened.

Just as Susannah was thinking of turning back into the darkness to wait, she saw the sister's face appear in the glass pane of the rectory's door. Susannah glanced across the clearing. It was empty. As she raced toward the door, icy drops of water began to fall from the sky.

"You've brought nothing with you, I hope?" Sister Mary Genevieve eyed Susannah carefully in the darkness of the cabin once she had ushered her inside.

"No, nothing but the clothes I wear," Susannah said, the lie tumbling easily out. "And this book." She held it out.

The sister took the book from her and stared at it. "I can make good use of this, but you'll need to leave it with me." She set the book on the table and crossed the small room. She opened a trunk, pulling out a black wool gown identical to the one she wore and shook it out. "Here. Put this on. We don't have much time."

Susannah hesitated, then reached for the laces at the back of her dress. With the injured fingers on her left hand still bound, she fumbled.

Sister Mary Genevieve sighed. "Turn around. Hurry up." Susannah felt the woman's cold fingers at the nape of her neck as she released the collar buttons one by one. "I don't have much hope for a successful escape if you're a prisoner in your own clothing. You are certain you've brought nothing else with you?" the nun asked again. Susannah nodded, a feeling of dread in her stomach. When the nun lifted the dress over her head, Susannah concealed the lump on her chemise with her hand. The sister helped her into the black gown.

"The life you have known ends today, and you must not carry any piece of it with you. Do you understand? He must have no reason to suspect you are still alive."

Susannah stared at her. "Then what *is* he to think? What are you going to tell him?" she asked, afraid to know the answer.

Sister Mary Genevieve tied a plain black bonnet beneath Susannah's chin. "That I saw you fall into the river."

Susannah's mind reeled, still unable to believe that she was really daring to try to leave, to believe that she could thwart Edward for good. Sister Mary Genevieve took up Susannah's dress and tore the sleeve away from the shoulder seam, then tore it again to make a ragged edge on the scrap of wool. She held it up. "I found this tangled in the brambles at the water's edge."

Susannah could see the tale unfolding and dared to hope that Edward might believe it.

"Father Adler has done this before?" Susannah asked. "What if Edward questions him?"

The sister threw the remains of Susannah's gown into the fire, and they watched it flare. "He is well practiced in dealing with men like your husband and cases like yours. He will say nothing that could give you away."

Susannah closed her eyes, praying that she could trust these strangers. "Where will I go?"

"You will go to the port tonight. In the morning, the first westbound boat of the season departs for Detroit, then Mackinac Island—do you know of it?"

Susannah nodded. She knew what most people in the East knew: the siege of the fort there in 1812, Indians and canoes, the fur trade that had made John Astor rich. But it seemed as remote as the moon.

"Good. There is a wealthy woman on the island named Magdelaine Fonteneau. She has agreed to provide refuge for you in her home. And to keep you safe until we are sure that your past has been put to rest."

"But why? Why would she want to help me?"

Sister Mary Genevieve gave her a solemn look. "Madame Fonteneau lost her own sister to a man's violence. Those who could have helped the girl stood by and did nothing."

Susannah swallowed. "He killed her?" She thought of the way she had seen Edward lose control of himself when he was in a rage. She knew there were no limits to what he might do.

Sister Mary Genevieve nodded. "Yes. But we are not going to let that happen to you."

"And what about you? What am I to you that you would take such a risk to help me?"

"You may think that no one knows the truth of what your husband has done, but I can assure you—people know."

Susannah winced. Once again she felt exposed, embarrassed. She felt that a stronger woman would have been able to keep the secrets of her household and maintain a graceful façade to the world. Or perhaps a stronger woman would not have allowed her husband to treat her so badly. Would not have allowed things to go so wrong.

The nun put her hand on top of Susannah's. "And yet until Marjorie came to me, no one had done a thing to help you. That, to me, is the worst kind of cruelty. Worse even, in a way, than the things your husband has done. I believe we will be judged—in the next life, but in this one too, make no mistake—by whether we do what we can to stop the suffering of others. Do we stand by and ignore another's pain? Or do we take action to end it?"

Susannah gave her a skeptical look. She had spent so much time alone with her suffering and now in one day two people, a whole network of people, really, were willing to help her. "And there's nothing in it for you? You must know that I cannot pay you. Edward is wealthy, yes, but I have no money of my own."

"Oh, no. I'm not looking for payment, though you are right that I do ask for one small thing in return."

"What's that?"

"Madame Fonteneau has been a loyal advocate for the church for many years, and we owe her a great debt. Her life has been difficult. She lost her younger sister, as I said, as well as her older sister, who disappeared from the island the same year. She became a widow at a young age, with a little boy to care for."

Susannah nodded. She thought of how shattered she had been when her parents died. Losses like these could become so big they swallowed you whole.

"We have arranged for a new house to be built for her—in fact, it should be complete by now—so that she may spend the rest of her years in comfort. But with so much distance between us, Father Adler worries about how she fares. Someday, when he can, he intends to travel there to see for himself. But in the meantime, in any way that you can, please try to be of use to her, to help her in return for the help she has given you."

"But what can I do for her?" Susannah said. "What does she need that I can give her?"

"I don't know. She has endured a great deal, and it is our wish to bring her comfort, peace. Perhaps when you arrive you will see what must be done."

"I don't know, but I will try."

"That is all that I ask," the nun said. "Now, we must address what you will call yourself.

Fraser was Edward's name, Edward's brand on her arm. "It hardly matters what I am called," Susannah said, "as long as it is something else."

"Of course it matters," the sister insisted. "Nothing has meaning unless we *give* it meaning."

Susannah smiled. "Those don't sound like the words of a religious woman."

"On the contrary. God waits until we act—not the other way around. It took me far too many years to learn that lesson." The sister laced her fingers together. "From now on you will go by *Miss Dove.*"

"Miss Dove." Susannah repeated the words as she heard the *clip-clop* of a horse and wagon outside the cabin, worn wheels creaking to a stop.

Sister Mary Genevieve tipped her chin to the door in recognition. "It's time." She stood. "The name is a protection, and a reminder: You are in flight."

Susannah nodded. Suddenly everything seemed to be speeding up again. She stole a glance out the window at the wagon. It was covered with a canvas tarp, the sort undertakers used to collect the dead. Susannah gave the nun a frightened look.

"No soul would dare to look for you here. Quickly now," the sister said, opening the door and hurrying Susannah to the wagon. Their breath bloomed from their mouths. Susannah hoisted herself up, one foot on the wet wheel well, curling her toes to keep her boot from slipping, and lifted the corner of the tarp, then climbed over the side. The wagon was full of clean straw. She didn't even get a look at the driver's face.

"Father Adler was very clear in his instructions," the nun said. "Once you get on the boat you are to find a priest named Father Milani. He will see you safely to the island. Do not speak to anyone else. If you are pressed by anyone, simply explain that you are traveling to St. Louis. The boat will make one stop, in the port of Detroit, but no matter what happens, stay on the boat. Do you understand?" The sister's eyes were stern, and she grasped Susannah's shoulder. "If you leave the boat, we cannot help you."

Susannah nodded. She was so afraid, her heart writhing violently within her, that she felt she might cry out. "Shouldn't we pray?" she asked.

"There isn't time. Remember my instructions. And be brave—*determined* to survive." Sister Mary Genevieve walked alongside the wagon for a few steps and began to lash the canvas in place, casting Susannah's hiding place into darkness.

"Good-bye, Miss Dove, and God be with you."

Chapter Three

E dward Fraser knew something was wrong when he returned home from his meeting in Black Rock to find a single damask tablemat at the head of his long dining table. Their hired girl, Marjorie, emerged from the kitchen with one bowl of stew and half a loaf of brown bread.

"Good evening," Edward said. "Is Mrs. Fraser ill?"

"No, sir," Marjorie said, turning her back to Edward to light a lamp on the sideboard. "Mrs. Fraser is not here."

"Isn't here? Why, it's"—Edward began, pulling out his pocket watch—"nearly nine o'clock. What do you mean she is not here?"

Marjorie waved his concern away with her hand. "You know how she likes her rambles. I wouldn't worry, sir—she knows those woods better than anyone."

Edward stared at the woman, dumbfounded. He had never thought her particularly bright, but this seemed foolish even for her. "I should say she does, well enough to know that she shouldn't be in them after dark. What the devil is wrong with you, Marjorie? Why didn't you send for me?"

"I'm sorry, sir." She looked at her shoes.

Edward took the hunk of bread from the plate on the table. "Keep that stew warm for me. I'm going to look for her. I can't imagine what she has gotten into her head." He stalked into the front hall and Marjorie followed, twisting her apron around her fingers.

"Perhaps she stopped to call on a friend?"

"And what friend would that be?" Edward barked. Both of them knew he didn't allow Susannah to have friends of her own. Edward shoved the crumbling hunk of bread into the pocket of his coat. He moved to leave, then hesitated and crossed back into the kitchen, where his musket hung by the hearth. "I won't be long."

He had yet to decide precisely where he was going, but only a fool would trudge into a dark wood unarmed. In the places Susannah liked to roam, he knew, there were wolves. Perhaps bears. One of the men who worked for him liked to tell a story of meeting a bear, six feet tall on its hind legs with blood on its teeth. But Edward made it a practice never to believe a story a man tells in which he comes out the victor in the end. In his experience, most men cried like children when forced to face something they feared.

He started out into the darkness heading north with his wool muffler wrapped tightly under his chin. Still the cold wind found its way to his skin and he shivered. Buffalo had grown at a breakneck pace, and houses now stood on land that just a few years ago had been uninterrupted forest. Edward knew that he was one of the men who had determined that this city, with its placement at the mouth of the lakes, should establish itself as the gateway by which crops and settlers would flow. Just ten years before, thousands of workers and their new machines had dug out the canal that connected Lake Erie with the mouth of the Hudson and, by extension, the Atlantic. In that time, Buffalo had swelled from a tiny village to a city of fifteen thousand souls.

Trees came down in huge swaths, for fuel, for building, and to clear roads, but dense stands of pine and maple remained at the outskirts of the city. Edward now skirted one, shouting Susannah's name. No one answered but a raven perched high in the canopy. Edward sighed. When they had first married, he had merely been amused by Susannah's willfulness and believed that his bride would succumb to her bridle. But time and again—there was her attempt to run away, her refusal to conceive a child—he had learned not to underestimate her.

It had been a day for all sorts of frustration. At the brickworks, he had broken up a fight in the yard when he saw from his office window a crowd of men converging around two workers. One had his meaty hands clenched around the other's neck. Edward had raced out of his office and down the hall to the door that led into the yard.

"What the devil is going on here?" he had shouted as he made his way into the crowd. Some of the men dispersed at the sound of his voice, but the fighters did not yield.

"I *said*, what the devil is going on?"

A young man so scrawny it seemed impossible that he could lift fifty-pound bags of sand all day said, with a little too much excitement in his voice, "It was a friendly disagreement, sir, until Colm started in on that fat one's mother."

Edward stepped up to the men and put his hands on their shoulders to pull them apart. Both men panted. Colm Riley, whom Edward had hired a few months back, rubbed his neck where the other man had gripped it. He spit a clot of blood and mucus onto the ground.

"Blasted Irish," Edward said. "Nothing has any use to you if you can't punch it. Or drink it."

Both men waited for him to say more, their hands hanging at their sides. All the nearby workers waited too. Edward hesitated. Some factory owners tolerated fighting as a part of this kind of business. It was rough work and you needed strong men to do it, men whose fathers' knuckles had beaten all the bright ideas out of them. But the knowledge that other men in his situation made allowances only redoubled Edward's anger. He felt it race up his spine, and his voice took on the eerily calm tone that signified his most intense rage.

"You're no better than garbage, both of you. As of today, you no longer work here. And I'll be damned if you ever work anywhere else in this city."

The men stood there, staring at him. Colm's bottom lip hung wet and swollen, like the underside of a slug. They were the kind of men you might see fishing on a Sunday morning, relaxed, patient, as if there were nothing else in the world to concern them. Edward had known that particular serenity as a boy: watching the surface of the water, the dance of the slack line in the sunlight as his small boat bobbed. Nothing pleased his mother more than a pail full of cold fish, and he loved feeling that he had done something, really *done* something useful to assuage her worry, even if only for an afternoon. But he had outgrown the hobby. His father's beatings had seen to that. He could only see his mother cower for so long before he lost respect for her, and for himself. The violence had warped him, made him see sympathy as a weakness. He learned that there was only one way to get power, and that was to take it.

Things got worse in the afternoon when Nathaniel Root came to inquire, his tone casual, without suspicion, about financial records the city needed in order to renew its contract with Edward's company for building supplies. He wanted information about Edward's backers for the factory.

This created a minor problem, for Edward's only backer was Edward himself. When he had borrowed all he could from the New York banks and they cut him off, the grim bankers shaking their heads, he drummed up credit elsewhere, in Pennsylvania and Ohio. These funds Edward used to expedite the construction of new homes, to build the jail he had boasted about at the dinner with Beals and Root. But the money only went so far, and profits were slow to come in. When the note on the loans had come due, he couldn't pay.

A lesser man, one without any gall, would have curtailed his projects, perhaps waited until the first crop of homes sold so he could pay off the loans, then wait some more while he saved enough to begin again. But Edward saw tremendous opportunity for gain, and he was loath to sit around while someone else grabbed it. He felt like the king of the city. His fingerprints were on every construction project, and thoughts of his legacy crowded out any impulse toward moderation. He understood that he was spreading himself very thin, but that was only in the short run. If only the banks could look down the line, consider the opportunities. But they were unwavering in their disdain for his plans.

"Suppose the market were to fall," a rat-faced man in Manhattan City told him. "Suppose we were to have trouble with Britain in the Northwest Territory again. Or Nat Turner's ghost incites the negroes to burn up all the cotton in Virginia. You've got no equity, no security. You must exercise some caution, Mr. Fraser. This boom cannot last."

It was lack of imagination, Edward thought. But then, they were small men, happy slaving their lives away in little offices, moving stacks of paper around. They weren't willing to take a risk on creating something important, something big that would outlast them all. But Edward was willing. No, he was more than that; he was determined. And so he found another source of funding, an unlimited source: his own hand, the steady, confident quill of the forger.

The woods yielded no sign of his wife, and Edward changed direction. There was another place, a place he dreaded most, where Susannah might be, and a musket might come in handy there too. He thought of the sort of men who populated Canal Street—illiterate dockworkers, drunks, toothless degenerates who would wager their own mothers in a poker game without batting an eye. And the women. They turned his stomach. Filthy, used-up whores, the lot of them godless, hopeless. It seemed impossible that Susannah even knew that place existed. But if she had taken up with someone—and Edward had suspected for a long time that she had—well, that was the place they would go. Where people would look the other way, mind their own business, and feel no moral obligation to inform a man that his wife had made a cuckold of him.

He didn't know the names of the people in this horde, but he was willing to bet they knew his. He almost smiled at this thought, despite his sour mood. There wasn't a soul in Buffalo who hadn't heard about his work. The people of Canal Street either worked for him or worked for someone who worked for him. But they didn't *like* him, not one bit. *A man like me*, Edward thought, *reminds them of everything they can never have, can never be.*

Before long, he had reached Canal Street. He saw the light of the open fires, the ramshackle buildings that seemed to sway with the drunkenness of the people inside them. If she was in one of them, he would find her.

The walkway along the canal was strewn with garbage and dotted with frozen puddles, and Edward moved slowly past couples and clusters of men who drank from all manner of crockery. He tried to get a look at their faces to see if he recognized any of his workers from the brickyard. But it was dark, and anyway he felt out of his element. A gang of men could rise up to beat him and throw him in the canal without a second thought. An undertaker's crude wagon passed on his right, almost knocking him off his feet. The driver seemed not to notice what he had done, only tipped his hat, his clenched fist of an Irish face cordial.

Edward knocked on doors. A saloon, then a sort of trading post that sold hats and tobacco. Each person scarcely listened to his description of Susannah before shaking his head, saying, "No, I ain't seen nobody like that."

It was after eleven when he approached the front path of Hawkshill with his gun slung over his sagging shoulder, like a man who had spent the morning hunting and come home without a kill. He was worn down by the search; the narrow alleys and sinister faces had been a whetstone turning his anger into fear. Where could she be?

Marjorie met him at the door. "Mr. Root is waiting for you in your study."

"Root? What's he doing here?" Edward's tone sounded more startled than he meant it to. He couldn't imagine why his maid had summoned the city attorney. It wasn't as if they were friends—Edward didn't have friends. He had hosted the recent dinner for Root only to gain favor he might use later on.

"I thought it wise to find someone to assist you. I hope I did right, sir."

Edward sighed with disgust, then peeled his coat from his shoulders and leaned the musket upright in the hallway corner. He strode into the study. Nathaniel set down his glass and stood. Edward rubbed his numb fingers together.

They shared a brief handshake, and Edward searched the

other man's face for any sign that he was using Susannah's disappearance as a pretense to get a moment alone with Edward's desk drawers.

"Marjorie sent word that you were out searching. Do you have news?"

"None. I've been to the woods north of here—it's her habit to walk there, nights, sometimes, though never with *my* permission. As far as I can tell, she hasn't gone to the slums either."

Nathaniel's eyebrows leapt. "Down at the canal—are you mad? I can't imagine Mrs. Fraser would have anything to do with such a place."

"I can't either," Edward said grimly. *What is this feeling?* he thought. *Guilt? Remorse?* He searched his chest for the anger that kept him solid, the way one searches with his toe for a stair in the dark. But Edward felt only hunger, exhaustion.

Nathaniel grasped his shoulder. "Whatever you need, I am at your service."

Edward stared at him. Nathaniel was younger than he was, Edward felt sure, maybe by five years. This was an irritating fact, as was his simple presence. Why couldn't Marjorie have sent for Wendell Beals instead, supplicating Wendell, who would do whatever Edward asked without a question? Edward wondered, fleetingly, what Nathaniel would do, if Susannah really was dead, about the loan documents. Would he insist on investigating a grieving man?

"I wonder," Edward said, the thought occurring to him for the first time. "Should we notify the constabulary? I thought for certain I would have found her by now."

"When was she last here?"

"This afternoon. Marjorie said she set out for her usual walk. Nothing seemed amiss."

Nathaniel looked at his watch. "If she left at three, that means she has been gone nearly nine hours. In the cold."

Edward sighed. "She's a willful girl, but to be honest she knows the hazards of the woods better than most. She wouldn't be careless enough to stay out there alone."

"Yes, let's go," Nathaniel said. "I'll just get my hat."

Edward walked over to his desk and pulled open the drawer where he kept money in a locked box. The constabulary was a volunteer force. In Edward's experience, men worked harder when they were getting paid. He filled his coin purse and dropped it into his pocket.

As he went into the hallway to join Nathaniel, there was a knock on the door. The men looked at each other, and Marjorie appeared.

"Well," Edward said, "Aren't you going to answer it?" Even now, in this moment of crisis, there was a way things should be done. A man like Edward Fraser did not answer his own door.

She turned the knob and a plump woman stepped inside. Sleet had begun to fall and her black shroud was wet on the shoulders.

"Who are *you*?" Edward asked rudely.

But Marjorie was bowing her head and whispered, "Good evening, Sister." She then backed out of the way to let the woman into the front hall.

The woman fixed her gaze on Edward. "Is this the Fraser household?"

"Yes," Nathaniel said before Edward could, his voice tight.

"The residence of Mrs. Susannah Fraser?" she asked.

"Yes," Edward barked. He glanced at Marjorie, noticing her recognition of the woman. He could feel the tension coiling in his shoulders. He hadn't known there were any nuns in Buffalo. "What news do you have?"

The woman reached for Edward's hand, but he wouldn't give it to her. Her eyes were intensely dark, the iris and pupil nearly the same color. The contrast with her pale skin gave her the unreal look of a doll. She wore a black bonnet, but a few wisps of her hair had escaped in the wind and they hung at her temples. "My name is Sister Mary Genevieve. I'm afraid I have to give you some terrible news."

He felt he had known it all along.

Nathaniel stepped closer and put his hand under Edward's elbow. "Hold steady, man," he muttered.

"Sir, there has been an accident. Mrs. Fraser has gone home to the Lord."

Edward drew a long breath. The air in the room felt suddenly thin, as if it were leaking away.

"What happened?" Nathaniel asked. He led the three of them into the study, guiding Edward onto the sofa as the nun took a chair. Marjorie stood by the door, her handkerchief to her lips as she began to cry.

"I was in Black Rock this afternoon," the sister began, "ministering to a man whose child is ill. Our church owns no carriage at present, so I set out for my errand on foot. When evening came, I headed south, along the water. The path was deserted."

Edward's face twisted with impatience. "Don't delay. Just tell me what's happened."

"I was on the section of the river where the bank overhangs the water on a small rise. As I said, the path was empty, but all of a sudden I saw another person walking toward me, a woman wearing a shawl over her hair. She was about a hundred yards away, ambling slowly along the edge of the water. I saw her drop something on the ground, but she did not stoop to pick it up, which I thought was strange. As I watched she seemed to step nearer and nearer to the edge of the bank—so much so that I thought to myself, *God protect that woman*. The wind was just starting to pick up then. And all at once, she went over," the nun said, her voice straining against tears. "The river just swallowed her up. I did not even hear her cry out. I ran to the bank. I could see the hem of her skirt rise to the surface, but the water was churning so, and the wind blowing. The current was terribly fast. You know it never freezes, no matter how cold the temperature. She stayed near the bank for a moment, but the part of her dress that was tangled in the brambles ripped, and she was swept away."

Edward turned to Nathaniel. "That current runs at fifteen miles an hour, even in fair weather. And it runs north, toward Niagara. Good God, Root, she will have gone over the falls." Then he turned back to the nun. "And you did *nothing* to help her?"

"Oh, please, sir, you have to believe me. It all happened so terribly fast. I screamed and screamed for help, but all the boats were moored for the night and no one was out. I could barely reach the brambles from the high bank."

Edward combed the woman's account in his mind, imagining the scene, watching Susannah's hair float out behind her as she fell. "But how did you know who she was? How did you know to come here?"

"When she went over into the water, when I saw I couldn't reach her, I kept running toward the place where I first saw her and the object I saw her drop. It was this."

Sister Mary Genevieve opened the soggy book, its pages smeared and clotted together like paste. It was the botany book Susannah carried on her walks. He had never understood his wife's fascination with something so mundane. The nun pointed to the name printed inside the cover, much of the ink washed away.

Edward knew this woman had no reason to lie, and yet his mind was determined to resist her story. He took the book, turned it over in his hand. "But this doesn't mean Susannah is the woman you saw go into the river. Perhaps she dropped this days ago and that woman happened upon it." As he spoke, Edward found he was convincing himself. "She has been known to roam deep into the woods north of here. Perhaps she found an old cabin or knocked on a farmhouse door."

The sister pulled a scrap of fabric from the pocket of her apron and unfolded it. She draped it over her hand. "Do you recognize this?"

Edward sighed, then shook his head. "I honestly don't know."

But Marjorie gasped. "Sir, that wool is from the dress Mrs. Fraser was wearing just this morning. I pressed it for her myself."

So this would be it, then, Edward thought. The moment when everything changed.

Nathaniel put his hand on Edward's arm. "My friend, at first light I will gather some men down at the port. We will find her body and bring it home."

Chapter Four

The straw in the wagon bed did little to cushion Susannah's shoulder blades from the rough ride on Buffalo's pitted roads. As the wagon pitched and shuddered along, she felt every bump and dip echo through her bones and clenched her jaw to keep her teeth from chattering.

After what felt like an eternity, the texture of the road changed. The scent of moss and wet wood and ordure wafted under the canvas, and Susannah knew they were at the port. The wagon slowed, rocking from side to side, and changed direction; the hoofbeats began to reverberate off close walls. Finally, the horses came to a stop and the front end of the wagon tipped up slightly as the driver stepped down.

He peeled back the canvas. Susannah blinked at him and then her eyes roved, taking in the details of where she was. A narrow space between two brick walls, the low light of an oil lamp mounted above a doorway. The walls were slick with damp, as if so many people clustered together in such tight quarters kept it from freezing.

"Strange cargo here," the man said, grinning at her with two teeth like arrows pointing in opposing directions.

Susannah gave him a frightened look.

"'Tis all right, miss. Ain't no one to see you but myself. Name's Connolly."

The driver's brogue was clipped and comforting. She thought of Marjorie as she sat up and touched the back of her head with her fingertips. Her shoulders ached. Mr. Connolly offered his hand and she pulled herself over the edge of the wagon, then smoothed her skirt with her palms.

"What is this place?" Susannah looked up at the doorway.

Overhead, a voice called, "Look out below," and the contents of a full commode rained down a few feet away from where they stood.

"Can't you tell? It's the finest inn in town." Mr. Connolly winked at Susannah and led her toward the doorway. "You'll pass the night in a room here."

Inside they took a sharp right up a narrow staircase that wound to the third floor. At the top, Mr. Connolly held Susannah back with his palm while he stepped out of the stairwell to have a look around the corner. Satisfied, he waved her into the passageway lined with candles in clouded glass globes. Four rooms down, he swung open a door, and she followed him inside.

Susannah took in the narrow bed, a cornhusk mattress half covered with blankets still twisted in the shape of the bed's previous occupant. A small window showcased a square of the night sky and Susannah stepped closer to it, looking first up at the stars and then down below at the lot behind the building. The flattened hull of a boat was splayed out on the ground and surrounded by piles of lumber. A group of men stood in a circle talking in the lamplight, each with his arms crossed in front of him. Every few seconds, one turned to spit tobacco juice over his shoulder.

"Where are we?"

Mr. Connolly looked up from where he crouched on the floor, sweeping the glass from a broken liquor bottle into a pile with his sleeve. He jumped up, crossed the room in one step, and pulled her by the shoulder back toward the bed. "*Miss*. Holy Mary, mother of— stay away from that window."

Susannah shook her head. "Of course. Forgive me."

Mr. Connolly sat down beside her on the bed, holding his hat in his hands. "The sister says, and I think 'tis best, that I shouldn't know much about you. And I don't. What I do know, I'll never tell." He gave Susannah an emphatic look. "You can count on that. But folks around here, well, they *know* who you are—or, were—just by the look a' you. What I'm getting at is that some folks wouldn't think twice to report as they'd seen you out walking the streets. And I believe you know better than I what Mr. Fra—or, *certain parties* would pay for information a' that sort."

Susannah closed her eyes, weariness descending on her once again. Even here she had to cower from Edward. She mustn't forget. He would be looking for her, might be looking already.

"Ah, don't worry, miss," Mr. Connolly said, patting her hand with his clumsy bear paw. "Soon as we get you out of the godfersaken town of Buffalo, a new life begins. Young and pretty as you are—well,"—he blushed, stood up, and donned his hat—"in no time you'll be starting anew."

Susannah shook her head. She wanted so much to believe it was possible, but the path seemed fraught with dangers at every turn. And yet these people wanted to help her try. *Why?* He nodded his good-bye at her and put his hand on the door.

"Mr. Connolly," Susannah said, and he paused. "You aren't supposed to know about me, but might I know something about you?" She felt her voice break open in her throat. "Why would you want to help me?"

He thought for a moment, rubbing the back of his neck with his hand. "Well, to your first question, there's nothing much to tell. I work in the yard down below, fixing up the boats. At times there's work loading and unloading the cargo." At that, he paused for a minute. But he wouldn't meet her eyes when he continued.

"And as for helping you, well . . . my da was a hard man. A hard man to my ma. I couldn't help her enough before she died. So it comforts me to help someone like you." Mr. Connolly stopped short. "I'm under strict orders from the sister to deliver you here. In the morning, the innkeeper's wife will come to the room and tell you where to go. Don't open the door for anyone else. Now, let's try the lock." He went out into the hallway and waited.

The lock on the door was crude—a simple strip of iron with a slot in the wooden door frame—but the sound it made as Susannah slid it into place was comforting. Mr. Connolly waited to try the door and, once satisfied it would hold, called his muffled good-bye and was gone.

Only then did Susannah notice that the stench of the room was so intense that she could hardly breathe. With her back pressed against the wall, she reached over and pushed open one of the shutters to let in the cold air. She turned to the bed and grasped the blankets, giving them a good shake, and tried not to see the cockroaches that spilled on the floor and scuttled toward the darkness beneath the bed.

Susannah's body was tired, but her mind hummed like a hive. She lay down on the bed, taking a deep breath to calm it. She wondered what Marjorie was doing—washing dishes? Edward would be home by now from Black Rock, would have found her missing. Where would he start his search for her? It all seemed surreal and dangerous, and she found herself praying for the lock on the door, that God would strengthen it, strengthen her own heart for whatever lay ahead.

Sometime in the early dawn, the rhythm of Susannah's ruminations must have lulled her to sleep, for she woke with a start to the sound of someone banging on a pot in the hallway.

"Coffee's on," a weary woman's voice croaked out. "Get up, alla' you, now. Time to settle up payment and get on your way." The woman made her way down the hall, banging on each door with her spoon.

Susannah sat up in bed, pulled her knees to her chest, and wrapped the shawl around them. A great commotion began; she heard yawning and mumbles of "good morning," boots on the bare floorboards, shutters opening. A dog barked viciously in the yard.

At the end of the hallway, the woman banged the pot

again. "Ten cents extra for every one of you who's late getting out," she called, and the pace of preparations quickened.

A door opened and a woman shrieked with laughter. "Jesus Christ, Michael Carp—your willy's hanging outta your pants. Wake up, man."

The men in the hallway hooted and laughed as they passed Susannah's closed door in one mass and made their way down the narrow staircase toward the smell of fried bread.

It grew quiet on the floor and Susannah sat still, waiting. Her mouth began to water and she realized she hadn't had a thing to eat in almost a day. She stood and approached the door, listening. Footsteps in the hallway startled her, and she backed toward the bed.

The spoon tapped gently on her door. "It's all right, girl. You don't have to be afraid. Gather yourself and come on out. I'm to see that you get on the steamer."

Susannah hesitated. "I don't have any money," she said through the door.

"And I'm Mrs. Astor," the woman said with a mirthless laugh.

"No, really—I don't," Susannah said, urgency in her voice.

"It's *all right*. Open the door."

Susannah pulled her shawl over her hair and clutched it beneath her chin. She slid the lock to the right and opened the door wide enough to peer into the hallway. The woman's gray hair tufted out at the temples beneath her white bonnet. Her lips curled to the side in amusement when she saw Susannah's face. "Terrible tragedy, what happened to Susannah Fraser."

Susannah cringed, realizing that not everyone was as discreet as Mr. Connolly. She wondered what people knew, or thought they knew. One thing was certain: She had to get out of Buffalo right away. "I thank you, ma'am, for your generosity."

The woman scoffed. "My name's Mrs. Tully and I don't do nothing for free. Tom Connolly paid your way, girl. Even left passage for you downstairs." The woman gestured behind her with her thumb. "As far as it concerns myself, I never saw you here."

Susannah nodded and opened the door the rest of the way. "I'm ready to go."

Mrs. Tully looked into the room behind Susannah and simpered. "Ain't you got a trunk?"

"No," Susannah said, touching her dress. "This is all I have."

"All right, then," Mrs. Tully said, shaking her head. "I won't ask any questions."

She turned to the end of the hallway and Susannah followed. Downstairs a dozen men were in the kitchen, some slumped on the few chairs and the rest leaning against the walls in groups of two or three, some with their suspenders hanging down around their waists. The food smelled so good, Susannah felt she could already taste it. She moved her tongue across the back of her teeth.

Mrs. Tully stopped short and held Susannah back with her hand. "Best if you stay out here. I'll get you some bread and you can take it with you."

Susannah nodded. When Mrs. Tully came back she pressed a cloth-wrapped bundle into Susannah's left hand.

Her mangled fingers ached. In her right hand Mrs. Tully placed a card that recorded a transaction for the ticket price and read *BUFFALO to MACK ISLAND*.

"Get on with you." Mrs. Tully explained how to get to the boat, called the *Thomas Jefferson*. "That packet leaves at seven sharp, whether or not you see fit to grace it with your presence."

Susannah crossed the yard behind the boardinghouse, clutching the wrapped bread between her elbow and ribs. Her blood was in her cheeks and she felt conscious that some of the men were staring, even as she knew they wouldn't recognize her with the shawl pulled so close around her face. The morning was a little warmer and the smell of the stagnant canal water hung in the air. She touched the hard place on her thigh where the necklace was hidden under the folds of fabric in her skirt. She was counting the seconds until she was on that boat and out of Edward's reach.

The sight of the *Thomas Jefferson* made her heart leap in her chest. The varnished white oak hull gleamed from stem to stern, its line interrupted only by the massive side paddle wheel. Three masts jutted into the sky, one flying the flag, and two stacks emitted thin lines of smoke as the boiler heated. A crowd was forming at the edge of the gangway. Susannah stood off to the side and slid her passage ticket inside her sleeve, then unwrapped the bread. The oil had soaked through the cloth and her hand was slick. Though she meant to take only a few bites and save the rest for later in the day, she couldn't fight the intensity of her hunger. The three pieces were gone in a matter of seconds. She shook out the cloth and folded it into a square, wiping her hands and feeling ashamed that she hadn't been able to hold out longer.

The crowd suddenly surged toward the gangway and began to board the boat. Near Susannah, a man and his wife kept a tight grip on the arms of their two young children. The boy was pulling so hard toward the gangway that he nearly wrenched his father off his feet.

The woman barked at her son, *"Eine minute!"* then turned to her husband with a pleading glance.

"Ja, ja," he said, counting the coins in his hand. He hoisted his daughter up on his hip. The little girl's hair was the color of corn silk, her eyes a pale green. In her hand she held the end of a dirty rope tied to the neck of a goat. They moved toward the line of people and the eager boy was suddenly frightened, clinging to his mother's hand.

Susannah felt frozen in place. Here it was, her chance to be rid of this town once and for all, and she could not move. She looked back at Buffalo rising up from the water's edge, her eye following the tops of the buildings. She could count at least six that Edward himself had coaxed up where there had been nothing before.

A basket slammed into Susannah's shoulder and she heard a clatter. A woman in faded homespun barked impatient words in a language Susannah did not recognize, swinging her basket of dishes to the side to get by.

The *Thomas Jefferson* blew her whistle, long and low, and Susannah found herself moving with the stream of people, stepping onto the deck of the boat. A man in uniform took her ticket and examined it a moment before pointing toward a narrow set of stairs that led down into the hold of the boat. "Steerage," he said.

The only other time she'd been on the water, it was on a vessel half this size, a ferry that ran along Long Island Sound and north toward Boston. She had been just a girl, traveling with her parents to see a cousin of her father's. They had a cabin to themselves with velvet drapes on the window and they took their tea in the stateroom. She remembered that the teaspoons had been edged in gold.

The deckhand pushed her roughly toward the stairs. "Get on—we got a whole line of people here."

Susannah nodded and moved with the people wearing layers of clothing, patched jackets and shawls. She saw a man carrying a dining chair with a broken seat over his shoulder, a woman with a washtub containing a folded quilt, a pair of steel shears looping out of her apron. When she noticed Susannah looking at them, she shoved them deeper into her pocket.

"Belonged to my mother," she said, staring Susannah hard in the eye. "Try to take them, and I'll show you the wrong end, if you get my meaning."

Susannah blinked at the woman, took in the dirt and sorrow that lined her face, and nodded. The engines clanked and thundered as they cranked up, and she plunged into the darkness, her hands empty.

Chapter Five

1835

Magdelaine Fonteneau dipped her paddle in Lake Huron, the net of writhing whitefish cold at her feet, as her canoe skimmed through the icy water back toward Mackinac Island. Behind a long smudge of clouds in the western sky, the sun cast a pale glow across the strait and the two peninsulas, Upper and Lower Michigan, that widened like mirror images to the north and south. Beyond them, the big lake opened its maw.

Four weeks earlier, before the thaw, she had tied her canoe to her sled dog Ani's harness and walked alongside him as he dragged it over the still-frozen stretch of lake to nearby Bois Blanc Island, where Magdelaine kept a large maple sugar camp. She claimed to be checking the progress of the syrup, but this was only the most recent in a list of excuses for making herself scarce all winter long.

Magdelaine was avoiding her son and trying with all her

might to avoid, finally, going to see the house that he had built for her on Mackinac's southeastern shore, overlooking the harbor she had been paddling in and out of her entire life. Jean-Henri, his chest puffed with pride, had announced that he would build the house for his mother as a gift. She should have a place to rest, he said, though at forty-six she was hardly an old woman. He wanted her to live in comfort and enjoy the fruits of her labor.

The gesture made Magdelaine wonder if her son knew her at all. If he did, he would know that she had no use for a big house, with bone china and feather beds. She slept well in her cabin at the sugar camp but even better in the tent she had traveled with for two decades along the fur trade route in the Michigan territory, and slept best of all under the open sky when the bats pitched up out of the trees into the pink dusk and her fire roared beside her. She feared nothing then, when everything was within sight and she was alone. Beneath her broadcloth skirt, she kept a long knife tied to her ankle, and she was well known for her ability to draw it with the speed of a hawk and plunge it wherever she had to: into the belly of a hungry wolf, confused and nosing around her camp; into the chest of a man who had it coming.

The lake was quiet this evening, keeping its secrets to itself. Ani stood at attention in the bow of the canoe as she paddled, his muzzle following the arcs of the diving gulls. Evenings like these were rare, now that steamboats from the East could travel to this region, fueled by wood cut along the way from the dense forests. Every few days one of the vessels slid into Mackinac's harbor and cast its enormous shadow on the beach, where Odawa families still came and went with the seasons, building their lodges at the water's edge.

They came to collect "gifts" to compensate them for the lands in Upper and Lower Michigan they had agreed to give up to the American government. Meanwhile, the French families, some mixed with Odawa blood back many generations, stayed all year in small cabins. The newest arrivals to the island were Presbyterians from the East, who kept cows and chickens and well-manicured gardens around their wood-frame houses. The old and the new—birch-bark canoe and hulking steamboat, Indian lodge and farmhouse porch— sat alongside one another, showing how much had changed on the island in her lifetime.

Magdelaine was not opposed to progress. She herself had taken a steamboat to Detroit and was enchanted by the speed and comfort of the journey. But she missed the quiet of old Mackinac, and she suspected Ani did too. The dog glanced back at her and the sun glinted off the beads of water in his wiry fur. He dropped his tongue, a request, and she pulled one of the fish from the net and tossed it to his end of the canoe.

She approached the harbor and fought to keep her eyes on the shoreline. Magdelaine had argued against the house until she could see that her son would not back down. Then she relented, asking only that he show restraint and remember that what she loved most in the world was the island itself, its bluffs like cresting waves, the craggy limestone façades crowned with lush green cedar. Magdelaine wanted to die on this island, but out in the open air—not choking in a bed with velvet curtains.

Ani shifted back and forth on his paws, eager to run to his pen and reunite with his brothers. Something white and hulking loomed up on the shore, and it filled Magdelaine with dread as she dragged her canoe out of the shallow water and up onto dry sand. Her thoughts cast about, trying to distract her from the matter at hand. There was plenty to do on the island now that spring was here, and of course she was eager to look for the mail and see whether she had received another letter from Father Adler.

It had been months since she had had any word from him, a year since the unfortunate business with the second Miss Dove. *Dear Madame Fonteneau*, his letter from Charlestown, Massachusetts, had said when he wrote to her for the first time five years ago. *The church has become aware of your grace and devotion, of your good works and service. It is with those traits in mind that I must call on you for help. I want to know whether you might consider offering refuge to a young woman who must escape a troubled situation . . .*

Magdelaine was chilled to the bone, her hands numb, but it was a pleasant, familiar feeling, her physical connection to dozens of winters giving way to spring, to mud, to sap pooling in tin pails that would boil to syrup after a long day over a fire. She felt her son was trying to take away the comfort of these things she had always known, since long before he was born. Ani barked and raced up the beach, leaving her alone. When she could avoid it no longer, Magdelaine raised her eyes.

The house stood two stories high, white clapboard with glass windows and *four* brick chimneys that jutted rudely into the path of the diving ospreys who built their nests on the bluffs. The hipped roof would hold against any storm the lakes could brew, and the house promised heat all year long and kitchen enough to cook for a whole army. A long stone path led from the beach to the front door. It was a sturdy slab of oak with iron hinges. Lanterns mounted on either side of the door were lit, wastefully, for the evening sun still shone brightly, gleaming off the white paint. Next door was her beloved Ste. Anne's, little more than a cabin beside a fenced-in yard of gravestones.

Jean-Henri smiled at her from the porch of the new house, his arms outstretched. His dark hair stood out against the white paint, and though he wore a coat and collar in the French style, his nose was the same as hers, the same as her Odawa mother's: wide and flat and brown from the sun, even in March.

She held his gaze for a long moment, then turned on her heel and strode back to her canoe. With her knee, she shoved its nose back toward the water and splashed in after it, hoisting herself roughly over the side. The canoe pitched back and forth, nearly tipping over, but Magdelaine hardly noticed as she paddled hard with her anger's rhythm. Behind her she could hear Ani barking in confusion on the beach. Her shoulders burned as she moved through the icy lake, back toward her camp on Bois Blanc. The water peeled away from her vessel like an animal's skin.

"Mother—wait!"

Magdelaine didn't stop paddling or even look back to where Jean-Henri stood, calling to her from the beach, the garish empty house behind him. She could hear him scramble, his steps uncertain and sliding on the beach, and although she didn't turn around to look, she knew the sand must be flying up behind him as he moved down the shore toward his own canoe. She imagined him pushing it into the water and leaping over the side, his paddle moving before he sat down. Magdelaine was strong for a woman, but she was no match for a young man of twenty-six. The distance between their canoes shortened, until he no longer had to yell to be heard.

"Mother, please. Wait."

"Let me be," she replied, panting. She lifted her paddle, held it across her lap for a moment, and took a few long breaths. Icy lake water dripped down her shins.

"You haven't even seen the inside." Jean-Henri was crestfallen. He seemed incapable of understanding why the house upset her.

Magdelaine shook her head and began to paddle again, ignoring the pain. Jean-Henri sighed. With little effort he increased his speed and stopped her canoe by pulling out ahead, then turning his boat sideways. His mother turned to the right to avoid him.

"Do you really want to tire yourself out this way?" he shouted. "You can't outpaddle me—I learned my technique from you. And my stubbornness."

Magdelaine ignored him and skimmed silently through the water, just missing the bow of his canoe. He sighed again, then turned and caught up with her. They paddled alongside one another for several minutes, the waves splashing rhythmically against the birch bark. Magdelaine's heart pounded with her exertion and she was afraid her muscles would give out, but Jean-Henri was right—she *was* stubborn—and she wouldn't let him make her stop if it killed her. Bois Blanc moved slowly toward them. It was pristine and undeveloped in the way Mackinac had been a long time ago. The cedar and maple and white pine seemed impenetrable, growing right down to the shore.

When Magdelaine's boat scraped bottom she threw her legs into the water and yanked it toward the shore. But she was exhausted. Her knees buckled and she pitched forward, nearly falling into the water. Jean-Henri had leapt out of his own canoe just in time and caught her in his arms. Together they moved up the beach to dry sand. He sat Magdelaine down, then went back to the water and pulled both canoes out of the waves. Back beside his mother he heaved himself down onto the sand. They both panted, shivering.

"You are," Jean-Henri began, his breath rough and his eyes wild, "the most *infuriating* woman I have ever known. I don't know how my father put up with you." He rested his elbows on his knees and rubbed his temples.

"I thank the Lord your father isn't here to see what you have done with his money."

"Mother, it's *your* money. You earned the bulk of it long after he was in the ground. He hasn't deserved the credit for many, many years."

"Ungrateful boy," she muttered, shaking her head. She had only continued what her husband, Henri, had begun: maintaining relationships with hunters and traders in Lower Michigan, using the advantage of her mother's Odawa blood and language to earn their trust. Yes, Magdelaine was good at it, but only because she had had no other choice as a widow with a son to care for. She glanced at the sky; it was later than she had thought. They would have to paddle back soon if they were going to make it to Mackinac before dark, though she remembered she still had the fish in her canoe if her pride compelled her to stay at the camp and order her son out of her sight. She wished she had whistled for Ani to come back with her to keep her company.

"If it's my money, then all the more reason I have to say I don't want that ugly house."

"It's a good house, Mother. A beautiful house."

Magdelaine nodded. "For someone else, maybe. Not for me." Disappointment clouded Jean-Henri's face. She could see that he had been eager to reveal his work to her, eager to gain her approval. It was all he wanted of her, but somehow she found she could never give it. There was a wall between them, a wall she herself had built long ago, and it kept her from feeling the things a mother should feel: tenderness, love. If she kept her distance, she would be safe from those things, and safe from the sorrow of losing them.

"Mother," Jean-Henri said, taking Magdelaine's hands into his own. A misting rain began to fall, and she felt it seeping through her hair to her scalp. "Please, for me, just come take a look at it. See what I wanted to do for you. And if you still feel that you cannot live there, well, we will do whatever you please with it and you can stay on at the cabin or this camp. I only want you to be happy, nothing more."

This last statement prompted a skeptical glance from Magdelaine.

"Truly, Mother."

She sighed. "What in the world ever made you think a house like that would make me happy?"

"Since I imagined you would be glad about the house, I wanted you to think the idea for it was mine alone. But in truth, it was Father Adler who first suggested it."

At this Magdelaine straightened. "Father Adler? But why?"

Jean-Henri looked out at the lake, afraid to meet her gaze. "It was after the first Miss Dove turned back at Detroit. And after the second Miss Dove was . . . discovered." Magdelaine closed her eyes. "I think he was concerned that you might give up helping him."

"*Trying* to help him, you mean. I've yet to succeed."

"You must not blame yourself. There was nothing you could have done to change things for those women."

Magdelaine did not disagree, and yet she felt the weight of her guilt like a yoke on her shoulders. She and Father Adler had exchanged many letters to prepare for the women to come to the island. She had suggested the routes they might take and how they might travel safely and avoid contact with nosy passengers. As far as she knew, the priest had followed all her instructions, but still she could not guarantee the safety of these women whose lives meant so much to him. Yet he hadn't blamed Magdelaine for the losses. He knew she was devout, he said. He knew that she had suffered and that through her good works she would find redemption. Magdelaine doubted whether that redemption would come to pass, but she knew she had to keep trying. "But how will a house make any difference?"

"He worries about you, Mother. As do I. Both of us would like to see you enjoy some peace, some rest."

"In my old age."

"Just the opposite. You are healthy and strong—no one disputes this! But while you can enjoy it, slow down. Let us give you some ease. The trading cabin is too small for a woman of your station."

"That cabin suits me just fine. It's only too small because my son plans to live with me forever!"

Jean-Henri looked a little wounded by this remark. She knew he had had his heart broken in Montreal, after he failed to gain a toehold in banking the way that she had hoped—and she had written to every one of her connections to be sure he would have ample opportunity. Magdelaine supposed he became a great deal less attractive to the woman who was to be his wife when he proved he could not become a success, but that was five years in the past. He always had been a sensitive boy, quick to cry or cower, and it seemed he was stuck now in his sadness, unable to set it free.

"I'm sorry," Magdelaine said. "You know I am sentimental about the cabin."

Magdelaine and her sisters were raised there near the island's fort. The cabin was a tidy, tranquil place, with creaky floors swept clean each morning by their mother's broom. It was attached to her father's trading post, where men like Henri Fonteneau exchanged pelts for the goods they would ferry south in the fall to the mouth of the Grand River: ax blades and knives, flour and coffee and brass kettles. Magdelaine and her sisters were half-breeds—*metis*, the island missionaries and other whites called them when in a polite mood, and indeed they were *mixed*. The sisters were devout Catholic girls who nonetheless knew how to sew the birchbark outwales of a canoe and gum the seams with pine pitch.

Their mother's Odawa people had no choice but to tolerate the government's tireless efforts to reform their heathen ways, but Magdelaine often felt that being a half-breed was an even more difficult path than being a full Odawa. At least her mother's people had each other, their traditions, their history. And of course her father's people had everything they wanted, and what they didn't have, they took. But Magdelaine was at once *both* French and Odawa, and *neither*. She never had the luxury of feeling like a part of anything, and so she made her own way in the world from a very young age. Her father had died when Magdelaine was fourteen, her mother just before she came of age. Then her husband had been killed. And of course, there was the matter of her sisters.

Jean-Henri touched her hand again. "I know how you feel about the trading cabin. That's why I left it alone and built the new house on an empty plot. You can have both—the old and the new. Don't you see? There's no reason to deny yourself these comforts. You aren't betraying the past."

Magdelaine gave her son a pointed look. Everyone on the island thought they understood her so well, even him. But there was so much they didn't know. Magdelaine sighed. She examined her fingers, chastened. Jean-Henri had gotten carried away, without a doubt, in making this house that was so much more than she could ever need. He loved working with his hands, building things, much as Magdelaine wished he would do something that could earn him a little more power and respect in the world.

But Father Adler's involvement changed things. If he wanted her to live in the house, she would do it, and the next time he asked her to ensure the safety of a woman who needed their help, she would take that new Miss Dove inside and bar the door against the world, hold it with her own shoulder. It was unusual for a man to take notice of the suffering of women, and more unusual still for a priest. But Magdelaine had learned that people had their reasons for the things they did, even if they kept those reasons to themselves. She had written to him for guidance about what to do about Jean-Henri, about how to instruct her students, and other matters of concern on the island. Always, he wrote back with wise words urging patience, prayer. Father Adler was the only truly holy man she had ever known, and she was determined not to let him down.

"Well, come on," Magdelaine said, standing up and starting toward the canoes. "It's getting late."

"So you'll look at the house?" Jean-Henri grinned and hurried to her side.

"I'll live in it." She pushed off into the waves and began the paddle home, and Jean-Henri quickly followed. The rain fell steadily now, and they raised their voices to be heard.

"Oh, I'm so glad, Mother."

She had relented, but she wanted her son to know it would be on her terms. If she could direct a trading expedition through dense forest, through sickness and nimbly around packs of wolves and into hostile Indian settlements without losing a man to the hatchet, she would direct the goings-on in this preposterous new house. "I will accept it on two conditions."

"Anything," Jean-Henri said.

"I want you to write to Bishop Rese and tell him that we will pay for improvements to the church, with a rectory and money for a permanent priest. That Father Milani comes and goes as he pleases and neglects his duties. Some say he seduces women—and he is a drunk. It's a disgrace to the faithful here. Perhaps the bishop will consider assigning Father Adler instead and we'll get him to come to the island at last."

Jean-Henri nodded. "Of course."

Magdelaine switched the paddle from left to right. "There are a lot of girls here who need schooling, and we can't leave it all to the Presbyterians. They think if they dunk these children's heads under the water and say a prayer, the work is done."

He smiled. "I'm sorry I called you infuriating."

"No need for apologies," she said, grinning at her son. "I took it as a compliment."

"You said there were two conditions. What else?"

"I want you to go back to the city and get yourself established. I have been corresponding with a former agent of Matthew Bell's in Trois-Rivieres, Mr. Greive. He may have a position for you in Montreal and I want you to take it. A man *must* make his way in the world."

Jean-Henri looked uneasy. "I think we both know I am not cut out for business. My place is here, on the island. I have plenty of work to keep me busy." Magdelaine had to admit that that was true. Jean-Henri had repaired wagons and sleighs and boats, helped build the new houses that seemed to spring up like weeds. He earned enough on his own. He never asked for anything from her. But it wasn't about the money. It was about pride.

"You are your father's son. His blood runs in your veins. If you try, really try, you *will* succeed. You are not meant to be a common laborer."

Jean-Henri sighed but said nothing. Their canoes touched bottom for the last time that day and they hooked the cross-beams over their elbows and dragged them up the beach. Ani trotted down to them to make sure Magdelaine didn't forget to pluck out the net full of fish. Then he circled and followed at their heels as they climbed the beach to the house. It was dark now and the windows in the first floor of the house glowed orange, illuminating a sitting room with fine furniture, shelves lined with books, a carved banister on the staircase that led to the rooms upstairs. Magdelaine looked at her son and shook her head in disbelief, yet again. The steps leading to the entryway felt firm beneath her feet, and as they climbed toward the door, it swung open.

An island woman stood in the doorway. Magdelaine recognized her as the daughter of one of Henri's men, Ansel Leroux.

"Mother, you remember Esmee, don't you?" her son said by way of introduction.

"Good evening, madame," Esmee said. She wore a pale yellow apron over a broadcloth skirt striped with intricate ribbon work. Her sleek black hair was divided in two loose braids. She held her back very straight.

Magdelaine took the girl's slender palm between her own rough hands. "Yes, of course."

"Esmee is going to keep house for you here."

"Oh, I don't think—"

Esmee looked at Jean-Henri, worry briefly crossing her brow. He held up his hand. "After all these years skinning whitefish on the flat side of a rock, you think you know how to take care of a house like this? Besides, this way you can come and go as you please. Otherwise, all of this will just become a burden."

Magdelaine nodded. Her son deserved perhaps a little credit for his foresight. "I see. Well. Welcome, Esmee."

Esmee relaxed. She glanced once more at Jean-Henri, and he nodded to assure her that her position was secure. When he looked away, her eyes lingered on his face a moment before she turned back to Magdelaine. "Are you hungry? You must be. I have a stew warming." She took the fish from Magdelaine, then Jean-Henri's hat and coat and hung them on hooks next to the door. "But I thought first, madame, you might like to bathe. It is so chilly out, and you have been traveling a long time. I've heated the water."

Magdelaine fought to keep eagerness out of her voice. There was nothing on earth she wanted more at that moment than a scalding hot bath in a warm room. She made a show of glancing at her dirt-caked fingernails, then touched the front of her greasy hair. "I suppose I could use a good scrubbing."

Esmee nodded and left the front hall to prepare the bath in the kitchen. Magdelaine glanced into the sitting room, where a large fire glowed between a sofa and chairs that sat on a thick carpet. Next to the window was another chair and a large brass cage shaped like a bell. It hung on a hook from a stand that curved to the floor. Inside, a white bird with a rose-colored head hopped from perch to perch.

"A bird?" Magdelaine said. "For a pet?"

Jean-Henri smiled. "A dove. A good-luck charm for the next Miss Dove."

Magdelaine watched as the dove marched in place on the perch, opened its wings and closed them again. "Who would put a dove in a cage?"

"Cities full of very wealthy women. It's the fashion now to keep a dove in the parlor—a mated pair if you can. I thought it would be difficult to catch one and coax it into the cage, but this little creature submitted quite easily. Maybe it wanted some company."

"Well, I don't like it at all—it's terrible."

Jean-Henri sighed. "Then give it away."

He climbed the stairs, disappearing into the mysterious house's seemingly endless rooms. Magdelaine heard the girl's careful steps in the kitchen, then entered the room and watched as she heaved two buckets of steaming water off their hooks on the crane that stretched over the fire. The water made a satisfying sound as it filled the tin tub. Beside the tub was a chair and on the floor next to it a folded fur-lined blanket and a clean linen shift.

"Madame, this letter came for you yesterday," Esmee said, handing it to her.

Without showing her surprise, Magdelaine broke the seal and recognized Father Adler's steady hand. He had written to tell her that he had found another young woman in need of help and had begun to make the arrangements for her journey. Magdelaine felt the weight of renewed worry in her chest. So she would have one more chance to try to set things right, one more Miss Dove to try to save.

"Well," Esmee said, turning toward the door. "I'll leave you to your bath. Just call for me if you need anything."

She nodded. When Esmee went out, Magdelaine ladled some stew into a bowl and set it outside the kitchen door for Ani. Then she slipped off her moccasins and untied the back of her broadcloth skirt, stiff with mud. She pulled off her leggings. A wide dark band marked her ankles, the especially soiled patch of skin between where the leggings stopped and the moccasins began. Once the water had cooled slightly, she stepped into the tub and lowered herself slowly down onto her backside. She felt her cheeks pinken in the warm room as she slipped the bindings off the ends of her braids and loosened her hair with her fingers. It was streaked with strands of wiry gray. She leaned back and dipped her head into the water. Steam ascended from the tub, masking the window that looked out over what, she saw now, could be a garden.

And now another woman in need of salvation, a woman named Susannah Dove, was traveling west at this moment. It was all Magdelaine could do not to dress and return to the harbor to wait for her. This time, she could not let anything go wrong. Father Adler had not disclosed the city where the woman lived, nor the route she would travel, and this of course was wise. The second Miss Dove's husband had intercepted a letter from Magdelaine and uncovered his wife's plan to leave. Father Adler later wrote to explain that the woman would not be coming to the island after all, that her husband had waited until she tried to board the boat, to see whether she would really try to go through with it, before he dragged her back home. There was nothing more they could do for her.

A heavy rain fell. The sound of it on the windowpane was like the sound of two strands of beads rubbing together, swinging around a woman's neck as she runs.

Chapter Six

It took Susannah's eyes a moment to adjust to the dark space of the steerage deck. The smell of the place hit her first: goats and pigs shifted in narrow pens, agitating their soiled hay. Acrid tallow candles burned in the glass globes that lined that wall. Susannah glanced at the faint orange flames that danced within each fixture, then back at the narrow staircase that held the only path to the open air. Everything within sight was made of wood. One candle tipping over could ignite the entire steamboat.

She located an empty berth, little more than a plank of wood, and sat down. Additional berths stacked above hers, three high to the ceiling. Already the top tier was occupied with reclining passengers, and she could see why the bottom was the least desirable place to be. Tobacco juice and apple cores rained down at regular intervals. The vessel shuddered with the building pressure in the boilers, and soon she could hear the enormous paddle wheel that propelled the steamboat start to churn. They were easing away from the dock. Up on the hurricane deck, which was open to the air, she could hear the first-class passengers, who sat on benches and stood waving at the gunwale. Their cries of "Good-bye!" rang out. A few steerage passengers climbed back up the stairs to join the chorus of farewells and wave at the people on the dock. But most stayed put. No one was there to wish them good-bye. Everything and everyone they had was with them here in the bowels of the steamboat.

In the opposite corner, a heavily pregnant woman sat on the lid of a trunk with a rosary draped over her hand. The nun had told Susannah to find Father Milani, and she thought she might as well start looking for him now. Susannah stepped toward the woman. "Good morning," she said. "Would you happen to know where I could find the priest?"

"Which one? There's a Father McCorkle on the boat. He was with us on the canal boat from Albany. I saw a few more get on today."

"Was one of them named Father Milani?"

The woman shook her head. "I don't know."

Susannah nodded. The woman's shoulders were slumped forward, the weight of her belly pulling everything off center. "Would you like to lie down? I'd be happy to trade places with you for a while."

The woman looked suspiciously at Susannah. Everyone here seemed poised to thwart thieves and swindlers, as if they had seen them too many times. "No, thank you. My husband is waiting for me in Detroit. He made me promise I would sit on my trunk until I got there, and that's what I'm going to do." Susannah nodded again at the woman, wondering if she understood that it would be more than a week before they saw Detroit.

Susannah asked a few other people sitting nearby about the priest, but all answered, some in broken English, that they had never heard his name. She thought about going to the upper deck to ask around, but it seemed dangerous to show her face just yet. Anyone from Buffalo might be on the boat, and anyone who knew Susannah Fraser would be traveling first class. And after all, shouldn't this Father Milani be looking for her too? It seemed *he* should be the one to know where to find his charge.

All afternoon, the people around her kept to themselves. Each family was a compact little unit—German here, Irish there, Norwegians and Swedes. Their children looked like little blond ghosts. They moved quietly, whispered to each other, and disappeared out of sight. The day passed slowly.

At dusk a deckhand rang a bell to signal that the men had to leave and go to their separate quarters for sleeping. Even families couldn't stay together after dark, and a worried look crossed the wives' faces as they contemplated spending the night alone in a room full of strangers. Once the men left, the women busied themselves with caring for the children. One kind traveler offered a blanket to Susannah, and she took it gratefully. Susannah lay down in her berth and as she turned from side to side, trying to get comfortable on the hard board, she heard a pair of girls giggle. She turned and saw them playing cat's cradle with a dirty piece of string. Susannah smiled at them with her cheek propped on her elbow. They stared back, and the girl who held the string stuffed it into her shoe.

Around midnight, Susannah began to regret that she hadn't saved some of Mrs. Tully's fried bread. The women had brought their own food for their husbands and children—cured meats and bread wrapped in cloth—and they didn't offer any of it to Susannah. The first-class passengers up on the enclosed main deck would have dined in the stateroom, with servants to pour their wine, and by now they would be settled in their private cabins until morning. Susannah turned once more onto her left side, feeling the hard shape of the necklace cut into her leg. Somehow despite her discomfort, her aching bones, sleep finally came.

She woke with a start some hours later, just before dawn, and slipped quietly up two flights of stairs, past the main deck to the hurricane deck, which was faintly lit with small lamps. The cold wind off the lake shocked her cheeks, and she rubbed them with her palms. The paddle wheels tirelessly churned the water, and the entire boat shuddered with the pressure of the boiler. Wood smoke poured from the stacks and disappeared against the black sky.

Standing at the gunwale, she looked at the moon hanging low in the sky, smooth and silvery. But it looked desolate too against the barren water that stretched over the horizon ahead of the boat. Once again Susannah felt a pang for the plants in her greenhouse. All her work cast aside, and for what? Where would she be in a month, in a year? She thought about ivy, how the path of its growth depended on what stood nearby. Next to a fence, it could grow tall. In the absence of structure, it would spread across the ground.

Just then, Susannah heard a man approaching, singing softly under his breath, and her fingers tightened on the rail.

Her nerves were like a bell rung too many times, its toll off-key. She could no longer remember what to be frightened of, where a threat might reside. With familiars? With strangers? Danger seemed to lurk everywhere.

The man leaned his elbows on the rail a safe distance from Susannah and she exhaled. He wore a heavy coat with a wide collar made of fine wool. His beaver hat hung down over his eyes, and Susannah saw only the tip of his nose and his lips moving with the words he sang.

> *'Tis seven years,*
> *I've been a rover.*
> *Away, you rolling river . . .*

His pipe interrupted his song as he took intermittent puffs. When it was spent, he tapped the ashes into the water and put it in his pocket.

Just then he turned to her. They were the only ones on the hurricane deck. The rest of the boat, it seemed, was still asleep.

"Good morning," he called out. He tipped his hat and it moved a little farther back on his head.

Susannah nodded her head in his direction, without quite looking at him. "Morning, sir."

He stepped closer so that he could hear her over the wind. "You must be very cold. This night air is relentless."

Sister Mary Genevieve's woolen dress was doing little to keep out the wind, and Susannah thought of the fine furs and capes hanging useless in her wardrobe back in Buffalo. She remembered the nun's instruction not to speak to anyone, but she wondered if rudely turning away might only draw more attention to herself. "It isn't so very bad," she said. "I was finding it difficult to stay in my berth. Couldn't sleep, and the air down there is . . ." She tried to think of a polite way to describe the smell of the animals, the unwashed people packed together in the dank steerage deck.

"Malodorous?" the man offered.

Susannah laughed. "Yes, sir."

"I can assure you that the men's quarters are even worse."

"Tell me, how many goats do you have there?"

"Several. And one very offensive snorting donkey." The man extended his hand. "Alfred Corliss." By imperceptible degrees, the sky behind them was lightening.

Susannah slipped her left hand behind her back and briefly pressed her right hand into his. "Pleased to meet you, Mr. Corliss." She looked out over the water and hoped that he would not ask for her name. As the sun crept nearer to the eastern horizon behind them, Susannah could see that land wasn't completely out of sight. Off to the north, a jagged strip of blackness formed the lakeshore, miles and miles of forest, birds, bears, wolves, Indians. Places untouched by white hands. To the south, the lake seemed limitless. She had never sailed across the ocean, but she couldn't think of how any body of water could seem larger than this one, spilling off the edge of the earth into nothing.

Alfred pulled his collar up closer to his ears. "I'm happy to make your acquaintance. Where are you traveling?"

She took a fortifying breath and remembered the story Sister Mary Genevieve had given her. "St. Louis," she said. And then to prevent him from asking whether she was traveling with a husband, she added, "With Father Milani." A man she had yet to meet, of course, but Susannah knew well enough not to share that fact with Alfred.

He nodded. "I myself am bound for the Wisconsin Territory."

Susannah looked at him in surprise. "That is such a wilderness. Is your family there?"

"No, I have only one brother left, but he is back in Boston."

"Oh," she said. "I see." For the first time she allowed her gaze to linger on his face. His brown hair was overgrown, and a thick lock of it persisted in falling across his eyes, though he pushed it back up under his hat again and again with his slender fingers. Beneath the hair was a pair of dark brown eyes. To be nearly alone in the world was very sad indeed, Susannah thought. But she realized all at once that she could say the same for herself.

Alfred waved away her sympathy. "Not so sad. I am free to take on the work that others who are bound by obligations cannot. I will be a teacher in the Indian country, at a small mission school."

A religious man, Presbyterian perhaps. And she had mentioned traveling with a priest. She realized that he, like Edward, like so many men of her class, might hold disdain for a woman he assumed was a Catholic. "And what will you teach them?"

"Well, I've been hired to imbue them with the Gospels, of course, but to be honest I am far more curious about what I might learn from them, about the native understanding of creation." He gave her an apologetic glance, as if this notion might upset her. "I don't mean that I will neglect opportunities for conversion, but . . ."

"You must come to understand what they know, what they believe, before you can hope to introduce them to a new way of life."

Alfred nodded gratefully. "Precisely—that's just the way I see it. If I have learned anything in my travels, it is that there are many ways to see the world. Take, for example, a common bird we see around us each day—a finch, perhaps. Now, how many times have we watched this bird take flight across a field, or from one rooftop to the next, without understanding just *how* the creature is able to do so?"

"Many times, of course," Susannah said, "for I have watched birds all my life and could not explain to you how they are able to work this miracle."

Alfred held up a finger. "Ah, but it is not a miracle at all. A bird's flight is, simply, a proof. The laws of mechanics exist, with or without our notice." He reached inside his coat and pulled out a small bound book and pencil. Dawn rose around them. In the east, fire seemed to be rising out of the lake. The light brought everything into relief: Mr. Corliss's expensive coat was frayed at the cuffs. His wild boyish hair was flecked with gray. He opened the book and flipped past several drawings—the *Thomas Jefferson*, seen from the dock; two gulls diving into the waves—to a blank page.

"Many a priest and minister on this boat would argue that God made the bird fly," Susannah found herself saying.

"Indeed." Alfred's eyebrows climbed with excitement. "To them I would say that God made the bird, and God also made the man and imbued him with the curiosity and fortitude needed to seek out this knowledge. Here—I'll show you." With one hand pressing the binding at the top, he held the book flat and sketched the wing of a bird quickly with his right hand. "A bird flies because of the force of lift combined with the force of thrust. That is, because a bird is heavier than the air around it, it must use the force of lift to overcome its weight. When the wing is spread, it curves in such a way that the pressure is greater beneath the wing than above it as it moves through the air." He drew arrows pointing up beneath the feathers. "That is lift. Once a bird has attained lift, it must use the force of thrust—created by the flapping of its wings—to propel itself forward. And *that* is how the finch moves from branch to branch."

Susannah nodded. No one had ever explained such a complicated thing to her so plainly.

He pressed his lips together, suddenly embarrassed, and put the book and pencil back in his pocket. "But understanding the physical properties that allow for this phenomenon does not diminish the wonder of it, nor God's hand in making it so."

"You, sir, will make a fine teacher," Susannah said.

"I intend to try." He glanced at her. "May I ask you a question that may seem intrusive?"

Susannah braced herself. "Of course, sir."

"Is your destination in St. Louis a convent?"

Susannah hesitated, knowing her answer could put her on the receiving end of the kind of scalding condescension for Catholics she had seen Edward dole out many times. Perhaps this man, this Mr. Corliss, might want to engage her in a theological debate about the falsehood of Purgatory, about the nature of the Eucharist. Or, worse, he would ask her a question to which she did not know the answer, and uncover her lie. But what else could she say? How else could she explain why she was on the boat?

"Yes," she said finally. "It is."

"May I ask, then—why you wear a bonnet and not a veil?"

Susannah was so relieved by this simple inquiry that she nearly laughed. "A perfectly good question, sir." She had wondered the same thing about Sister Mary Genevieve, but now that she had taken on the guise of a nun, the answer was clear. "I will answer your question with a question," she said. "You are a Presbyterian?"

"Unitarian by birth, actually. Presbyterian by employment." He gave her a sheepish smile.

"Well, many sisters have found that it can be difficult to predict how people of Catholic faith will be received in mixed company. Though they do not hide who they are, they see no reason to invite inquiry and disdain. Many prefer to wear a simple bonnet while traveling."

"That seems a sensible tactic, Sister."

Susannah shook her head, constructing her tale as they spoke. "There I must correct you. I was not born into this faith but am considering it as a way of life. My name will change only if I decide to take the vows."

Alfred smiled gently. "Change the name you will not tell me, you mean?"

All at once Susannah realized she had been talking to this man for too long. He seemed harmless enough, but she knew better than anyone not to underestimate Edward's reach. They were scarcely out of Buffalo and she had already been careless. "Sir, I must be going now."

"Oh, please don't go. I do apologize if I gave offense. It's only that I've enjoyed talking with you, and this journey is a long one. If I do not know your name, how will I find you again?"

"Good day, Mr. Corliss."

She hurried back down to the steerage deck without looking back and tried not to panic. She would have to stay away from the main deck now if she hoped not to encounter Mr. Corliss again, but then how would she find the elusive Father Milani?

In the late morning they encountered one of the storms for which Lake Erie was famous. A woman came down into the sleeping quarters to report that the sky had grown suddenly dark and the captain had spotted lightning in the distance. The crew was forced to drop anchor and wait out the weather. The steamer lurched from side to side and many of the passengers felt the effects of seasickness. Another smell to add to the overpowering stench of the steerage deck.

Susannah didn't suffer from the waves, but she was hungry. When the storm passed and the boat began to move once more, she went upstairs despite her fears of being seen. She walked the perimeter of the steamboat, asking around for the priest, and once again she was surprised by the ferocity of the winds that whipped across the deck.

A colored man wearing a deckhand's tarred hat passed her on the right. He carried a bucket of water and a wooden cup and scouted embers in the after-dinner hours, when men stood smoking pipes and cigars all over the boat. Fire appeared to be a constant threat.

"Excuse me," Susannah said to him. "I'm looking for someone—maybe you could help me."

The man turned back. "Name, please?"

"He is a Catholic priest," she said for the third time that day. "Father Milani."

The deckhand shook his head. "Apologies, miss, but . . ." He thought for a moment. "Well, now, they *is* a man who be calling hisself a priest, but from what I seen he only a priest in the Church o' Rye."

Susannah gave him a confused look, then followed the direction in which his finger pointed, to a heap of brown wool slumped next to the paddle wheel housing in the center of the deck. "There?"

"Yes'm. Like I say, I don't know who he really is, but he say he a priest. He take his drink *awfully* hard."

Susannah nodded her thanks and the deckhand continued on, stopping every ten feet or so to splash a fresh cup of water on a smoldering plank. Susannah approached the brown heap. On closer inspection, the back of a man's head was visible, his hair bushy and dark. He snored loudly beneath his cloak.

"Excuse me," Susannah said, crouching down and touching his shoulder. He did not stir. "Excuse me," she said louder, shaking him. "Are you Father Milani?"

The man groaned, then rolled over and pried his eyes open. Susannah swallowed her surprise. She had expected a bloated old man, but the priest was slight, with a lively complexion despite his current state. He couldn't have been more than twenty-five.

"Perhaps," he said with one eye closed. "Who are you?"

"Father," she said, the address sounding strange for a man so young. "I am Susannah Dove."

He shrugged. "Pleased to meet you, Miss Dove. Now, if you don't mind . . ." He rolled back over into the dark corner of the wheel housing and pulled the cloak over his head to block out the light.

"Father, are you ill?" she asked, though she knew exactly what the trouble was. Even if the deckhand hadn't mentioned it, the priest reeked of liquor.

He groaned again. "How can I help you, Miss Dove?"

"Father, Sister Mary Genevieve instructed me to find you on this boat. Yesterday, in fact, I looked all over for you, but was . . . unsuccessful."

"*Madonna!*" Father Milani sat up, casting off his cloak. He was very thin, with lanky arms and legs, and beneath the cloak he wore a black frock coat made for a much heavier man. It hung on him. "Miss Dove, please forgive me. I have failed the sister and you. It will not happen again."

"I thought," she said, "that you were on this boat to escort me to Mackinac. But perhaps I misunderstood."

The priest blanched. He blinked his pale green eyes a few times. The left one was marred with a spot of brown in the iris, and both of them were bloodshot. "Do you think you need a doctor?" she asked.

Father Milani gave her a solemn look, then shook his head. "I believe I had some spoiled meat for supper last evening. But I am feeling much better now." He rubbed his eyes, then stood. "How have you found your journey so far, Miss Dove?"

"Well," she said, "I find myself fairly hungry at the moment, Father. As you may know, I have no money for food."

"*Madonna!*" he exclaimed again quietly. "Then we shall address that presently. Follow me." Father Milani wrapped the cloak around his shoulders with a flourish and descended the stairs to the stateroom in the center of the boat. He walked at a good clip, his long stride nearly leaving Susannah behind, and as he moved the cloak's generous fabric billowed out behind him.

As they approached the oak doors with cut crystal handles, an usher stepped toward the priest, glancing back at Susannah. "May I see your tickets, sir?" He had the weary look of having turned away this particular priest before.

"I don't want you to be ashamed, my son, when you finally learn that I am indeed who I say I am, Father Giovanni Milani, born in Italy, lately of Manhattan City and more lately Mackinac Island. This holy woman here is Sister Susannah Dove. We are en route to do God's work in the heathen interior, and we have dispensation to take our meals in this stateroom on account of Captain Crowell's deep generosity."

The usher shook his head. "That so." He glanced between the priest and Susannah, seeming to note her soiled dress. "Well, then you won't mind my summoning him to confirm your status. I can hardly afford to take your word for it twice. Wait here, please."

The usher strode out of sight and Father Milani reached

for the door. Susannah put her hand on his arm. "I can't go in there," she said. "Someone might recognize me."

Father Milani nodded. "Go to the door on the other side and wait for me."

"Is that true what you said, about the captain providing your meals?" she asked.

"Real cosmic truth, my dear," he said as he swung the door open with considerable effort, "is a matter of infinite mystery."

Susannah went to the other end of the stateroom and watched through the window as Father Milani moved among the tables covered in white linen, crystal, and silver. Stewards made efficient rounds with wine. One pushed a cart with a platter heaped with bread and a steaming silver coffeepot. She had walked among fine things like these at Hawkshill just two days before without paying them any heed, but now her attention was rapt.

Father Milani moved slowly, nodding his solemn priestly approval to the finely dressed men and women the stewards served. On a table near the window was a pound cake iced with sugar and heaped with strawberry preserves. With the cloak shrouding his arms, Father Milani moved his hand at waist level in a gesture of blessing as he worked his way among the tables.

He nodded one final time, then made the sign of the cross and joined Susannah back out on the deck. "Follow me, Miss Dove. And hush while you do it." They walked halfway around the exterior of the stateroom, back toward the entrance, and Susannah noticed that the usher had returned with the captain. The captain spoke harshly to him, then glanced around, clearly looking for Milani.

Milani pivoted on his right foot and Susannah followed. They took the stairs up to the hurricane deck and strode to a windy corner empty of other passengers. Father Milani removed his cloak and laid it carefully on the deck to reveal several rows of bulging pockets. He motioned for Susannah to sit on the deck and pulled out a few slices of bread, then a glistening slice of beef, and handed them to her. Her eyes wide, she pressed the beef between the bread, then opened her mouth to take a bite.

"One moment, Sister." She closed her mouth and paused in deference to the priest, embarrassed that she had forgotten to pray. From an especially large pocket, he plucked a dinner plate and a setting of silver, then arranged them on the bird-dropping-mottled plank at her feet.

"We are not animals, are we?"

Susannah's eyes widened and a laugh leapt from her lungs. She tried to press it back in with her hand, but it kept coming, filling up her chest and tumbling out. The priest began to laugh too, high and shrill, and the peculiar sound only made her laugh harder. Her eyes spilled over and she cut into the food with the silver knife, its handle inlaid with mother-of-pearl, and shoveled the still-warm beef into her mouth.

That night Father Milani retired to the men's quarters belowdecks and Susannah lay in her hard berth sleeping fitfully, dreaming of the clanking silverware in the stateroom. Then the dream shifted, and she was standing on the hurricane deck, bracing herself against the pitch of the lake. She glanced to the lookout perch at the top of the wide ladder beside the stacks, and there was Edward, appraising the lake in all directions. A wave washed over the deck in her dream and she shot up and gasped in the dark room full of sleeping passengers. It took a moment for the terror to subside—she felt sure he had found her—but finally she convinced herself that it had been just a dream. Edward was back in Buffalo, at least for now, and Susannah was still on the boat, moving farther away from him day by day.

Seven days passed, a tedious sentence of waiting. She met the priest once a day for food. Twice he was so late that she feared he had gotten too drunk and fallen overboard, but eventually he always came and passed her the stolen meals wrapped in a napkin. He was not allowed to stay with her in the women's quarters, and both of them agreed it was best that she stay out of sight, so she spent much of the time alone in her berth. One of the women near her was unraveling a moth-eaten sweater, then winding the yarn into skeins and knitting squares to be sewn together into a blanket. Susannah gestured with her hands an offer to help—the woman did not speak English—and she nodded happily, producing a second pair of needles for the task. Still, the time passed slowly.

A few times, when she couldn't bear the stench of her quarters, Susannah allowed herself a brief escape up the stairs to the main deck. They were fortunate not to encounter another large storm, but they were forced to stop twice to take in wood. The first time she watched as the ship stopped near a sandy beach and a dozen men spent five hours flinging logs from a smaller boat into the wood hold. Two days later they stopped again. One of the women told her she had heard that the first load of wood turned out to be too green. And so another day was lost to delay. Finally, on the ninth morning, a noise woke Susannah with a start and she glanced at the rectangle of light coming down the staircase. She tried to identify what it was that had startled her out of her dream, then realized it was not a noise but the absence of noise. After so many hours on the boat she had become accustomed to the fidgeting and coughing of the boiler, the incessant rush of water beneath the paddle wheels. But now everything was still. She sat up on her berth and listened as the bolts that held it suspended from the ceiling creaked with her movement.

The steerage deck was mostly empty, and Susannah wondered how long she had slept. She stood and smoothed her dirty hair back as best she could—she had found enough water for washing up only twice since the trip began. The sister's black gown certainly had been an appropriate choice. Susannah knew the elbows and the hem were soiled, but it didn't show. She wrapped the borrowed blanket over her shoulders and climbed the stairs into the fresh morning air.

Gulls circled in the sky and as Susannah ascended, she saw that the boat had docked. A deckhand was emptying a cask of kitchen remains into the water, fish heads and other scraps, and the birds were in a frenzy over it. She glanced at the shore. A handful of motley buildings, some little more than shacks, lined the docks, just as they did in Buffalo's port. She had a feeling that maybe no place near the water was any different from the next.

Beyond the anonymity of the port, distinctive features of the city came into view. Against the sky, church spires and towers were illuminated in the morning sun like a celestial city. The *Thomas Jefferson* was docked in a strait between Lake Erie and a much smaller body of water, the narrow entrance to which was clogged with the chaotic traffic of canoes and sailing vessels. The small lake opened to Lake Huron. This was Detroit.

The deck was as busy as a Manhattan City street. A few children darted between the other passengers, chasing a ball. Others stood at the gunwale, leaning out, calling to the people on the dock. The deckhands slid a gangway into place and the crowd on the deck shifted toward it. They shouldered bundles and packs. Tired women leaned against the arms of the men they had come with or the arms of the men they had acquired on the boat.

Not everyone was bound for Detroit, however, and some passengers held their children back by the shoulders to keep them out of the way. Susannah stood among them and watched the scene, hugging the thin blanket against her arms. It was then that she saw a man ten feet away from her, dabbing his forehead with a crisp white handkerchief. Her fingers clenched in recognition before the syllables of his name could form in her mind: Wendell Beals! Edward's loyal employee had been on the boat with her since Buffalo. She felt a cold terror wash down her back.

Susannah touched the black bonnet to be sure it covered her hair, then backed away from the rest of the people while watching Wendell out of the corner of her eye. She tried to understand what was happening. Had Edward sent him

after her? How had he known where she would go? There
wasn't time to find Father Milani or ask for his help. Wendell
was not moving toward the gangway, and she remembered
then what he had said at the dinner party—it seemed like a
thousand years ago—about going to visit his cousin in Green
Bay. So he hadn't come at Edward's bidding. But he would
surely relish the chance to discover her and bring her back to
him. If Wendell was going to stay on the boat, Susannah had
to get off.

With her heart pounding in her ears, she pushed her way
into the crowd and tried to put as many people as possible
between Wendell and herself. She didn't know if he had seen
her, but she didn't dare look back to find out. The departing
passengers shuffled down the gangway at an unbearably slow
pace. Susannah hugged her arms against her chest, counting
her steps to keep the panic down. Finally they reached the
dock and she broke away from the crowd and ran, the way
she would run from a wolf at her heels. Her boots pounded
the hard dirt as the distance grew between the whipping
ends of her hair and the boat, one more link that tried to pull
her back to Edward.

Chapter Seven

"What is hope?"

Magdelaine read the question from the cloth-bound book that lay open on her lap, then looked up at the four girls who sat before her in the sitting room and waited for an answer. For all her resistance to the house, Magdelaine was willing to admit that it had its benefits. When she had held her catechism class in the trading cabin, the girls shivered on cold days and argued over who would get to sit in the single chair. Now they were arranged comfortably on the sofa and in the high-backed armchairs, a fire warming the room, and each held a copy of the text and followed along. At noon, they knew, Esmee would serve them a meal at the dining table, and the promise of the food kept their minds from wandering too far from the lesson.

Three of the girls had been her students for nearly a year and Magdelaine was pleased to see their progress. They were half-breeds just as she was, all around fifteen or sixteen years old, living in cabins with dirt floors with mothers who waited for their husbands to return at the end of the trading season. The women knew very well that their men had white wives and children back in Quebec or Detroit. The Indian women were "summer wives," and the men treated them with as much respect as they would a servant or slave. Yet the mothers gave their children French names. They were no fools, these summer wives. They had seen what white blood and a white name could get a person in this world, and they were determined their children should claim their due. These girls came to Magdelaine for lessons never having held a book, with no concept of how to read the words on its pages, but they were hungry to learn from her. The mere fact that she owned dozens of these mysterious objects made her, in their eyes, wealthy beyond belief.

And now she had acquired a fourth student, a taciturn girl named Noelle who, somehow, already knew how to read. She wore a large dress that hung on her shoulders and swam around her body, and her face was often flushed. Despite this she was arresting, with curling black hair and porcelain skin. She rarely spoke in front of the other students, but she always knew the answer to the catechism's questions.

Magdelaine waited for the answer to her question about hope. "It is a virtue infused by God into the soul," read Amelia, whose father treated his island children better than most. Amelia had a chance, Magdelaine thought, of marrying well, climbing up to a different kind of life. Though Magdelaine loved Mackinac down in her bones, she knew that a grim life awaited these girls if they didn't try to improve themselves and their lot.

They continued on through the questions. Three times, Amelia rushed to answer ahead of the other girls, and finally Magdelaine raised an eyebrow at her. She sat back slightly in the armchair and pressed her lips together. Marie managed to stumble through a line without too much help and grinned at her teacher, showing off the gap between her front teeth. Pauline and Amelia took turns then and pronounced the words one syllable at a time, without intonation, without comprehension. Only Noelle refused to read aloud, shaking her head, her lips arranged in a perfect little circle of fear. She followed along, her mouth moving, as the others read, but the nature of her face changed as each question probed some aspect of the faith. Unlike the others, she was considering the words she read.

"Why is morning so fit a time for prayer?" Magdelaine read.

When the others remained silent, she nodded at Amelia. "To open the windows of the soul to the light of divine grace . . ."

"Marie, what do you think that means?" Magdelaine asked.

Marie's eyes dropped to the page. She scanned the left, then the right, then back again, her finger trailing along the margin. She colored, blinking, and chewed on her lip before she apologized. "Madame, I seem to have lost my place."

"My dear, the answer is not on the page. I am merely asking. *Why* do we pray in the morning?" Marie bit down harder on her lip and Magdelaine turned to the others, but a compelling spot of carpet or drapery held each one's attention. She sighed. "All right. Here is another question, perhaps more difficult than the last. Why do you think I ask you to read this catechism?" She could hear them breathing, the sound of a frantic ankle tapping against the leg of a chair. Near the window, the preposterous dove rustled in its cage, and Magdelaine willed herself not to look at it. "Girls, come now. Show a little courage. You have minds—use them."

Amelia cleared her throat. "Because you want us to learn to read and write?"

Magdelaine nodded. "Well, yes, that's true. Those skills will set you apart, give you the chance to learn about things you might never see. But I have other reasons too."

Marie whispered her answer once, and repeated it when the others couldn't hear. "Because you want us to become Catholics, madame?"

Magdelaine nodded. She had seen what happened to the Odawa who dug their heels in, insisted on keeping to their old ways of living. You had to be pragmatic. It was a way of being shrewd, as one had to be shrewd in business. It was a way of surviving. But what she was trying to teach the girls had little to do with religion. "There is yet another reason. A bigger reason."

"You want us to be careful," Noelle said, holding Magdelaine's gaze to avoid the sudden stares of the other girls. She rested her delicate hands on her lap one atop the other. The sleeves of her too-large dress nearly engulfed them.

The answer was vague, but something in Noelle's expression communicated absolute understanding. "Yes," Magdelaine said. "That's precisely it. I want you to be careful, careful in what you say and what you do, what you allow your life to become. I ask you to read these questions because you are valuable to me. Your life is valuable to me, and it should be valuable to you. It is *certainly* valuable to God. And, if you can know this, perhaps you will think differently. Perhaps you will be careful, as Noelle says."

She wasn't sure how to make them understand. Women had little say over their fate, and half-breed women on this distant island had less say than most. But if they knew their worth, they might insist on respect, or kindness at the very least. They might have the wisdom to know the difference between a good man and a man who cared only for himself, who saw a woman as a thing to be used and discarded. Magdelaine couldn't help but think of her sisters. Josette and Therese had been so valuable to Magdelaine. She should have let them know—should have made sure they knew.

Therese had been born first, and then Magdelaine, just one year later. But nine more years passed before Josette joined them. Their mother lost many babies in those years and had all but given up hope that she could birth another healthy child. When Josette finally arrived, she was greeted like the miracle she was. Magdelaine and Therese were in awe of her. Once she was old enough, they took Josette with them everywhere they went—their baby, they called her, their *petit lapin*. When Josette took her first steps, it was from Therese's arms to Magdelaine's that she toddled, on the sand of the beach Magdelaine could see now from her sitting-room window.

Magdelaine glanced up to see Esmee waiting patiently in the doorway that led to the dining room. Her apron was dusted with flour, her fingertips stained a purplish black from the elderberry preserves she had baked inside tarts as a surprise for the students. "Madame, the dinner is ready." Magdelaine nodded and the girls went to the table. Esmee served the stew and each girl raised her spoon primly, careful not to slurp, as they knew that dining at the table too was part of their lesson. All except Noelle, who scooped the broth to her mouth twice as fast as the others. It dribbled down her chin and she leaned forward over the bowl.

"Noelle," Magdelaine said. "There is no need to hurry."

She nodded as she shoveled in a few more bites and wiped her chin with the back of her hand. "I'm sorry. I don't know why I am so hungry."

Magdelaine gave her a weak smile. They all were hungry, in one way or another, and she felt it acutely each time they were in the same room. She worried for them, and she worried for Miss Dove, who still had not arrived. The previous night Magdelaine had stood on the front porch and watched as a boat docked, then waited to see if she would be able to identify Miss Dove from afar. Men disembarked and walked up the beach—a few soldiers, a group of plain-dressed men who were probably missionaries coming to see Reverend Howe—but not one woman. Magdelaine wondered whether Miss Dove was still making her way west, or whether she would be like the others Father Adler had sent to Magdelaine, women who desperately needed help but stayed just out of reach.

Since she had first learned of Miss Dove's impending arrival, spring had come to Mackinac. Magdelaine had been busy, first with settling in to the house and then overseeing production of maple syrup on Bois Blanc. She and Jean-Henri had tapped most of the trees themselves back in

March, then hired a dozen men to work in shifts boiling the sap down in pots on an enormous fire over several days. These days, it wasn't hard to come by men in need of work on the island. The beaver, which had made many white men very rich, was almost entirely gone from the region, and the men who made their living trading its pelts were now out of work.

After the girls had gone home, Magdelaine and Jean-Henri paddled over to Bois Blanc to bring back the last of the syrup. The grocer would sell some of it on the island to women who would use it in their cooking. The rest would travel on the next southbound steamer to Detroit and beyond, packaged as a souvenir of the quaint and backward Indian country, where they took their sugar from trees instead of cane.

The heavy pails of syrup were sealed closed with pine pitch, and Jean-Henri and Magdelaine lifted them one at a time into the canoes, then pushed off. They paddled slowly, careful not to rock their vessels, which rode low in the water from the weight.

"*Mon fils*," Magdelaine said to Jean-Henri. "When you write to Mr. Greive, be sure to tell him that you are able to depart for the city immediately, now that spring is here. We want him to know that you are a man of expediency." She was anxious to get back and finish their work in case a boat should arrive before the sun set. "Not a moment to be wasted, your father always said."

Jean-Henri sighed and said nothing. She glanced over at him. In the afternoon light he looked handsome but tired, with the beginnings of wrinkles fanning out from the corners of his eyes. He was no longer a young man, and she had known it for a while. But when had it happened? It seemed he had been a child—a trying child at that, full of fears she could never placate, nothing at all like his father—and then, suddenly, he had become this man who appeared before her, already worn down by the world. Where was his ambition, his pride?

"You *will* write to Mr. Greive, Jean, will you not?" He was running out of time. Soon it would be too late for him to start again. "Do you know how many letters I had to write to persuade him to consider you?"

Jean-Henri nodded. "Yes," he said. "I know."

She tipped her head back in frustration, then exhaled. "Is there something you are not telling me? Something that is keeping you here?"

"No. I don't know how to make you understand."

A thought occurred to her, and she brightened. "Do you have a lover? Because a grandchild could change my mind." He was so morose, and she knew she only made it worse by prodding him. Loneliness oozed from him. She didn't understand why he would want to stay here without a reason.

He shook his head. "There are girls. I know you think I've lived as a monk since Celine called off the engagement, but it isn't true. There are girls. But I do not love them."

"Love grows, over time. You are looking for perfection."

"You and Father had very little time, but you had love, did you not? Do you not wish the same for me?"

Magdelaine scoffed. "I met your father when I was fifteen, married him at eighteen, buried him at nineteen. By the time I was your age I was a widow with a seven-year-old son."

"What does age matter?" he said, almost to himself, as the paddle skimmed the undulating waves.

Her son was right. She and her husband had had love from the first day Henri passed through her father's trading cabin after a long winter in the interior. He saw Magdelaine wring the neck of a chicken in the yard, her lean arms taut, and before she could look up at the sound his boots made on the gravel, he was beside her. He had a strong chin, wild curling hair filthy with months of work, with sleeping on the ground, and hands so dark with dirt they looked burned. He came back each year. One spring she had poured a cup of wine for him at the feast to celebrate the traders' return, and Henri let his fingers linger on her wrist for a moment before he took the cup and drank it down. They married the following year. The wedding took place in the fall, and they left for the winter together and traveled as partners, despite his men's grumbling. Magdelaine was no summer wife. When she left the hot heaven of Henri's bedroll she gave orders—she learned how to oversee the care of the dogs, how to plan the day's journey, how to ensure that they had enough food and fuel to make it to the next safe camp for the night—and the men had no choice but to obey. When Henri died that first spring, shot by an Indian to whom he had refused to sell liquor, she led the men back to Mackinac herself, Henri's body in the bottom of her canoe and Jean-Henri already growing in her belly.

She wanted her son to have it, that kind of love, but Magdelaine suspected that not everyone could. It was reserved for the bold, the sure-footed, who seized a thing before they thought about the consequences. Magdelaine had known the joy of it. But Jean-Henri took after his Aunt Therese—he was cautious, hesitant. He waited so long to choose his course that it was chosen for him, or the path was closed off. This failure to act could lead merely to disappointment and missed opportunities, or, in Therese's case, to an abdication with disastrous consequences.

Thinking about her sisters renewed Magdelaine's anxiety over Miss Dove's safety, and she let Jean-Henri's silence rest between them for now as the last word on the subject of Montreal.

"*Mon fils*, if Miss Dove arrives tonight, I will want to write to Father Adler directly and let him know. He will be anxious to hear. Will you see that the letter gets on the first southbound boat?"

He straightened up and dipped his paddle with a little more force, relieved that the subject had changed.

"Of course."

They reached the shore and pulled the heavy canoes up onto the sand. The hired men walked down the beach to help and, two at a time, lifted the casks of syrup onto a wagon that would take them to Market Street. Ani circled in the dune thistle, then trotted over to them and moved among their boots, looking for Magdelaine. She whistled for him and he came over to her, then sat down at her feet and gazed up, his head cocked, his eyes inquiring. He was the strongest dog she had ever had, beautifully trained and completely obedient. Dogs were so much easier to raise than sons, she thought. Jean-Henri had been a man for a long time, but he floundered still, purposeless here on the island.

"You know, Mother," Jean-Henri said. "Things will work

out this time, with Miss Dove. It will be different. I know it will."

"Oh, Jean," she sighed, her hand massaging the thick fur at the nape of Ani's neck. "I hope you are right."

Inside the house, Esmee was sitting in one of the armchairs, with white fabric draped over her lap. She stood when they entered the room and reached to take Jean-Henri's hat.

"Monsieur, I am finishing the last of your shirts. If you'd like to try one on, I can check the length of the sleeve to be sure it is right."

Jean-Henri gave her a confused look, then turned to his mother. "What shirts?"

Esmee looked down. "Forgive me, madame. Did I speak out of turn?"

"What shirts?" he said again to Magdelaine, his voice edged with irritation.

"I asked Esmee to make you some shirts, for your new position. You will have to wait until you get to the city to have a proper jacket made." Though Esmee was skilled at embroidery, she wouldn't know how to make a French jacket for a man any better than she would have known how to make down shoulder puffs for a gigot sleeve or elbow-length silk gloves. She had never been off the island, never seen what French men and women wore, except maybe in a picture. Island girls learned from their mothers how to sew broadcloth cloaks and skirts, buckskin mittens lined with fur. Even the shirts wouldn't be fine, but Magdelaine wanted her son to have something of his own, something to remind him of home. Perhaps it would bolster him and keep him from giving up this time.

Jean-Henri shook his head slowly, then laughed, not with amusement but with frustration. "Infuriating," he said to his mother for the second time that spring. "Infuriating and relentless. I have yet to write to Mr. Greive and you have already packed my trunk. Why did you waste Esmee's time with this nonsense? Why can't you let me be?"

Silence stretched between them in the sitting room, taut as a wire. Perhaps Esmee could no longer bear it, because she leapt a few rungs above her station by speaking up. "Well, either way, you will be able to wear the shirts, monsieur. Whether you stay or go."

Jean-Henri looked at her in surprise, as if he had forgotten she was in the room. "Well, yes, I suppose that's true."

Flush climbed up Esmee's cheeks and temples. "Forgive me," she said, afraid to look up into his face once again. "I only meant that you should not worry that my time was wasted."

Jean-Henri nodded at her, then looked at his mother one last time and shook his head again, before stalking out of the room.

Esmee returned to the fabric on the chair and folded it into a neat square. The sewing basket contained the finished shirts, as well as a half dozen handkerchiefs embroidered with Jean-Henri's initials and two pairs of moccasins, one plain hide and one lined with rich blue wool, expertly embroidered with silk ribbon and white glass beads around the cuff.

"Esmee," Magdelaine said, as she appraised the work. "These are very fine. But really, the shirts would have been sufficient."

"Oh, I don't mind." She wound a loose piece of thread around her forefinger. "No good comes from idle hands."

"I don't think my son will appreciate the care and effort. But thank you."

Esmee bit down on her bottom lip in a kind of shy smile and shrugged. "You must be hungry after all that work. Let me fix you something to eat."

Just then Jean-Henri called down from the top of the stairs. "Mother, a boat is coming into the harbor."

Magdelaine went out onto the porch to wait. From there she could see the boats and the figures of the people who disembarked, though not the details of their faces. Magdelaine stood frozen in place as the passengers walked down the dock. She had waited so long to make good on her promise to Father Adler. She tried to imagine Miss Dove's face and saw someone with black hair and big dark eyes. The image made her cringe. She was imagining Josette's face, Josette's eyes. She felt the impulse to sigh and withheld the breath. This Miss Dove would be no ghost. She was a living, breathing woman who needed her help.

Once again, though, Magdelaine was disappointed. Miss Dove was not on the boat.

Chapter Eight

Susannah ran, her boots thundering on the wood plank sidewalks into the heart of Detroit. When she felt her chest would explode, she stopped and doubled over to catch her breath. In the road, horses pulled crude open carriages that carried men in pristine white collars and new hats. The barefoot servants who rode on the back platforms dragged their heels in the dirt. Wagons stacked with crates shuddered by too; in the crates were onions and potatoes and tallow, nails and glass bottles jangling together, horseshoes and firewood and a cluster of inert pheasants tied at the feet. One wagon contained a gleaming grand piano nestled in a bed of hay.

She backed out of the street and into an alley between two tall buildings. Her mind continued to race. Had Wendell seen her? No matter what happened now, the question would dog her. One letter from Wendell to Edward would send her husband after her, and she would soon be back in Buffalo.

Susannah felt her stomach lurch when she realized she had a more immediate problem. Sister Mary Genevieve had told her to stay on the boat, no matter what, because if Susannah left it, the nun wouldn't be able to help her. And now here she was, alone in a city where she didn't know a soul. She had no food, no place to lay her head, and not a penny to her name. She still had the necklace, but in order to make use of it she would have to find someplace to sell it.

She realized with equal parts remorse and relief that she had brought the blanket with her. She hadn't meant to steal it. Back in Buffalo, quilts and comforters puffed with goose feathers sat folded in a closet, but this filthy square of coarse wool was more precious to her than any of them. Susannah had never really been cold in her life, she had never been dirty, nor had she even worn the same dress two days in a row. And she had never, in all of her life, been so alone.

There was no one to help her now. No maid to bring her some food, no kindly nun or Irish carriage driver or priest to take her elbow and lead her to safety. She had made a disaster out of her plan for escape. Susannah sank to the ground with her back against the cold brick wall and stared at her hands. For a moment, despair took over. She might as well turn back to Buffalo, save Edward the trouble of having to come find her. But then she felt that hard rock of resolve in her chest, the determination that had helped her escape. She couldn't give up.

Several hours of daylight remained, she told herself, enough for her to sell the necklace and find a meal and a room for herself in a boardinghouse. Then she would write to Sister Mary Genevieve and explain what happened, and hope that the woman would forgive her mistake and find a way to help her. She would take the cheapest room she could find and try to make the money last as long as possible. What she would do tomorrow, or the next day, felt too daunting to imagine.

Susannah glanced up and down the street, knowing that a goldsmith had to be somewhere in the city. Her stomach churned with hunger, and she felt she would do almost anything for a little food and a pail of hot water to wash her face and hands. Her dress was crusted with white around the armpits and the collar. She walked a mile before she spotted a shop.

Crouched in an alley between two buildings, Susannah hitched her dress up to her waist and tore away the handkerchief that held the necklace. Glancing around once more, she took a breath and unwrapped it. The crisp lines and brilliant color of the necklace splashed over her like cool water. The garnets were deep but clear, the goldwork delicate. It was plain to see that this had been not just her mother's favorite piece, but also the most valuable one.

Martha Brownell had been the sort of woman who was so sure of herself and her place in the world that she was like an ancient tree, rooted and immovable. To Susannah, it seemed her mother knew everything—botany and natural philosophy, the mythology of the Greeks, Shakespeare's mysterious dark lady. But unlike most women, Martha didn't learn these things to further her reputation or earn the praise of her peers. She studied the world as if it were a fleeting thing. And it was. The sheet music Susannah's father, Phillip, bought her was a puzzle to be solved; she played the piano for the pure joy of it, with the windows thrown open, even when there wasn't anyone home to hear it.

But one wet, cold November week, Martha developed a fever that rendered her delirious. She cried out thanking her husband for all that he had given her: passage to America, a fine home and beautiful clothes and trinkets, a daughter. After that fit, she fell comatose for weeks. Phillip and Susannah took turns at her bedside reading her stories, spooning broth between her lips. Father and daughter were astonished when she finally emerged from the episode, blinking with clear eyes at the morning sun that spilled across her quilt. But their relief was short-lived. Soon it became clear that the prolonged fever had left its mark on Martha's mind. She was dim, forgetful. The books she had raced through, her index finger trailing the page, sat unopened where she had left them before the illness. The kettle had become an enigma to her and she watched it, questioningly, as Susannah fixed her tea. To see her intelligent mother reduced to a heap of need, of childlike wanting for sweets and enchantment with the tumbling tail of a kite in the wind, was a horror.

Phillip devoted himself completely to his wife's care. He summoned doctors from across the city, from Boston and Philadelphia, and even once brought an Indian healer to the house. He hired a nurse to live with them and answer Martha's every request. His patience and tenderness were without limit, as he led his wife from room to room, helping her to relearn the names of her favorite things: *Lavender. Calico. Velvet.* Occasionally, she would have a flash of sudden understanding and ask, "I wasn't always this way, Phillip—was I?" in a hushed voice, as if it were a terrible secret. She would begin to cry and he would hold her hand and whisper words to her: *Helpmate. Ardent friend.* Until she knew what they meant, until she knew they were meant for her. She had come back from the brink of death, forever changed, only to die a few years later from cholera, alongside her husband, leaving her daughter alone in the world.

Susannah wrapped the necklace back up and held it in her palm as she crossed the street and rang the bell at the goldsmith's. A slight man with an upturned nose answered the door.

"Yes?" he said, his eyes scanning her dress. He kept a grip on the door. "I don't have any food to give you."

"No, sir, I'm here about a necklace of my mother's. I'd like to sell it."

"It belonged to your mother, did it?"

"Yes, sir."

"Your own mother, flesh and blood? Because I don't buy stolen jewelry."

"Sir, I assure you—she left it to me when she died."

He eyed her a moment longer, and then his face softened. "All right, then. Come in."

Susannah stepped into the workshop and over to a table next to the window. She unwrapped the necklace and laid it down.

The goldsmith shut the shop door, sliding the bolt into place, and then joined her. He whistled long and low. "I see you have recently experienced a reversal of fortune. A woman dressed like you, with a necklace like that!"

Susannah felt a jolt of hope. Maybe it would be worth

even more than she thought, enough to buy passage on the next boat to Mackinac.

He draped the necklace over his palm. "These are . . . two, four, six, eight," he whispered as he counted. "Twenty-eight garnets set in gold." The goldsmith looked up at her again, his eyes stern. "Are you *certain* you did not steal this necklace?"

"Please, sir. I am certain."

He stepped to another table containing a tray of tools and a loupe. He poked at the stones with a small pick, then held the necklace up with his left hand and wedged the loupe between it and his eye. His shoulders relaxed and he gave a slow sigh of recognition.

"My dear," he said, looking satisfied that the world had fallen back into line with his expectations. "I am sorry to tell you that these stones are paste."

"What do you mean?"

"Stones made to imitate garnets. And a very good job too. I wouldn't have known without the magnification."

"That can't be," Susannah said. She felt suddenly that she was underwater, the walls of the workshop undulating, the jeweler's tools seeming to drift menacingly toward her. "My father gave my mother that necklace. He was not the sort of man to buy fake gems." Susannah's knees buckled and she gripped the table in an attempt to stay upright. "Do you think he was swindled?"

The goldsmith came around the table and cradled her elbow. "Miss, are you all right? Why don't you sit down?" He led her to a chair. She stared down at her boots, taking shallow breaths. Her hunger was making her weak, and the weakness was like a veil over her eyes.

"It's possible that he was swindled," the goldsmith said. He crossed the room to a pail of water and dipped a brown mug beneath its surface. Water dripped onto her hand as she took the mug and drank. Sweet and cool, it soothed her stomach for a moment. "But there's another possibility. Forgive me for asking, but did your father experience any . . . alterations in his financial situation?"

She thought back to the week after her parents' deaths, when Edward spread her father's papers across the desk in the study, dredging through file after file as creditors called at the house with sheepish looks on their faces for hounding the daughter of a man not yet cold in the ground. Her father had been cautious with his money, until his wife took ill. Then he spent every penny he had on her care. "Yes."

"Well, it is customary, when fortunes are strained or lost, to squeeze money from every corner of the household. There are ways to do so without losing face. As I said, this imitation was done by an expert jeweler. Your mother could have worn it to ten balls and no one would have suspected."

"I see," Susannah said. It hardly mattered, all the things her father had bought for her. Her mother hadn't danced at another ball after the fever stole her mind. The jewels sat in their velvet boxes. When her father needed money, it made sense that he would go to them first.

Of course, the forgery mattered now, mattered in the most immediate and tangible way, as her aching head and rumbling stomach reminded her.

"So you can give me nothing for it, then?" she asked, suddenly feeling strong enough to stand.

"Well, very little, I'm afraid." The goldsmith crossed the room to where the necklace lay on the table. "I might be able to give you enough for a few meals." He held the magnifying glass up to the stones again. "I must say, this is a *remarkably* good forgery."

She saw then that he would try to pass the necklace off as authentic and sell it at a high price to an unsuspecting customer. Or perhaps all of it was a lie. Perhaps the stones were real and this man was the swindler. If she had been wearing one of Susannah Fraser's fine gowns, this man would have dealt fairly with her. Most people cared nothing for right and wrong but only what they could get away with when they thought no one who mattered was watching.

"No, thank you," she said, snatching the necklace out of his hand. She stepped toward the door, feeling stronger for the moment, her head clear.

The goldsmith stepped in front of her. "Well, now, wait a minute. Perhaps I spoke too—"

"I must be on my way," Susannah said.

But the goldsmith didn't move. "Perhaps . . ." He put his hand on her shoulder. "We can come to some sort of an agreement." He was only a few inches taller than Susannah and she looked hard into his eyes. She could hear his breathing quicken.

Over his shoulder the bolt on the door held her in and the rest of the world at bay. Where was it more dangerous? Out there? In here? In a heartbeat she was out in the street, the door slammed shut behind her, and off running. Running again.

For hours, she shuffled through the streets in a famished daze. That no one stopped to try to help her was proof of how accustomed respectable people were to the sight of beggars in this city. As darkness fell, she rapped on the door of a magnificent white stone church, but after a long time an irritated minister came to the door, a linen napkin tucked in his collar, and shooed her away.

Susannah found her feet carrying her back to the wharf. She stepped carefully to avoid the drying mounds of horse dung in the road. The surface of the river reflected the lamplight from the windows, and its greasy surface was pocked with the detritus of travelers: a lost boot, a length of rope.

She passed a saloon with a sagging front porch and from the shadow of a tree watched the place. She heard a fiddle, the rhythmic thud of boots on a wood plank floor stepping in time with the music.

Susannah dipped into the darkness along the side of the building and crossed around to the yard in back. Tables stood in three rows beneath a canvas awning. Candles flickered in the glass shrouds that kept out the wind. At one table four men passed cards in a circle around a pile of coins in the center. A larger group gathered around a wire enclosure. When a bell sounded they began to shout, some shaking fistfuls of paper bills in the air. Two boys in the front stepped away to get a view from the other side, and Susannah saw what they all watched. A large orange rooster held another in the dust with its curved talons. It pecked the eyes of the losing bird with ferocious speed.

One of the card-playing men glanced up at her. He was about eighteen, his right cheek stretched over a wad of tobacco. He elbowed the man next to him. "Would you look at this creature here?" Then, to Susannah, he said, "My lovely, you look lost." He spit a long arc of juice in the dirt at his feet.

She stared at him, frozen.

"Don't be afraid. This is just the sort of place people might come when they're lost."

Susannah turned toward the road, and he called out after her. "That's a lovely dress. Perhaps I can persuade you to lose it in a game of poker!"

She wanted to keep running, but her body was against her, her throat burning with thirst and her nose running, and when she came to a building a few stories taller than the others, with lamps in the upstairs windows, she sank onto the porch steps and leaned her cheek against the weathered baluster. *Just for a moment*, she thought. *Let me rest just for a moment.* Before she slipped away she heard a husky woman's voice cry out. "Ah, Christ Almighty. Bettina, get out here!"

Chapter Nine

Susannah inhaled and opened her eyes, sleep receding like a tide. She glanced around. The room was small, with bare walls and a ceiling of mottled boards. A low lamp burned on a table in a corner. Underneath it, twin black shapes loomed in the darkness. She sat up. A pair of boots, connected to two long, motionless legs. Then she heard it, the sound that had in her sleep become the sound of the steamboat's engine: a snore.

Susannah screamed. Helplessly, she reached for her head, and found that her bonnet was gone. Her hair hung loose around her shoulders. Someone had removed her pins. She touched the sleeve of her dress, where she had tucked the necklace after running from the goldsmith. It was still there.

The door opened, and a petite woman wearing only a corset and petticoat knelt down next to the bed. She had dark eyes and the pert nose of a storybook fairy. She put her hand on Susannah's shoulder. "It's all right. You're all right."

"Where am I?"

"It's all right. You're safe here."

"Who are you?"

"My name is Clementine, but the men call me Tiny. What's yours?"

"What men? Is he one of them?" Susannah gestured toward the man snoring on the floor.

"Christ Almighty!" Tiny turned her face toward the door and shouted into the hall. "Bettina!"

A plump girl with cheeks caked with rouge appeared in the doorway. "What?"

"Did you leave Amos Sharp in here with our poor scared foundling?"

"What—him?" Bettina shrugged. "He needed to sleep it off and Molly said we was wasting enough rooms taking in street trash."

Tiny shook her head. "Can't you see this girl's awake? She can hear what you're saying."

Bettina pursed her lips. "Why should I care?"

Tiny raised a slim dark eyebrow. "Get that drunk weasel out of here before I tell Molly you've been giving it to Sam Clark for free."

"But he's sweet on me!" Bettina whined, her jaw slack.

"Get!" Tiny shouted again, as if at a rat that had found its way into the kitchen.

Bettina scrambled over to the man and wrenched one of his legs up off the floor. She tucked it between her forearm and the breast bulging out of the top of her dress. Like a child pulling a wagon, she dragged the man across the floor. His headed thudded over the threshold and he moaned softly but didn't wake.

"Where am I?" Susannah asked again. She raked her fingers through her hair and then began lacing it into a braid.

"You really were out cold," Tiny said. She reached into her pocket. "Here—your pins. Where you are is Molly's. Finest house of entertainment in Detroit."

Susannah coiled the braid and pinned it in a bun. The black bonnet lay upside down on the table beside the bed, and she pulled it on. Tiny nodded at what she was doing. "That's a good idea. The men who come around here would be awfully interested in that red hair of yours. Are you hungry?"

Susannah's eyes filled at the mere thought of food.

"Well, come on then." Tiny helped Susannah out of the sagging bed and they crossed into the hallway and down the stairs to the parlor. Upholstered chairs lined the perimeter of the room. A few were empty but men sat in most of them, holding their hats on their knees. One was looking through a large book of drawings. He came to one he liked especially well and showed it to the man next to him. Susannah could see only half the picture: the curve of a woman's bare behind. The second man turned the book on its side and leered.

Tiny pulled out a chair at the end of a table, farthest from the men, and motioned for Susannah to sit down. "I'm going to get you some food. Don't talk to anyone, you hear?"

Tiny came back with a piece of fried whitefish on a plate and a bowl of soup, potatoes, and beans. Next to the fish was a hunk of bread slick with butter. Susannah looked at her in disbelief, then spooned the steaming soup into her mouth. The beans were tender and smooth, sweet with butter and onions. She tore into the bread, sopped up the oil from the fish, and shoveled it in.

"Molly makes sure we eat well here. To keep up our strength. Am I right, boys?"

"Right you are, Tiny," said the man with the book.

Tiny winked at Susannah, then lowered her voice. "Now then, why don't you tell me about yourself." She glanced at Susannah's bandaged left hand resting on the tabletop but didn't ask about it. "Underneath all that grime you're a looker. You're not in the market for a job, are you? Because, if you are, Molly always wants—"

"No, thank you," Susannah said quickly, glad her mouth was full of food to hide the mortification in her voice. She chewed, swallowed, marveled at the fact that she was at this moment concerned about offending a prostitute. "I mean, thank you, really, thank you for all of this. But . . ."

"Oh, I know," Tiny said with a laugh. "I'm just having a good time at your expense."

The floor creaked behind Susannah's chair. "Oh, why'd you bring her down here in that widow's garb? She's gonna ruin the mood." Bettina scoffed as she walked around the table. "What's she doing here anyway?"

Tiny sighed with the weariness of Job. "Bettina, you . . . daft . . . cow." She spoke slowly. "Let me explain something to you. These men"—Tiny gestured at the other end of the room—"are drunk or on their way to getting there. And money isn't the only thing they've got in their front pocket for you. *Mood* isn't really on their minds." Bettina pursed her lips, and Tiny shook her head. "I'm sorry if I took the romance out of it for you, girl. If you don't get out of my sight this instant you'll lose your day off. I'm trying to have a conversation here."

Bettina opened her mouth to respond, then thought better of it. She turned to the men. "Daniel Burke, I believe you're next."

A man with his sleeves rolled up to the elbows and dark hair that curled over his collar jumped to his feet, then tried to cover up his eagerness. He followed her out of the parlor.

Susannah watched them ascend the stairs. She could hear Bettina's chatter. "Now, see here, Daniel. I'm going to be Lady Worthington and you're the duke. And you're very, very rich . . ."

"Anything for you, Bettina," Daniel said as he swayed on the stairs.

"I said Lady Worthington!"

"That's right. Okay."

Tiny was listening to the exchange too and shook her head. "We all have our crosses to bear," she said to Susannah. "And that girl is mine."

The food was easing the pain in Susannah's stomach, sweeping the dust out of her mind, and she felt warmth coming into her cheeks. "Clementine," she said, the words awkward. "I don't know what I would have done if you hadn't—"

Tiny waved her hand. "I only did what anyone would when they saw a woman passed out on their front steps."

"Not one person—not one—would help me today. I think I've wandered every inch of this city."

Tiny pursed her lips. "Well, I suppose I was raised right." She laughed. "So, where did you come from? I don't even know your name."

Susannah wondered what, if anything, she had confessed in her stupor. Now that she was in Detroit, the story she had told the teacher on the boat no longer made sense. If she really was on her way to becoming a nun, why hadn't she gone to a church for help? If she was bound for St. Louis, why had she gotten off the boat in Detroit? And why didn't she have a penny to her name? She decided she would simply tell the truth, or a sort of truth, which, Susannah was discovering, was the only real kind.

"Susannah," she said. "I'm trying to get to Mackinac. But all my money is gone."

Tiny appraised Susannah's dress. "Are you a missionary?"

"Something like that. You of all people must understand the importance of secrets."

Tiny giggled. "What, me? I'm an open book. Raised in the lap of luxury. Always dreamed of growing up to become a whore. It's a marvelous life." Her voice turned hollow on the last part, and Susannah must have winced because Tiny rushed to say, "It's really not so bad here. I make more money than my father ever did, and he was a cordwainer for twenty years."

"In New York?"

Tiny shook her head. "In New Hampshire. Concord." Then her face spread into a devilish grin. "Or Portland, or Boston, or Springfield, or Albany. Depends on the night. Depends on the man. Sometimes I ran away from a girl's school. Sometimes my mother was killed in a fire. Sometimes my family warned me out of town because I was a bad seed, right from the start." She lowered her voice to a throaty whisper. "A very, very bad seed."

"Well, which story is the truth?"

"Does it matter?" Tiny looked tired. The early-morning sun shone through the window and revealed wrinkles in the corners of her eyes.

"It should," Susannah said. She suddenly wanted very much for Tiny to trust her, but her words sounded like a reproach.

"Fairly haughty for a woman who dresses like a nun but isn't one, and won't say why she's traveling north."

Men began to clomp down the stairs, tucking in their shirts as they went. They passed through the parlor and turned toward the kitchen, where a back door would let them out into the alley.

"Funny," Tiny said. "They always come *in* through the front door, but they never leave that way."

"Morning, darling," said a portly man in a silk waistcoat. He nodded at Susannah, then placed his hat on his head.

"Good morning, Jim. See you Friday." When they all had left the room, she looked at Susannah. "If you need money, you could try it out here for a while. It probably seems impossible to you, but you'd be surprised what you can get used to."

Susannah gave her a weak smile. "What do you do now, this time of day? Washing and things?"

Tiny held up the back of her hands to Susannah. "Do these hands look like they've seen the washboard? Wouldn't touch it with a ten-foot pole. We have servant girls who do that for us. They cook too, bring wine up to our rooms in the evening. Now's the time of day when we sleep. Molly's not going to let me keep you around here eating our food for free, but why don't you stay long enough for a rest before you go?"

Susannah meant to demur, but she was so tired. "It sounds wonderful." They rose and pushed their chairs in beneath the grand dining table, then moved toward the staircase. The banister curved toward a landing on the second floor, its surface slick from the thousands of palms that had passed over it, some belonging to eager men, some to hesitant men, visiting Molly's for the first time. The house was as quiet as a church now, all the visitors gone home except for Lady Worthington's duke.

When Susannah and Tiny were halfway up the stairs, the front door swung open and the knob crashed into the wall behind it. They turned back to see a man swaying in the door frame.

"Now," he said, "which one of you is going to give me back my money?"

"Oh, Christ," Tiny said under her breath. "Sir, we are closed until the evening."

"You're not closed until I get my money."

"Do I know you? I don't think I've seen you here before."

"No, I'm only passing through. But I passed here last night and was the victim of a grievous theft." He slurred the last few words.

Tiny glanced at Susannah. "This is why I tell them to lock the damn door, but do they listen?" Then, to the man, "You were dissatisfied with your service here?"

"The blasted girl stole my wallet. I had money in it when I arrived and now it's all gone."

"Perhaps," Tiny said, approaching him slowly. "Perhaps you indulged a bit too much in our fine spirits and cannot recall how many hours you spent with your . . . What did you say the girl's name was?"

"Rosie. Dark hair and . . ." He cupped his hands at his chest. "Tall."

Tiny nodded and stepped off the bottom stair. "I see what's happened. All the row houses on this street look alike. The place you want is two doors down. Alice's. That's where Rosie works."

The man squinted at Tiny. In one swift motion he reached for her shoulder and yanked her against him, his arm locked around her torso, holding her back against his chest. Her feet hung a foot above the floor. "I know where I was last night. Right here."

Susannah stood frozen at the banister. Tiny shrieked, kicking her legs. "Let me go."

"Don't scream."

Tiny turned her face toward his upper arm and bit at his sleeve, but he jerked his body away before she got her teeth into him. He grabbed her jaw with his free hand and squeezed it.

"Oh, please," Susannah cried. "Don't hurt her."

He laughed. "Oh, how you'll be sorry for that bite. I'll say it once more. I want my money."

"Rot in hell." Tiny spit on his shoe. He gave her petite frame a violent shake. "I can't breathe, you beast."

Susannah saw the light glint off an object in his left hand

before her mind registered what it was. He pressed the flat side of the blade against Tiny's throat and her eyes widened. She looked at Susannah.

And suddenly Susannah knew what she had to do. "Sir, I have something for you, if you will just please let her go." She unrolled her cuff. "This necklace is worth probably a hundred times what you say you lost last night."

He narrowed his eyes at it, then looked at Susannah as if for the first time. "What the hell kind of whore are you, dressed like that?"

"Please take it, and please let her go."

He hesitated, weighing his options, then finally cast Tiny toward Susannah, and she fell to the floor at the foot of the stairs. He grabbed the necklace with the knife still in his hand. The stones gleamed in the morning light as he slipped it into his jacket pocket along with the knife. "I cannot wait to leave this wretched city." He stepped out into the street and closed the door behind him.

Susannah helped up Tiny, who rubbed the skin of her throat with her fingers to confirm that it was still intact.

"Are you all right?"

"I'm fine," Tiny said. "What a maniac. If you had that necklace all along, why didn't you try to sell it?"

"I did try, yesterday, but the goldsmith told me it was a fake. It belonged to my mother."

"A fake? It certainly looked the part."

"Well," Susannah said, the reality of what she had done in giving it away beginning to sink in. "The gold was real. It *was* worth something. Maybe he'll give it to his wife."

Tiny giggled, then threw her head back to laugh. She

swept a handkerchief out of the top of her corset and dabbed her eyes. "Wives. They bear the brunt of it, don't they? At least I get paid to put up with these men. I'm willing to bet that weasel's wife is at home this minute, up to her elbows in flour or waddling around with a ripe belly."

"We're blessed then, aren't we?" Susannah said softly. "Not to be wives."

Tiny regarded her, then nodded. "You saved my life, Susannah. That man could have killed me."

"I've settled my debt to you, then."

Tiny shook her head. "Wait here." She went up the stairs and down the hall. Susannah heard a door open and close. She pressed her cheek against the ornate wallpaper that lined the stairwell, no longer tired—the man with a knife had seen to that—but merely stunned by all that had taken place since she found Sister Mary Genevieve's feather waiting on her table in the greenhouse. She thought about Mackinac and whether she would ever see it, wondered what kind of wildflowers grew there, wondered whether they were different from those she found in Buffalo. The fall might come earlier there, the ice crunching underfoot before the last leaves had drifted to the ground.

Tiny came back down the stairs and pressed a wad of notes into Susannah's hand. "*These* are authentic, to be sure."

Susannah glanced at the money. It was enough to purchase a ticket to the island and a few meals besides. But when she thought about what Tiny had been forced to do to earn it, Susannah felt her stomach turn. "This is too much," she said, trying to hand some of the money back to Tiny.

"Don't waste my time refusing. I can make it back in one night."

Susannah clutched her hand. "Thank you, Clementine."

"Easy come, easy go," she said, smiling. "Now, I've got to get some sleep. If you'd like to stay I can set up one of the empty rooms for you."

"Thank you," Susannah said. "But I have a ticket to buy."

She rolled the money into her sleeve and opened the row house door. The morning was bright and cool, and she felt a little astonished to be seeing it at all after what she had endured in the last two days. If she had known how hard she would have to fight for her own escape, she might have stayed right where she was in Buffalo, tiptoeing around Edward Fraser until he killed her. But instead of exhaustion or fear she felt a little trill of hope in her chest. For the first time in her life Susannah had found a way to take care of herself—she wasn't waiting on anyone else to do it for her. She was so much sturdier than she had known.

Back at the port she purchased her ticket and a mug of hot, black coffee, along with some bread and cured meat. The boat to Mackinac would depart in an hour, a smaller vessel than the *Thomas Jefferson*, but one that, she hoped, did not contain anyone who knew Susannah Fraser. Still, she wasn't going to take any chances this time. As soon as she was on board she would find a quiet corner and stay there, out of sight, until she reached her destination.

When the deckhands slid the gangway into place and started letting new passengers board, Susannah returned the empty mug to the vendor and started toward the boat. Just then she felt a hand on her elbow and gasped. But she spun around to find, not Edward, but Father Milani.

"Miss Dove! Thank heavens," he said. "I have been looking for you all night long. Why on earth did you leave the boat?"

He looked peaked, sick from either drink or worry, or both. So perhaps he hadn't spent the *entire* night searching, she thought with a smile. Still, she regretted any trouble she had caused him. "I saw a man I know, an employee of my husband's, and realized he had been on the boat with us since Buffalo. I didn't stop to think—I just ran."

Father Milani nodded. "I saw you running, and I rushed off to follow you, but you disappeared into the city. Do you think the man on the boat recognized you?"

"I don't know." Susannah prayed that she had looked to Wendell like merely one more immigrant in the crowd. If he had seen her, though, Edward would soon be on his way to Detroit. "But I certainly don't plan to wait here and find out."

"Of course," Father Milani said. "Let me just buy our tickets." He turned toward the ticket window.

"You need buy only one," she called to him. "I have paid my own way."

Chapter Ten

After two weeks of searching for Susannah's body with his men, Nathaniel returned to Hawkshill as the sun was setting. He found Edward standing at the window in his study noticing the change in the angle of light, now that spring was upon them. Soon, the leaves would burst out of their buds.

Edward had always believed that drink was ruinous, that it was foolish for a man to dull his ability to perceive, to react. But he had poured himself one glass of scotch after another since his wife disappeared and by now had come to understand its appeal. He hadn't expected the way drink would put him at arm's length from himself, give him a rest.

When Marjorie led Nathaniel into the room, Edward could see immediately from his posture that he had nothing new to report. And what did it matter? he wondered in the bare room of his drunkenness. The girl had been nothing but trouble to him since he had met her. First there was the shock of her father's debts, then the realization that she was not a typical woman, content with parties and gowns. Instead she spent hours alone in the woods gathering flowers and writing about them in her little books. He had wanted a showpiece, a wife who would relish being on his arm, but Susannah seemed indifferent to status and wealth. He had thought many times of simply disowning her—she had no family left to challenge him, and it could be easily done with a claim of infidelity or, better yet, insanity. Divorce was unseemly, but a man of his connections and station could find a judge who would dispense with a wife quietly. Susannah could go back to Manhattan City, or wherever she pleased, for all it mattered to him. And he would have been free to begin again with someone new.

And yet the idea of pursuing divorce had unsettled him. It had felt a little too much like admitting a mistake, a defeat. Susannah would be destitute, at the mercy of strangers, but Edward got the idea that the prospect of poverty didn't bother her as much as it should. The *unfairness* of that shocked him. He had given her so much—yards and yards of silk and taffeta, a home full of the finest crystal and mahogany and lace, that damned greenhouse—and all he asked for in return was her compliance. It seemed like such a small thing.

"Edward." Nathaniel stood in the doorway of the study, only the toes of his soiled boots touching the ivory carpet. "Our crew has searched the perimeter of Squaw Island and everything in the vicinity north of Black Rock. We haven't seen a sign of her."

Edward felt he was peering at Nathaniel from behind a haze, and his mind wandered to the notion that he detested Nathaniel's appearance. The young man was, regularly, a careless dresser, creased and rumpled, his jackets badly tailored. He and his foolish wife had once told Edward and Susannah that they cared little for fashion, as if one could simply choose not to enter the contests that determined everything.

Nathaniel took a step into the room, his face full of fear. "I'm sorry, Edward, but I think we can only conclude that she is lost."

Dead, Edward thought, the syllable plunking down like a bass note. He stood very still. Edward had vowed to conquer Susannah, and now she was certainly conquered. What relief he would feel now, he thought, careful not to let any evidence of his thoughts creep onto his face. And yet, as he waited for that relief to take hold, it did not come.

Nathaniel stood before him, anxious to provide friendship in his time of grief. He glanced at Edward's empty glass and quickly refilled it from the decanter on the sideboard. Nathaniel was a *good* man, in the most tiresome way, Edward reflected. He believed that laws—man's and God's—could save men from themselves. As if that were what every man wanted at the last, to be saved.

Edward took a step back and sat down on the sofa. *So I am free of her.* But instead of relief, he felt the irritation of a man bested in competition. It felt unfair to be robbed of the chance to keep up his efforts to reform his wife. He had believed that in time she would yield to him. And now she was gone.

Nathaniel was eyeing him cautiously, clearly trying to assess his mind. It occurred to Edward that Nathaniel was afraid of him, the way Wendell feared him, the way men at the bank, the men who worked in his brickyard, the nun, his own wife—the way they all feared him. He had not spoken since Nathaniel said the words, and he searched himself for what he felt just now, knowing that Susannah would not return home. It wasn't grief but instead something like a cousin to grief. Disappointment. Loss.

Nathaniel sat down beside him and put his hand on Edward's shoulder. "Forgive me. This is very difficult for me to say. The pools at the base of the falls are quite deep. The currents strong and competing. There's little chance—" He stammered here, afraid to go through with it. "Edward, I believe we should conclude the search and move forward with a . . . a service at the church."

Edward jerked his head in Nathaniel's direction. He hadn't said the word *funeral* because there would be no body to bless and bury.

"When the Middleton boy went missing last year, Reverend Webster held a sort of remembrance for the family."

Edward felt his fingers touch his forehead. His hand seemed to move of its own volition.

"Is there anyone to whom I may write?" Nathaniel asked. "You've said her parents have passed. Has she any family at all?"

"None," Edward said, his mind coming into focus. "I suppose we should send word to Eliza Beals. Then we can count on all of Buffalo knowing by the morning."

"And there are no friends of Mrs. Fraser's to whom you'd like me to write?" When Edward shook his head, Nathaniel said, "How curious. She was such a lively girl and yet so alone—" He clamped his mouth shut when something a little wild flashed across Edward's eyes, then tried to soften his words. "Of course, you haven't been in Buffalo long."

Edward turned a cold gaze on Nathaniel. "Some men allow their wives to roam about, doing as they please." He thought of Nathaniel's wife, Sylvia, her incessant talking and infuriating presumption that her mind was exceptional. "But in my opinion that reflects poorly on the wife *and* her husband. Susannah knew her place."

Nathaniel nodded, accepting the slight. "I will go to Reverend Webster's office directly and see that preparations are made. You have only to send for me if there is anything else I can do for you."

Nathaniel stood and turned to go, but stopped him. "Root, before you leave. Would you pour me another drink?"

Not long after, Edward called Marjorie in to give her the news. She reacted with a wail, a little theatrical in Edward's opinion, since the news couldn't have come as a complete shock. Hadn't they known for days that this was how it would turn out, since the nun, that harbinger of doom, had appeared dripping wet at the door? He eyed Marjorie a moment, then told her to go home to her husband.

By the time Edward realized he was drunk, he was very drunk indeed. The room swam before his eyes and he swam in it; the house seemed to rock gently, like an immense cradle of brick and beam. He moved into the hallway with his hands gripping the doorframe to his study, then set his sights on the stairs. He thought he'd like to have a drink of cool water from the pitcher beside his bed, then lie down.

As he leaned into the banister, Edward thought of his mother, long dead, and the way she always pinned her dark hair away from her face to reveal her clenched Calvinist jaw. The house pitched left and Edward sank onto the stair. Suddenly, he was six years old, clutching his mother's hand as they hurried across the square of the Ulster town of Ballymena toward the church. He noticed a man sitting on the ground in front of the pub, propped up against a pole, his hands folded in his lap and his head hanging to the side in sleep. A line of drool shone through his blond whiskers.

"Mother," Edward had asked her. "Why does that man sleep on the ground?"

She yanked Edward so close to her that his cheek rubbed the coarse wool of her cloak. "That's what a man looks like when God has gone out of him," she muttered. "When God goes out, the Devil comes in."

Her words had frightened and confused him. As he watched the man's chest rise and fall with his breath he wondered if there was a cavity there, somewhere beneath the man's lungs, where an ethereal presence like God or the Devil or a ghost could enter and leave at will. Edward had touched his own sternum with his child's starfish hand and shuddered at the thought. Was there anyone there, inside him?

With his cheek pressed now against the plaster that lined that staircase at Hawkshill, Edward touched that same place on his chest, his fingers long now, his knuckles shadowed with dark hair. The memory shifted something inside him. For decades, so many carefully constructed layers had hardened him against recollections like these: anger and distance and time and wealth. But the drink had somehow sliced through them all. A knife going right to the bone. For a moment he felt his mother's harrowing eyes set their gaze upon his life as it was today. What she saw appalled her heart. He was a thief, a covetous, malicious man bound for the inferno.

Edward sat on the stair, blinking. He was unraveling now because he had lost control of Susannah, and controlling her kept everything else in its place. He could choose to give in to defeat and come clean, or he could summon up the hardness that had so long sustained him.

In a moment he was on his feet, moving toward Susannah's bedroom. His head was suddenly clear. A pile of a dozen dresses was draped across the bed, shimmering fabric of pink and green and peach, like the feathers of an exotic bird, and they mocked him. They had been delivered two days ago by the girl from Madame Martineau's shop. When he saw the glint of Susannah's shears resting on the lid of her sewing basket, he laughed. In a moment the shears were in his hands. The hems feathered out as he sliced through each layer of fabric, cut through the lace sleeves, split the bone buttons with a sharp pop. The massacred dresses rustled as they fell to the floor in pieces, confetti of stiff satin and taffeta and slippery silk.

But Edward wasn't appeased. He yanked the feather bed off its wood frame then, casting it against the wall and knocking the lamp to the floor. The glass globe broke and oil seeped out into the carpet. Edward felt the thrill of destruction, crossing the room to the wardrobe. He threw the clothes on the floor one armful at a time, tore the ribbons off all the bonnets. With his elbow, Edward shoved her mother's jewelry box to the floor. Its hinge popped off and the contents spilled out, a sparkling metallic wave sluicing across the floor.

When he paused to catch his breath, he glanced again at the jewelry. A laugh bubbled up in his lungs. Susannah had an astonishing quantity of it for a woman of her age, most of it, aside from a few pieces Edward had given her, inherited from her feeble-minded mother. Phillip Brownell had been a fool in all things, Edward thought, but mostly in his boundless generosity. Edward shook his head, the obvious thing to do so plain before him. He would sell it all, each and every piece, and get a small shard of recompense. Yes, that was what he would do. But not right now. For now he would lie down for just a moment, to stop the room from spinning.

Hours later the scent of lilac soap roused Edward from a frantic dream that had him tightening his hands into fists beneath the pillow. He pried open his swollen eyes, took in the pale pink and yellow quilt. He was in her bed but her bed was on the floor. And she wasn't there.

The sunlight coming through the window was bright, and he realized he had slept very late. Edward propped himself up on his elbow and gazed about the room. The truth of it all rushed Edward's mind, and he exhaled. *This is one of those moments that tests a man's mettle.* Would he allow meekness and grief to gain footing within him? Hardly. Nothing but a nuisance, this was, and it would soon be past. He decided that if there was any scotch left in the decanter, he would pour it out. What he needed was a plate of eggs.

He stood up and crossed the room to the basin and splashed cool water on his face. He wondered if Marjorie had been into the room and seen the mess, then remembered he had sent her home. He checked his watch. Noon already. She would be downstairs, fixing some food, too afraid to approach him. He sniffed the air. Bread.

As he stepped over the mess toward the hallway, Edward remembered his vow to sell the jewelry. He forced himself to smile, knowing that that smile could freeze the remorse that oozed within him and demanded to be acknowledged. He could act in opposition to his conscience—he had done it many times before. It was merely a little game, finding ways to outsmart that tiresome urge toward guilt, shame. He knew how to lock it up and throw away the key. Of course, he would have to be careful, so soon after his wife's death, lest people judge him callous. But he could begin the preparations now.

In the rubble next to the bureau he found a tablet of paper and an ink pen. Edward sat on the floor and began to sift through the twisted mass of necklaces, bracelets, brooches, and earbobs. He pulled the most valuable pieces out first—a string of pearls with a gold clasp and matching pearl earbobs—then made a note of their size on the tablet. He appraised the enamelwork on a string of coral flowers but decided they weren't worth the effort. There was a bracelet of carved ivory he had always admired, and he set that aside with the pearls. The real prize, he knew, was the string of garnets. Susannah refused to wear them. They were enormously conspicuous, the sort of piece that demanded attention and courted disdain from women of lesser means. When he asked her why she never wore it, she told him that she preferred more modest pieces. But Edward knew too that the necklace was precious to her, having been her mother's favorite.

It had to be somewhere in the clutter, but as he dug and sifted he didn't find it. He went about the room righting the furniture and returning the feather bed to its frame. He searched each drawer of the bureau, looking among the folded clothes and pressing his hand into the fabric to feel for the hard shape of the jewels. Nothing.

Had the wretch gone behind his back and sold it? What reason could she have? She didn't want for any comfort here. Then another thought occurred to him. What if she had not fallen into the river, but jumped? What if she set out in the rain that night determined to end her life? Would she take the necklace with her as a talisman, hoping she would soon see her mother again? He tried to picture Susannah succumbing to that dark impulse but could not. For in whatever ways she was unhappy with him in this house, this life, Susannah loved the world. Her work in the greenhouse was ongoing, her little plants depending on her. She would not take her own life.

Reverend Webster presided over the memorial service. He prayed, and the congregants prayed along with him, that Susannah would somehow miraculously return to them, and if it was God's will that she should not, the reverend prayed that she would sleep peacefully in her watery grave.

Edward sat in the front pew as he always did and felt a hundred pairs of eyes boring into the back of his skull. There was a curiosity in them, a morbid fascination. Would this man so central to the business of the city allow himself to break down, to succumb to grief? Had he loved his wife deeply? Would he marry again—and when?

With his head bowed in prayer, Edward could nearly hear the chatter crackling in the minds of the people sitting around him. *What of the circumstances of Mrs. Fraser's death? Why was she out walking alone?* The town's gossips were surely in their glory. Edward glanced from side to side. Eliza Beals, accompanied by a nephew resembling his uncle Wendell, sat with her plump arms in her lap and worried a handkerchief in her fingers. Sylvia Root was stoic and sad next to Nathaniel, who glanced nervously at Edward, then nodded when their eyes connected. At the very back of the church, under the shadow of the choir loft, sat that peculiar nun, Sister Mary Genevieve. Had Nathaniel invited her?

It was only appropriate that she would attend the service, of course, since she had been there when Susannah died. *That's her,* the gossips would be saying. *She's the one who saw Mrs. Fraser go down into the river. She's the one who raced to Hawkshill to give the awful news.*

He looked back again at the shadowed nun, and though he could not see her face he saw the fabric of her veil sweep forward off her shoulders and understood that she was bowing her head toward him, a gesture of supplication or sympathy or blessing. It made his skin crawl, and not just because he was wary of her religion. Something was odd about this whole business, Edward thought. Something nagged at him about the nun, her story of Susannah's death, all of it. She was keeping something from him.

The reverend read a psalm. *Hear my cry, O God. Attend unto my prayer. From the end of the earth will I cry unto thee, when my heart is overwhelmed: lead me to the rock that is higher than I.*

Edward laced his fingers together to keep them occupied and glanced impatiently at his watch.

After the service, he walked across town and into the woods to the rectory cabin next to the Catholic church, expecting to meet this Father Adler, the priest Sister Mary Genevieve claimed to work for. But instead he faced the nun herself when she opened the door. A brief flash of panic crossed her face, but she brought it back under control. Edward wondered, fleetingly, if the priest and the nun were lovers. The prospect amused, then appalled him. He felt he was corrupting from the inside out.

"Mr. Fraser," she said, stepping aside to invite him in. "How can I help you?"

"I've come to speak to the priest."

"I'm sorry, sir. He is away in Lockport for a baptism."

Edward stepped inside and removed his hat. The ceiling hung just a few inches above his head, and in the dim light the nun's face floated before him. Behind her, near the hearth, was a small white statue of the crucified Christ, his elongated face ghoulish and contorted in agony. Edward couldn't help but stare at it—contemplating it, as the nun would likely say—and wonder who had carved it so painstakingly from soapstone. These Catholics and their fetishism, Edward thought. He felt he'd like to break the statue with an ax.

"I wonder if you can tell me, Sister," he said, exaggerating his deference, "whether Mrs. Fraser was wearing a necklace when you saw her fall?"

The nun shook her head. "No, sir, I couldn't say. As you will remember, it was raining that night and your wife wore a heavy shawl."

"And when she fell, you said you heard her cry out?"

The nun hesitated. "Yes, sir."

"You heard her scream?"

"Well, I—"

"That is *not* what you said the night you came to Hawkshill. You told me then she made no sound."

"Perhaps," the nun fumbled. "Perhaps my memory is failing me. It all happened so fast."

Her eyes, he could see, were not really black after all but very dark brown, with flecks of umber. "Do you doubt what will happen to you if I learn that you are deceiving me?"

Sister Mary Genevieve held his gaze, though her face was full of fear. "No, sir, I think I know very well. But what reason in the world would I have to lie?"

Part Two

Refuge

Chapter Eleven

The northbound steamer traveled up Lake Huron, and as the paddle wheel churned the water Susannah watched the shore with its endless expanse of cedar and beech and maple stretching on forever, not a clearing or a house in sight. It felt as though the boat were taking them not just deeper and deeper into the wilderness but back through time, so that she could see everything that men had done to the land be undone, all the ways in which they had broken it be unbroken. Susannah knew it should have terrified her, and yet she was not afraid. The trees, the bears, the wolves—whatever creatures waited in that forest—were absolutely indifferent to her existence. And that was something else altogether from a man who meant her harm.

Detroit had done something to her, loosened the strings that held her fear tethered in her chest. She could have died there at the hands of the man with the knife, and yet she had survived. In fact, she had survived every day since she had married Edward Fraser, despite everything. The wind off the water was cold and fresh, and she inhaled it as if she could take the whole lake into her body. But the relief would be short-lived. Escaping Buffalo, she knew, was only the first leg of this journey. Edward might be only a few days behind her. And even if she had succeeded in leaving him behind, she had no idea what to expect of her future.

The journey from Detroit had taken nine days. The boat moored at the north end of Lake St. Clair to take on wood, which cost them a day. Bad weather delayed them further as they crossed Saginaw Bay, as did an argument between a steward and an Indian on shore over the sale of a fresh-killed deer. The steward had offered to pay in whiskey only, but the Odawa hunter wanted money. Several men got involved in trying to sort it out, including the only white man ashore for a hundred miles, who tended the Thunder Bay lighthouse.

But finally the journey came to an end. Susannah registered the scent of the island before she saw it creep over the horizon as dusk took hold of the sky: wood smoke, the mossy smell of earth. There were three islands, in fact, two of them densely forested. The third had been cleared on the southeast shore and had the marks of a long history of human use. This island at the end of the world, in the middle of all this nothing, was lit up with gas lamps and lined with bridle paths and cabins and a white church with a belfry. A dock jutted out from the middle of the flat brown beach, and it was crowded with a dozen canoes and two schooners. A line of rude cabins surrounded by tall fences stood beside Indian dwellings clustered around small fires. Behind the small cabins was a row of more permanent homes, and, behind those, farther up the bluffs, was the military fort. There flags whipped in the wind like something alive. But Susannah heard no bugle, saw no marching. It had been twenty years since the war with the British. A lone soldier stood in a lookout, his arms draped over a rail, smoking a pipe.

She couldn't have imagined a place like this, in all of her avid daydreaming, and no words would come when Father Milani explained that they had to be quick in departing the boat, for it would soon press on to Chicago. Susannah stepped down from the dock to the footpath as if stepping into a dream.

She followed Father Milani to a large white house, and several dogs in a wooden enclosure began to make a terrific noise, barking at the newcomers. But they went silent when a woman in her midforties came out to the porch and shouted a command. She too was a singular sight. She wore a narrow black skirt over red leggings, a calico blouse fastened at her throat with a silver brooch that complemented the gray streaks in her coiled braids. They ascended the porch and approached her, Father Milani making the introductions as the woman he called Madame Fonteneau took Susannah's hand.

"Miss Dove, welcome." Susannah tried to cover her surprise at the woman's appearance. She was an Indian, or part Indian, at least, with dark eyes and a wide brow. When the nun told Susannah that Madame Fonteneau was wealthy, she had imagined a white woman, of course, in fine clothes and jewelry—someone a little like the woman Susannah Fraser was supposed to have been. But it seemed that perhaps wealth meant something different here. "You have journeyed a long way. Please come inside and get warm."

Father Milani stepped toward the door to follow them inside, but Madame Fonteneau turned back to him. "Thank you, Father, but I'm sure you have much to attend to at the church, having been so long away." She held his gaze a moment. Susannah watched something pass between them, as if Madame Fonteneau were daring him to ask for her deference so that she could deny it. Perhaps she knew something about the priest's drinking habits. All the swagger Susannah had seen Father Milani display on the boat disappeared in the woman's presence, and he nodded.

"Indeed, I have much to do," he said, not quite able to meet her gaze. "I am sorry to have to decline your hospitality."

Magdelaine held up her hand. "Before you go, tell me— did you encounter any problems on the boat? Do you have any reason to believe Miss Dove was followed?"

Susannah held her breath as she waited to see whether the priest would tell her about Wendell Beals and the detour in Detroit. She didn't want to conceal the truth, but Madame Fonteneau was an intimidating presence. Susannah feared she might wash her hands of the whole endeavor if she learned of the setbacks on the journey, that Susannah hadn't followed the nun's instructions to the letter.

But Susannah needn't have worried. Father Milani had no interest in prolonging a conversation with a woman who clearly had nothing but disdain for him. "Our journey was long and uneventful," he said. "Miss Dove was a patient traveler."

He touched his hat and bid them good evening, then started back toward the lane. Magdelaine opened the door and gestured for Susannah to step inside. The front hall was spare but warm and dry. A lamp sat on a small table at the far end, casting everything in a soft yellow glow.

Inside Madame Fonteneau gestured apologetically. "This really is my son's house," she said. "I only live here to appease him."

Susannah untied her black bonnet and pulled it off, then cleared her throat, unsure how to say what needed to be said. "Madame, I cannot tell you—"

"Magdelaine."

Susannah gave her a confused look.

"Call me Magdelaine, please. If I may call you Susannah?"

Susannah nodded and took in the sitting room. There was a thick carpet and a stack of books resting on a table beside an armchair. A flowered pillow embroidered with yellow thread sat in the chair. Four pairs of moccasins warmed beside the stone fireplace, and in front of the window a dove rustled in a cage. Magdelaine and Susannah stood at the base of the staircase that led to the second floor. Thick drapery shrouded the window on the landing.

"Thank you," Susannah whispered, trying again to express her gratitude. "Thank you for taking me into your home. What you have done for me—"

Magdelaine waved the rest of the sentence away with her hand. "Don't thank me until you decide whether you like living here in January, when there is snow up to the windows and the lake tries to blow the island off the edge of the world. We've prepared a room for you upstairs. I know you must be tired, but first, come meet my son."

Susannah's mind raced to keep up with Magdelaine's words. January was nine months away. All through her journey from Buffalo she had thought only of escaping from Edward and surviving from one day to the next. Now that she had made it safely to the island, now that the worst of the danger seemed to be passed—at least for the moment—the wide-open expanse of the future was coming into existence. How long would she need to stay here, and where would she go next?

They went into the kitchen where a man who looked just like Magdelaine was washing his face and neck over the sink. He dried off with a towel and turned to them.

"Miss Dove, may I present my son, Jean-Henri Fonteneau."

Susannah held her bandaged hand back against her skirt. Jean-Henri took her other hand and gave her a warm smile. "Miss Dove, welcome. We are all so relieved you have made the journey safely." Susannah noticed that while he shared his mother's features, his face was softer than hers, though still handsome. Magdelaine was stern, exacting, but Jean-Henri looked merely preoccupied.

"Try not to get too accustomed to his company," Magdelaine said. "He will soon be off to Montreal."

Jean-Henri's shoulders deflated slightly, but Magdelaine seemed not to notice. She pulled Susannah farther into the kitchen. "And this," she said, putting her hand on the arm of a young woman who stood at the table chopping onions, "is Esmee."

"Your daughter?"

"No," Magdelaine said. "Esmee is far more indispensable than that. She runs this house, sews, feeds us, washes our clothes. We would not last a day without her."

Esmee smiled at Magdelaine, then turned to Susannah. "Welcome," she said quietly. Her eyes lingered a moment, and Susannah felt the woman examining her face, the loose strands of her red hair that fell across her shoulders. Esmee's eyes flicked up to Jean-Henri, as if to measure his response to the newcomer, before they turned back to her work at the table.

"You must be very weary," Magdelaine said. "Would you like me to show you to your room?"

Susannah nodded, suddenly aware of her exhaustion. She could feel it all the way down in her bones.

"Esmee," Magdelaine said. "Will you please bring some hot water upstairs for Miss Dove?" On the boat Susannah had only been able to splash cold water on her face and hands, but she hadn't gotten clean. Her fingernails were dark with grime, and she knew she smelled of sweat. The notion of clear hot water and a fresh cake of soap, a thick clean cloth, made tears form in the corners of her eyes.

Esmee pulled a brass pitcher and bowl down from a shelf above the sink and ladled steaming water into it from the pot that boiled on the fire. She climbed the stairs, her steps careful and silent, and Susannah and Magdelaine followed her.

The room contained a narrow bed with a wooden head-board and a thick wool blanket. A small dresser stood against the opposite wall and the dark window reflected in its mirror. Susannah could see the pier, hear men singing around a bonfire on the beach. "Now, you will need something to wear," Magdelaine said. Esmee set the water on a table and went out of the room as Magdelaine pulled open one of the dresser drawers and removed a freshly pressed linen shift with fine white edging. Behind the wardrobe door hung a few simple calico dresses, and she pulled one down. "I hope these will do until we can make you something better." She held the dress up to Susannah's shoulders. "I am afraid it will be a little big."

Susannah would have been happy to wear a flour sack if she could remove the black wool dress once and for all. "This will suit me just fine."

She sat down on the blanket, pressing her palms into the soft feather bed. Magdelaine glanced out the window for a moment, still wondering, Susannah knew, whether Edward might be lurking outside the house. She pulled the chair in the corner over to the side of the bed and sat down across from Susannah. "I know you must be very tired."

Susannah nodded. Her head felt so heavy she could barely hold it up.

"But we must speak for a moment about your journey. Father Milani seemed confident that you were not followed on the boat. Do you feel safe now that you are here?"

Susannah swallowed. It had been so long since she had felt anything resembling safety. "I know that I am safe here, but I still feel afraid. It's hard for me to believe that I've really escaped him, that he isn't searching for me."

"Perhaps your wariness is justified. Boats arrive every few days, and your husband could be on any one of them," Magdelaine said. "Until we can confirm that he believes you are dead, we must be very careful."

"I will do whatever you think is best," Susannah said.

Magdelaine glanced at Susannah's bandaged hand.

"Would you like me to call for Dr. Biddle to come take a look at that?"

"No. It looks worse than it is."

"Did *he* do that to you?"

Susannah sighed, feeling her eyes well up once again. She was so tired—tired of being afraid, tired of holding back when she longed to weep.

Magdelaine's jaw tightened, and she seemed to measure her words. "That time is over now. No one is going to do anything like that to you again. Do you understand me?"

Susannah nodded. She thought of what the nun had told her about Magdelaine's sisters, how she had lost them both. That had happened long ago, but the anger in Magdelaine's voice was as fresh as if it had happened yesterday. It was clear that she was determined to protect Susannah from meeting the same fate. It had been so long since someone had looked out for her, the very feeling made her dizzy. She wanted to sink into Magdelaine's embrace and the safety it offered.

Magdelaine stood up. "You need to rest now. In the morning we will talk about how you plan to spend your days. But know that you will stay here until we are sure you are safe." She lit the candle beside Susannah's bed. "There are more of these in the drawer. And books downstairs. I will send Esmee up with some food, if you can stay awake long enough to eat it."

Susannah shook her head. "I don't think I can."

"Very well. Tomorrow, then. Sleep well, Susannah." Magdelaine slipped out of the room and pulled the door closed behind her.

Susannah's eyes were heavy, her head nodding like a doll's as she pulled the soiled dress off. She carefully unwrapped the soiled bandage from her fingers and peeled the splint away, then washed her face and arms with the hot water and white cloth Esmee had left. With the last bit of strength left in her body, she pulled back the blanket and collapsed into bed, her toes curling in satisfaction for one brief moment before she dipped into the blackness.

In the morning, long after the sun rose, Susannah finally woke and sat up with a start before remembering where she was. She changed into the fresh shift folded on top of the dresser and pulled on the calico dress. It hung loose and comfortable around her waist, so much lighter than the dresses and corsets she had been accustomed to wearing back in Buffalo. In the kitchen, Esmee stood barefoot with her back to the door, kneading dough at the table. Her feet were wide and brown, and though the rest of her body was slight, the feet seemed to announce a kind of stability. Susannah traced in her mind the narrow arches of her own feet, white and smooth on the bottom from a lifetime of slippers and rides in carriages.

"Good morning," she said to Susannah. "How did you sleep?"

"Very well. For the first time in a long while."

Esmee smiled and gestured to the table. Susannah sat down in the chair, and Esmee held the dough in one hand and wiped the table with a rag in the other. "Good. But you must be famished. Would you like something to eat?"

Susannah felt her stomach lurch. "Yes, thank you. I feel like I could eat a horse."

"Lucky you won't have to do that!" Esmee moved with measured grace from the cupboard to the pot on the fire, then over to the table, and placed a steaming bowl in front of Susannah, along with a spoon. Black wild rice, whitefish, and pale green leeks floated in an inky broth. Susannah sipped it carefully from the edge of the spoon, unsure of what to expect, then felt her throat relax as the flavor bloomed in her mouth. She realized that the color of the broth came from the rice, and it tasted fresh, almost of grass, with a sweet pucker from the leeks. A satisfied smile broke out on Esmee's face when Susannah began taking large bites of fish, slurping a bit in her rush to eat the food.

"Coffee?" Esmee asked.

Susannah nodded without stopping to speak.

The door off the kitchen opened and Magdelaine came inside, carrying a basket of chopped wood. She unwrapped her shawl. Esmee set down the coffeepot and hurried to the sitting room, then came back carrying a pair of moccasins. Magdelaine stepped out of her wet boots and into the dry moccasins.

"Thank you," she said. "And good morning, Susannah. I see you have been introduced to Esmee's wonderful cooking." Magdelaine wore a fresh blouse with the sleeves turned up to her elbows and her long black and gray hair in two loose braids. "How are you feeling this morning?"

"Rested," Susannah said, setting down the spoon with some embarrassment. She had emptied the bowl in a few short minutes and longed for more. Before she could ask,

Esmee whisked it over to the pot and brought it back brimming with stew, then set coffee and hot milk before them both.

"I'm glad," Magdelaine said, sitting down and folding her hands on the table. "Because your journey is over, but we face a new challenge. What will you do, now that you are here?"

Susannah thought back to Magdelaine's comment the previous night about the weather in January and felt again the same uneasiness about her future. What *would* she do? How would she fill her time, with what purpose? "Forgive me," Susannah said. "But I have no idea."

"Well, what *can* you do? Do you know how to cook?"

Susannah shook her head, conscious that Esmee had paused in her work at the hearth in order to hear her answer. "No. There was always . . . someone always did it for me." Esmee seemed to relax then, reassured that she wouldn't have any competition for her position. Susannah thought of Marjorie back in the kitchen in Buffalo, kneading a small loaf of bread for Edward alone. She had been Susannah's only friend, really—and of course it was her concern that had set Susannah's escape into motion.

"How about needlework? Could you mend? Do the washing?" Magdelaine held a smile pressed between her lips, and Susannah saw that she was teasing her. "I suppose someone did that for you too."

"Yes," Susannah said, studying her cup. "It seems I am fairly useless."

Magdelaine shook her head. "That's not true. Perhaps you had an education. Could you teach?"

Susannah brightened then. Indeed her father had made

sure she had good tutoring from the time she was young. In recent years, books had been her only companions, books and her plants. "Yes, I would be glad to try my hand at that."

Magdelaine nodded. "Come on. I have some things to show you."

As they stood to go to the sitting room, Esmee was one step ahead of them, kneeling at the fire to stoke the banked coals and warm the room. "I teach a small group of island girls the catechism, as well as some geography and figures."

She pulled two books down from the shelf. One was small enough to fit in a pocket; the other was wide, with thick pages. Susannah opened it to see columns of handwritten numbers. A ledger.

"I always kept very careful records," Magdelaine said. "Sales, inventory. Now I use them to help these girls learn sums. Heaven knows no one else is teaching them."

Susannah nodded. "I would be glad to help you."

Esmee had moved from the fire to the birdcage near the window. She scooped food from a lidded pail and poured it into a dish. Susannah hadn't known she was listening to their conversation until she spoke. "But what will you tell the girls, madame? About Miss Dove?"

Magdelaine nodded. "Esmee's right—we don't want a lot of rumors starting about where you came from. I suppose I will simply tell them I hired you to assist me, that I brought you here from the East. They know so little about the rest of the world. I don't think it would occur to them, or anyone else on this island, to question it."

Esmee smiled. "That is probably so."

Susannah gestured to the cage. "That's a beautiful dove," she said to Magdelaine.

"Do you think so? It was a gift from my son. I think it seems awfully cruel to keep it penned in that cage. Every time I come into the room and see it, it upsets me."

"It isn't cruel. Many women in New York keep them as pets."

"That's what Jean-Henri says."

"They are bred to live in cages. I don't think it would occur to them to expect another kind of life."

Magdelaine smiled. "The women, or the doves?"

Susannah grinned back at her. "I see your point."

"This one was wild once, until Jean-Henri caught it. He said it was a good-luck charm, and keeping it might help you to arrive safely. I was willing to try anything! You aren't the first Miss Dove I tried to help, you know. But you *are* the first one to successfully make the journey."

Susannah remembered the nun telling her that Father Adler had assisted women like her. "What happened to the others?"

Magdelaine was quiet for a moment. "The first Miss Dove managed to leave home—she was coming from Quebec—but when she got to Detroit her fears got the best of her. The unknown seemed worse than the suffering she knew. She returned home. We don't know what happened to her after that."

Susannah's eyes widened. It had never occurred to her to stop and turn back once she'd slipped away from Buffalo. Nothing could be worse than returning to that house.

Magdelaine grimaced as she continued. "The second Miss

Dove was desperate to make the journey, but we were care-less in our planning. Her husband intercepted a letter that included too many details, and he quickly understood what she meant to do. He waited to see whether she would follow through with it. When she turned up at the port in Boston, ready to board a boat to New York, soon to follow the path you took here, he was waiting for her. She never made it out of the city."

"And the third Miss Dove?" Susannah asked.

Esmee moved at the edge of the spotless room with a broom.

"Is you," Magdelaine said. "So you can see why we must be careful, why we must explain your presence to anyone who might otherwise gossip about your arrival."

Susannah was coming to understand just how much was riding on her escape, and how much she owed Father Adler, Sister Mary Genevieve, and Magdelaine. She was glad to be able to earn her keep by helping with the teaching, but still, a question nagged at her. "How long am I to stay here?"

Magdelaine shook her head. "That is up to you. You are my guest, not my servant. You are not indentured to me. I imagine that after what you have been through, you'd like some time to rest. And we will want time to be sure you are safe, that you won't be followed. But soon you will begin to think about your future. When you are ready to move on, we'll help you. Though I'm sure you know that you can never go back where you came from."

Susannah nearly laughed at the prospect. "Nothing on earth could compel me to do that—believe me."

Even in her certainty, Susannah felt a pang of homesickness. Not for Edward, of course, but for her childhood home, for the Manhattan City she might never see again, for the plants surely dying of thirst in her greenhouse.

She tried to imagine what it might be like to stay here on the island, or if she didn't stay here, where else she might go, but her mind came up empty. Never in her life had it occurred to her to wonder about who she wanted to be; the script always had been written by someone else. First she was a daughter, deeply loved but protected, directed. Then she became the wife of a man who controlled each minute of her day. His desires, his plans, were necessarily hers. And there was no room for anything else. For the first time, Susannah's future was like a book with blank pages, waiting to be written. It was a terrifying prospect.

She thought then of the promise she had made to Sister Mary Genevieve, that she would try to be of use to Magdelaine. Perhaps the answer to her future lay there. The woman had been through terrible tragedy—one sister killed, the other vanished. Maybe if Susannah could learn more about what had happened all those years ago, she would understand what she could do to help Magdelaine, how she should focus her efforts.

"I know you have your reasons for choosing to help me," Susannah began. She felt a stir of anxiety that she might be broaching a sensitive topic, but she pressed on. "I am so sorry for what happened to your sisters."

Esmee paused in her work, then leaned the broom up against the wall and left the room.

Susannah glanced after her, feeling tension swell between herself and Magdelaine. "I apologize," she said quickly.

Magdelaine's expression remained calm, but Susannah saw her throat move as she swallowed. "I don't like to talk about the past."

"Forgive me."

"There's no need for forgiveness. We must focus on the future now." Magdelaine stood, reclaiming control of the conversation. "I would like you to stay close to the house for now. If there is anything you need, any sort of food, or a book that I do not have here, one of us can go to Market Street or send for it. You are welcome to get outside for fresh air, of course—we can't have you cooped up in the sitting room. But please, be careful. Try not to get yourself noticed. If you'll excuse me, I have some things to take care of."

She went upstairs, leaving Susannah alone in the sitting room. Maybe it was the tension she had caused, but suddenly she did feel cooped up, in need of fresh air. She crossed into the front hall, then out the door onto the front porch. With her arms crossed against the chilly breeze, she looked out at the lake. In the distance she saw a schooner with its sails ballooning in the wind. The lake was a serene gray under a white sky; it seemed completely different from the day before, when it had been dark, and the day before that, when it had been as blue as the Caribbean. The variety was a wonder, or perhaps a terrifying kind of changeability. Like the beasts that lurked in the Michigan forest she had watched from the deck of the boat, the lake was indifferent to the story of one woman, indifferent to the story of five hundred on a boat that it could smash in the shallows with one leaping wave.

Around the side of the house was the wooden pen that contained Magdelaine's four dogs, and they leapt into a barking frenzy as soon as they caught a glimpse of her coming their way. Susannah froze. Dogs had always scared her. As a girl, she had cowered from the ones that roamed the alleys in Manhattan, feral and hungry. The barking made her feel as though she were choking on her own heart. But she tried to talk herself out of the fear of these dogs, secured in a pen. Though they threw their bodies against the door, its lock held.

"Don't be afraid. They really are softhearted, in spite of the way they sound." Jean-Henri appeared, carrying two pails across the yard. "And they are only interested in these," he added, holding up the buckets.

Susannah watched as he carefully unlatched the door to the pen and squeezed his body through the small opening without letting the dogs escape. The howling ceased as they descended on the pails of food.

Jean-Henri wiped his hands on his trousers and secured the pen before crossing back over to where Susannah stood. "I gather you never had a dog of your own, Miss Dove?"

Susannah laughed. "No. Not even a tiny terrier."

She glanced around the yard beside the house. The ground was mostly bare, with patches of brown grass lying down here and there from the weight of the recently melted snow. Along the house, small green shoots had begun to sprout—little weeds and the earliest spring flowers. The bare branches of two apple trees laced together like long, dark fingers. They were only a few weeks away from budding, but the fruit would be poor if they weren't pruned soon. Susannah flexed the fingers on her injured hand. The pain was still there, but it was receding. The hand would never be the same, but she felt she soon might be able to put it to use. She wanted badly to ask about the trees but was afraid of giving offense.

"Mr. Fonteneau, is your mother . . . fond of gardening?"

Jean-Henri laughed. "In a word, no. My mother dislikes anything that requires her to stay in one place for too long. You should have seen the struggle I endured simply getting her to live in this *house*."

"I see," Susannah said.

She had seen the island from a distance as the boat approached. Only this southern edge seemed to have been cleared of trees. The interior was sure to hold botanical treasures. And there was the possibility of growing peas, radishes, herbs, and potatoes, right here in the yard.

Jean-Henri followed the path of her gaze and winced. "It must not seem like much, to you. I get the feeling you are accustomed to something much grander."

Susannah shook her head. "What I wonder, sir, is whether I might try my hand at the work. I intend to make myself useful to your mother. I would like to start a garden here."

He looked at her in surprise. "You want to plant a garden?"

"If you think that would be all right with your mother."

"I think she will be very surprised. And pleased."

"Is there . . . do you have a shovel I could use? And a saw for the trees?" And all at once Susannah recognized a new difficulty: The small amount of money she had left from her exchange with Tiny would soon run out. In Buffalo she never once thought about the cost of tools, or the wood that kept the fire going in the greenhouse so that it would stay warm all winter and her plants could thrive while icicles hung from the eaves at Hawkshill. She would have to ask for yet more generosity from this family until she had a way to repay them.

"You want to begin now, today?" Jean-Henri asked with a delighted laugh. "Yes, of course. I'll get you whatever you might need. How about seeds?"

"Where can I get them?"

"Morin will have some at his store. He sells goods that come in on the boats and sorts the mail too. I was planning to go there now for a few things—I'd be glad to ask him about the seeds." Jean-Henri stacked the empty buckets beside the house and pulled his collar up against the chilly wind. "What do you want to plant?"

Susannah shrugged. "Anything he has, I suppose. Peas, pumpkin, lettuces . . ." She thought of the wild carrot seeds she had chewed faithfully each day back in Buffalo, the sharp hulls sticking between her teeth. "But no carrot—please."

He gave her a curious look but nodded. "I'll be back soon," he said, and set off down the lane. As Jean-Henri disappeared around the curve of the island, Susannah stood in the bare yard in her plain dress and felt again a sense of being completely unencumbered by possessions. She reached for a coin purse, a silver mirror in her pocket, and there was none; she felt at her throat for her brooch and there was nothing there. She had only the pins that were tucked in her hair when she departed for her journey. In Buffalo she had owned crystal vases, paintings, embroidered pillows, rugs, egg cups, tiny forks whose sole purpose was to pull a steamed snail out of its shell. Everyone she knew in that former life envied her possessions; for Edward, each one was an emblem of his success, his dominance. And yet she had walked away from all of it without one backward glance. Now, unadorned, unencumbered, she felt weightless, invisible.

But she knew that she was not invisible. The previous evening, leaving the boat with Father Milani, she had felt the triumph of surviving alone in Detroit and somehow managing to make it to the island. She had hoped she could leave her fear behind in that chaotic place, and yet it had followed her here after all. She could not forget that Edward might be searching for her. If he had learned of her escape he could soon be here. If Wendell Beals had written to him about seeing her on the boat in Detroit, Edward might have received the letter by now. Her hostess was right; she had to stay near the house and be careful.

Susannah tried to shake off her fear by making plans for her seeds based on the pattern of sunlight and shade in the yard. Magdelaine's house faced south and the front of the yard would be the best place for corn. Lettuce might fare better near the apple tree. She stooped down and dug her index finger and thumb into the earth. She was pinching up a bit of soil to feel its consistency when she sensed someone was standing behind her. She shot up and turned.

"I'm sorry—I didn't mean to startle you."

Susannah drew in a breath she hoped the man didn't hear and cast her eyes down in panic. She knew him—he was the teacher from the boat, the one who had made her the sketch of the bird. He wore the same coat with the upturned collar he had worn that day, the same cheerfully curious expression. What was he doing here?

"I'm looking for Mr. Fonteneau," he said, glancing at the house, then back at Susannah, tilting his head in recognition. "Why, I know you. I am Alfred Corliss—I believe we met on the boat."

Susannah swallowed and looked up at him. She felt the damp soil clinging to her fingers. "Yes, hello. I remember."

Alfred took off his hat and pushed a hand through his hair, then put it back on again. "Forgive me for being rude, but I do not believe you ever told me your name."

"Miss Dove," Susannah said. Her mind raced to recall what she *had* told him on the boat, the details of her supposed plans—that she was bound for a convent in St. Louis. How would she explain her presence here?

"How remarkable!" He clasped his hands together. "I am very glad to see that you are well. I looked all over the boat for you when we departed Detroit, but you were nowhere to be found. I feared you had taken ill."

Susannah took a breath to calm her nerves, reminding herself that Mr. Corliss had no reason to be suspicious of her, to want to catch her in a lie. He was, simply, a kind man on a journey of his own. "Father Milani, the priest who was escorting me to St. Louis, had some sudden business in Detroit," she explained, concocting the story as she told it, "and we stopped there for a few days. Then he was needed at the church here, and asked me to delay the rest of my trip to spend some time here."

Mr. Corliss smiled. "I can't imagine that you would mind, now that you've seen this place. Isn't is lovely?"

Susannah nodded, trying to think of a way to end the

conversation without being rude. Magdelaine had told her to keep from being noticed, and here she was standing in the yard talking to a stranger.

"You might remember that I was headed to the Wisconsin territory," he continued, oblivious to her anxiety, "but on the boat I met Reverend Howe, the head of the Presbyterian mission school here. He insisted that I consider teaching there instead, and the man *is* persuasive. So I agreed." He glanced behind him, in the direction of the school. "Though now that I'm here, I am not sure I endorse his methods. He is a force. You should meet him, take a tour of the school—he will be fascinated and more than a little bedeviled to know how the Catholics lured you away. He may very well try to convert you back to Calvin's way of thinking." Alfred smiled. He didn't seem too concerned about her affiliation himself.

"That is kind of you," Susannah said. "But Father Milani has found me a position helping Madame Fonteneau with her own teaching, here at the house. I expect that commitment will consume most of my time."

"I admire your focus. I think I have decided to stay on here as well. The school needs a . . . moderating force if it hopes to succeed at its aims." He took off his hat again and the curls slipped down over his eyes once more. "Of course, my brother wants me to come to my senses and get back to Boston immediately. We are charged with running my late father's factory together, but neither he nor my father ever understood my interest in this kind of work. Most people don't, do they?"

She gave him a weak smile.

"Isn't it something that providence has brought us together again when we planned to end up in such different places?"

She wanted to return his friendliness, but she couldn't afford to. Instead, she brushed the dirt from her hands. "I wish you well in your work, Mr. Corliss, but now I must get back to mine." Without waiting for him to say good-bye, she turned toward the house.

"Miss Dove—one more thing. Do you know when Mr. Fonteneau will be back? We have a leaking roof at the school and I hear he is the man to see for help."

Susannah nodded. "You might try back in a few hours," she said. She would be sure to spend the rest of the day inside, so she wouldn't risk seeing him again.

Chapter Twelve

How long has she been out there?" Magdelaine asked the next morning as she placed the pail full of fish on the kitchen worktable. She crossed into the front room to where Jean-Henri stood at the window. She had seen Susannah working in the garden when she returned from the lake. The young woman was crouched down with her back to the lane, hacking at the hard-packed soil.

"I woke at dawn and she was already out there, though I don't know how she could even see what she was doing before the sun came up. Esmee took her some coffee a while ago because she didn't want to come inside for breakfast."

Magdelaine shook her head. "Yesterday afternoon she wouldn't leave her room. Now she won't come back inside?"

Susannah ascended a ladder and worked with methodical confidence in the boughs of the apple tree. The small saw Jean-Henri had given her was in her right hand.

"She says it is safer for her to work very early when most people are not yet out and about."

"She is probably right about that. Not that we get many visitors here."

"True." Jean-Henri straightened then. "But yesterday the new teacher at the mission school came looking for me. He wants me to fix their roof."

"And what did you tell them?" She was a little surprised they would deign to let a Catholic make the repairs. When the reverend and his wife first came to the island a few years back, Magdelaine had tried to extend a welcome, inviting them to the Christmas celebration and other feasts, but they never came. They were interested only in saving souls, and saving them in a very particular way. She had heard they took boys from their families, cut their hair, and forced baptism on them like pouring a tonic down a sick child's throat.

"I told them I'd be glad to do it, of course." Her son turned to look at her. "I thought *you* would be glad to hear that someone must have recommended me to Reverend Howe. My work speaks for itself—I'm building my business. Isn't that what you want?"

Magdelaine gave him a weak smile. "You know what I want—I want you to get to the city, seize a *real* opportunity." She put her hand on his shoulder as a concession. "Let's not argue about it now. I'm glad for you about the job. Be careful not to fall through into the sanctuary when you are working on the roof—you might get converted by accident!"

They both laughed then. The sun was coming out. Susannah had her calico sleeves unbuttoned and rolled up over her elbows. Her fair skin would burn, even in the weak sunlight of spring, but she seemed not to know or care. She moved the saw to her left hand, but when she tried to grip it, it sailed to the ground. The injured fingers still weren't ready for work.

Magdelaine glanced at the ground where the saw had fallen and was alarmed to see that it was littered with dozens of small branches. "*What* is she doing to my tree?"

Jean-Henri laughed. "A month ago you would have nothing to do with this house. Now you own a tree that has been here for fifty years?"

Magdelaine narrowed her eyes at him. There was nothing worse than Jean-Henri when he was right. "She's going to kill it."

"She says it needs pruning. She says she can double its output of fruit if she trims back those overgrown branches and thins it out before it buds. I believe she knows what she is doing."

Magdelaine watched as another heavy branch fell to the ground. Odawa men thought that growing food was women's work, and since Magdelaine had spent her life doing the work of men, she knew little about it. "Perhaps she does."

In just the one day, Magdelaine had learned that Susannah knew more about everything than she had expected she would. She thought back to the awkward moment in the sitting room the day before, when Susannah had tried and failed to get Magdelaine to talk about the past. It made sense that Father Adler would tell Susannah about Josette and Therese—he needed a way to explain why a stranger would be willing to take her in. Magdelaine didn't have to wonder how he himself knew of the sad tale. When Josette had been killed and Therese disappeared, Magdelaine had put out the call to every priest between Wisconsin and New York, begging for information on the sister who had vanished. Surely Father Adler had heard about it then.

She was still torn between opposing beliefs about Therese: Part of her believed that her older sister was dead. Jean-Henri, just a little boy then, had told his mother he saw Therese take her own life. But Magdelaine wasn't sure whether to believe him. Then, the following year, Esmee's father, Ansel Leroux, who had worked for Henri and then Magdelaine, told her that he saw Therese walking down the street in Quebec City. Magdelaine had scoffed and pretended not to believe him. But later she went to Quebec City in secret to see for herself, looking at every face, checking every doorway. But of course Therese was nowhere to be found. Still, she couldn't be certain that Ansel had been mistaken.

They watched as Susannah climbed back down the ladder once more and removed her bonnet, revealing her striking red hair. She shook out the twigs and slivers of bark that had fallen into her skirt from the branches.

"She is very unusual looking, isn't she?" Jean-Henri said.

Magdelaine turned to him, amused. "Beautiful, you mean?"

"No." His tone was earnest. "Well, yes, perhaps she is. But what I meant is that she is conspicuous. That red hair is very . . . distinctive. I don't know if I've ever seen a woman with hair quite like that before."

"All the more reason we must be careful," Magdelaine answered. Susannah's hair had been on Magdelaine's mind since she arrived. If anything marked her as a visitor, if anything drew attention to her, it was that hair.

Magdelaine glanced at her son and wondered for a moment if she was going to have a new problem: Jean-Henri in love with Susannah. She pushed the thought away. He wouldn't be so foolish—would he?

Magdelaine left him at the window, shaking her head as she came back into the kitchen. Esmee was sweeping the ash out of the fireplace with a wide broom and collecting it in a kettle to boil for soap.

"I believe Jean-Henri is more than a little taken with our guest," Magdelaine said quietly, casting a worried glance back at the sitting room.

Esmee's face stayed blank, though she paused for a moment in her work. "I hope she is worthy of his interest, madame."

Magdelaine laughed. "*I* hope she is a very patient woman, for my son can take a lifetime to make the simplest of decisions."

Esmee continued sweeping, then tapped the last of the ashes into the kettle. She kept her eyes on her work, her hands moving. "Indecision and prudence," she said without a hint of impudence in her voice, though her words laid it bare, "might, at times, be easy to confuse."

Magdelaine raised her eyebrows at Esmee and expected the girl to wilt under her gaze. Although Magdelaine was standing in the kitchen of the house she never asked for and still felt was a burden, a house she would be happy to turn her back on tomorrow so that she could seek solace in the deep woods on Bois Blanc for the rest of her days, Esmee was still her employee. Yet she faced her haughtily, then turned away and moved gently through the motions of her work as if nothing were amiss. Why in the world would she defend Jean-Henri's passive nature? She was one to watch, this girl.

"I keep thinking about her hair," Magdelaine said, turning back to her concern. "I think we need to do something about it before it gets her noticed."

Esmee shrugged. "What can we do? Her hair is her hair. She wears a bonnet when she is outside."

"I know, but still—how many women with red hair have you seen on this island? People are going to talk about her. If anyone is looking for her, that hair is how he'll find her. I wonder . . . is there some way we could tint it darker?"

"With a dye, you mean?" Esmee raised her eyebrows. She placed a lid on the kettle.

Magdelaine stepped into the pantry and moved her hand over the jars and canisters that lined the shelves. "Manoomin water probably wouldn't work. And beets would only make it *more* red."

Esmee stepped in behind her and reached for a jar of nearly black preserves on the top shelf. "What about elderberry? It stains everything it touches."

Magdelaine took the jar. "It could work," she said, nodding. "Now we just have to persuade her to let us try."

When Susannah came inside a while later, Magdelaine and Esmee were waiting for her in the kitchen. Her cheeks were bright pink from the wind, her hands caked with soil. She removed her bonnet. "Esmee, may I wash up at the sink?"

"Of course," Esmee said, rushing over to help her. She poured hot water from one of the kettles they kept over the fire throughout the day into a bowl and gave Susannah a clean cloth. Susannah winced as she dipped her hands into the water and wiped them with the cloth.

"We'll have to get you some gloves," Magdelaine said. "Did you cut yourself?"

"No," Susannah said. "They are just raw from the wind. I lose myself in the work. I don't notice how tired I am until I stop. I have always been that way."

"Well, aren't we lucky," Esmee said, "that we will reap the benefits of your hard work this summer. It will be a beautiful garden."

Esmee and Magdelaine exchanged a glance. A compliment was as good a way as any to open this discussion, Magdelaine thought. She pulled out a chair and gestured for Susannah to sit down.

"Do you remember, on the night you arrived, when you said that you would do anything I asked you to do, if it would help keep you safe?"

Susannah glanced nervously between them. She nodded.

"I think we must do something about your hair."

Susannah's hand drifted up to the back of her head. "You want me to cut it?"

"We want to dye it."

Susannah's eyes widened. She looked at the jar of elderberry on the table, then at Esmee, who nodded her encouragement.

"All right," she said, and reached up to remove her pins.

"Here, let me help." Magdelaine stood and stepped behind Susannah's chair. One by one she pulled out the pins that secured Susannah's long hair in a twist at the back of her head. It uncoiled and spilled down her back in soft, shining waves, like the waxy red of maple leaves in autumn.

Esmee handed Magdelaine her hairbrush and Magdelaine swept it through Susannah's hair with long, steady strokes. As Magdelaine watched the motion of her own hands, she remembered the last time she had done this task, nearly twenty years ago, when she had brushed and braided Josette's hair for the last time. It was before she had left for the winter the year Josette died. The old sorrow rushed up. It would never leave her, that sorrow, no matter how much time passed.

Magdelaine shook off the memory and tried to focus on the matter at hand. "Is it ready?" she asked Esmee.

"Yes." Esmee brought the pot over from the fire. They had decided to add vinegar to the preserved fruit because that was what fixed the dye to wool.

"It smells terrible!" Susannah cried.

Of course they had no idea whether the dye would work the same way on a woman's hair, but they didn't dare let Susannah know they had never done this before.

Magdelaine smoothed the preserves on in sections until Susannah's whole head was covered. Then Esmee wrapped a rag around it while Magdelaine tried to wash the fruit from her hands. The color remained beneath her fingernails when she sat back down at the table across from Susannah to wait. Esmee made another pot of coffee, then joined them.

"I hope you aren't too sad," Esmee said, putting her hand on Susannah's. "It will grow out. Eventually."

Susannah shrugged. "I know. It's only that I've had this

hair my whole life." Her tone was wistful, but Magdelaine could see that she was trying to shirk the sadness. "But it doesn't matter now. It's just one more thing that ties me back to him."

Esmee gave her a vigorous nod. "That's right. Good riddance."

Susannah still didn't look convinced. Magdelaine turned to her. "A woman who endures is a woman who does what must be done," she said sternly, then softened her face into a smile. "You should be proud of yourself. From now on, *you* decide your fate. *You* decide who you will be."

Susannah's eyes welled and she nodded, taking a deep breath.

When another half hour had passed, they helped Susannah lean over a large basin and rinsed her hair until the warm water ran clear. They squeezed out her hair with towels and snatched them quickly away before Susannah saw that they had turned a disconcerting shade. They sat her next to the fire and combed the hair out once more.

When it finally dried, Susannah's hair was a strange color. Not black, but not brown exactly. The striking red was gone, replaced by a washed-out shade of very dark purple.

Magdelaine and Esmee exchanged a glance, and Susannah looked at them with wild eyes. "What? Tell me."

"It is certainly . . . changed," Magdelaine said.

Susannah pulled a lock over her shoulder and in front of her eyes, then winced. "I want to see it."

They led her into the sitting room, where a mirror hung above a small table. Susannah let out a shriek and clapped her hand over her mouth. Across the room in its cage, the startled dove shot up and began to bash against the bars. She reached for a section of hair and examined the strands in the dim light of the room.

"Shh," Esmee soothed the bird, crossing the room to comfort it.

Susannah smoothed the hair back into place and took a deep breath. "It doesn't matter," she said. "It is only hair."

Magdelaine stood behind her in the mirror and placed her hands on Susannah's shoulders. She set her jaw and lifted her chin, the way she had done countless times when fear or sorrow threatened to take over. Susannah studied Magdelaine a moment, then squared her own shoulders, lifted her own chin. If there wasn't so much time between then, Magdelaine thought, they could almost be sisters.

Each morning for the next three days, Susannah worked on her garden. Magdelaine watched as she first staked out a large rectangle of earth to receive all the seeds she had to plant. Then she cleared out brambles and cut back the tall grasses that obscured the yard from passersby. She dug beds, one for vegetables, one for herbs, and one for native flowers she said she hoped to find when Magdelaine felt it was safe for her to take walks in the early morning. For now, Susannah asked Jean-Henri to dig up two thimbleberry bushes so she could transplant them to the garden.

Susannah rose in the dark each morning and dressed in her room, then emerged with her disastrous hair coiled tightly at the back of her head beneath the black bonnet. Only a little of the deep color showed around her brow.

When Father Milani called to tell them he was bound for Detroit once again, that he would return sometime in the fall, he glanced twice at Susannah, perhaps noticing that something was different, but said nothing.

"Good-bye, Madame Fonteneau," he said, taking her hand. Magdelaine held his gaze, examining his unusual eye, with its half-brown and half-green iris. Perhaps the split had something to do with the half-truths he told to the people of the island. He had always looked a little fearfully at Magdelaine, as if he knew she could see through his façade. Indeed, Milani's secrets might come in handy, she thought. They would certainly keep him quiet about Susannah.

She squeezed his hand back. "Safe travels, Father."

Monday morning brought a heavy rain and a fog that billowed up over the limestone bluffs like smoke off a fire. It was not a day for working outdoors. But her students were instructed to come, rain or shine, and Magdelaine thought about how she would introduce them to their new teacher.

"You have worked wonders already in the garden," she said to Susannah while they waited in the sitting room for the girls to arrive. "I never could have imagined the possibilities you have seen for this little plot of land."

Susannah shook her head. "I've done nothing yet but make room for the new plantings. I hope we will have vegetables by the fall."

Magdelaine cared very little whether they would. They hardly *needed* the food. She had always fared very well on wild leeks and whitefish, and the Presbyterians grew enough vegetables that the grocery was always well stocked in the fall. But she sensed that aimlessness was Susannah's enemy now. She needed work to do with her hands, and with her mind, which the teaching could provide.

They heard the girls chattering as they came walking up the path. Amelia carried a basket of corn cakes still warm from the fire in her cabin. In the front hall they removed their cloaks and hung them to dry. Esmee whisked their moccasins away and placed them in a line in front of the fire in the sitting room. They padded in wool stockings to take their places on the sofa and chairs.

"Good morning," Magdelaine said. Just as she had expected, the girls seemed startled by Susannah's presence. They glanced at each other, then at her. "Girls, this is Miss Dove. I have asked her to come live with me so that she can help me with our lessons from now on. She is a very special teacher and you are very fortunate to have her here."

"Welcome, Miss Dove," Amelia said, her reliable confidence on full display. Pauline and Marie smiled shyly but couldn't find their voices.

"Now," Magdelaine said, unfolding one of Henri's old trade maps and spreading it on the floor, "let's begin with—wait, where is Noelle?"

Marie and Pauline looked down at their laps. Magdelaine turned to Amelia, who continued to sit up tall, her chin in the air, but she too remained silent. Magdelaine held up her hands. "Well?"

"Madame, she won't be returning," Amelia said.

"Why not?" Magdelaine tried to keep the irritation out of her voice. The girls were free to attend the lessons or not, and over the years she had seen students come and go. There was a large Odawa village a few days' travel south, where Lake

Michigan met the mouth of the Grand River, and often the island's summer wives traveled there to visit relatives. It was not remarkable to lose a student. But Noelle was unusually bright, if shy, and Magdelaine had begun to look forward to her presence at the lesson.

"I know not, madame. Her mother only told us this morning that Noelle has gone from the island and won't be coming back."

It could have happened for any number of reasons, and Magdelaine's first instinct was to go to Noelle's mother to find out more, but she knew from experience that the errand would be a waste of time. They had probably sent Noelle off to be married, and that was the end of her story.

Susannah stepped in to turn the girls' attention to the map. "What do we have here?" she asked them.

"The Michigan Territory and beyond," Marie answered in her mousy whisper. "That's where we are right now."

Susannah smiled. "I see. Where in particular is the island?"

Marie pointed to a small circle between the two large peninsulas. Outside, the dogs howled, then barked in sharp bursts at something near their pen. The sound startled the women and they paused to listen, then turned back to the map.

"We left off last time listing the towns along the river," Magdelaine said. "What is this one called?" She pointed to the place where the river joined Lake Michigan at the western edge of the land.

"Gabagouache," Pauline said.

Magdelaine nodded. "They call it Grand Haven now."

"And what about you, Miss Dove?" Amelia asked. "Where on the map do you come from?"

Susannah and Magdelaine exchanged a glance. Susannah shook her head. "That place isn't on this map," she said.

The dogs began growling once more, a vicious, frightening sound. Magdelaine stood.

"Girls, please excuse me a moment. Continue going over the map with Miss Dove."

She left the sitting room and went out to the yard through the kitchen door, Esmee trailing at her heels. Jean-Henri was standing at the door of the pen, peering between the slats at the dogs as Magdelaine and Esmee rushed over.

"They're fighting," he said.

Magdelaine shouted a command for silence, but the dogs did not heed it. The steady rain had subsided to a stinging mist she could feel on her cheeks. She opened the door to the pen and saw in the dim light the dogs tumbling over one another in a pile, claws and teeth flashing smooth and white amid the chaos of gray and brown fur.

She whistled again and Ani looked up, finally, and backed away from the pack, through the door of the pen to her side. But the other dogs continued the fight.

Finally Jean-Henri stepped into the fray and pulled two dogs out by the scruff of their necks, his whole body engaged to control their strength. Sled dogs were all muscle and will, bred to pull hundreds of pounds over the snow for hours at a time without stopping. The worst thing you could do to them was try to keep them still. Out on the trail they would pull and pull, the harness slicing into the flesh of their chests, until they died.

The fourth dog barked and spit by itself in the center of the pen. It leapt from its back up onto its haunches, then lowered its head and growled at them, its teeth dripping with foam.

Magdelaine understood at once. "Rabid," she said. "*Mon fils*, we have to get your father's musket."

Jean-Henri pulled the two writhing dogs through the open door of the pen and let them run across the yard, then slammed it shut with his hip and forced the latch into place. He nodded.

"Esmee, run, please, and get it. But carefully—it is loaded."

She nodded and took off running.

Jean-Henri examined the scratches on his forearm, then pushed his dark hair out of his eyes. A moment later Esmee bolted back through the kitchen door with the weapon swinging in the crook of her elbow and Susannah following behind her.

Esmee held the butt end of the musket out to him. "Please, monsieur, be careful."

Jean-Henri took the musket, first wiping his hands on his trousers to dry them, then letting the weapon rest lengthwise on his open palms. He glanced over his shoulder at the pen, the rabid dog howling inside.

"Jean, hurry!" Magdelaine hissed at him. "It has to be done now. You know that latch on the door is loose."

He opened his mouth to reply but closed it again, and didn't move. Magdelaine felt her jaw tighten and her eyes grow wide with fury. She was ashamed on his behalf, since he didn't seem to feel the shame he should himself. How he hesitated! Any man worthy of his place on the trade route knew that a sick dog could bring down an entire pack within hours. What was there to consider, to pause and reflect upon? It was a moment for action, but he could not do it. Was it too much to ask that her son behave as any man would, as Magdelaine herself had behaved many times? The world issues its threats and one must answer them, and quickly, or pay the price. What would Henri say if he could see what his son had become?

Magdelaine wrenched the weapon from her son's hands. She heaved it up to her shoulder, then crossed to the door of the pen and lifted the latch. Inside, the dog paced back and forth along a small semicircle in the dirt, breathing with a low pant. The light was dim but the dog's eyes were bright in the dark nest of fur, and Magdelaine aimed an inch above the patch of brow between its eyes and fired. The powder in the pan popped and the animal made a high-pitched cry and fell, just as the charge in the barrel echoed like a thunderclap.

She came back out through the door of the pen. Ani was at her side in an instant, peering between the slats of the pen to confirm that the danger had passed. While the other dogs had moved far away across the yard, he had tracked Magdelaine's movements the entire time with absolute loyalty, anxious to protect her.

"Since you could not perform the deed," she said to her son as she handed him the spent weapon, "you may have the honor of reloading this and putting it away. And burying that carcass. We will have to watch the other dogs carefully now to see if any of them grow sick as well."

Esmee and Susannah glanced between them. They were embarrassed for Jean-Henri too, Magdelaine assumed, as any woman would be. Esmee had defended his hesitant nature before, but would she persist in doing so now that she had seen the danger in it? Susannah murmured something about the students, and she and Esmee went inside.

Jean-Henri did not notice them go. His eyes were not on them but on his mother, challenging her. "Did you even think to ask if *I* was bitten?"

The rain had stopped and a garish sun began to burn through the remaining clouds, causing them both to squint. Magdelaine shielded her eyes with her hand. "But it was clear you were not."

Jean-Henri emitted a hard little laugh. "But did it occur to you once to *ask* whether the dog had bitten me?"

She glared at him, allowing the hard shell of her anger to cover her surprise. In fact, she had not thought to ask him, had not thought to worry for his sake.

He shook his head, then tried again. "Let me ask you this: Would you have moved so quickly to fire if the rabid dog had been Ani?"

Magdelaine did not have to think about her answer. "Yes."

Jean-Henri nodded. "Yes, that's what I would have said too. You would have done it just the same."

"And you fault me for that?"

"It does not trouble you at all, that you could with great *ease* put down this beast who has been your loyal companion for years? Who has traveled with you to the sugar camp and back, kept wolves away from your bedroll, worked tirelessly pulling your sleigh? It does not trouble you at all?"

Magdelaine shook her head. "No." She felt no conflict

between her words and what was in her heart. It was because of her love for the dog—and even as she thought of the word *love* she felt ashamed, how silly it was to love a beast—that she would be willing to put him down. For her own sake and for his, that he would not be able, in his derangement, to hurt her, the one he loved most of all. It would be an act of mercy.

"That, Mother, is the difference between you and me."

Chapter Thirteen

The rain came back the next day and Susannah was forced to delay her work in the garden once more. The girls came again for their lesson and after it had ended and they had left, Magdelaine went to inquire—against her better judgment, she said—after Noelle, the girl from her class who had gone missing. Susannah settled in the sitting room with a book and tried to read, but her mind kept leaping to matters off the page.

She had been careful to avoid the mirror on the wall of the sitting room so that she would not catch a glimpse of her hair. She tried hard not to think about it or wonder how long it would take for the color to grow out. Magdelaine was right that it was time for her to seize control of her life, to do what must be done to survive. Changing her hair ought to be a small price to pay for her safety.

She tried to focus not on what she had lost but instead on the effect her work in the garden seemed to be having on the rest of her body. Every muscle in her back and arms, each small tendon in her hands, everything ached with fatigue. But it was a marvelous ache. She found the work hypnotic, like a deep prayer. She had never gotten down in the dirt and planted a garden of her own, a garden that waited on the rain and the sun—forces outside her control—to act upon the plants and bring them to life. Now finally it seemed she was putting all her study in the greenhouse to use. She thought of Magdelaine's students, hard at work trying to understand the idea that their island was only a small dot on a map, and that map only a portion of the region, the continent. She thought too of Mr. Corliss, wondered if he was teaching the physics of birds to the children at the mission school. A small part of her had hoped that he would call again after the day she encountered him in the garden, but she knew she should be grateful he had stayed away.

When Esmee finished her work in the kitchen she joined Susannah in the sitting room, pulling her chair up close to the fire for light. At her feet was an open sewing basket containing spools of thread and brightly colored porcupine quills. Susannah watched as Esmee slid a quill into her mouth for a moment to soften it, then pressed the flat side against the newly sewn moccasin in her lap and sewed it into place with a back stitch. She folded the quill back and forth in the shape of a letter Z, then repeated the steps with a quill of a contrasting color.

"I'd like to have seen the porcupine who wore such a fanciful coat," Susannah said.

Esmee smiled. "There's an old woman on the island who dyes them. The same way we dyed your hair, in fact."

Susannah leaned across the hearth and touched the patchwork of color. "So beautiful. Are you making them as a gift for someone?"

Esmee didn't look up. "Making and repairing the clothes is part of my job."

Susannah couldn't help but press her just a bit more. "So you don't take a little more pleasure in making things for a *particular* member of this household?"

Again, Esmee would not look up, but she twisted her mouth to the side to prevent a smile from sliding into place.

"You have set your heart on him, haven't you?"

"I didn't know my feelings were so plain," Esmee said. Finally she looked up at Susannah. "Do you think he knows?"

"I honestly don't know. Jean-Henri seems like a good man, but he also seems lost inside his own head sometimes, doesn't he? And more than a little defeated by things. Perhaps he would never think to hope he could be with someone like you."

Esmee shook her head. "I doubt that very much!"

"Well, he would be a fool not to return your affection." Susannah wondered how it was possible that Esmee didn't know how lovely she was—that long black hair, the dark eyes, her delicate chin. Surely she had received attention from other men, proposals even. But there was something else about her that was even more appealing than her beauty: a steadfastness that calmed anyone who was fortunate enough to be in her presence. She knew what was important and what was frivolous, and she didn't waste any time on the latter. Esmee had decided that Jean-Henri was the man she wanted to marry, Susannah could see, and she had known it for a long time.

But perhaps his uncertain plans for the future were beginning to wear on her patience because she seemed anxious now, even despondent. She set the embroidery down. "It hardly matters. He will be gone to Montreal before the summer is over."

"Esmee, I don't think he wants to go."

"But *madame* wants him to go, and so he will. He would never defy her. He will come back once every few years until she passes. And then I don't think he will come back any more."

"Perhaps he would take you with him," Susannah said. She couldn't understand why a grown man like Jean-Henri allowed his mother to have so much power over his fate. He seemed to be trying to gain Magdelaine's approval, and she seemed determined to withhold it from him.

Esmee gave her a shy smile and shook her head. "I don't dare to think of such an outlandish thing as that. Besides, I could never leave this island. It is my home."

"And you don't think you could"—Susannah hesitated— "*tell* him how you feel?" Esmee gave her a doubtful look and Susannah nodded. "Of course. I understand." She couldn't think of anything to say that might offer comfort. It was an unavoidable truth that most people had very little say over whether they would get the thing they wanted. Jean-Henri might love her back, but he might leave anyway. Or he might stay on the island but set his sights on another woman. There was no telling. Esmee could only wait and see.

Susannah stood and walked over to the window. She

looked out at the gray beach and longed for the rain to stop so that she could get back to the garden. Her attachment to it bordered on desperation. In its cage, Magdelaine's pet bobbed its head up and down, watching Susannah.

"What do you feed this dove?"

Esmee took up the embroidery once more and glanced at the cage. "Cracked corn," she said.

The dove used its beak to pick at its feathers, then dipped it into the dish that held the food. Susannah thought about how Magdelaine had said that the mere sight of the bird in its cage upset her. She had been puzzled by the comment but found now that watching the bird filled her with a strange dread. Her throat felt tight as she asked Esmee, "Are its wings clipped?"

"I don't think so," Esmee said.

"But you do not ever take it out and let it fly around?"

"I think Magdelaine is more upset by the idea of giving the poor thing a taste of freedom and snatching it away, than she is about leaving it in there all the time."

"I wonder why she doesn't just let it go," Susannah said.

"I've wondered the same thing. She never asked for that dove, you know," Esmee said. "But now that she has it, it's hers. She feels responsible for it, for whatever fate might befall it."

Susannah wasn't unaware that she had plenty in common with this bird. "I think I'm going to take a walk."

"In the rain?" Esmee gave her a confused look.

Susannah shrugged. "That way no one will be out. And don't worry—I won't go near Market Street. No one will see me."

At the kitchen door she took a shawl that hung from the hook and wrapped it over her hair before stepping outside. She gulped the fresh air. The dread she had felt for the dove remained, but she knew it was really just dread for herself, for the future. Worrying about how she could continue surviving as Edward's wife had filled every minute of every day. Even though she had escaped, she still feared him. She dreamed about his boots thumping up the stairs to her room, his eyes flashing with anger. She examined her memory of what had happened at the port in Detroit, wondering whether the man she had seen on the boat really was Wendell Beals and, if so, what he would tell Edward he saw. Her future brought new uncertainties too. Who would she be now if she wasn't that fearful wife, afraid of her own shadow? What would rush in to fill the void?

She surveyed the garden. It was coming along, though most of it still existed only inside her head. She had pruned back the apple tree as far as she dared, and not a day too soon, for the buds had already appeared and now the tree could direct its energy into producing more fruit instead of wasting it sending leaves to its overgrown branches. Beneath it and along the perimeter of the tall fence, Susannah had dug beds. She expected she could find lady's slipper and sweet pea growing wild, or at least in a nearby garden owned by someone willing to share a cutting. She could plant them midsummer. For the kitchen garden Susannah had put in the grocer's lettuces and peas, corn and squash. She had been concerned about water, but now after three days of rain, things were looking up. Still, the growing season this far north must be short. The squashes would be small, tender.

Taking the stone path that ran along the back of the house, Susannah crossed out of the garden and through the gate into the churchyard next door. Rain washed the faces of the small gravestones that leaned like a line of crooked teeth, a grim smile. One, shaped differently than the others, caught her eye and she crossed over to it. The top right corner of the stone was crowned with a small statue carved in the shape of a rabbit. The face read: *Josette Savard, 1799–1816.*

Seventeen short years, Susannah thought.

The rain began to come down harder and the church looked deserted and dry. Ste. Anne's, Susannah could see, was the plain little sister of Magdelaine's house. It too was made of white clapboard but it stood only a story high, with a pitched roof and a wide door on iron hinges. She hurried to the other side of the yard and tried the door, feeling a wave of surprise that it gave so easily.

Inside, ten pews fanned out from the middle aisle, five on each side. The only light in the space came from the two small windows cut into the clapboard on either side of the altar—a simple low table covered in an embroidered cloth. On the floor next to the altar was a tall likeness of the Virgin, carved into the face of a log and varnished to a dull sheen.

Susannah moved into the last pew on the right side and slid all the way to the end, where she nearly disappeared into the darkness. She rested her hand on the back of the pew in front of her, then lowered her forehead down on top of it, listened to the whisper of her breath, smelled the damp fabric of her dress. Nothing moved. Nothing shifted or whispered back. She heard only the tapping of the rain and felt herself sheltered from it by the sound construction of the roof. If a church could do nothing else for you, it seemed it could do that.

Just then she saw motion in the front pew. A man who had been bowed down praying in the darkness sat up and turned.

"Forgive me," Susannah said, standing to leave. "I didn't know anyone was in here."

"It's all right," Jean-Henri said. "Please. Stay."

She lowered herself uncertainly back into the pew, and he walked down the short aisle and sat down beside her. "I came in to get out of the rain," he said.

She nodded, feeling like an intruder. "So did I."

A silent moment passed. Jean-Henri folded his hands in his lap, glancing down at them, then back up at the altar. Susannah tried not to think about the last time she had seen him, cowed by the rabid dog, as well as his mother's impatience. She wondered again why he couldn't seem to seize control of his life. He was a man, after all. What could stop him?

"I hope that the dogs didn't frighten you yesterday." He seemed to read her thoughts. "It's very rare for us to have trouble like that."

"It *was* frightening to see that dog's nature change so quickly, but I knew I wasn't in danger," Susannah said.

Jean-Henri pursed his lips. "Because of my mother, you mean? The way she takes things in hand?"

Susannah didn't want to say that his mother seemed to be the one capable of protecting them, while Jean-Henri had faltered. "She is a remarkable woman," she said instead, answering a question other than the one he had asked. "But it seems she is very hard on you."

He laughed. "Yes, I suppose she is. But I haven't ever known any different."

"And you never think to speak up to defend yourself?" The question was out before Susannah could stop it, before she could choose her words more carefully.

He winced. "I haven't done a very good job of staking my claim in the world the way she had hoped I would. I hoped for it too. But I'm not much for business—my father was, but I am not. My mother called in every favor she could to secure a position for me in Montreal when I was a young man, but I could not succeed, despite my best efforts."

"I am sure you were better at it than you think."

He laughed. "No. I wasn't. I lost my mother's associate a good deal of money. And now she wants me to go back and try again. To make my mark. But I can't bring myself to do it."

"And you can't tell her that?"

"Believe me—I've tried. But she won't listen." Jean-Henri shifted in the pew and squinted at the front of the sanctuary. "What my mother doesn't understand, what she will never understand, is that there is more than one way to leave your mark on this world. What about a man who has not founded a village, has not made a fortune in trade, but has, simply, tried to live a good life? Doesn't that life leave its own kind of mark?" He paused, then shrugged. "I love this island. I love the people here and I like helping them fix things that are broken—roofs, wheels, boats. But she wants something else for me, something that doesn't *mean* anything to me. I feel like I know the answers to questions that nobody is asking."

"Nobody?" Susannah replied, thinking of Esmee, who was at this moment making a plain shoe into a beautiful object because it meant something to her.

"Well, not my mother anyway. She sees no value in my way of living. She is determined to make me leave."

Susannah thought about that determination. Was Magdelaine trying, as Jean-Henri believed, to control him—or was she afraid?

"Do you think," Susannah began, remembering that her attempt at discussing family history with Magdelaine had not gone well, "that her insistence has something to do with what happened to your aunts?"

He looked at her in surprise. "How do you know about that?"

"The nun who helps Father Adler in Buffalo told me a little, only that one of them died and one of them disappeared. It's so sad."

"Our story has spread, I see."

"Josette Savard," Susannah said. "Is she one of them? I saw her stone outside, the one with the rabbit."

Jean-Henri nodded. "*Petit lapin*—that's what they called her. I was only seven years old when she died. Some of it I remember, because I was there. But some of it I only learned later on."

Susannah realized that this was the closest thing to an invitation she might get. She felt she had to know. "I hope you won't think me rude to ask, but what happened to them?"

Jean-Henri sighed, laced his fingers. "There was a man, Paul, who set his sights on my Tante Josette. She was only a young woman and didn't know what some men were capable of. My mother knew, and so did my Tante Therese—their older sister. Mother went away for the winter, as she did each year after my father died. She always left me in Therese's care while she was gone. That year, in addition to charging Therese with looking after me, she made her promise to keep Paul away from Josette. They warned her about him, but she didn't listen."

Susannah was beginning to understand. "And Paul killed Josette. So when he did, Therese ran away? Because she thought she was to blame?"

Jean-Henri nodded. "Yes, she did run. But she didn't make it very far. Here's what I remember: I was alone in the cabin, sitting on the floor stacking blocks. It was a gray day, and inside the cabin it was very dim. It was the day Josette died—I didn't know that then, but I realized it later. Tante Therese came in, and I remember noticing how strange she seemed. She was moving slowly, her hands down at her sides. She sat in the chair beside the fire and stared at nothing. I went over to her and took her hands to try to get her attention, but she didn't seem to see me."

Jean-Henri cleared his throat, then rubbed his palms together. "Her hands," he said, "were wet. After a minute she seemed to get her bearings. She looked at me and nodded, then took me by the hand and walked me to the neighbor's cabin, and asked the woman to look after me. When I saw the neighbor's expression change—her eyes went wide—I looked back at my tante. We were out in the daylight then and I could see that the front of her dress was soaked with blood. Her hands too. And the blood was on my hands from where I had touched her."

"Because she had found Josette . . . afterward?"

"Yes."

Susannah put her hand over her mouth. She thought again of the times Edward had threatened her. She could have met the same fate as Josette. Jean-Henri looked haunted by the memory alone, his face pale. "What a thing for a child to see. You must have been so afraid."

"I was, but I didn't understand any of it. I was mostly confused. The neighbor took my hand and pulled me close to her skirt. Therese turned and walked away, very slowly. I remember thinking how cold she must have been because she wasn't wearing a cloak or boots, and there was still snow on the ground."

"So she left the island that day?"

Jean-Henri shook his head. "She disappeared around the curve of the lane, walking away from the port to the back half of the island, where it was deserted. The neighbor woman ushered me inside, but when she had her back turned, I slipped back out and followed Therese, though I don't think she ever saw me. But I saw." He paused to clear his throat, to steady his voice. "I saw what she did. She walked down the beach and out into the lake. She just kept walking in that slow way until the water covered her up."

"So she didn't disappear," Susannah whispered. "She died."

He squinted again at the altar. "That's what I saw."

"And you had to tell your mother when she returned? She must have been heartbroken."

"I'm certain she was, though she never let me see any sign of it. I don't know how much of my story she believed. No one ever saw Therese again after that, so my mother must have decided eventually that I was telling the truth. But they also never found her body. And no one else saw what I saw, as far as I know. So some people were left wondering."

Susannah shook her head. To think he had carried the weight of this story, all his life. At least one thing made her different from Josette—if Edward had done to her what Paul had done to Josette, there would not have been anyone there to see, to carry on her memory.

"We never spoke of it again, of course," Jean-Henri said. "My mother took it the way she takes everything, absorbed it all inside of her and showed a stoic face to the world. It's only in her private moments—her time alone at the sugar camp, I think—that she must let her sorrow show."

Susannah shook her head. "And she wasn't worried about a young boy seeing such a terrible thing? Her own son?"

"I think she thought it would make me strong, the way men must become strong," he said bitterly.

"But you were so small then. Surely she must have shown you some tenderness, some warmth."

"Tante Therese did that. She was there every morning when I woke, she sang to me, played games with me. She did the kinds of things a mother does."

Susannah thought of her own mother's soft, pink cheeks, her rosewater scent. Susannah had delighted in her, and she in Susannah. *Thick as thieves*, her father would tease them as they giggled together over a game or whispered over a book. Oh, how she missed her. "Why?" Susannah said almost to herself. "Why couldn't Magdelaine do those things with you?"

"I think I reminded her too much of my father. I think I reminded her of how she lost him, of how she was alone. And she couldn't bear to be reminded. And then she lost her sisters. Loss after loss. It's why she's worked so hard to get me to leave the island. She says she wants me to succeed, but I think she wants to protect her own heart."

Susannah exhaled, marveling at Jean-Henri's insight. "There is so much sorrow here."

"But it's old sorrow," he said. "It's hard to explain, but I've seen a change in my mother since you arrived. She wanted very much to help you, wants to keep you safe. It's very important to her."

Susannah thought again of the dove in the sitting room, rubbing up against the bars of its cage. She felt a swell of satisfaction knowing that her arrival had helped Magdelaine somehow, that it had perhaps eased that old suffering. She had promised the nun that she would try to be of use to Magdelaine, and she wanted more than ever to keep that promise now that she knew the details of what had happened so long ago. Though she felt sorry for the boy Jean-Henri had been—abandoned by a woman too hurt to love him—she found herself admiring Magdelaine all the more. How strong she was! No matter what troubles she encountered, she bent them to her will or shoved them away. For as long as she could remember, Susannah had felt herself merely caught in the eddies. She had no control over what happened to her. She wanted to learn to be stronger, like Magdelaine. To fight harder.

Still, there was a price to pay for that too. Why couldn't Magdelaine fight her fights *and* love her son? Why did love have to be a weakness?

"I should think you would *want* to leave," Susannah said, "the way she treats you."

Jean-Henri shook his head. "This is my home, the only home I've ever known. And she is my mother, the only one I've had since my Tante Therese died. In her own way, she does care for me. I know she does. Perhaps you are important here, Susannah. Perhaps helping you will finally bring her some peace."

Back in her room upstairs she slipped out of the damp dress and sat in front of the mirror in her cotton shift, one of three new ones Esmee had sewn for her. The one she had worn on the boat had been torn up for rags. She thought of the threads that still hung from it where she had sewn her mother's necklace to the fabric, then wrenched it away with the hopes of buying her safety. That transaction had failed, but safety had come to Susannah in another way. That was the way of the world, surprising you. It was indifferent to your needs, but once in a while it dropped a morsel in your lap.

Susannah loosened her hair and brushed the damp sections into one sleek wave over her shoulder and thought about the peace that had eluded Magdelaine all these years. Jean-Henri was a loyal son, wanting to please his mother, willing to give up so much in order to do it, but Magdelaine couldn't see it. And then there was the mystery of Therese— dead, but maybe not dead. As Susannah knew very well, sometimes women went into the water and came back out again. Sometimes a story that seemed to be over had not yet ended.

In the morning, the sun finally came out and warmed the garden. By evening, the buds on the apple trees had shed their brown sheaths and soaked the sunlight into their little clenched white fists. They seemed to hesitate, to need to wait for the promise of just a little more sun, and when it came the buds unleashed their frills, the fleshy pink blossoms like open mouths singing a hymn.

Chapter Fourteen

Noelle had gone to visit family. That was all anyone would tell Magdelaine about the girl's absence, and eventually she gave up trying to find out more. Even Magdelaine couldn't win *every* fight. Noelle might return to the lessons, or she might not. There was no telling. That was the way of things.

The first of May arrived like a contented sigh. The flowers relaxed into color and the bees rose up from wherever it was they spent the cold months. Magdelaine was up early as usual, sitting at the writing desk in the sitting room to answer some correspondence. She wrote to a bookseller in Detroit to request a volume of English poetry that she wanted to read with her students. Then she wrote a long-overdue apology to Mr. Greive of Trois-Rivieres about Jean-Henri's delay. She didn't say when or whether he would arrive in Montreal—she didn't want to damage her reputation with this man any further with a lie. She addressed the letters and set off down the lane to Morin's store.

"Good morning, madame," Morin said when he saw her coming. He wore his buckskin coat and stood behind the small counter under a canvas awning. It was still early in the season for vegetables, but he had a few bunches of winter greens tied with string, and onions and potatoes in a wide basket. A sack of manoomin sat open with a tin cup beside it.

Magdelaine smiled as she passed out of the bright morning light and into the shadow of the awning. "Good morning, Mr. Morin. What do you have in from the boats?"

The man drank coffee from a steaming cup and read a week-old Wisconsin newspaper. He used it to gesture to the shelves behind him. "New sewing needles, some new calicos. A few tools. And then the usual: coffee, chocolate."

"I'll take a tin of coffee, please." She glanced at the new tools hanging on hooks along the wall. One was a small saw—not like the crude one Jean-Henri had given Susannah to use on the apple tree, but one that was finely made, with small teeth, for making precise cuts. Jean-Henri would appreciate the care someone had taken in making it. "And the saw," she said, "as well as these letters."

Morin nodded, took the letters, and wrapped up the saw. Magdelaine counted out coins but he waved them away. "You're settled up and then some, from the syrup."

She nodded and took the package.

"Oh, and I have a letter for you," he said. "From Buffalo."

Magdelaine felt the nape of her neck prickle.

"It came yesterday." He handed it to her. "Enjoy the sun. Another month of this and I'll finally thaw out," he said.

"And a few months after that, freeze again," she said with a smirk, and waved good-bye. Out in the lane she tucked the package under her arm and tore open the envelope. Inside was a sheet of stationery and a piece of newsprint, folded in half. She read the letter first.

My dear Madame Fonteneau,

It is with great happiness that I send this letter to thank you for your assistance in the matter of Miss Dove. I have enclosed a notice that seems to suggest we are successful.

I pray that fortune will soon bring me to your island. I am yours in gratitude,

Father Adler

Magdelaine unfolded the newsprint to find an obituary for a woman named Susannah Fraser, dated April 11. She felt an enormous wave of relief wash over her. Finally, she had done it. Father Adler was happy. Susannah was safe. She knew that the heavens didn't keep score—at least not that way. Saving Susannah couldn't bring Josette back. Still, she had prevented the loss of one more young woman. That had to count for something. Father Adler had signed the letter the way he always did, with that tepid hope that one day he might find himself on the island. She wondered if this time, though, the words would carry just a bit more weight. They had been corresponding for so long and now they had done this good thing together. Shouldn't they meet and shake hands at last?

Magdelaine glanced out at the placid lake that reflected the sunlight like a mirror. It was so bright her eyes began to water and she shielded them with her hand. For nineteen years, Josette had been in the ground, she thought as she folded the letter and tucked it in her pocket. Would her little sister sleep more peacefully now? And what about Therese, wherever she was? Did Susannah's saved life make any difference to her?

Magdelaine sighed. The obituary should be happy news, and it was, but beneath the relief was that same foundation of uncertainty. What had happened to Therese? Magdelaine closed her eyes and took a deep breath of the spring air, repeating the same answer she always did when the question reared up once again: She would never know. There would be no peace on the topic.

Back at the house she greeted Susannah in the sitting room, determined to put the past back in its grave, at least for today. Something good had happened, and she wanted to relish it. "I have some happy news for you," she said.

Susannah closed her book and set it on the table. She wore her hair loose, and it hung nearly to her elbows. The color from the elderberry had faded some, but the bright tones of her natural red were still subdued.

Magdelaine handed her the obituary. "You are dead."

Susannah held her gaze a moment before she looked down at the clipping. Magdelaine saw her hand tremble a bit as she held it, but Susannah clenched her fingers to steady it. Her eyes moved as she read the text. "This may be the strangest moment of my life," she said, "reading my own obituary. I am dead."

"You are dead," Magdelaine nodded. "And yet . . ."

"And yet, here I am." Susannah nearly whispered it. She

glanced back at the clipping. "They held a service for me. I had not thought to imagine *that*."

"You see what it means, don't you?" Magdelaine said. "He is not looking for you. You really are safe now."

Susannah nodded, and her weak grin broke open into a real smile, maybe the first one Magdelaine had ever seen on her face. Her youth showed in the smile; sorrow and worry had made her seem far older than she was.

"Now that we know this, I think you should feel free to expand your range a bit, explore the island, if you wish."

"I like the sound of that," Susannah said. "There are only so many times I can make the circuit from my room to the kitchen to the garden and back again."

"Why don't we take a walk to celebrate, and I'll show you around?"

Susannah coiled her hair in a loose twist and covered it with the fraying black bonnet. They set out back down the lane toward Market Street, and Magdelaine tried to see the island through Susannah's eyes. They passed three small clapboard houses, each separated by a swath of shrubbery and vines and a few small trees budding with leaves. To the left, the beach stretched in a crescent dotted with Indian lodges and canoes. As they neared the main street, the gravel lane grew more crowded with horse-drawn wagons. Spring and summer brought many newcomers to the island. Some wore native clothes, some French. Even a few women moved in the crowd, their wide skirts absurd alongside the men's more practical attire.

They passed the new church, as Magdelaine thought of it, the one the Presbyterians had built when they set up their mission school on the island just a few years back. As she tried to think of something friendly to say about the reverend, she noticed Susannah's somewhat mournful gaze at the building.

Magdelaine suddenly realized her oversight. "I never thought to ask," she now said, "whether you would like to attend Sunday meeting. You must be missing it. We can arrange for it now."

"Oh, that's not it," Susannah said. "I suppose I was just admiring the building. My husband was the one who insisted on attending each week back in . . . well, before. Though I believe it was mainly to court clients and conduct business. I hope you won't take offense if I say that religious feeling has always eluded me."

Magdelaine was quiet for a moment. She had felt that same absence ebb and flow over the years. "I understand the feeling. When so much of life is a struggle, it's hard to imagine that anyone is looking down."

Susannah nodded. "Have you talked much with Reverend Howe?"

"No. Jean-Henri has helped with some repairs on the building, but the reverend will have nothing to do with me. He has been here a few years now but never reciprocated the welcome we tried to extend when he first arrived. I believe he is afraid our Catholicism is contagious—like a typhoid. He is very severe. The girls tell me that he treats his students poorly, is determined to convert them at any price, whether they understand what any of it means or not."

Susannah raised her eyebrows. "He has hired a new teacher, a man from Boston."

"Really? How do you know that?"

"I had a brief conversation with him on the boat to Detroit. And once he came to the house, looking for Jean-Henri."

Magdelaine gave her a wide-eyed look. "And you spoke to him?" She reminded herself that Susannah's husband had printed that obituary. As far as he was concerned, his wife was dead. He wasn't looking for her.

"Don't worry. I didn't reveal anything of myself. He was the one who hired Jean-Henri."

"So he deigned to consort with us?"

Susannah smiled. "Perhaps he is more liberal than his employer."

As they neared the crowded lane, Magdelaine sensed Susannah hesitate. Fear was not an easy habit to break. Perhaps she would need a little more time to get used to the idea that she was safe.

"Let's go this way instead," Magdelaine said, gesturing to an empty path that led to the fort. They climbed the steep hill, the sun at their backs. Magdelaine felt perspiration dampen her upper lip and she panted some with the exertion. She noticed that Susannah did too, but neither of them seemed to want to stop. Cedar trees grew out to the edge of the bluffs, some even jutting sideways out of the limestone façade. In the open spaces, wildflowers covered the ground. Susannah stooped to collect a specimen of each one.

"Spring beauty," she called a star-shaped white blossom. The trout lily was yellow with a little white beard beneath the blossom. "Those are the anthers," she explained to Magdelaine. "They distribute the pollen."

They walked to the edge of the bluff. There, Magdelaine showed her one of the island's most prized features, a limestone arch about a hundred and fifty feet above the beach. When they looked down at the lake through it, the blue expanse and the line of the horizon filled the entire arch. It was as holy a place as any church, Magdelaine thought.

On the way back home they cut through the meadow behind Ste. Anne's and crossed the churchyard. Just as they were about to pass by Josette's stone, Susannah slowed her pace. She let her fingers run over the carved stone ears on Josette's rabbit, the curve of its back. Magdelaine felt a twinge of uneasiness. She never allowed herself to visit her little sister's grave—she always forced herself to walk by it without a glance.

"Come on," she said. "There is much to do at home."

"Magdelaine," Susannah ventured in a small voice. "Why is it that Josette has a stone, but not Therese?"

"Didn't I tell you"—she snapped, then inhaled through her nose, softened her tone—"that I don't like to talk about the past?" She wasn't ashamed, exactly, of their sorrows, though maybe she was a bit ashamed to have to admit that she had been absent when Josette needed her most. It had taken weeks for word to reach her, and the journey home would have been arduous enough on its own, without the agony of the terrible news. Magdelaine felt the old regrets surge: If only she had returned to the island sooner, things might have been so different.

"Therese has no stone," Magdelaine said finally, "because there was no body to bury."

"But she *did* die that day?" Susannah asked.

"Why do you want to know?" Magdelaine asked.

"I suppose I am just trying to understand what you have been through."

Magdelaine hesitated. Jean-Henri had seen Therese go under the waves. There was every reason to believe it was true. And yet how could she explain to Susannah that all these years, part of her still doubted, still hoped that somehow Therese was alive?

Magdelaine had never told anyone that she had gone on that fruitless search to Quebec City, and she wasn't going to tell Susannah now. Hope was nothing but a thing that plagued her, and she prayed that it would leave, once and for all. Magdelaine knew all too well that wanting an impossible thing didn't make it so. She answered what had to be true, despite her hopes. "Yes," she said. "Therese died that day."

Susannah nodded. "And—forgive me—even if you couldn't have a headstone, you didn't want something in her honor? A statue? Something?"

Magdelaine pressed her lips together. "If you're wondering whether I blamed Therese for what happened to Josette, the answer is yes. I did. For a long time. But I don't blame her anymore. It wasn't her fault—whatever happened. She couldn't have stopped that man." She looked at Susannah. "Knowing you, knowing about other women like you, has certainly taught me that."

"I suppose I was wondering," Susannah said, "whether you blamed *Josette*. Because you had warned her about him and she went against your wishes, and then she wasn't strong enough to get away, the way you would have if you had been in her shoes. She wasn't smart enough to see what was coming."

Magdelaine touched Susannah's elbow. "Is that how you feel? That you should have been able to stop your husband?"

"I didn't fight back. I gave up hope. If it wasn't for your help, I would still be there, still be accepting that as my lot in life. I'm not strong the way you are."

Magdelaine shook her head. Susannah had it all wrong. She had mistaken a failing in Magdelaine—hard-heartedness—for something good, something noble like strength, courage. Susannah seemed to her far more courageous than she had ever been. "You're here, aren't you?" Magdelaine said to her. "You *did* escape him. You're stronger than you think you are. Real strength isn't in the fight. It's in the enduring, the going on even when it seems like all hope is lost."

Susannah shrugged, then nodded at Josette's grave. "You have endured plenty yourself," she said.

"It was the worst day of my life—and I wasn't even here." She surprised herself by allowing the words to spill out. "Worse than the day my husband was killed. Worse than the first time I had to leave my son behind on the island."

Susannah looked at her in surprise. "Leaving Jean-Henri was difficult for you?"

"Of course. He was my son."

"He still is, isn't he?"

"What do you mean by that?"

Susannah shook her head and seemed to try to muster the courage to say what she meant. "It is only that you seem awfully determined to make him go away. Though you *must* know that he truly does not want to go."

Magdelaine gave her a hard little laugh. "You don't have a child. You don't understand."

Susannah's face clouded over for a moment with pain, and Magdelaine instantly regretted her words. She realized she did not know whether Susannah had lost a child, whether she longed for one or not. She might never have the chance to have a child now, given her circumstances. "I'm sorry," Magdelaine said. "That was a terrible thing to say."

"I may not be a mother," Susannah said, "but I've been a daughter. I know how much my mother meant to me, how much I mourned her when she died."

"Maybe I have regrets," Magdelaine said. Was that true? she wondered. "Maybe I didn't care for him the way that I should have. Maybe I punished him for things that weren't his fault." She was losing control of her voice. A kind of strangled sound was climbing up her throat, threatening to break into a sob. Who was this person speaking out through her mouth?

Susannah took Magdelaine's hands and, with more authority than she had ever heard the wisp of a woman muster, said, "They are gone, your sisters. But your son is still here."

Part Three

Homecoming

Chapter Fifteen

E dward sat behind the massive desk in his study and surveyed the piles of paper that needed attention. He had stopped opening the letters weeks ago when he could no longer muster the energy to read them, much less respond to their requests. Bills languished in those piles, Edward knew—increasingly terse requests for overdue payments on his loans, invoices from suppliers, timid appeals from workers for back pay. And the condolence letters! Every woman in the county, it seemed, be she the wife or mother or aunt of one of his workers, had written to say how sorry she was to hear of his wife's passing. They fell all over themselves to express this sympathy, all for a woman whom they did not know. Of course, they were trying to inquire, in the only way they knew how, after the sanity of the man who employed their men, the man who could decide, on a whim, whether they might eat this winter.

Edward relished the opportunity to ignore them all. Back

in the spring, when the news of Susannah's death had first shocked him into a rage, he had vowed not to drink anymore. But he found the stuff more difficult to resist than he could have imagined. His defenses, once ironclad, were down now as October ushered in fall's chill, and he began yet another month of rambling around the big empty house. What Edward hadn't expected was the pleasure drink brought. It was the ritual he liked: the sound of its pouring, the color like late-summer honey. When it slid to the back of his tongue and worked its scald on his throat—well, that was something to long for. He understood it now, why some men would do anything for it. After three glasses he felt he was looking at the world through a stained-glass window. Everything was dappled with bubbles and pink hued.

He saw too that it wasn't drink itself that had ruined so many men but what the drink unleashed. It was like a crowbar that pried the locks off the door—pried the very hinges, so that it could never be closed again. Losing Susannah had showed him just how little real control he had, and that realization sent a shudder through all of his endeavors.

In September, Marjorie had announced in a whisper that her husband finally had saved enough money to settle the scrubby little plot of land in Illinois they had been lusting after, and she would depart.

"Yes, fine, as you wish," Edward had mumbled, hardly looking up at her.

He gave her an extra two weeks' pay without complaint, as it helped to dispense with her more quickly. He had come to dread interactions with anyone and wanted to be alone in the house.

But after a month without her, Hawkshill showed signs of serious neglect. A woman from the Presbyterian church brought him a pot of stew a few mornings a week. He knew how to reheat the food himself over the fire but not how to wash the pots, and he left them crusted in a heap on the board in the kitchen. Flies got to be a problem. One evening he sat dozing before a low fire in his study, his glass listing to the side and cold scotch soaking through the leg of his trousers. As he wrenched his eyes open he saw a pair of mice making off with a heel of bread, the last he had in the house until some other woman took pity on him and brought more food.

He had been the most careful man he knew; now he was careless, and he was surprised to find he didn't really mind it at all. The brickworks he had worked so hard to build kept on running without his management of the day-to-day affairs, it seemed. He had always taken great pleasure in controlling every detail of work in the hot yard of hard-packed dirt. The yard belonged to him and he could summon things out of it. That fact had always been a comfort to him. But no longer. When the inquiries into this decision or that began to irritate him, he found a squat and malicious little man named Rache, shorter and crueler than Napoleon, to carry messages from the house and oversee the workers. After that, Edward seldom put in an appearance there.

Still, he was well aware that his debts far exceeded the sums he could raise if he had to by selling the factory and the homes he had built, even by selling Hawkshill. He was spread as thin as a sheet of ice and it was only a matter of time before it cracked.

And yet he tarried. His indifference to the impending collapse, and the drinking, were symptoms of a notion that had infected his mind, though at first he could not articulate just what it was. Each day he rose late and roamed the house in his nightshirt, now yellow with sweat, prowling cupboards and closets in search of some clue as to what had become of his life. He dressed and went to dinner at a tavern, though it was wearying to endure the silence that engulfed the clusters of men who sat over their glasses of ale. People were talking about him, he knew. They wondered how long he could go on as he was. Everyone thought he was overcome by grief at the sudden loss of his wife.

In the afternoons he walked through the dense woods to the clearing in which the Lamb of God Church sat. Workers and their weary-looking wives came for a kind of Mass most days of the week and always on Sunday, though they led the service themselves. He had asked Marjorie once why the blasted priest was never in his own church, and she explained that Father Adler was assigned not just to Buffalo but to the whole of Erie County and beyond. He traveled in the good-weather months, taking communion to villages that hadn't seen a priest or been given the sacrament in a year. All that for a magical crust of bread, Edward thought. What a waste.

He watched Sister Mary Genevieve from his hiding spot as well, though he wasn't sure what he was looking for. She sat alone in the rude cabin reading for hours, then moved about at the hearth to stoke up the fire and cook herself a meal. Once a week she washed clothes and linens and hung them on a line. Once or twice he saw the priest's vestments hanging alongside her kitchen towels, but by the time he could concoct a reason to inquire after the priest, he was told the man had departed for some other remote place once again. Edward had intended to speak frankly with the man about his suspicion of the nun, that she knew something she wasn't telling about his wife's death. But he never could get an audience with Adler.

One afternoon as he crouched in the dense undergrowth beneath a stand of pines, his hands and cheeks now ravaged with a poison oak rash despite how careful he had been to avoid the leaf Susannah had once warned him about, the nun finally varied from her routine. Around two o'clock she pulled on her black bonnet and set off toward town with a stack of letters in her hand.

Edward shot up from his hiding spot, then forced himself to hang back a good distance before following her. He waited until they both were on the road among milling shoppers and children darting underfoot with their games before approaching her.

"Sister, good afternoon," he said.

It was clear from the look that came over her then that she did not know he had been watching her. She glanced behind him, wondering, Edward knew, where he had come from. Hawkshill was on the far opposite end of town.

"Good afternoon, Mr. Fraser," she replied, her voice steady and her eyes on the road. She glanced up at him, then let her eyes flit nervously away again. "Are you well, sir? You look poorly."

He nodded. "It is my grief, you see. For everyone else, six

months have passed, but for me, not a single day. I am trapped forever in the memory of the night you delivered the terrible news."

She seemed to consider what to say next, then simply nodded. There was nothing in his voice that sounded grieved, he knew. It was full of malice.

"The Lord offers healing if you will turn to him," she finally said. "Healing for any affliction."

She was talking about the drink, and this galled him. "Where are you from, Sister?" he asked.

"My work has taken me to many places all over the East and Northwest."

"So, not from here? Not from New York?"

"No."

"You've no family nearby? How very lonely you must be."

"Sir, when a religious woman takes orders, she renounces the ties to her blood family so that she may devote herself completely to the Holy Family. Everywhere I have been and everywhere I will go, this family is with me. There is no loneliness in that."

He laughed. "Indeed. But say you were, one day, to disappear. Do you think anyone would notice that you were gone?"

She stopped walking and turned to him with wide, fearful eyes. Two men, one in front of the other, passed by them carrying a rolled-up rug on their shoulders. Sister Mary Genevieve glanced at the backs of their heads, then to the other side of the road, where a woman stepped carefully around a muddy spot in the road, a baby on her hip. Her eyes met Sister Mary Genevieve's and the nun tipped her chin slightly. The woman hurried inside the tavern behind her.

"I'm not sure I understand the purpose of your question, Mr. Fraser."

He shook his head, changed course. "You . . ." He laughed again, rubbing his forehead with his palm. "You are a slippery one. You think you hide behind holiness, but I see you for what you really are. A liar. A derelict."

"You treated Mrs. Fraser like a dog in the street," the nun said, her face reddening. "You nearly killed her yourself, probably more than once. How dare you mourn her? How dare you threaten me?"

"How dare *I*?" he shouted. A few people stopped their nearby conversations and turned to look. A year ago he would have cared about propriety, about rumor. But now he didn't care a whit for any of it.

"Even now I see that though you claimed not to know my wife, you were in fact acquainted. That she told you lies and played upon your sympathy, you, a person who is nothing—a lowborn, a *Catholic*, for God's sake. Did you ever stop to think about why she might talk to you? To question whether she was telling the truth, whether she was even sane?"

"I'll say no more on this matter." The nun's shoulders seemed to relax as a man came walking toward them from the tavern. "It is past. Let the dead rest in peace."

"Sister," the man said, "is everything all right here?" He had broad shoulders and wore a white shirt and waistcoat with no jacket. Broken blood vessels coursed his wide, red nose, indicating a few decades of hard drinking, and the singsong clip of his voice was unmistakably Dublin. He was one of a handful of micks who called themselves the "volunteer constabulary." Edward knew this one, in fact, from a fight the man had helped him break up in the brickyard. And he had paid him a time or two to do his bidding.

"She's perfectly fine, Padraig," Edward said.

"It's *David*, actually, you smug son of a bitch."

Edward waved his hand, a gesture to dismiss the man's insubordination. "I have business to attend to at home."

"So you will go there directly, then?" David said.

Edward didn't answer. Sister Mary Genevieve stood next to her protector, her chin raised, her eyes blazing. Edward chewed his bottom lip while he held her gaze a moment longer, then turned to go.

"And you'll not be bothering the sister again, Mr. Fraser?" David called after him. "Won't be lurking outside her cottage?" So she had seen him after all, and told her friends about it.

It took everything in Edward's power not to answer this challenge. The world had gone crazy, and no one saw it but him. What kind of a world was this where someone like that would speak in such a way to someone like him? There were people who counted and people who didn't count, but suddenly it seemed the nothings were taking matters into their own hands. Edward was the one who needed protection. Everyone wanted something from him. They wanted his money, his power, his wife. They wanted to make him into a Papist. That was what it was. They wanted to shove Rome down his throat like a tonic for a disease he didn't have. The colors of the road—the mud, the mustard-hued manure between the ruts, the vivid red of maple boughs arching over the footpaths—all of it blurred in his field of vision. He felt he was losing control of his mind, but he no longer cared about control. The world was a chaotic place, and he knew he had to be willing to do anything in order to survive in it.

Bad news came in threes, so Edward wasn't the least bit surprised to find Nathaniel waiting for him in his study back at Hawkshill.

"You let yourself in, I see," Edward said.

Nathaniel let his eyes roam the room without moving his head. Beneath the plates of decaying food, the half-empty tumblers, were the items Edward had purchased to furnish this big house. There was the gleaming oak desk and bookcase, a hand-carved sideboard, an oil painting of two pears tipped askew in a blue china bowl. "You are cavalier with your possessions, sir," Nathaniel said.

"What better way is there to relish ownership of a thing?" Edward asked. "It is mine, so I may break it." He hadn't grown up with money. It wasn't until after he married Susannah that his business took off, aided, of course, by his many frauds. Now he had the house, the possessions that he had long felt he deserved, and he would be damned if anyone was going to take them away.

Nathaniel's jaw tightened. Edward was going to make him struggle through this task. He wouldn't make it easy on him. "Edward, I am here as a courtesy. To give you one last chance to tell the truth."

"The truth about what?"

Nathaniel sighed. "If you don't, in about an hour some men are going to come here to arrest you. I have a file full of evidence on my desk, depositions from lenders who will testify that you falsified documents to secure loans, claiming properties you do not own as collateral, using false names, failing to pay taxes . . . the list goes on."

Edward sat very still. In the golden haze of afternoon light, Nathaniel's face was positively childlike in its earnestness. Edward felt charmed by the display, and a little embarrassed for Nathaniel, a city *attorney*, obviously an intelligent man by all accounts, but one who, it seemed, knew nothing of the world.

"Nathaniel, between the brickworks and my construction projects, I employ most of the working men in this town. The working, taxpaying, *voting* men."

Amusement broke out over Nathaniel's face. "And a good many of them are owed back pay and have witnessed you breaking numerous laws. If you really think they will be loyal to you now, you are even more deranged than I thought."

"Their word against mine before a judge? Preposterous."

"Edward, do you understand what I'm telling you? It's not their word against yours. I have hard evidence. You're going to jail."

Edward shook his head. He couldn't let reality intrude— not yet. The truth was that losing Susannah had been like the rock that starts the avalanche. He knew he couldn't stop it now. "No, I am not."

Nathaniel looked up at the ceiling, then threw up his hands. He put on his hat. "I tried. I really tried to help you. I hope you will remember that. It's all I can do."

It didn't seem like it took them a full hour to arrive, but Edward couldn't be sure. He hadn't looked at his watch in days. He had always, in his quest to transform his efforts into wealth, carefully monitored the passage of time, as if without him, it wouldn't go on. But now Edward understood the secret mechanism by which the world worked, and it was nothing so systematic as the gears of a watch. Instead it was like Erie, where you tried to hook as many writhing fish as you could, and they were all too heavy on the line. A fish flopped into your boat and back out again; it took your line and pole and arms back in the water with it up to your elbows. Or you clubbed a fish and it lay still for a while, then revived. Or you slit through its gills with your knife before it came to and you skinned it and pulled out the bones and even fried it and consumed it beside your fire, but the next time you were near the lake you saw that there were always more fish surfacing to pluck gnats out of the air, and your boat was too small, your arms too weak, to get them all.

When they came and made the arrest—two men in blue coats, one fat, one thin, like twins who had not divided evenly in the womb—he went quietly along, and because he did not argue or try to fight them off they left his hands unbound. They put him in a black carriage with no windows. There was just the light that came in through the spaces between the planks, and doors that bolted shut on the outside. The conveyance had no seat, and so Edward sat on the floor with his knees pulled up and bounced around like a kernel of unpopped corn.

Edward watched through the gap between the boards as the officers pulled the carriage up in front of the squat brick jail he had spent so much time building. The thin officer went up the stairs to the front entrance and inside, perhaps to unlock the cell door and ready it for him. Edward recalled the weight of those iron bars. Three workers had strained to carry them into the building. Though it had only ever been used to house drunks while they snored through their hangover and, once, a thief with a weak grasp of geography who thought he could ride the Erie Canal from Albany all the way to Chicago, the cell had served the city of Buffalo well.

Word of his arrest traveled fast, and Rache came straight from the brickworks to the jail when he heard. After a loud argument with the jailer, Rache was admitted to visit with Edward, but they were not allowed to talk in private. There would be no telling Rache what papers to burn, and so their conversation consisted of Edward's directive on what to say to the men.

"The truth will come out," Rache said, as a way of reassuring Edward, but it did little to ease Edward's anxiety. The truth *would* come out. And what would he do then?

Edward shuffled through the mail the man brought him and almost cast it all aside when his eye caught a glimpse of Wendell's handwriting on an envelope. The paper was badly battered, as if the letter had been sent many months ago, was lost and then found again. Wendell, ensconced as he was in the remote outpost of Green Bay, might be the last man from Buffalo not to know of this turn of events. Wendell, who had always been loyal, if weak, nonetheless knew the world for what it was. Perhaps his words would provide some encouragement or, if nothing else, some distraction.

My dear friend,

I write to you with a heavy heart, sharing in what I know must be a time of great sadness for you. Mrs. Beals received word that Mrs. Fraser is feared dead after my boat departed for Green Bay. Her letter was carried on a small steamer that followed my boat all the way to Detroit. I remember noticing its gleaming red wheel wells, newly painted, and debated with myself over whether this was mere ostentation. So much in our time is, and thus it can be difficult to recognize true beauty.

But true beauty, sir, was within your dear wife, and it shone out in her countenance, her kind voice, and her bright and active mind. I tell you nothing of which you are not fully aware, I know, but I must tell it nonetheless.

We docked at dawn in Detroit, and a deckhand from our shadow boat raced aboard to deliver his bag of letters that we were to take on to points farther north. Some passengers were roused from their beds for urgent letters but I was long awake, at the rail, watching Detroit's steeples ease into view. Hence I received her letter right away, and how great was my sorrow when I read your sad news! The weight in my heart extended to my limbs and I felt frozen. The bell in the tallest belfry began to ring just then and I felt our Creator himself rang that bell to remind me that, though lost to us for a time, your dear wife is in a happier place now, where her garden might bloom perpetually and know no winter.

The gangway had been extended to the wharf and passengers bound for Detroit streamed off the boat. Mrs. Fraser was so much in my mind just then that my eyes played tricks on me: I saw her face in the crowd, a woman remarkably like her in demeanor and gait met my gaze. And I swear, sir, that she recognized me too.

I started, dropped my letter, and bolted toward her, but

*the crowd converged and the woman disappeared. How
cunningly truth eludes us, when our mind is bent by our
heart's desire. I felt so keenly your dear wife's absence that my
mind conjured her image. She was but a mirage, of course—I
knew it in an instant. I feel certain that you too have seen
this mirage, my friend, and I join you in grief as*

*Your constant friend,
Wendell*

Edward held the letter pinched between his fingers and
stared at the words. *A mirage of Susannah on a westbound boat.
A mirage of Susannah in Detroit.*

How was it possible? And yet hadn't part of him suspected it all along, been unable to accept her disappearance
and the idea of her death? Edward thought of Sister Mary
Genevieve standing in the road earlier that day. She hadn't
been afraid of him.

A wave of rage crashed over him and he glanced up wildly,
first at Rache's meaty grimace, then at the bars between them
and the stone walls that enclosed his cell. Edward had built
this jail, and he knew better than anyone that there was no
way out.

Susannah had tricked him—and ruined him. She was
alive and walking free, while Edward was here, behind these
bars. But they couldn't hold him forever. Now that he knew
the truth he could bide his time, wait for his chance. And
then he would find her.

Chapter Sixteen

Fall on the island was a brief and brilliant affair. The trees seemed to change color overnight and burn gold and rust-red for just a day or two before icy rain stripped the branches. Magdelaine had told Susannah that the men who had once worked tirelessly as traders—those who had not returned to Quebec or found new homes elsewhere—were unengaged now that the demand for pelts had ceased. Mainly they fished, in bobbing canoes anchored off the beach. They were trying to take as much as they could from the lake before the surface froze and they would have to cut their way through for fresh fish. The women worked just as hard, drying and preserving the whitefish and trout so that in January they could summon a halfway decent stew.

Susannah's garden yielded a small harvest of potatoes, squash, and oats, plus a good crop of apples and a thimbleberry bush draped with red jewels. She took it all in its time, and Esmee helped her turn the berries into preserves. She traded seeds with a Presbyterian woman in exchange for crocus and snowdrop bulbs and planted them in rows in the beds closest to the lane. When the weather turned cold, she set her sights on putting the garden to bed for the winter. She had plans for the spring, ideas about how to make the most of the medicinal herbs, and had ordered from a catalog seeds to start with next year. The little wooden box arrived on the last boat of the season, the seeds in five burlap pouches nestled in a bed of hay. The safety of that dry place gave her a peaceful feeling. The seeds were tucked away, suspended from the moisture that could set free their lolling, searching roots.

Despite the arrival of her obituary back in the spring, Susannah still had not felt that she was truly safe from Edward's reach. It wasn't until October, when the frost came and the boats stopped running, that she finally allowed her fear to recede. He believed she was dead—after all, he had held a funeral for her, had printed the details of her life in the newspaper. And even if any part of him still doubted her death, he could not get to her here. The frozen lakes were keeping her safe.

Esmee taught Susannah her ribbonwork technique for embroidering skirts and cloaks and moccasins, and they sat by the fire late into each night, working the layers of silk in silence. In the time it took Susannah to embellish the cuffs of a pair of mittens for herself, Esmee completed three wool capes. The first two came quickly, one for herself and one for Magdelaine. On the third garment the rhythm of her fingers slowed as she switched to a small needle and fine thread and peered over a French book Magdelaine had given her as a gift, trying to copy a climbing vine shown in the picture.

This cape was larger than the other two, and Susannah knew without asking who would wear it.

She had assumed Esmee would expect her to make her own new clothes, but one chilly night at the end of October, Susannah retired to her room to find a muslin-wrapped package on her bed, tied with a bow. Inside was a simple dress of fine red wool, the collar, cuffs, and hem edged with flowers in black satin ribbon. A Mackinac dress for a Mackinac winter.

The next day Alfred Corliss knocked, and when no one answered—Magdelaine and Jean-Henri had gone to Market Street, Esmee was at church, and Susannah only watched from the upstairs window—he wrote a quick note and stuck it under the door. It was addressed to Susannah, an invitation to come tour the school and have dinner with the reverend and his wife. And Alfred too. She wrote back a polite but terse decline, and asked Jean-Henri to walk her note over to the mission school. Alfred posed no danger to her now, but she had lied to him about who she was and it felt too late to tell the truth, too late to try to explain it all.

It was a mark of her settling in that Susannah had allowed herself to make plans for the garden, planting those bulbs for the spring. Whenever she felt uneasy about her own future, she remembered her promise to Sister Mary Genevieve and her gratitude to Magdelaine. What she wanted now was to help Magdelaine find some peace. While the woman hadn't exactly softened toward Jean-Henri, Susannah noticed that she mentioned Montreal less. They didn't discuss the sad story of her sisters again after that day in the churchyard, but Susannah felt that some kind of uncertainty lingered there. If she needed an explanation for why fortune had brought her to this place, perhaps it was to be the one to help this family settle the past, once and for all. Only then could Susannah think about what lay ahead for her. She tried to be satisfied with this plan.

Still, she felt the familiar melancholy that always set in this time of year. Daylight grew shorter, the sun setting before they sat down for their evening meal, and everything seemed to be dying. Winter meant waking to the cold morning. It meant day after monotonous day stuck indoors, sealed away from the weather.

November had brought icy rain; December brought the snow. Susannah watched from Magdelaine's warm sitting room, the fire roaring beside her chair, as snow drifted from the wind off the lake until it obscured the front porch, piled up to the windows, wrapped itself around the thimbleberry bushes like fleece. Magdelaine brushed the front steps clean each morning with a broom and cleared a path to the dogs' pen. Esmee was careful to set the water pump's handle high each night and wrap it with a blanket to keep it from freezing.

Despite the weather, Magdelaine's students came faithfully each week to read from the catechism together, to study their figures and Magdelaine's maps. Susannah assisted with it all and helped the girls practice reading in English. They all spoke French at home, and some of them Odawa, and in comparison the English was difficult, puzzling. But French was the language of the island's past, Magdelaine told them, and English was its future. Whites from the East came regularly now on things they called pleasure trips, journeying just for the novelty of sleeping in the well-appointed cabin of a steamboat, of seeing the last of the real-life savages before they were all pushed west. A shop had opened on Market Street to sell Indian curiosities to the travelers: cornhusk dolls, woven mats and baskets.

The Americans might be strange, Magdelaine said, even ridiculous, but they had money, and they were coming. The girls had to understand what they could expect for their futures. Magdelaine was patient but stern and didn't hesitate to make them repeat over and over the question about the fifth article of the Apostles' Creed: *What benefit have we by the resurrection? It confirms our faith and hope that we shall rise again from death.* She seemed to want the girls to understand that it meant not just the final death that waited for them, but the many deaths that would precede it, the setbacks and disappointments that would require them to begin again with new hope.

But the girls, of course, were girls. They had never left the island and never wanted to, and they cared little for what might come or go from it. The affairs of men, French or American, meant nothing to them. They did not understand that those men might become their husbands, and then their affairs would matter very much indeed. The third week in December would be their last meeting before the Christmas Eve Reveillon, and they anticipated the party with as much excitement as Magdelaine had hoped they would direct toward their studies. But she confessed to Susannah that she could not blame them—it was a joyous time of year.

Their discussion veered quickly, when Magdelaine gave them license, from eternity to *pattes d'ours* stuffed with stewed rabbit, to melted chocolate with cream and tart apple preserves. The girls and their mothers would cook for days in preparation, Magdelaine explained. They would burn through piles of firewood in the small hearths of their trading cabins. When the fire on the beach was ready, they would bring the food out on large tables and cook the rest outdoors. The girls would make crepes for the young men they fancied and show off their skills. Everyone said no girl was fit to marry until she could turn a crepe.

The morning of the feast, Susannah heard Esmee lay the fires and begin her work in the kitchen before dawn, and she rose to join her. It had snowed again in the night, and the windows shimmered with frost in the candlelight as Susannah buttoned her red wool dress and tied a fresh apron around her waist.

Esmee showed her how to roll out the dough and cut it into rectangles for the pies. As she worked, Susannah noticed how sure her hands felt as she moved the rolling pin in careful arcs. Her work in the garden had made her arms at first sore, but then, the more she kept at it, strong. She had brought the garden to life with these hands, and the accomplishment satisfied a thirst she hadn't understood was there. Here in the kitchen, working beside Esmee, she thought of nothing but the dormant bulbs, the resting branches of the apple tree. She was happy.

"Susannah, how did you celebrate Christmas as a child?" Esmee stirred the pot of stewed meat that would go into the pies.

"Quietly," Susannah said, calling up memories from a lifetime ago, back when her parents were still alive. Before Edward had taken her down such a different path than the one she had hoped for. "We would go to church. My mother would always send our cook home to be with her own family, and she would make something for us herself. A goose or a turkey. Buttered potatoes. She had been a farmer's daughter and knew her way around the kitchen."

She marveled at Esmee's skill with spooning just the right amount of meat to fill the pies, folding the dough so that the corners matched perfectly and pinching it closed. She rounded the edges with her knife to make the pie resemble the bear paws for which they were named. "I suppose you have been making these same pies for many years."

"Yes," Esmee replied. "My mother taught me how. But we didn't have the same sort of family celebration you describe. We never lived in the same house as my father—my mother was a summer wife, to be sure. My father worked for Monsieur Fonteneau, and then madame for many seasons, and I only saw him a few times a year. He had another wife, other children, in Montreal, and spent Christmas out on the trade route or in the city with them."

Esmee did not relay these details with bitterness but only as matters of fact. Hers was a common story that had been played out many times on the island.

"I didn't know," Susannah said, "that your father had worked for Magdelaine." Susannah had spoken to Jean-Henri about Therese, and Magdelaine herself, but she had never asked Esmee about it. Of course, the young woman would have been just a baby when it all had happened. "Was he with Magdelaine when she learned what happened to her sisters?"

Esmee paused in her work and looked up at Susannah

with wide eyes. She wiped her hands on a towel and crossed the kitchen to peek into the front hall. "I've never spoken about this with madame," she said in a low voice, returning to the table. "She might be angry if she hears us."

Susannah nodded. "Forgive me for bringing it up."

"No," Esmee said, "it's all right. Jean-Henri told me you have taken an interest in his family's . . . history. The answer is yes, my father was there. He was the one who buried Josette in that churchyard."

"Oh," Susannah sighed. Somehow she had not thought to imagine the burial, and the fact of it made the story even sadder. She had come to view Josette as a version of herself, the Susannah who couldn't escape from Edward; she could almost feel the dirt piling up on her, raining down from Esmee's father's shovel. She took a deep breath to remind her lungs that she was still here. "How very sad it must have been for Magdelaine."

"She was beside herself, according to my father. Even a year later, when he tried to get her to go looking for Therese, he couldn't wake her from that spell of her grief."

"Look for her where?" Susannah asked. "I thought Therese died that day too."

Esmee gave her a confused look.

"Jean-Henri said—"

"Ah, yes. Well, he was a little boy then. No one was sure what to think of what he said he saw. Therese's body never washed up, but that's not unheard of in cases like these. It's a big lake and currents can carry bodies a long way. For a while, according to my father, people accepted Jean-Henri's story. But then the next year my father was in Quebec City and he saw Therese walking down the street."

"He did? Are you certain?"

Esmee nodded. "The way he told it, he approached her. She looked very different, he said. She was much thinner and her hair was pulled severely back under a black bonnet. But it was her. She pretended not to know him, told him he had her confused with someone else. When she walked away he followed her until she came to a building and went inside. It was a convent."

Susannah felt a twinge of recognition, but of what she could not say. "And he was *sure* it was her?"

"Yes," Esmee said. "He didn't tell me about it until many years later, of course. As soon as he returned to the island that spring, he told Magdelaine what he had seen. But she didn't seem to believe that Therese could be alive."

"How could she not want to know whether it was true?"

Esmee shrugged. "You have to understand. She was still very angry at Therese then. Whether she was dead or alive. Perhaps Magdelaine felt that if Therese had chosen to leave the island, she should not interfere with that choice. She felt that, either way, Therese was dead to her. Or perhaps she simply didn't believe my father's account."

"But why would he lie?" Susannah's mind was racing to catch up. She thought back to her conversation in Ste. Anne's with Jean-Henri, how Therese had been like a mother to him when his own was away. "And Jean-Henri—does he know about this?"

"I don't know," Esmee said. "I have no idea what my

father said to him, and I certainly would never bring it up. I try not to interfere. This is not my family, not my business." She said this wistfully, as they both knew Esmee longed to be a Fonteneau. "Unless Magdelaine told him—and that's hard to imagine because she wouldn't have wanted to give a little boy false hope about finding his beloved aunt—I would guess that he does not know."

Susannah clutched the rolling pin. Again she felt that twinge of recognition, a sense that she had known something about this story before Esmee told it to her. She tumbled the details through her mind once more. Was it Esmee's father she recognized? But how could she? Was it Quebec City, a place to which she had never been? Then suddenly she realized what it was: the convent. The woman he had seen, the woman he thought was Therese, had escaped him by running inside a convent.

Susannah sank into a chair, letting the rolling pin clatter onto the table. Therese Savard was alive, and Susannah knew where she was.

"What's wrong?" Esmee said with alarm. "Are you all right?

Susannah swallowed and nodded, then stood back up and took up her work with the dough once more. "I'm fine." She wouldn't say anything yet, not until she decided what to do. She sensed that Esmee was watching her, but Susannah wouldn't meet her gaze.

They heard footsteps on the stairs. Jean-Henri stumbled through the kitchen in his sleepiness, pulling on his boots as he went out to attend to the dogs that howled for their breakfast. Susannah stole a glance at Esmee as he passed by her without so much as a word of greeting. But Esmee was well practiced in hiding her tenderness for him. She might as well have been invisible.

The dogs' howling quieted and a few moments later, Jean-Henri returned to the kitchen. Without asking whether he wanted it, Esmee poured coffee into a mug, then added hot cream and handed it to him. The sun was coming up, light coming into the kitchen. It would be a clear day, just right for the celebration in the evening. He gave Esmee a benign smile, murmuring his thanks.

Magdelaine joined them in the kitchen. "Good morning," she said. She poured a cup of coffee for herself.

Susannah tried to imagine how Magdelaine would react if she blurted out the words: *Therese is alive.* She wasn't the sort of woman who liked surprises. Susannah knew she couldn't say anything yet, not until she knew whether her suspicion was correct.

Jean-Henri sipped his coffee. "We'll need more wood before tonight," he said. "The pile is low."

Magdelaine sighed. "And you had not thought to check it before now?"

Jean-Henri laughed in frustration. "If I had, you would have complained that I concerned myself too much with the management of this household, that my attention should be on my business. Whatever I do, you will find a way to be dissatisfied with it."

Magdelaine glanced at Susannah as if to say, *See what I must endure?* But Susannah only smiled back. She thought Jean-Henri had plenty to endure himself.

Magdelaine set down her cup and smoothed back the

wiry gray hairs that had escaped from her long braids. "Let me dress and we will harness the dogs."

Esmee cleared her throat. "Madame, why not let Susannah go instead? She hasn't yet seen the other side of the island. Or really seen what the dogs can do." She turned to Susannah then. "Have you?"

Susannah shook her head. All summer and fall the dogs seemed to lie indolent in their pen or in the sunshine when Jean-Henri let them wander in the yard. As Magdelaine's favorite, Ani had the most freedom. Magdelaine had told Susannah that she suspected Ani had given his heart to one of the children enrolled in Reverend Howe's school, as the dog waited outside the door each day for the students to emerge. But even Ani had seemed bored in the heat, aimless.

"Just wait," Magdelaine had said to Susannah many times. "Just wait until you see them in the winter. When they are in their glory."

"I would love a chance to go," Susannah said now to Jean-Henri.

Esmee nodded. "You must."

Jean-Henri shrugged, still irritated with his mother. "You will need warmer clothes."

Esmee lent Susannah a pair of loose wool stockings and tall, fur-lined boots that laced up with a leather cord. They were too large for Susannah's feet, but she didn't complain. Over the wool dress she fastened Esmee's hooded cloak, then shoved her hands into large stiff mittens. She looked strange, she knew, but she had come to think differently about clothes since she had arrived on the island. In Buffalo her dresses were made of the finest silk, cut close on the body and finished with exquisite detail. Here clothes simply provided protection from the elements. In its own way, this new ensemble had a kind of beauty. It performed a task. Here, the value of a thing came from what it did for you, not how it appeared or whom it might impress.

Outside Jean-Henri showed Susannah how to help him harness the dogs. They slipped leather straps over the dogs' heads and across their chests, then buckled them at the back and clipped them to the reins. She expected the dogs to yelp and shuffle as she had seen them do so many times before, but they stood completely alert, their bodies like coiled springs. The covered sled was painted green, with sloping sides and wide black runners that held the seat aloft. With a short chain, Jean-Henri attached a flat sled to the back, which they would use to carry firewood back home. He attached the harnessed dogs to the front, then helped Susannah in, showing her how to stretch her legs out straight inside. Then he pulled one blanket over her shoulders and another over her lap.

"These dogs are born to do one thing," Jean-Henri said. "And that is *pull*. Do not reach your arms out. Do not sit up high. Keep your back and head low. Understand?"

Susannah nodded and pulled the hood of her cloak up over her head.

"Then we are off." Jean-Henri stepped around to the back of the sleigh. Susannah felt the sleigh shift as he stepped up with one foot and then the other onto the wide runners. He held the two handles that jutted out behind her shoulders and shouted. "Yah!"

The dogs jolted forward and the sleigh was in motion.

The carriages Susannah was used to sat up high, on wheels
that rolled across the road, slowed down in mud. Horses
were trained to walk at a slow clip, and even when they trotted, a carriage could only move so fast. But these dogs pulled
at a mighty pace, and the dry, packed snow offered little resistance to the slick runners. In a flash they reached the
wooded path and the dogs increased their speed once again.
Jean-Henri shifted his body weight onto the right runner
and the dogs made a distinct right turn, following the curve
of the shore. The frigid wind shocked the senses and Susannah's eyes teared up. As the droplets escaped across her temples, they froze against her skin. Back in the yard Susannah
had been able to smell the dogs' matted fur, but the air on
the lake was so dry and cold that she smelled nothing, even
as the dog closest to her evacuated its bowels on the ice,
never breaking its stride. The excrement flew to the side and
Susannah understood the real reason for Jean-Henri's instruction to keep her head low.

They reached the back half of the island in just a few
minutes. The dogs headed right for a dense stand of trees. At
the shore they pulled with all their might up the incline, and
the sleigh slowed enough for Susannah to take a breath and
look around. The sky was a pale gray, almost as white as the
ground. A row of cabins churned wood smoke into the sky;
behind them the bluffs were green with pine and cedar
boughs frosted with snow. Jean-Henri navigated an opening
in the trees where a man stood splitting logs and throwing
them onto the huge woodpile behind him. His ax made a
thwap and *creak* with each split. The dogs slowed as Jean-
Henri pressed on the iron lever that created a drag in the

snow. They continued to pull against it a moment, then relaxed, their breathing hoarse.

Susannah climbed out and together they stacked several bundles of wood on the sleigh. The dogs would have to work harder to pull the extra weight, but she didn't doubt they could do it. She felt the color in her cheeks from the wind and the exertion, her heart pounding beneath her cloak. Jean-Henri paid the man for the wood, and the two of them walked back to the sleigh and leaned against the nose to catch their breath before they departed.

"I wish we had the time to go all the way around the island," he said. "There is so much to see this time of year. But we should get this wood back." He took a pipe out of his pocket, and then a small birch-bark box embroidered with quills, from which he scooped a portion of tobacco.

Susannah pointed to the box. "That is very fine."

"Esmee makes these," he said.

Susannah watched his face for some clue of whether he returned Esmee's feelings. Only a truly unseeing man could be blind to the things she did for him in the hopes of winning his favor, but he seemed to be unaware of her motives. His mind was too much on his own problems to see anything else.

Jean-Henri lit the pipe and puffed on it for a quiet moment. "I am going to tell my mother today, for the last time, that I am not going to Montreal."

"She already knows—she must," Susannah said.

She thought back to what Esmee had said in the kitchen, that Jean-Henri probably didn't know that Therese might be alive and well. It would be cruel to bring it up now, to taunt him with that hope when she wasn't even sure if it was true. But she couldn't resist bringing another potential source of happiness to his attention. She felt a little guilty for the manipulation in her next words, but someone had to make him see what was right under his nose. "Your mother will not stand in the way of the match. I'm sure of it. She is very fond of Esmee."

Jean-Henri turned quickly to her and furrowed his brow. "What match?"

Susannah smiled. "You *are* in love with her, aren't you? Isn't that what's keeping you here?"

"In love with Esmee?" Jean-Henri studied the box in his hand as if he were seeing it for the first time, as if he were considering the idea of love itself for the first time in his life.

"I may be speaking out of turn in saying this—in fact, I'm *sure* that I am—but you do know, don't you, that Esmee is very much in love with *you*?"

"With me?"

He appeared to be truly dumbfounded by this news. Now it was Susannah's turn to laugh. "Can it be that you honestly did not know? A girl as beautiful as she is, still unmarried, finding every far-fetched reason to cook for you, give you gifts, embroider for you! And you *really* did not know? I saw it the day I arrived."

Jean-Henri's face was growing red, redder even than the chill had made it. "You are mistaken."

"I don't mean to embarrass you. I'm sorry." She put her hand on his sleeve. "But this is not speculation. I know it to be true. And I know her to be despairing that you will never return her affection for you."

"For me?"

Susannah nodded.

He shook his head. "I suppose I always assumed she had a beau. She is a good deal younger than me, you know. I thought I must seem old to her, and not much of a man, still living in my mother's house, no vocation to speak of." Jean-Henri looked at the birch-bark box. Esmee used a very sharp needle when she worked with the quills, sometimes pricked her fingers and bit down on them to stanch the blood. "Me? You are *certain*."

Susannah laughed at the way he kept repeating the question. "Oh, yes. Quite. You do not think her beautiful?" She was teasing him now. A dead man might claw his way out of the ground to be the object of one of Esmee's glances.

He looked at her and a smile took hold at his temples, but he pursed his lips to keep it from ruling his face. She could see what he was thinking: first, that he was delighted; but next that acting on this news, to seize it and make something of it, terrified him a little.

She thought back to the way he had hesitated the day the rabid dog had attacked the others in the pen. Magdelaine had been so exasperated with him, and it only made things worse. Jean-Henri wouldn't ever be a bold sort of man, but the world was full of bold men. He was something else: cautious, thoughtful. He took his time with things, Susannah thought, but he was true to the ones he loved. Esmee had made a wise choice to set her sights on him.

"I think we should be getting home now," he said.

On the ride back he was silent, contemplating. Susannah felt herself growing eager, as they drew near to the house, wondering how he would announce himself to Esmee, whether he would ask her to walk with him so that they could speak in private, or perhaps take her hand right there in the kitchen and make his feelings plain before them all.

But when they returned he led the dogs to the pen, methodically unhooking each one from the harness, then fed and watered them, and climbed the steps to his room without a word to any of them.

Chapter Seventeen

That afternoon it snowed a little more, and then the sky cleared first to blue and then to purple dusk and then to an inky black shimmering with stars. The purpose of Reveillon was to stay awake and greet the early morning on Christmas Day, and, while waiting for its arrival, to celebrate what the world had to offer—game and casks of wine and hot fires and music, friends and love and the blessing of children, each one steeped in the hope that he would fulfill the promises of the Prince of Peace. And each one, in his own time, falling short.

Magdelaine knew something about this. She had stopped pestering Jean-Henri about his plans because her inquiries yielded no new information nor revealed any ambition on his part. Though on every other day of the year she bemoaned the state of things with her son, the holiday pried open her heart just a bit and she was able to be happy, as Susannah had urged her to be, that he was nearby.

She almost never let herself think back on the time when Jean-Henri was a baby. It had been a terrifying chapter in her life. A man shot Henri in the chest and she watched him sink into the river reeds, his torso gored as if by the antlers of a buck. She paddled slowly home with his corpse in the bottom of the canoe. His men paddled their own vessels nearby but gave her a wide berth, waiting patiently as she stopped along the way to retch into the river. She believed it was her body rejecting the images she had seen, for what woman—even a woman like Magdelaine—could bear it? She did not know then that the baby was there too amid the sickness, probably the cause of some of it.

And perhaps because it was Christmas, that tricky loosening holiday, perhaps because she and Esmee had shared some wine as they carried the last of the food out to the tables on the beach, Magdelaine allowed her mind to linger on the image of her baby boy. What pure openhearted joy he had worked up in her, like a mania. He had a mouth like a little fish, wide and hungry, and her breasts had ached with the weight of her milk, never enough to satisfy him. He rooted and rooted, his dark eyebrows expressive from the first day, arching peacefully in sleep, then ramming together in anguish, then tipping up, questioning. She slept ten minutes at a time and woke with a start in case he might have vanished somehow into the night, chasing after his father. But he was there, still in her arms, wrapped like an ear of corn in his swaddling. The blinding love she felt for him was a terror, a nightmare of vulnerability after what had happened to Henri, and she pushed it away as hard as she could, her elbows locked. Sometimes, though, it found its way back in anyhow, an exquisite wound.

And now he was a man and she had wished him gone so many times that the words of the wish had become a kind of prayer she repeated, not even thinking of its meaning. But today, a day for reflecting on joy, she knew that she wanted Jean-Henri to leave because someday he would go anyway, and forever, the way the others all had, and for once she wanted to be able to control the timing. In truth she was surprised each year he continued to live at all. Her life took place in a forest with the swinging ax of death felling all the other trees. It never reached her. That was the true suffering. It only took everyone else.

Women began to arrive with baskets of food. They spread cloths on the tables and unpacked the dishes, arranged partridges on spits over the fires. Their children, clutching dolls and games, chased each other in and out of the darkness. Tonight they would eat whatever they wanted from the tables loaded with food, and they could run at top speed and scream with laughter and fall into a heap beside the fire to listen to the men play and sing. Sometimes Christmas Eve was so frigid the celebrants had to move indoors, fractured into the few parlors large enough to hold them, but this year the weather was in their favor. The night was almost mild, and everyone on the island arrived bundled in their warmest clothes and gathered around three large fires on the beach.

Susannah and Esmee stood together near a man playing a fiddle and singing a carol. When the music finished, they clapped and Susannah shook the musician's hand, her smile bright in the firelight.

Father Adler had insisted in his letters that Susannah needed Magdelaine's particular assistance to ensure her safety. But she wondered now as she watched Susannah if he didn't have something else up his sleeve, an idea about what Susannah might do for Magdelaine. Susannah had gotten that garden to yield more food and flowers than Magdelaine ever could have imagined. And it wasn't just that. Somehow her arrival had shifted things between Magdelaine and Jean-Henri, between Magdelaine and her own memories. In offering Susannah refuge, Magdelaine had found a kind of refuge for herself. Of course, when the thaw came Susannah would be free to move on, and yet Magdelaine found herself hoping that she would stay.

She felt a tap on her shoulder and turned to see her student Noelle, who had slipped out of existence the previous spring. Her mother had told Magdelaine she wouldn't be returning, and yet here she was.

"Madame," she said. *"Joyeux Noel."*

"Joyeux Noel! We have all been wondering whether we dreamed you. Where have you been?"

Noelle's eyes skidded across the fires. "I was visiting family in Sault Ste. Marie. I'm sorry if I gave you cause to worry."

The girl looked thinner and tired, hollow in her eyes. Magdelaine tried not to probe her face too openly. "We missed your contributions to the class. The others look to you to guide their thinking, you know."

Noelle's mouth hardened. "Well, they should not. They should think for themselves."

"I agree. But as I'm sure you know, many cannot, and many more do not want to. It is not an easy way to live."

Noelle shrugged. The shrug seemed to ask, *What good is an active mind for a woman in a place like this?* But then such a thought was for an older woman, not a girl. As if to show Magdelaine she had imagined it, Noelle's face lightened. "Certainly I missed seeing you, madame. And I thank you for thinking of me while I was away, and for your kindness. You are nothing like my mother."

"Your mother is angry with you?"

Noelle shrugged again. "For things she doesn't understand."

Magdelaine nodded. She didn't doubt it.

"I cannot live in her home any longer, she says."

"So you will not be rejoining our class in the new year?"

Noelle shook her head. "Maybe you've heard—Bishop Rese has opened a school for girls in Detroit and I am determined to go. Perhaps they will let me assist the teachers. So it is back across the lake for now and then south in the spring."

"Oh, how wonderful, Noelle!" Magdelaine smiled—she had always known Noelle had potential. "But why don't you come and stay with me until you leave? The empty rooms in my house feel like a sin."

Noelle gave Magdelaine a gentle smile. It said *yes, yes, yes, let me stay*. But when she spoke she said it was impossible. "My family is expecting me. It is time for me to leave this place for good."

Magdelaine nodded. "There is nothing for you here." Noelle winced when she said it, and Magdelaine softened her tone. "What I mean is that your life is ahead of you. Will you promise me something?"

"Yes."

Magdelaine took Noelle by the hands. She thought about how the same stories kept repeating, over and over, and she knew they would keep on repeating long after she was gone. All a person could hope to do was change the ending. "Promise me that you will be careful, that you will never forget what your life is worth."

Noelle nodded, her eyes filling, and she looked away. *Something is wrong here*, Magdelaine thought. *This girl should be happy—her life is just beginning and she has nothing but freedom and time*—but Noelle seemed full of sorrow.

"Did something happen, Noelle? Something you are not telling me?" She shook her head, but Magdelaine wasn't convinced. "Come and eat. You will need your strength." She led Noelle by the hand to one of the tables heaped with food, then began stacking meat pies on a plate for her.

A small sound escaped Noelle's lips. Magdelaine held the plate in one hand and put the other one gently on the girl's elbow. Noelle could not hold back her tears any longer. She collapsed against her with a sob, pressing her cheek into Magdelaine's collarbone. Magdelaine's hand went to the back of the girl's head, touched the soft fur of her hood. A few revelers glanced at them, and Magdelaine led her away from the people again before she said, "What can I do to help you, Noelle?"

Noelle pulled away and as quickly as the wave of weeping had overtaken her, it subsided. She wiped her eyes, sniffed. "You have already done it. I cannot stay now. I only came to say good-bye, and thank you."

"I don't understand."

"I hope you will not be angry with me. I chose you because of what happened to your sisters. Because you will not be careless. So many people are."

Magdelaine stiffened at the mention of Josette and Therese. For nearly twenty years, no one had dared to mention their names, until Susannah began to ask about them after her arrival. And now Noelle, who must have heard the story from her mother, as it all had happened long before she was born. Magdelaine wondered how much of the truth people knew, and how many details they had invented to satisfy their own curiosity. She knew that people whispered tales about Therese, that she was not really dead. Jean-Henri had seen one thing and Ansel had seen something else. Magdelaine had been forced to accept that she would probably never know what had become of her sister.

She shook off the memories and turned her attention to what else Noelle had said. "Noelle, what do you mean you *chose* me?"

"I have to go now," she said, then whispered to herself, "Oh, Mary, help me." She opened her cloak and wrapped the pies in a handkerchief. She put them in the pocket of her dress, then tied the cloak closed again.

"Bon voyage, Noelle," Magdelaine said, embracing her once more. "Keep a strong heart."

The girl set off into the darkness, hunched against the cold with her arms crossed in front of her. She clutched her elbows as if she were bracing herself for a blow.

Magdelaine watched her go, then saw Esmee and Susannah approaching.

"Was that Noelle?" Esmee said.

Magdelaine nodded. "She came to say good-bye. She is leaving for Detroit, to try to get a job as a teacher. But I think something is wrong. Perhaps I should . . ."

"Did she ask for your help, madame?" Esmee asked gently.

Magdelaine gave her a warning look, but then considered the question. "It is strange, but she said I have helped her already. She thanked me. But I don't understand . . ."

"Perhaps you should wait, then. Wait and see."

Magdelaine chewed her lip a moment. She wondered if Esmee was talking about Jean-Henri as much as Noelle—Magdelaine's tendency to make plans for other people's lives, whether or not they wanted her intervention. She nodded. "Yes. I suppose my help isn't always welcome."

Esmee took her hand. "Let's have some wine. And get close to the fire. I am chilled. Susannah, are you coming?"

Susannah hadn't heard the question. Her attention was focused on the far side of the gathering, where a man with a neatly trimmed beard stood laughing in the crowd.

"Who is that?" Magdelaine asked.

Susannah's eyes darted to her mittens. "What do you mean?"

Magdelaine laughed. "I mean the man over there, who seems to be holding your attention."

"Oh," Susannah said. "That's Alfred Corliss, the new teacher at the mission school."

Magdelaine looked at Esmee, who responded only with a coy smile and a shrug. Magdelaine thought back to the walk they had taken in the spring, when she had caught Susannah gazing at the mission and mistook her wistfulness for religious feeling.

"Susannah," Esmee said, "how long has it been since you've spoken to him?"

"Oh, I haven't at all." Her eyes darted to Magdelaine's. "I haven't. I promise."

"Well, I don't see why not. He is a newcomer here, just as you are. It is our duty to make him feel welcome. Let's go wish him *Joyeux Noel*," Magdelaine said.

"Yes," Esmee said, taking Susannah's elbow. "Let's."

"I—" Susannah tried to protest, but they had her by the arm and the two of them marched her toward the group of men, swinging by a table along the way to pluck up a jug of wine. They could have been any three women in the world approaching Mr. Corliss and he wouldn't have known them in the shadows of their hoods.

"Are you enjoying our Reveillon, Mr. Corliss?" Magdelaine said as she pulled the hood from her head. The men let out a cheer when they saw the jug, then held out their empty cups so she could pour for them.

"You must be Madame Fonteneau," he said, taking her hand. "I have been looking forward to the chance to meet you, finally. *Joyeux Noel*." He looked at her companions.

"*Joyeux Noel*," Esmee said.

"Thank you, miss," he said to Esmee. Susannah let her

hood slip off her head, and when he saw her his eyes widened into a smile. It was too dark now for anyone to see, but Magdelaine had noticed earlier in the day that the dye had finally faded from Susannah's hair. "Miss Dove. I didn't recognize you."

"I've let my friends dress me up for the occasion." His eyes shone in the light from the fire and his cheeks were pink. Though his hands did not hold a cup, Magdelaine wondered if he had thrown off his temperance for the holiday and gotten into the wine. She hoped so.

"Tell me, Madame Fonteneau—have you found that Miss Dove makes a competent teacher?" Magdelaine saw that Mr. Corliss had already formed an opinion on this topic. She wondered just how much the two of them had talked on the boat.

"I feel fortunate to have found her," Magdelaine said. "I have more students than I can handle. This region is full of girls who would like an education, but it seems I am the only one willing to give it to them."

"The Reverend Howe *does* enroll girls in the mission school," Mr. Corliss said.

"And where is he tonight, the reverend?"

Mr. Corliss replied with an embarrassed shrug. "I suppose you could say he disapproves of the French style of reverence."

One of the men standing nearby, the grown son of a trader named Luc, raised his fingers to count the ways in which they celebrated. "Revere the wine," he said. "Revere the food. Revere the *belles femmes*." He gestured toward Susannah and Esmee, laughing.

Magdelaine smiled. "I will never understand that way of

thinking. It's so unpleasant. How can one revere life by taking every pleasurable thing out of it?"

Mr. Corliss nodded. "I will agree that he has a singularly rigid point of view."

"Indeed. You say he enrolls girls, but it is only to teach them sewing and to memorize verses they do not understand," Magdelaine said. "Honestly, I thank the Lord that Reverend Howe will not take them as regular pupils. The girls tell me he insists on cutting their brothers' hair, then converting them whether they want it or not, and turning them back out again if they will not submit to his ways."

"I cannot speak to the past," Mr. Corliss said. "But since I arrived at the school that hasn't been true. My sole focus is literacy for each student. I leave the theology to Reverend Howe. In fact, I would be glad to give you a tour." He hesitated, glanced between Magdelaine and Susannah. "I was disappointed to hear that Miss Dove didn't have time for one when I invited her back in the spring."

Back in the spring, of course, Susannah had been terrified of her own shadow, too terrified even to tell Magdelaine, it seemed, that Mr. Corliss had shown interest in her. Now, things were different. Magdelaine glanced at Susannah, trying to read her thoughts.

She turned back to the teacher. "Mr. Corliss, I'm sure we can arrange something."

"Please excuse me," Susannah mumbled. She turned and hurried away from them, up the beach.

"I fear I have upset her," Mr. Corliss said to Esmee. "I didn't mean to insist—"

"Nonsense," Magdelaine said. "She mentioned earlier

that she was not feeling well. I should have heeded her concerns and seen her home. Please, go back to enjoying the feast. Esmee, could you help Mr. Corliss find something hot to drink?"

"Yes, of course, madame."

Magdelaine nodded to them and went off after Susannah, catching her by the elbow and gently turning her around. "What is the matter?"

Tears streamed down her cheeks. *The second young woman I've brought to crying this evening*, Magdelaine thought. *Heaven protect them from me.*

Susannah pulled a handkerchief from her sleeve and blew her nose. "Why did you force me to speak to him? It only makes things more difficult."

"I don't understand," Magdelaine said. "You are safe here; your old life is in the past. Mr. Corliss seems genuine in extending a hand of friendship. There's no reason why you shouldn't be able to accept it. If you want to."

"But that's just it—my *old life*, as you call it, can never really be past. The little I have told Mr. Corliss about myself has been a lie, and I am too ashamed to tell him the truth. What good is a friendship based in deceit? Don't I owe him more than that?"

Magdelaine patted Susannah's hand. "My dear, I don't think he is asking for an account of your activities—I don't think he supposes you *owe* him anything at all. I think it is much simpler than all that. He likes you. That is all."

Susannah shook her head. "Don't you see? I am trapped by the past. I may have escaped the dangers, but I cannot erase what happened. I cannot start fresh."

Magdelaine thought for a moment, choosing her next words carefully. "Why did you come here, Susannah? Why did you leave behind everything you have ever known, to come here, to an island you've never seen, full of people who know nothing about the real you. Why did you do it?"

Susannah did not hesitate before she answered. "For safety. To save my life before my husband took it."

"That is what I thought too, in the beginning. That is what I thought would have protected my sisters. Safety. Caution. I have thought for so long that if only I had been more careful, if only I had stayed vigilant—that somehow I could have stopped that brute from killing Josette, could have stopped Therese from taking her life."

The mention of Therese's name seemed to call up a question in Susannah, and she opened her mouth to ask it. But then she seemed to lose her nerve. Susannah was quiet for a moment before she said, "It's an awful thing to believe in, but isn't it true?"

"No. I don't think so. Not anymore. And I don't think you came here for safety. You may believe that, but it is not so. I think you came here because you wanted to be *free*—and that's a different thing. You wanted out of that prison your husband kept you in, the prison of loneliness and fear. You wanted freedom."

Susannah watched her mouth and the words that came out of it like birds flushed out of a tree. She took a small breath. "That *is* what I wanted."

"Mrs. Susannah Fraser has been dead since April. You saw the obituary yourself."

Susannah swallowed and nodded.

"So there is no reason why you should not have your freedom. But you cannot wait for *safety*. There is no real safety, not for any of us."

Susannah seemed to be rolling these words over in her mind. She needed time, Magdelaine saw. She hoped Mr. Corliss was a patient man. Susannah's gaze flicked to something behind them and Magdelaine turned to look, expecting to see the figure of Mr. Corliss at a distance, engaged in jovial conversation. But instead, in the darkness at the lip of the water stood Esmee and Jean-Henri. They did not touch, but her son's head was inclined toward Esmee's and they whispered to one another.

"What is this?" Magdelaine asked, turning back to Susannah in surprise.

She gave Magdelaine a knowing look. "You wondered whether your son was in love. Now you know."

"I don't believe it!"

"Neither did he. But as you can see, he learns quickly."

"*You* are responsible for this?" Magdelaine's shock subsided into a swell of happiness. She smiled at Susannah. "You matched my son with my *servant girl*?" She was joking, of course, suddenly filled with a lightness of heart. She had already come to love Esmee as a daughter. How could she not have seen what was brewing between them?

"It was not my doing, I promise," Susannah said, clearly relieved to be talking about someone else's entanglements. "I only acted as messenger, relayed what she had told me. I knew he couldn't help but love her back. Esmee was nearly sick with feeling for him and he did not see it."

They stood side by side, watching the lovers. Magdelaine

laughed at her son's cluelessness, at her own. "Now *that* I will believe."

Susannah leaned her head against Magdelaine's shoulder. "I helped them because they needed help—it was plain to see," she said. "But I had another reason. It will bring *you* happiness too, I hope?" Susannah looked at Magdelaine. "Your family is growing."

Magdelaine nodded, and her breath caught in her throat as she watched their figures in the moonlight, blue-black and silver. They passed a mug of wine back and forth between them, sharing it. Esmee took a drink and when she handed it back to Jean-Henri he cupped his hand beneath her wrist, just as Henri had done so many years ago when it was Magdelaine's wrist, Magdelaine's cup. She thought again of Jean-Henri as a small boy who longed to run faster than his legs yet knew how. Joy in the smallest thing—a robin peeking out from the maple boughs, a shimmering icicle on the cabin window—would rise up in him and he would call for his mother to come and see, so that they could rejoice together in the gifts the world kept giving, over and over and over.

Chapter Eighteen

Nothing was quieter than a Mackinac house on Christmas morning. Revelers slept as if enchanted into stasis by a spell, their bellies full of wine, their hearts full too.

Susannah peeked from the doorway into Magdelaine's room to see the woman lying on her back with her limbs spread wide and her hair tangled around her head like a crown. She pulled the door closed. Down the hall, Jean-Henri's door was closed, and Susannah felt sure that if she checked Esmee's bed, in the small room off the kitchen, she would find it empty.

With the quiet house to herself, Susannah finally had time to reflect on the conversation she had had in the kitchen with Esmee. She realized that she needed to get a letter to Buffalo so that she could find out whether Sister Mary Genevieve might actually be Magdelaine's sister Therese. Mr. Morin wouldn't be in his store today, but maybe tomorrow. She would walk the letter there then. Today she would have to force herself to wait and rest.

But first she wanted some fresh air. Susannah dressed in her red wool and tiptoed down the stairs and into the sitting room. She placed new logs on the banked coals, then pulled on her cloak and stepped out to the front porch, feeling the chilly wind run its fingers up her scalp. A dusting of snow had fallen in the early morning, and she swept it from the stairs with the broom. Her motion disturbed a brown rabbit hiding beneath the thimbleberry bush, and it sprang out across the white expanse, racing for cover in a sleepier yard. She thought of the carved stone rabbit on Josette's headstone, how it had weathered so many winters in the graveyard. But this rabbit was terrified, vulnerable—real.

Something else moving through the snow caught her attention, and she looked up to see Alfred Corliss come around the curve of the island on the lane, then raise his hand to Susannah in greeting. She longed to lean the broom against the porch and hurry back inside, but instead she waited as he came nearer.

"Good morning, Miss Dove. I was just now debating whether it was too early to call when you stepped outside."

She let her eyes graze his shoulder but couldn't quite bring herself to look into his face. "Good morning, sir. Merry Christmas." It was much colder now than it had been the night before, and Alfred's nose was pink, his eyes tearing from the wind's bite. She couldn't very well leave him out in the snow. "The rest of the house is still sleeping," she said. "But will you come in for something warm to drink?"

"I wouldn't trouble you," he began.

"It's no trouble, Mr. Corliss. One must not be cold on Christmas morning."

Susannah shook the snow off the broom, and they went inside. She hung her cloak, then took his hat and overcoat and hung them on the adjacent hook. She glanced up the stairs. "Perhaps we could talk in the kitchen, so we do not wake the others."

He pulled a chair up to the worktable, and Susannah pushed the kettle over the flame. They didn't speak as she made the coffee. Alfred looked out the window, laced his fingers together on the table. She carried their full cups over on a tray and sat down in the opposite chair.

"I imagine your household will attend the Christmas Mass together later today?"

Susannah nodded. Magdelaine and Esmee and Jean-Henri would go, of course, but she wasn't sure about herself.

"And you, sir?"

"Reverend Howe will preach at noon. And again at two. And again at four." Alfred laughed. "He is fond of preaching, and the fondness seems quite independent of the response of his flock. He has a captive audience in these students, you see. They board at the school. Home is far away for some of them."

Susannah responded with a close-lipped smile. Alfred's easy way with conversation made her nervous. She had once known how to conduct herself during a simple social visit: when to nod, when to smile, how to interject a charming aside without shining the spotlight on herself. But now it all felt silly. And perilous. Alfred was here because he wanted to ask something of her, she knew. Something impossible.

They passed a few awkward moments staring into their cooling coffee, and Susannah felt her uneasiness growing. Perhaps if she made him uncomfortable enough, he would simply give up and leave.

"You must be looking forward to the spring," he said, trying again at conversation. "And your garden? You did remarkable things with it earlier this year."

Susannah looked up in surprise. His observation made her wonder whether he had been watching her from afar, and she didn't like the notion. "Thank you. I have some ideas about what I'd like to try next year. The growing season is short, so my choices are limited."

He nodded. "Reverend Howe believes in teaching gardening to the young men. I have found that most of them are excellent foragers with a vast knowledge of the local plants, but they have little experience with planting itself. I myself have little experience. My father was a businessman—more comfortable at his desk with his ledger than he was outside. Everything I know about planting I learned as a boy, from my mother. But it has been years since I've spent time digging in the dirt, and I don't wish to misinform my students."

Susannah nodded, still avoiding his gaze.

Alfred sipped his coffee, then cleared his throat. "I wonder if you might be willing to spend some time with us in the spring? Help ensure the students are on the right course with their garden?"

Perhaps that was all he wanted, assistance with the lessons, Susannah thought. Well, that was something she could provide. "I would be happy to help if I can, sir."

He nodded. "I appreciate that, Miss Dove. While the

weather keeps us indoors, I am hoping to teach them something about the anatomy of a seed and how it germinates. That way in the spring they will understand what is happening when the seed is buried in the ground. Do you have any suggestions?"

Susannah thought for a moment. "Well, you might try sprouting some peas. You could place a handful in a damp cloth and keep it somewhere warm. Be sure the cloth doesn't dry out. Check every so often. It will take a few days for the sprouts to emerge. You could examine them, label the parts. But keep a few back for planting. You'll need a pot of good soil. Keep them well watered, on the windowsill. You want sunlight, but you don't want them to get cold. The students could chart the progress, and in the spring you could plant them outside . . ." She trailed off when she noticed that Alfred was grinning broadly at her. "Have I said something amusing, sir?"

"Forgive me, no. It is just that I think this is the most I've ever heard you say. And I am enjoying listening very much."

His compliment made Susannah feel self-conscious. Suddenly her dress felt too tight and she straightened the collar, touched the handle of her cup but did not pick it up for fear of spilling it. Beneath the table she worried the skin around the thumbnail on her left hand. Time had lessened the pain in her fingers, but sometimes they still ached. And they would never again straighten out. She knew some people were unnerved by the hand's appearance, and she often kept it hidden from view. "I am not very good at conversation, sir."

He smiled. "That is not true. It is only that there is much you do not say."

She responded with a weak smile of her own. Part of her was afraid he would linger here in the kitchen. But she realized that another new and frightened part of her was afraid he would go.

He cleared his throat again. "Miss Dove, I get the feeling, sometimes, that I make you uneasy, and I regret that. I want you to know that I have no desire to invade your privacy. I would never ask you to reveal your secrets—though there's something about you that makes me want to tell you mine." He smiled. "I may have mentioned that my brother disapproves of my work here, wants me to return to Boston and the factory. There is more than that. I ran away, you see—couldn't take another day of that life. My brother doesn't know where I am. You are not the only one hiding here."

She took a small breath and met his eyes. She wondered what he knew, what he thought he knew.

"But I am not going back. This is where I belong. My family is not my destiny. I can choose the life I want, and that life is here."

Alfred seemed to be waiting for her to respond, but what could she say? She couldn't begin to explain herself when there was so much about her past that she could not tell him.

He sighed. "I know what you are feeling," he said. "The world can be an awfully cold place." His cup was empty, and he slid it a few inches away so that he could rest his elbows on the table. He tried to begin again. "It gives things and then it takes them away." She thought of her happy years as a girl in Manhattan City. Of her mother and father. "And loneliness can engulf us."

"Yes," Susannah said, before she could stop the tiny word from slipping out.

"And we might like to have someone to call on, for counsel, for friendship—"

If it was God he meant, Susannah thought, he could save his breath. "*That* particular friend is deaf to my troubles." *I have prayed a thousand prayers*, she wanted to say. *And not one of them was answered.*

She saw from his amused grin that she had misunderstood him. "I wonder, Miss Dove . . ." Alfred said, then winced. He twisted up his mouth, pushed the flop of curls off his forehead. "I wonder if you would let it be *me*. Let it be me you turn to in times of trouble."

She opened her mouth in surprise, then closed it again.

Alfred pressed on, in danger of losing his nerve. "Ever since we met on the boat I have thought of you and wondered how you fared. And then we saw each other again, even though it seemed impossible we ever could. I cannot explain why, but I feel, somehow, that I know something about what you are carrying, whatever secret thing it is that you are afraid to let anyone know. And I suspect it is something you think terrible, and yet I want to tell you that whatever it is, I could never think badly of you—"

Susannah felt anxiety climbing her lungs, and she stood up from her chair, took a step away from the table. She couldn't allow what was happening now to continue. "You speak out of turn, Mr. Corliss. You know nothing about me."

"Please, forgive me, Miss Dove, but I must say this to you. I would never *insist*, you see. I would never insist on . . .

well, anything, really, from you, and certainly never that you would tell me something you do not wish to tell."

He stood and came around the table to her side, approaching carefully, the way one might step toward a frightened animal. He reached for her left hand, and though she flinched slightly she let him take it and lift it up onto his palm. Then he ran his thumb over the two crooked fingers, the hard piece of scarred bone under the skin.

"This hand, for instance. You injured it, maybe as a girl, maybe in some other way. If you ever want to tell me how, I'd like to know. But only because I am interested in the story of you, Miss Dove. Not because I wish to *do* anything with the knowledge."

She saw then that he knew, that somehow everything she had hoped to hide was laid bare.

"Don't you see? It's all right. I don't need to know everything about you, if there are things you cannot tell me. I already know everything that is important."

She wanted so badly to nod in agreement, to say that she wished to know him too, that she wished to pass the time together. But his kindness—for that was what it was, and nothing more? The feeling was so unfamiliar, she had trouble naming it—his kindness felt like a threat. She was still married, not in her heart but according to law. She had run away from home, was lying about her name, her past. He would never be able to accept her if he knew the truth. And of course there was always the risk that if she told him the truth, somehow word might reach Edward and he would come after her. She pulled her hand from his grasp and slipped it into the pocket of her apron.

He sighed. "I've said too much. Please forgive me. I'll leave you now." He turned toward the front hall, and Susannah followed him.

As he lifted his hat from the hook, she said, "Mr. Corliss, wait. Let me try to explain."

He turned back to her, and she made herself look directly into his eyes. It seemed very important to her just then that she make him understand, once and clearly. "You are a very kind man and I seek, along with Madame Fonteneau, to be a good neighbor to you and the others at the mission."

Alfred drew his bottom lip between his teeth, then looked down at the floor.

"Should you need a cup of rice," Susannah said, her voice surprising her by growing thick with tears, "or should you need to borrow our ax while your own blade is out for repair, we would be happy to oblige you, sir."

Alfred's eyes were full of baffled concern. Her tears unnerved him, and he reached for her elbow.

Susannah stepped quickly away from his hand. "But you must never again come here to call on me, in particular, you see. And you must never think that we could be anything other than neighbors. Do you understand?"

Edward himself might not be chasing her, but the mark he had left on her life would be with her forever. There was no freedom from her past, however far she traveled from it. It was foolish to think she could start again.

Alfred shook his head. "No, Miss Dove, I do not understand. If your heart is set so hard against me, then why do you cry? Understand me—I am not making a proposal of marriage! Only a proposal of friendship, friendship with the smallest hope that perhaps, in time—"

Susannah shook her head roughly. "No, sir. Please do not say any more. I cannot bear it. If you have any feeling at all for me, you will go. And do not come back."

Alfred waited another moment, watching her, but when Susannah did not falter he placed his hat on his head and, defeated, left the house without another word. The door closed and she glanced up the stairs. No one stirred. She stepped carefully back into the kitchen and tipped hot water from the kettle into the sink so that she could wash their coffee cups. Then she sat down at the table, put her head in her hands, and wept.

She thought about how close he had been, thought about how he had touched her fingers. The most frightening thing of all was that, when he had asked what had happened to her hand, she had almost told him. Alfred Corliss was a kind man who could be trusted with a secret, who might, in exchange for the honor of revealing herself to him, offer company, counsel. Here was God offering to assuage her loneliness, and she had turned away from it. But what Alfred was asking was impossible.

After a while she returned to the sink to finish the dishes. When she placed the second cup on a towel to dry, she heard a peculiar sound coming from the yard. Susannah dried her hands. The sound stopped for a moment, then began again, a high-pitched whine. After the dogs had hauled the wood back the previous day, Jean-Henri had let them rest. At the Reveillon, Magdelaine had indulged Ani with scraps of the rich dishes of food. Perhaps he whined in sickness now as so many others on the island were sure to be whining this morning. Too many sweets. Too much meat and wine and butter.

The sound came again, this time grinding, picking up steam. Susannah remembered the growls of the rabid dog Magdelaine had put down, but this sound was only urgent, not so frightening as the sick dog's barking had been. She took a cloak from the hook by the front door, then passed back through the kitchen and went out the door to the dog pen.

She padded across the snow in her moccasins and carefully swung open the door. The dogs lay in a heap, snoring in the dim light inside the pen. Up high near the roof of the enclosure was a platform Jean-Henri had pointed out to her, where they kept new puppies away from the rest of the dogs. Ani had found his way up there somehow, and he lifted his head and glanced sleepily at Susannah before putting it back down on a bundle wedged at his side. The whine—a little sputtering, revving cry—came from the bundle, warmed and cosseted by his fur and warm canine breath. Smooth flesh, a pink mouth open, mewling. A baby.

Susannah drew in a breath and stepped closer, her mouth hanging open in surprise. The child wore a hat of gray wool that covered its ears and brow. Only the small dark eyes were visible, the peach-colored nose, the wet, open mouth. The baby twisted its shoulders back and forth and back and forth against the swaddling, whining in frustration; finally a tiny bare arm popped out and the crying stopped. It sucked noisily on the thumb, nestled into Ani's fur, and went to sleep.

She reached up and pulled the warm bundle from its bed. The baby's eyes opened and searched Susannah's face, the thumb still planted firmly in its mouth. It didn't appear to be in pain, or injured, or the least bit cold or uncomfortable. She almost hated to take it away from its protector, and Ani watched her carefully as she did. She opened her cloak and tucked the small body next to her chest, then closed the cloak. Ani trailed behind her as she stepped quickly across the yard, then back into the kitchen, closing the door before she shouted for help.

Chapter Nineteen

The baby, who looked to be about two or three months old, lay atop a folded blanket on the table in the kitchen, and the four of them—Magdelaine, Susannah, Esmee, and Jean-Henri—stood over it, staring. It stared back at them, the thumb planted securely in its mouth. Magdelaine felt her chest fill with dread. How could Noelle have done this?

"A baby," Susannah kept whispering, over and over.

"Is it a boy or a girl?" Esmee asked.

"I was too afraid of the cold to check."

Esmee nodded. "Well, perhaps we should now. Jean, will you stoke up the fire?"

He crossed the room to the hearth and went to work with the poker. Magdelaine stared after him, then back at Esmee, still surprised by her use of *Jean*. Esmee wasn't even conscious that she had addressed him in such a familiar way. It was what she called him in private, Magdelaine saw, and she no longer felt she had to hide it.

Esmee unwrapped the swaddling. Beneath it, the baby wore a cotton gown cut down from a garment for an older child. She lifted it, then put it back down. "A boy! And this is soiled. We need something else to wrap him in."

"So he has eaten lately, then?" Susannah said. She went into the pantry and began pulling out linen towels.

"Yes, you're right. That is a blessing." Esmee glanced at the pile in Susannah's hands. "No, the red one, I think—yes, it will absorb the most."

They unwrapped the boy and he opened his mouth in surprise at the cold air on his skin, letting the thumb fall away. Only then did he begin to wail. Esmee moved quickly, wrapping him in the towel and tying it with twine, then in the large wool blanket from the sitting room. She helped him get his thumb back, then placed him in Susannah's arms. The long tail of the blanket hung down to the floor.

Jean-Henri spoke over his shoulder as he balanced another log atop the blaze. "He can't have been there more than a few hours. I put the dogs in the pen at midnight."

Magdelaine tried to imagine how Noelle had kept the dogs from barking when she sneaked in with the baby. Perhaps she brought food for them, something to placate their tempers, and sat on the damp straw to wait for them to settle to sleep. The baby would have been wrapped inside her cloak, latched one last time to her breast, his tiny palm drifting absently over his own cheek, his fingers touching the contours of his ear. And behind Noelle's breast, her heart tearing, frayed like a root ripped out of the ground.

"Either way, he will be hungry soon. We'll have to think of how to feed him, madame."

Magdelaine glanced up at Esmee with a start, then at the baby, looking at his features for the first time. He had sleek black hair, like an otter, and long dark lashes rimmed his green eyes. His cheeks were covered in red scratches. "He isn't staying here," Magdelaine said.

"You don't think the dogs did that, do you?" Susannah asked, touching the scratches.

Magdelaine shook her head. "I don't know."

"Do you believe it, madame? A baby in our manger, on Christmas morning? Is it some kind of sign?" Esmee smoothed his hair with her fingers.

Magdelaine wondered why no one seemed to have heard her—the baby couldn't possibly stay here. But then she realized what Esmee had said, and snapped her reply. "Certainly not." She looked again at the boy's eyes, noticing a familiar brown mark in the iris of his left eye. She had only ever seen eyes like that on one other person. The situation became clear to her. "This is no immaculate child." With that she walked out of the room and back up the stairs, then opened her wardrobe and began to dress.

Esmee was right behind her. "Where are you going, madame?"

Magdelaine shook her head. "I won't say anything until I am sure."

Their eyes met, and she could see that Esmee too had noticed the brown mark in the baby's eye. Very little got by her; Magdelaine understood it now. Esmee saw things about Jean-Henri that Magdelaine herself could not see, and, seeing her son through his lover's eyes, she liked him more. She wondered whether, at last, Jean-Henri would show some decisiveness, and marry her. Perhaps if Esmee accompanied him, he would go to Montreal.

"I'll be back in a few hours."

Esmee nodded. "He will deny it."

"Yes. Even on Christmas Day."

"But you will try him nonetheless?"

Magdelaine shrugged. "What else can we do?"

It was, of course, futile, Magdelaine thought as she trudged through the snow to Ste. Anne's. Still, it was a relief to get out of the close quarters of the kitchen. She could barely look at the child. Why hadn't she understood what Noelle was trying to tell her at the feast? Her words were so plain—if only Magdelaine had been paying attention to the girl instead of letting her thoughts linger on the past and all that was dead in it. She could have reasoned with her, tried to change her mind.

She reached the door and pulled it open. If Father Milani were any kind of priest he would be there now, preparing to give the Mass later in the day. But the sanctuary was dark and cold. He had let the fire in the back go out. Magdelaine sat for a moment in the pew and walked her mind through the steps she could take, had she more energy and more hope, to try to put things right. Somewhere on this island Milani was sleeping off drink, likely in a warm bed some devout man or woman had given up for the comfort of the priest. Magdelaine could search the Catholic homes until she found him. It was a small island. She could confront Milani as she had longed to do so many times. He had neglected every duty he was charged with, from ministering to the sick to presenting himself for burials to comporting himself with a little dignity and keeping to his vows. But the truth was that he couldn't be more than twenty-five years old and probably had been assigned to this remote territory without ever having laid eyes on it. He couldn't minister to these people, and he couldn't be held responsible for their undoing, not solely.

She pushed herself to her feet and went to make a fire. She might have better luck trying to change Noelle's mind—after all, the girl had told Magdelaine where she planned to go, and Sault Ste. Marie was only a day's journey by sled across the ice. How Noelle would live to regret what she had done! How she would look back on this day for the rest of her life and see the face of that infant frozen in time, while he grew and grew in the care of some stranger who might love him, but never as well as Noelle. Her own son, abandoned!

Magdelaine stacked the logs on the grate. She could tell Noelle something about sons, how you wrung your hands over them and yet could never at the last shake the longing you had to hold them, even when they grew to be men. Of course, she hadn't touched Jean-Henri in a decade, except to lean on his arm that one time when he had outpaddled her to Bois Blanc the previous spring. And then because the only other option was to collapse into the water. Still, the longing was there, always, and she didn't dare give into it.

The sanctuary began to warm. In a few hours, the devout and those they dragged along with them would begin filing into this space and look to the altar for guidance on how they should contemplate this day, the anniversary of the birth of the man who would save them. He was difficult to access, that man. You had to go through men like Milani to get to him, and that, Magdelaine thought, was a shame. Father Adler would be dismayed to hear of what was happening on the island, but of course Magdelaine couldn't imagine actually writing to him of the details. Milani was still a priest, after all. And there were things one couldn't say about a priest, even if they were true.

Magdelaine pulled up her hood and went back out into the snow. Noelle's family might be persuaded to take the child, but she doubted it. The girl had the sort of mother who turned her daughter out when she learned of her condition. She wondered if Noelle's mother knew of the priest's involvement in the matter. Probably so. Noelle had no doubt argued her case to her family and found no sympathy there. They would deny the child. But Magdelaine would try reasoning with them anyway, for all the good it would do.

Chapter Twenty

Soon after Magdelaine left, the baby began frantically pressing his palms against his open mouth and wailing with hunger. Susannah and Esmee took turns trying to soothe him. They walked from the kitchen to the sitting room and back again, passing the windows and showing him the intricate patterns the frost made on the glass, the soft fringe on a wool blanket, but nothing would calm him.

Esmee and Jean-Henri listed aloud the names of the families they knew with small children, but they couldn't think of a woman on the island who had recently given birth and might be able to nurse the child. People came and went with the seasons, and this time of year the population was at its lowest.

Someone could be sent for, but it would take time. To make do, Esmee instructed Jean-Henri to heat cow's milk over the fire, nearly shouting to be heard over the boy's screams. They allowed it to cool and then spooned a few

drops at a time into his mouth, and after several long minutes the wailing subsided to a whimper. Soon the baby was
quiet but alert, his eyes studying the curve of Esmee's fingers
on the spoon. The sun was shining through the small kitchen
window and made a bright square on the table top. The baby
watched the light as it moved in a liquid swirl on the wood.

Now that he had finally calmed down, Jean-Henri took a
close look at the baby's cheeks. "He seems so well taken care
of, except for these scratches. I wonder what in the world has
caused them?"

"The dogs would have done much worse damage than
this," Susannah said. She took the spoon from Esmee and
handed it to the baby. He tightened his fist on the handle.

"Is there something we could put on his cheeks?"

"I have a salve upstairs," Susannah said.

"I wonder . . ." Esmee said as she unwrapped the blanket
from the baby's shoulders and pulled out one bare arm, then
reached for the baby's hand. "That's what I thought. Look
at these fingernails!" The little white slivers were long and
jagged.

"I can get my knife," Jean-Henri said. "Though his fingers are *awfully* small."

"No, Jean," Esmee said. The baby watched her as she
leaned over him on the table and gently pried open his fist.
There were cuts on the heels of his hands too, from where he
had dug his fingernails into them in his distress. She kissed
the red half moons, kissed the soft chub of his palm. Then
softly, steadily, she took the tip of each tiny finger into her
mouth and nibbled on the nail.

It was so quiet in the room that they could hear Esmee's

teeth tapping softly together. She removed each nail and spit it onto the floor, then smiled at the baby. He did not smile back, but the square of light no longer held his attention; instead it was Esmee's dark eyebrows, the pale part in her black hair.

Susannah noticed that Jean-Henri stood beside the table, captivated by the way Esmee seemed to know just what to do, how she solved the problem with such assured calm. She finished with the baby's right hand and moved to the left. Jean-Henri took the newly groomed fingers in his hand and examined them, then turned his gaze back to Esmee. His closed mouth stretched into a secretive smile, as though something had occurred to him that he wanted to keep to himself for a while, to relish.

The gaze reminded Susannah of the way her father had looked at her mother while she was absorbed in some task—reading a book, turning a stitch in her embroidery with the tip of her tongue pressed between her lips in concentration. Susannah was delighted to see that Jean-Henri might adore Esmee in this same way, but beneath her joy was some anguish too. She was certain no one had ever looked at her in quite that way. Not every woman was so lucky as her mother had been, as Esmee was now.

Susannah stood from her chair to usher these maudlin thoughts away. She had so much to be grateful for, and she was determined to be glad for the couple. They seemed to be yearning for a moment alone, so Susannah mumbled something about going to check the fire in the sitting room and stepped out.

All of them were gathered there when Magdelaine returned a while later through the kitchen door. The baby slept on a pile of blankets near the fire. Susannah went to the kitchen to meet Magdelaine as she came in and realized that she had been holding her breath for news of what would become of the baby. Magdelaine bent to pull off her fur-lined boots, and one of her long braids swung down over shoulder. She flung it back with a sigh, then stood and stepped into dry moccasins. Only then did she acknowledge Susannah with a nod, and they walked in to the sitting room to be near the fire.

Magdelaine fell into the empty armchair. She looked more exhausted than Susannah had ever seen her. Her eyes were heavy. The lines around her mouth creased into a deep frown.

Jean-Henri sat forward with his elbows on his knees. "Well?"

Magdelaine closed her eyes for a moment, then opened them. "No one is going to claim this child."

Esmee put her hand to her mouth and looked at the boy. In sleep, his mouth moved as if he were suckling, and he furrowed his brow with the seriousness of the task.

"Do you know who his mother is?" Jean-Henri asked. He didn't ask after the father because it was a pointless inquiry. If the father wanted to be known, he would have married the girl or at the very least provided for her care, as the traders had done for the summer wives to whom they were not actually married. Babies came into the world all the time without fathers, especially on this island, Susannah had learned. The possibility that the mother might be unknown, or that she would shrink from the task of caring for her own child—now there was a novelty.

"Yes, I do."

He waited to see if she would tell him the name, but she did not. "And her parents will not claim him either?"

"They say it is impossible that they have a grandson. They say I am mistaken."

"But there is no chance," Esmee said, sounding mysteriously convicted, "that you are mistaken." She and Magdelaine shared a glance.

"No."

The boy opened his eyes and glanced around the room, then at the dancing light of the fire. He watched it a moment, fascinated, then examined his own hand. His mouth turned down into a pout and he began to whimper. This cry was unlike his earlier wails of hunger; it churned plaintively as if he were reflecting on his own loneliness, the uncertainty of his future.

Esmee went over and lifted him from his makeshift bed. She held him on the inside of her forearm, with the back of his head resting in her palm, and cooed to him. The crying eased some as she swayed her arm back and forth. The room was otherwise quiet as they all watched him. Susannah wanted desperately to ask what they would do with the child—the air was heavy with the question—but somehow she could not find the words.

Jean-Henri stood too and peered at the baby. He stuck out his tongue and the whimpering stopped altogether. The little creature examined the grown man and the complicated workings of the parts of his face. "May I?" he said to Esmee.

She glanced at him in surprise. "Yes, but have you ever—"

"Surely I can figure it out," he said.

She passed the boy into his arms. Jean-Henri tried lifting him upright so that he could see the rest of the room, but his floppy head wrenched to the side and he began to cry once more. Quickly, Jean-Henri swooped him down into the cradle of his elbow and rocked him as he had seen Esmee do. The baby sighed and chomped at the air in search of his thumb.

"You say no one will claim him," Jean-Henri said, his body rocking back and forth like a canoe on the lake. "Well. *I* will claim him."

Susannah watched as Magdelaine tried to comprehend her son's meaning. She blinked at him. "What are you talking about?"

Jean-Henri kept his eyes on the boy. "If he has no father, I will claim him. I will be his father. And Esmee will be his mother."

Esmee did not react with any sort of surprise but simply ran her hand over the baby's silky hair, then grinned at Jean-Henri. The two of them had conspired to do this—not just to adopt the baby but to join together to thwart life's disappointments and injuries. It was audacious and it made Susannah's chest expand like a bellows. What was love if not a conspiracy, an alliance? You agreed to fight together against a common enemy, to let nothing come between you. Affection was the least of it. This was a kind of soldiering and you did it with a strong shoulder and with a fearlessness that anyone who knew something about what life did to you would have a hard time mustering.

"Oh, *mon fils*, don't be ridiculous. You don't have to do this. Someone on the island will take him in, or someone in one of the villages."

Jean-Henri shook his head. "I have made up my mind. Esmee and I will be married. And we will raise this boy as our son."

"You don't know what you're saying. What about Montreal—how will you earn a living here?" Magdelaine's voice grew shrill and Susannah took a step toward her, placed her hand beneath the woman's elbow. It had been a while since Magdelaine had brought up the subject of the position in Montreal; now, faced with this venture that was completely out of her hands, she clung to it.

But Jean-Henri seemed different somehow, certain in a way Susannah had not seen since her arrival. Magdelaine's protestations wouldn't dissuade him. If only she could see what a blessing this was, Susannah thought. Her son, who was devoted to her, wanted to stay near her, wanted to make a family with the woman Magdelaine thought of as a daughter. Susannah would give anything to be a part of a family like this one.

"What kind of life can you have if you stay on the island?" Magdelaine asked.

Jean-Henri laughed. "What kind of life? The kind of life *I* want—that's what kind. You tell me all the time that I should be more like my father, that I should have his courage, his conviction. But I have to hear about these things from you because I never knew the man myself. The only father I ever had is the one who exists in tales you tell me, and you only tell me those tales to illustrate the ways in which I have failed."

The remark sent a flash of pain across Magdelaine's face. "That's not true."

Jean-Henri shook his head but softened his voice. "Don't you see?" he almost pleaded. "I can do something he could not do. I can be more than just a man in a story."

"Be hopeful, madame," Esmee said gently, then kissed Magdelaine's cheek. "Or if you cannot, let us be hopeful in your stead. Good things will come from this."

Magdelaine seemed to know she was losing the argument, and as a last-ditch effort she looked to Susannah. "Do you believe these two could be so foolish? What in the world can I do to stop this?"

Susannah took her hand. "Forgive me, but are you sure that you want to stop it? Life has taken so many people from you, left you with so much grief. But here it is offering you a wonderful gift. Listen to them. Listen to what your son is telling you about what he wants to do. *I* think it is very brave."

Magdelaine glanced from Jean-Henri to the baby, then let out a deep sigh.

"Cheer up, madame," Esmee said. "In a few years he'll be strong enough to paddle. And carry the pails at the sugar camp."

"You can teach him to fish," Jean-Henri said, his mouth twisted into a crafty smile. It wasn't often that he got to taste victory in a battle with his formidable mother, and he was going to relish it.

Magdelaine put her head in her hands and took a deep breath, then walked over to the window and looked out at the lake. Susannah glanced at Jean-Henri, and he shrugged slightly as they waited to see what she would say.

A long moment passed before she spoke. "Mark my

words," she said. "Some day you will be standing at this window trying to persuade that child not to do something disastrous."

Jean-Henri laughed. "I suppose you are right about that."

Magdelaine turned around and stepped toward them, shaking her head. "What will you call him? My grandson needs a name."

"Henri?" Jean-Henri suggested, with a noticeable lack of commitment.

Magdelaine pursed her lips. "No. Let him have a new name."

"Madame, we want you to choose," Esmee said.

"We do?" Jean-Henri cut his eyes at his soon-to-be wife.

The new grandmother thought it over. "How about Raphael? Raph."

Esmee smiled a dreamy smile. "Patron saint of lovers," she told Susannah.

"And lunatics," Magdelaine said.

"Well, then, Raphael seems just about right. Now," Jean-Henri said, touching Esmee tenderly on the back of her neck and holding her gaze, "I will go roust Father Milani from his bed. No point in waiting when there is a marriage *and* a baptism to perform on the same day."

"No," Esmee and Magdelaine said at once.

Esmee cleared her throat. "No, Jean. I think we must have someone else."

"But—this island hasn't seen another priest in years. Do you want to travel to do it?"

"No, but—"

"Father Adler," Magdelaine said.

Susannah drew in a breath at the mention of his name. She had been waiting for the opportunity to confirm her suspicion about Therese, and here was her chance.

"It should be Father Adler," Magdelaine said. "We should write to him. If this doesn't get him to come, finally, to the island, then nothing ever will."

Jean-Henri wrote the letter, and the next morning Susannah volunteered to walk it down to Market Street. When she went up to her room to put on a warmer dress, she pulled a sheet of paper from the drawer in the table beside her bed and wrote out a letter of her own to accompany Jean-Henri's. If her hunch was right, this letter could set into motion the answer to some very old prayers. If she was wrong, Father Adler could tell her himself when he arrived on the island.

Mail slowed almost to a stop during the winter months, with the boats not running, but occasionally men made expeditions to settlements in the south of the Michigan Territory, or beyond to Detroit, and they never left the island without taking the mail with them in sleds light enough to whisk across the frozen lake. From Detroit, the letters might find their way to a boat traveling over the treacherous shoals at the western edge of Lake Erie, then along its southern bank. A wagon transporting furs or grain might make room for a bag of mail, though delivery to the eastern cities could be delayed by rutted or washed-out roads, downed tree limbs, cracked spokes, disease of man or horse, spring blizzard, winter thaw, bears, wolves, Indian attack, or plain old incompetence. It was a miracle, really, that any correspondence ever met its destination. At best, it would be weeks until the letter made its way to Buffalo, and weeks more before they might hear word from Father Adler or Sister Mary Genevieve.

As Susannah buttoned her cloak and pulled the hood up around her ears, she overheard a conversation between Magdelaine and her son in the kitchen. She was warning Jean-Henri to be cautious with the woman who was not yet his wife, lest they find themselves with two babies to take care of. Already Magdelaine was trying to take the situation in hand, control the uncontrollable. She was nothing if not consistent.

Still, Magdelaine seemed to have accepted Jean-Henri's decision and had even taken the child into her arms for a while. She walked him around the sitting room and showed him the pictures that hung on the walls. Then she took him to the dove's cage. He watched the bird as it hopped from one perch to another, never quite opening its wings in the small space of the cage. It bobbed its head at Raph, curious about this small new person. Susannah thought back to the first time she had met Alfred on the boat, when he had explained the mechanics of flight so clearly to her. The force of *lift* combined with the force of *thrust*—that was what the dove needed in order to fly. But it didn't have the space for either inside the cage.

Magdelaine pressed her nose to the boy's cheek, and Susannah hoped she was coming to see that if she did not fight so hard against everything that challenged what she thought was true about the world, she might have some peace. The newly formed family might bring her a great deal of joy for the rest of her years, if only she would let it. But as Magdelaine's circle tightened, Susannah wondered about her own place in it, whether there was a place for her here at all. She felt there was no reason to believe that they needed her as much as she had come to need them.

Magdelaine had told Susannah from the first day that she could stay as long as she needed to, but she had only meant until the danger had passed. Once that obituary arrived, they all knew that Susannah was safe. Perhaps it was time to begin making plans for the spring. She would see this matter through—welcome Therese back home or learn that she had been wrong and welcome Father Adler instead—and then she would leave the island. She could find work somewhere. She knew that Magdelaine would help her.

The snow in the lane was crowned with a layer of ice, and it crunched beneath Susannah's boots. She walked in one of two wide troughs made by the runners of sleighs and stepped carefully around the leavings of horses and dogs. The lake seemed to be encased in a thick pane of glass, but she knew that beneath the ice it moved, its currents tumbling stones as old as the world. Now and again the frozen surface would groan with the pressure of the invisible surging of the water. Along the beach, waves had frozen in great arcs, one on top of the other, like icing along the edge of a cake.

She trudged to Morin's store with the letter to Father Adler in her hand. Susannah had planned to slide the letter under the door but was surprised to find Morin there on such a cold morning. They exchanged smiles of solidarity, both their noses red from the cold.

"A letter to go out, please," she said and handed it to him.

Morin nodded, his teeth clamped on a pipe. "Maybe next week."

"That's sooner than I had hoped. Thank you." She turned back toward the lane.

"Miss?" Morin said, calling her back. "I believe I have a letter for you."

She stepped back under the awning. "For Madame Fonteneau?"

"No, for you. 'Miss Dove.'" He read the name from the envelope.

She thought with a jolt of Edward, but of course he would not have called her by this name. Then she thought of Sister Mary Genevieve. How strange that Susannah was sending a letter to Buffalo just as one was arriving from the same place for her.

But no, when she opened the envelope she found that the letter was not from Edward and not from the sister. It was not from Buffalo at all. In fact, it was not a letter at all, but a drawing sketched by a careful hand she recognized as Alfred's. The drawing showed a simple pot sitting in a shaft of light. The pot was empty, but she knew what was hidden inside it. A planted pea, taking root in the secreted damp of the soil.

Chapter Twenty-one

In the first week of February, they received a reply from Father Adler that he would come as soon as he could after the thaw, when the boats finally started running again. Magdelaine decided that she would not tell him of Raph's true origins, and instead would let him believe that the baby really did belong to Jean-Henri and Esmee. What good would it do to say otherwise? He *was* theirs now, and she felt it was their duty to protect him from the truth of his origin.

Father Adler had advised them in his letter to baptize the child as soon as possible and not wait for his arrival, for if he was delayed and God forbid the child died, he should not want the separation from eternal peace on his conscience. The idea of asking Father Milani to bless his own bastard child filled Magdelaine with bile; still, she knew that Father Adler was right. The baby had to be baptized, and the sooner the better.

"Good morning, madame," Father Milani said as she came into the church.

Off the sanctuary was the small alcove where he slept—or purported to sleep, at least—and it contained a narrow desk where he sat writing a letter. His voice was jovial, the voice of a swaggering sinner who knew that he could spend his time any way he pleased and never once worry his head about what consequences might come his way. He laid down his pen and stood, noticing for the first time the pale-eyed baby she held in her arms.

"And who do we have here?"

"Father Milani," Magdelaine said, anger making her tongue slow to work. "This is Raphael Fonteneau and I would be grateful if you would perform his baptism."

The priest glided over to them, the tails of the preposterous scarf tied at his neck fluttering a little behind him. He touched Raph's cheek. "Of course."

She watched him carefully as he looked the baby over, waiting to see if he noticed the boy's eye, if recognition might spark. But if he was aware of the link between them, he did not show it.

"I had not heard that Jean-Henri had determined to take a wife." He smiled. "Of course, a child's arrival will force a man's hand to the bond. As it should."

"Indeed," Magdelaine said. The muscles in her shoulders felt coiled like a spring, and her head began to ache. "I would not have expected you to know. Certainly you are too much occupied with your duties to give your ear to island gossip." Magdelaine was trying to shame him, but of course it would never work. "Yes, my son will marry Esmee Leroux." She had prepared the next part in case he insisted on performing the wedding first. "We are waiting for the thaw so that some of her family might be present. But I'm sure you'll agree that the matter of the child is more urgent. He has not been well." That too was a lie. But this was a man who had no use for the truth.

Milani nodded again. "Yes, I see. Let me consult my appointment book," he said, turning back to the desk.

"Father, I would be grateful if you would perform the sacrament today. Now."

"Now? I'm sorry, madame, but I am engaged at the moment in some correspondence . . ."

"Please, Father. I ask you as a faithful member of this congregation. It means so much to me that it would be today."

He pressed his lips into a line and looked back and forth between Magdelaine and the child. "It is highly unusual. Where are his parents?"

"Both of them have been ill, and I fear for the child." In truth, Esmee *had* been sickened at the thought of Father Milani's devilish hands touching the boy she now felt earnestly in her heart was her own son, as much as if she had given birth to him herself. She had explained their theory on Raph's paternity to Jean-Henri, and the news had made him furious, then more protective than ever.

"But where are the godparents?"

"I will be his godmother. And he will have to make do with just me."

Father Milani considered her request. After a moment, his face softened. "He resembles you, madame."

She swallowed. "I hope he will take after my son. His father."

"I'm certain he will." He excused himself to go to a cabinet and remove the necessary items to perform the ritual. They waited beside the fire in the back of the sanctuary as he warmed the holy water so that it would not chill the child on so cold a day.

Magdelaine watched him work. "Do you know, Father, the thing I find most useful about our religion for the people of this island?"

He glanced up at her, curiosity in his eyes. Perhaps he had some ideas of his own on that front.

"Though I understand that we must have a priest's guidance in matters of our faith, it is also true, as you know, that this part of the world does not yet have nearly enough priests. And much of the time, the faithful are left to their own determination to stay true to their religion."

"It is true, and I lament it."

"But what I find useful is that the faithful may do this because even without a priest, there is God himself, watching us always, listening to the words we say and the words we do not say. He sees everything, in the day, in the night, he sees inside our secret hearts. We cannot hide a thing from him. Do you not find that a comfort, Father?" If he didn't understand her meaning now, she thought, then he really was a fool.

He looked at her, stricken by her words, but he soon covered this reaction with his carefully constructed façade.

Milani cleared his throat. "You are right. It is a great comfort, madame. Now, let us introduce this new soul to the Lord's keen attention."

* * *

As Magdelaine's household waited eagerly for Father Adler's arrival, more drawings appeared for Susannah. She had asked Mr. Corliss not to come back to the house, and he was respecting her wishes by sending them through Morin's store. One arrived every couple of days and Susannah handed each, wordlessly, to Magdelaine. She could see that he was trying, in his gentle way, to remind Susannah that he was waiting for her, should she have a change of heart. Each drawing depicted the same pot on the same windowsill, but time changed its contents. As with all creation, in the beginning, there was nothing. But then there was *something*, and that something thrived. The second picture showed merely a shift in the soil. The next, a tender shoot, like a green knuckle, emerging. The shoot then uncurled and stood up. It split its two leaves like a woman letting down her hair.

That was the thing about a seed. It hardly waited for man to intend anything upon it. The impulse toward life was so strong, the potential coiled so tightly within the seed coat, that the little vessel needed very little encouragement to begin. If a few drops of water seeped into the bin where onions were kept, the inert bulbs would come alive, each wide root slick like a tongue. If a jar of dried beans sat too near the steam and heat of the kettle, one would open the lid to find a dozen yellow-green worming roots, coursing against the edges of the dank glass in search of soil.

"My dear," Magdelaine said after Susannah showed her

yet another drawing, "I don't see how you can continue to ignore this poor man's attempts at kindness. Won't you at least allow me to invite him over for a meal?"

It was the last week of February and they had just returned from a trip by sled to the other side of the island. Susannah folded up the drawing and slipped it back into her pocket.

"To what purpose?" she asked. "It will only give him false hope." She knelt in front of Ani and unbuckled his harness, releasing him into the yard, then released the other dogs. Magdelaine noticed that her hands moved deftly now on tasks like these. Susannah no longer hesitated or tired easily with the work—she seemed at ease, confident. What's more, her injured fingers seemed finally to have healed, though they were dreadfully misshapen. She joined Magdelaine at the back of the sleigh as they moved the bundles of wood to the stack beside the house.

Magdelaine wondered if Susannah really had made up her mind about Mr. Corliss, or if, beneath the dread and weariness in her heart, some part of her was still hoping to be convinced. "And tell me again *why* you can't consider the possibility of mere friendship with this man? The danger has passed—your old life is dead and buried. And you are free to do as you please."

Susannah sighed. "I know that what you say is true, but somehow I still cannot believe it. Besides, there is too much I would not be able to explain to him. How could I ever tell him the truth?"

"I don't suppose you have to decide that yet," Magdelaine said. "But it's not impossible that he might be more understanding than you think." Susannah gave Magdelaine a dubious glance that made her laugh. "I am not saying it would be easy," she said.

Susannah cleared her throat and looked away from Magdelaine. "The real reason, you see, that I have been avoiding Mr. Corliss," she said, "is that I do not expect I will be staying here past the spring."

Magdelaine paused in her work, her chin resting on top of the rough wood she held in her arms. "Oh." She felt a pang of sadness that another loss was upon her. One more person she had allowed herself to care for was going away. Magdelaine tried to hide her disappointment. It made sense, of course, that Susannah would want to move on. There was nothing tying her to the island. Her time here was always meant to be a temporary arrangement. How could Magdelaine expect her to stay, just for her own benefit? She cleared her throat. "As I told you when you arrived, I will be glad to help you move on when you are ready."

Susannah's shoulders fell slightly, but then she nodded too. "Yes," she said. "I think it is for the best. Perhaps I will go to Detroit, to that school Noelle told you about. Do you think they would have me as a teacher?"

Magdelaine smiled. "Certainly—if I tell them you've converted." They laughed.

Susannah grew quiet again as they finished unloading the wood, brushed off their hands, and headed inside.

"Whatever you want to do, I will help you," Magdelaine said.

*   *   *

B aptism seemed to agree with Raph and as February gave way to March, he awakened to his new world. He was a solemn baby but watchful too. When Magdelaine held him on her lap in the sitting room, his eyes darted from her face to the fire and back to her face once more, then to the fringe on the wool blanket that hung on the back of the chair and back to her face again. He seemed to be asking whether Magdelaine too saw the miraculous blue-orange flames, asking how her fingertips found the rough wool each time she reached for it. Every once in a while a smile would flash across his face that was pure Jean-Henri, the top lip stretched higher on one side. And she had to remind herself that this baby wasn't really her kin.

In mid-March Magdelaine packed two traps, a sack of dried fish and leeks, and a pouch of rice in a small bag, and sharpened her knife. Dressed in two layers of worsted beneath her broadcloth skirt, she hitched Ani and another dog to the sleigh and left for her sugar camp on Bois Blanc. She spent the first few days at the camp alone and tapped many of the maples. The stand of trees was so dense that she could forget the grove was surrounded by an enormous lake, boats moving to and fro. There was nothing but the trees. The sun set early and she worked until the dim light began to make her squint. She heard the *thwap* of one of the traps and a rustling in the grass.

Ani raced toward it and barked wildly until she reached him. As quickly as she could, she cut the rabbit's throat. For a long time she had not been able to eat rabbit at all, after what had become of Josette, but the dried fish would not be enough to satisfy Ani, and she had spoiled him for so long she doubted whether he could hunt successfully on his own. As the thawing sap plunked slowly into the pails, she skinned the animal and gave a few pieces of the meat to Ani and the other dog. The rest she cooked in a stew and ate it straight from the pot, burning her tongue as she watched the cloud cover recede and reveal the stars.

It had pained her to leave Raph behind so that she could escape to her camp—though she couldn't think of a more competent mother than Esmee. The longing for him was familiar. After all, she had felt the same about leaving Jean-Henri behind all those years ago. She thought about Raph all the time she was away from her house. She had made a habit of narrating her actions when he was around—"This is a spoon and you use it to stir"; "This is a book and you hold it like so; here, feel the pages"—and she found herself hoping that Esmee wouldn't forget to do the same. Of course Esmee did things in her own way, and in truth it was a better way, with more patience and trust in the child.

Magdelaine thought about Susannah too, her plans to leave, and the prospect made her feel uneasy. Everyone who needed saving had been saved, she supposed—Susannah, Raph, Noelle perhaps—and that was a fact to celebrate. But something had happened to Magdelaine since she had rescued Susannah. Susannah had rescued her back. The past would always be with Magdelaine, but her friendship with Susannah made her see now that today mattered too. She felt lighthearted, hopeful. And she didn't want it to come to an end.

Magdelaine typically lingered at the camp for two weeks or more, but this year she could not fight the temptation to return home after five days. The hired men had begun to arrive at the sugar camp, and they no longer needed her assistance. Last year she had stayed because it was a way of escaping from Jean-Henri and the house she didn't want. But now she found that she wanted to be there in the ostentatious house with the big fire and the snow falling outside. She wanted to be among them, before things changed once again.

She packed up the few items she had brought along. The sack of food, now empty, she rolled up and slipped into her bag. During her time there the ice had begun to crack open. She would have to leave the sleigh behind on the island. Ani and his brother trotted with her to the canoe and she pushed off, her paddle knifing the icy water. Her shoulders knew the motion the way her hands knew how to come together in prayer. When the port came into view she saw that it really was spring—the first boat of the year had arrived. At the beach her feet crunched over the ice that remained. A family of grebes swam in an arc away from her.

At the house she found Susannah and Raph asleep together in the big chair in front of the window. The baby clutched a lock of her red hair in his fist.

Susannah opened her eyes. "Welcome home," she whispered. She shifted Raph in her arms so that she could lift him without waking him up and set him gently on his bed of pillows, near but not too near the fire. He stirred and tossed his head from one side to the other before he found his thumb and settled back to sleep.

Magdelaine gazed at him. "It seems impossible but he has changed so much, in just a few days."

"He will be happy to see you when he wakes up."

"Where are his parents?"

"Gone to the port to meet the boat," Susannah smiled. "Today might be their wedding day."

Anticipation fluttered in Magdelaine's chest, but she tried to tamp it down. Father Adler might have been detained, might have to delay his journey, for a dozen reasons. She didn't want to let herself believe just yet that he really might arrive.

"Have you heard any more from Mr. Corliss while I was away?"

"More of the same," Susannah said, her voice plainly sad. "But I have not replied."

Magdelaine followed her gaze to the cage beside her chair. Inside, the listless dove stared back at them. Jean-Henri had told her the bird would be a good-luck charm—a dove to help them in their efforts to save Miss Dove—and perhaps he had been right. Here was Miss Dove, safe beside the fire. If the dove was a charm, it had worked its magic. And yet the cage still seemed like a cruel home.

Susannah seemed to share her thoughts. "Magdelaine," she said. "Have you ever thought about releasing that poor bird?"

"Nearly every time I see it," she said.

"Well, if that is the case," Susannah said, her voice nearly angry, "then I wonder why you don't do it."

"I suppose I worried about what might happen to it. It was born wild, but it has been in this cage a long time now—what if it doesn't know how to survive?"

Susanna shook her head and Magdelaine saw that tears were welling in the corners of her eyes. She swallowed, then tried to steady her voice as she said, "It should have the chance, though, to try. Shouldn't it?"

"Yes, indeed, it should." Magdelaine looked at Susannah with concern. It seemed very important to her that the dove should have its freedom, just as she finally had hers. And yet it was clear that freedom had not brought Susannah happiness. Magdelaine felt again how much she longed for Susannah to stay.

"*You* should do it, Susannah. You should let the dove go." She straightened in her chair. "Are you certain?"

"Yes," Magdelaine said. "Absolutely certain." She opened the box on the floor where Esmee kept the sack of cracked corn they fed the dove and when the bird heard the rustle of the grain, it snapped to attention. Magdelaine shook the bag again and the dove leapt from its perch inside the cage.

Moving slowly so as not to startle the bird, Susannah lifted the latch on the door and swung it open. The dove stared at her, then hopped to the end of the perch and paused again, perhaps wondering whether the invitation was a trick. At last the dove hopped onto the back of Susannah's waiting hand and allowed her to touch its head with her fingertip.

Susannah glanced at Magdelaine, who nodded, and together they walked into the front hall and opened the door. Magdelaine cast a handful of grain on the front steps and the dove fluttered down to it. They watched together as it picked at the corn, then lifted its head to look around. The breeze off the lake lifted the feathers on the bird's back. A long moment passed as it seemed to survey the house where it had come from and the long forgotten wider world beyond. Then all at once the dove opened its wings and sailed off, around the side of the house and out of sight.

Magdelaine moved to follow it, but Susannah put out a hand to stop her.

"Don't you want to make sure it's all right?" Magdelaine asked.

Susannah shook her head. "I can't really bear to know, either way. If it is killed, I will feel responsible. If it survives, I will envy it." They stood in front of the open door on the front steps staring out at the lake, at the empty air the dove had flown through.

"Susannah," Magdelaine said. "Do you *want* to go to Detroit?"

She thought for a moment before she spoke. "I want . . . to be of use."

Magdelaine nodded. "I know that feeling well. It has organized my life, really. Seeking out what there is to *do* and seeing that it is done."

Susannah shook her head. "Sometimes I wonder whether you have ever in your life hesitated, whether you've ever had a moment of doubt. You are so sure of yourself. I've never known that feeling."

Magdelaine pressed her lips into an amused smile. "Just because I am skilled at hiding my doubts doesn't mean I don't have them." She folded her hands in front of her. "I doubt whether I have really helped you at all—you seem so unhappy. I wonder why you feel you must go to Detroit to be of use, as you say."

"To begin again," Susannah said. "To make a fresh start."

"And *there* you will not feel compelled to lie about your past?"

Susannah looked at her and then sighed. "I don't know."

"We take ourselves with us, wherever we go. I learn this anew each year when I try to escape to my sugar camp with Ani. I think we are going alone, but everyone is there in my mind, in my memories and fears and dreams—my sisters, my husband, my son. Some things you cannot run from."

Susannah's eyes were welling again. She could not speak, merely shook her head.

"Mr. Corliss would certainly be disappointed if you left the island."

An exasperated laugh burst from Susannah's lungs. "Him again? I've told you—what he wants, I cannot give him."

"All right," Magdelaine said, patting the back of Susannah's hand. "Let's leave Mr. Corliss out of it. Let me tell you what *I* wish." Magdelaine took a breath before she pressed on. A year ago she would not have admitted to loneliness. She would not have been brave enough to take the risk. "I wish you would think about staying. For good, I mean."

Susannah looked at Magdelaine in surprise.

"Stay and live here with me," she went on. "Jean-Henri and Esmee will need a home of their own, and I don't want to live in this big house by myself. We could take on more students, make this into a real school. You would certainly be of use then, to those girls." Magdelaine forced herself to say the last part. "And to me."

A smile slowly took hold of Susannah's face. "I would like that very much," she said. Just then she saw Jean-Henri and Esmee coming around the curve in the lane with a woman wearing a black cloak.

Susannah drew in a sharp breath. "Magdelaine, there's something I have to tell you. About Father Adler."

Magdelaine looked again at the three people walking toward the house. She nodded. "I know," she said, feeling her shoulders sink with disappointment. "I can see that he isn't coming."

Susannah shook her head. "No." She took Magdelaine's hands. "He is not. But there is something else."

"Mother!" Jean-Henri broke into a run when he saw them standing in front of the house. "Something's happened—you won't believe it!"

Esmee kept pace with the newcomer and as they drew closer, step by step, Magdelaine felt her lungs begin to constrict, as if someone were squeezing them. She tried to breathe. She could not tear her eyes from the face of the woman who walked beside Esmee.

Inside the house Raph began to cry, and Susannah went in and brought him out to the porch. Jean-Henri reached them then, panting from the run. Joy spread across his face like an open flower. "It's a miracle," he said.

Esmee held the woman's hand. As they approached the front steps they slowed down, then stopped.

Though the woman smiled at her, Magdelaine continued to stare. Time moved in reverse across the woman's face. She felt her whole field of vision fill with it until the familiar brown iris expanded and subsumed her completely. It was too much for her. Magdelaine, the woman who had faced her husband's murderer and his musket, who could skin a buck and paddle three miles without stopping to take a breath, fainted on the front steps of her house, right at the feet of her dead sister Therese.

Chapter Twenty-two

When Magdelaine awoke they were standing over her. She blinked, her eyes darting among their faces, anxious to see whether the ghost remained.

"Are you all right, Mother?" Jean-Henri said, crouching down, his hand clutching her shoulder and shaking it. "Can you move?"

Magdelaine brushed his arm away. "Of course I can move."

She wrenched herself into a sitting position and waited for the room to steady. There was a humming in her ears not unlike the sound of church bells ringing from far away, and she took a deep breath. Here was her son, Esmee, Raphael, Susannah—and, yes, here was Therese Savard, back from the dead, transformed into a middle-aged woman.

"Esmee," Jean-Henri said. "Let's get her up to her bed."

Raphael began to bawl, and Susannah swayed with the boy in her arms while the rest of them helped Magdelaine to her feet and up the stairs to her room. They settled her against the pillows, and Esmee took the whimpering baby from Susannah's arms and walked him over to the window. Jean-Henri stood on one side of the bed, and Therese and Susannah on the other.

"Susannah," Magdelaine whispered. If she was having visions, if she had lost her mind, she trusted Susannah the most of all of them to tell her. "Do you see this woman standing here among us?"

Susannah reached over and put her hand on top of Magdelaine's, rubbing the knuckles. "Yes, I do, Magdelaine." Susannah grasped the newcomer's fingers with her other hand. "She is the nun who helped me get out of Buffalo. I didn't know it then, but now I understand—she is your sister."

Magdelaine felt her disbelief well up again and flood her eyes with color. This time, though, she held on to consciousness. She swallowed, nodded, allowed herself, finally, to meet Therese's gaze. Her voice came out in a whisper. "I always knew you were alive."

Therese's eyes searched Magdelaine's face. "You did?" She wore a black wool gown and a plain black bonnet, beneath which her hair was coiled in a tight bun. Her jaw was the same stern bone that had rarely allowed her mouth to smile as a girl. Two deep vertical lines marked her brow.

Magdelaine shook her head. "Well, I wasn't sure *what* to believe. But I hoped."

Therese sat down on the edge of the bed, then hesitated and reached for Magdelaine's elbow. Her hand trembled. "Yes, I am alive. But also full of regret."

Emotions marched one after another across Magdelaine's heart: first shock, then gratitude, then confusion. "All this time, you have been—where? And you never wrote to us? Never let us know that you were all right?" She felt anger begin to take over. "How could you let this go on so long?"

"I can hardly believe that I can finally say it now," Therese said, glancing at Susannah, who nodded. She turned back to Magdelaine and cleared her throat, placed both hands on top of her sister's. "What I have longed to say for so many years. I am sorry. I am so very sorry for what happened to Josette. I am sorry that I was too afraid to face you, to tell you that she died because of me."

Magdelaine struggled to keep up with Therese's words. "But how could *you* be responsible? It was Paul's knife, and when my men confronted him he confessed."

Therese shook her head. "Yes, he killed her. But only because I told him where she was. I was jealous of the attention he gave her. I wanted her to pay a price for having what I could not have." She tried to steady her ragged voice. "I didn't know, though, what he would do—I hope you can believe me."

"Oh, Therese," Magdelaine said. She pictured her forlorn sister the last time she had seen her, the October before Josette died and everything changed. Therese had been so serious, so timid. But bitter too. She was just twenty-seven years old, but somehow life had passed her by. Inaction had seized her and she could not plot a course in the world. Magdelaine thought of how many times she had criticized her son for the same behavior. They were alike in many ways. "Of course, you didn't know what he would do. *That* is why you stayed away all these years, and let me believe that you were dead? Because you thought I would blame *you*?"

"I blamed myself enough for us both. But you must have blamed me too. Didn't you?" Tears spilled down Therese's cheeks.

Magdelaine took a breath, hesitating before she spoke. She couldn't lie. Not now. "Yes, for a while. But I was only angry with myself, that I was not there to try to stop it, that I could not stop you from taking your life."

Jean-Henri gave Therese a handkerchief. "Thank you, *neveu*," she said.

Magdelaine looked at her son. He was a nephew again, after all this time.

Raph began to whimper, and Esmee brought him over to meet his great-aunt. Jean-Henri introduced them and Therese brushed her finger along the baby's cheeks before Esmee took him out of the room and downstairs for some milk.

Susannah stepped toward the door. "I should go too. So that you can catch up."

"No, Susannah," Magdelaine said. "I want you to say. You know that you are much more than just a guest here now. In fact, you really are the reason Therese is here. Jean, bring her a chair." He pulled a chair from the hallway and one from the corner of the room for Susannah and himself. Therese stayed where she was, perched on the side of the bed. She tried to give Jean-Henri his handkerchief back, but he waved it away.

"I still cannot believe you are here," he said. "I *saw* you. I saw you go into the water. But perhaps I only imagined it—I was so young."

Therese shook her head. "You did not imagine it."

"Tell us, Therese," Magdelaine said. "Tell us what happened."

She took a breath. Magdelaine could see her gathering all her strength before she began.

"After I discovered Josette, I was wild with grief. I hardly remember any of it, except the running. I know I stayed off the lane. I ran through the woods—I remember that. I surprised a wild dog eating his kill, but he must have sensed how far out of my mind I was because he let me be. It took all afternoon but I made it to the back half of the island. There was no one in sight—Jean-Henri, of course, I didn't know you were following me. I walked straight out into the water. It was freezing. I kept walking until I couldn't feel the sand beneath me and then just let myself sink. The water rushing in was like fire behind my eyes, and it took everything I had not to struggle against it. Finally everything went dark and I felt victorious. I wasn't going to have to live in the world alongside what I had done, how I had failed my sisters."

Jean-Henri nodded. "That's when I ran to get help. But when I came back, you were gone."

"A while after I blacked out—I don't know how long—I opened my eyes to find that I was lying on the rocks next to an overturned canoe. My whole body was numb, but I was alive. I couldn't believe that I had failed even at ending my life. I should have seen it for what it was, a miracle of survival, God's hand keeping death at bay, but all I could think was that I could never face you again. I did not know who owned the canoe and whether he had helped fish me out of the waves, but when I looked around there wasn't a soul in sight. I didn't think—I had no money, no food, no change of clothes, but I pushed the vessel into the water and began to paddle. I was never as fast as you, Magdelaine, but eventually I made it across to St. Ignace."

Therese explained how, once she had made up her mind to live, the world seemed to open to her. In the village at St. Ignace she met a man who had organized a party planning to travel to Quebec City—planning, in fact, to set off just as she was coming up the beach. She told him that she had nearly drowned and that, when she came to, she remembered nothing of her past but saw only visions of the Virgin Mary calling to her from across the water. He could see from her ice-crusted hair and blue fingertips that she was not lying, at least not about the cold-water plunge. She could pay him nothing, but if he was a man of faith—and indeed, he nod-ded, he was—he could help her get to a convent where she could put her calling to use. And he would be rewarded for his good deed in the afterlife.

He did not need much convincing and shouted to the men that their departure would be delayed by a few hours. He took Therese home to his wife, who shrieked when she saw the shivering young woman and ushered her inside the rude cabin and close to the fire. She sent the men out and ordered Therese out of her sodden clothes. Wrapped in a coarse wool blanket she crouched on the floor and rocked on her heels so she would not give over to the cold while the woman heated water for a bath. A while later, dressed in bor-rowed leggings and a woolen cloak over her dry dress, Therese departed with the men.

She braced herself for cruelty—perhaps the men would not share their food—or a frightening encounter with a drunk who might try to take liberties with her, but she needn't have worried. The men believed her to be a woman who had had visions and was perhaps herself a conduit of holiness. They felt it was their duty to see her safely to Quebec, and they took that duty seriously.

Six weeks later, Therese explained, she arrived at the Convent Ursuline in Quebec City. Again, she prepared herself to be cast out, her lie uncovered, and sent back to Mackinac to face Magdelaine and what the world would be like without Josette. But again, this reckoning did not come. The Ursuline sisters welcomed her into their world. They clothed and fed her. They took Therese at her word that she had seen a vision of her calling. They did not ask where she came from nor what she was leaving behind.

The sleeping quarters in the girls' dormitory was a tiny ten-by-ten room with a hard bed and a window the size of an open prayer book. There was no fire, but the other postulants pooled their yarn and knitted a thick pair of stockings for her to wear beneath the black wool garb the convent had issued her. There was a small library in the building, and she conquered her shame to admit to them that she could not read or write. The next day, they began to teach her.

Some of the other postulants had been sent to the convent by angry fathers, and they felt trapped in the life of sacrifice. For Therese, though, the convent did not feel like a prison. Instead, it offered the very sort of escape she had prayed for as she'd walked into the icy waves off the island. She could begin again in this quiet space, buffeted by four walls and the space for contemplation of anything other than the life she had left behind. If it was devotion the Ursuline sisters wanted, she would give it to them. She would devote herself to whatever they asked, as long as she could stay there forever.

"You wanted to forget us," Magdelaine said. It was an accusation, but her voice was soft with sympathy.

Therese shook her head. "I wanted to forget myself."

And for a while, she told them, it worked. She studied and after a few years took her orders and became Sister Mary Genevieve. Somewhere along the way the story she had invented to persuade the man in St. Ignace to help her get to Quebec became the truth. She began to feel a sense of calling to the life of sacrifice and service. She taught classes to students. She read. She prayed. And, with time, she was almost able to forget.

But then, she said, she started to dream about Josette. Josette as a little girl and Therese as a grown woman. They walked together around the island, sometimes through the snow with a stoic gray dog loping beside them, and other times in the heat of summer, the smell of fish wafting up from the beach. Josette held Therese's hand and they did not speak, but when Therese looked down to catch her sister's gaze, the girl's eyes were always focused on something else, never seeing Therese. They walked with purpose, unsmiling, as if they were headed somewhere important, but they never reached the destination before Therese bolted up, shivering, in her bed. She knew Josette was trying to show her something, to take her somewhere, but Therese refused to be reached. She wouldn't let herself be sucked back into the past.

"But Josette would not let me go so easily," Therese said.

The following fall, a woman arrived at the Ursuline convent, a frail young waif in a fine yellow dress. Her face was drawn but pretty, and as she came into the sunlight pouring through the room's one window, Therese saw that her left cheek was yellowed with a bruise. A man wearing a snow-white silk cravat held her elbow and led her into the room, then quietly described his predicament to the Mother Superior.

"Lucretia becomes hysterical, has visions," he said. "She invents awful things, then harms herself and accuses me of having done them. Last week she threw herself down the stairs." The nun wrote as he spoke, nodding. "And said that I had—" Here he hesitated, as if the words were too awful to say aloud. "That I had *pushed* her."

"Yes," the nun said. "Please do not let her accusations trouble you. They are obviously the product of a deranged mind. We have seen this before, cases of spiritual or mental vexation so severe they lead a woman to see a thing that isn't there."

"You must do something with her," the husband said. "You must compel her to tell the truth. I will be back for her in a month's time, and I expect she will be changed."

Therese offered to help Lucretia get settled in her room. As they walked the long hallway together, she nodded toward the bruise on her cheek. "That looks bad," Therese said. "Does it hurt?"

"Not too much anymore," she said. "My husband did it. No one believes me."

Therese stopped in the hallway and took Lucretia's hands. "I believe you."

It was as if Josette herself had sent the woman to the convent, and Therese said she knew then precisely what she would do to begin a kind of penance.

When Lucretia's husband came back for her at the end of the month, his impertinent young wife was gone.

"You were right, sir," Therese told him. "She was deranged. A few days ago she ran out and down the road and before I could catch her, she threw herself in the river. We have no hope that she will be recovered."

He seemed surprised to hear of this terrible turn of events, of course, even blamed the sisters for carelessness, but he believed the story. As he packed his wife's clothes and stepped up onto the carriage that would take him back home, Lucretia was on her way to Montreal, where Therese had found work for her in a laundry. She had a new name and a new life. The successful thwarting of that awful husband was a bittersweet victory. Therese had intervened and saved Lucretia from a terrible fate.

"If only I could have done the same for Josette," Therese said to Magdelaine. "But time moves in only one direction."

Therese explained that she had continued her work at the convent, teaching, nursing the poor and sick who came to their doors. It wasn't as though she sought out wives who wished to leave their husbands. But every now and then one came to her, whether because of violence or neglect or some other reason. She never insisted they explain themselves, and she did everything she could do to help them.

But the work didn't seem to be enough to satisfy Josette. The dreams of her little sister continued. In them, Josette never grew older, and, walking together, they never got any closer to their destination, nor did Therese learn what was the object of Josette's gaze. She was trying to show Therese what she could do to make amends for what had happened on the island, and Therese was trying to interpret what that was. Helping Lucretia and other women like her wasn't enough, it seemed. The years passed, and, Therese explained, she continued to feel unsettled, continued teaching and working and waiting.

Then one winter day, after she had been transferred from the Quebec convent to one in Charlestown, Massachusetts, Therese offered to take the morning chores for a sister who was ill. She got the kitchen fire going, kneaded the bread and put it in the brick oven to bake, boiled the coffee. And when the bell sounded she went out into the cobblestone alley beside the convent to meet the man who delivered the milk. The wind howled between the brick walls, and the air was full of small pellets of ice that clung to her sleeves. Therese took the heavy ceramic jug he lifted down to her and handed him the coins. When she looked up into his face to smile her thanks, she saw that he wore a fine beaver hat and that beneath the hat his cheeks were warm and dry. The pelt that made his hat could have come from Mackinac, and thinking of that place nearly made her fall to her knees on the cobblestones.

Even Josette, from whatever otherworld she was watching, must have known that it was impossible for Therese to go back to Mackinac. So why had she brought the milkman and his hat across Therese's path? Perhaps in the urgent dreams, Josette's gaze was on the women Therese had yet to meet, had yet to find a way to save. So she redoubled her efforts to find them, and when she did, she made arrangements to send them to the island. If she could not bring Josette back to Magdelaine, she could send these women in her place. She had to try to return what her sister had lost.

Magdelaine understood now. "The other women I tried to help, before Susannah—*you* were the one who sent them?"

"Yes," Therese said. "As you know from my first unsuccessful attempts, it wasn't easy." It was one thing to send a woman from Quebec to Montreal, or Boston to New York, she said. But sending a woman alone deep into the Michigan Territory was another thing entirely. There were setbacks.

"I felt my failures were only making things worse. Here I was, upending women's lives to try to save them, all because I was having dreams that my dead sister wanted me to do it. I began to question my sanity. I determined to withdraw from the world. I left Massachusetts on my own and went to the tiny parish in Buffalo."

"But Father Adler came with you, and he wouldn't let you give up," Magdelaine said with a satisfied nod as she saw the story begin to click into place.

Therese glanced at Susannah, then turned back to Magdelaine and shook her head. "Magdelaine, you don't understand. There is no Father Adler. He is a figment, a name I created to use in helping make arrangements for these women. It's hard for a woman on her own. But when I tell people that I am writing on behalf of a priest, or traveling, or requesting assistance, of course they never question me. It costs money to make arrangements for these women. No one would give *me* anything. But they give readily to a man of God . . ."

"But—" Magdelaine said, trying to get her voice to work. "All the letters I exchanged with the father. All those thoughtful replies. That was—"

"That was me. I wrote them."

Now it was Magdelaine's turn to grasp her sister's hands and fight off tears. She felt at once the loss of the man she had admired—and the shock that he had never really been there at all!—alongside this gift: *Therese* had been there, all these years. She had never really lost her. It was almost too much to comprehend, to realize how completely she had misunderstood her own fate.

"And I thanked God for the chance to speak with you," Therese said. "If only from a distance."

Magdelaine shook her head in wonder, her cheeks wet now.

"It took a long time for me to realize," Therese said, "that I was wrong about what Josette was looking at in the dreams. She wasn't tugging on my arms to show me all these unfortunate women, though she did want me to help them. She was tugging, pointing, leading me to you, Magdelaine. She wanted me to come back to you."

Magdelaine opened her mouth to speak but found she could not. That image of Josette as a girl, whole, walking and talking and scheming in the afterlife to get her sisters to reconcile in this world was both a comfort and a rebuke. All these years she had been haunting Therese. Why had she never once visited Magdelaine?

Therese sat down on the bed. "I spent many years begging, in my heart, for Josette's forgiveness. I see now that she gave it long ago. But what I don't know is whether *you* will forgive me, Magdelaine. For failing to help Josette, for leaving you alone, a widow with a son, to shoulder it by yourself. And for staying away so long. I have tried penance and self-denial and teaching and praying and forgetting, and none of them have worked. When you sent the letter asking Father Adler to come to the island, Susannah included a letter of her own, in which she told me that she knew who I really was. I realized that I could not wait any longer. I had to come back here and simply ask you, as I should have done long ago, will you please forgive me?"

Magdelaine tipped her head to the side in sympathy. She thought back over the twenty years that had passed since Therese's disappearance. How might they have been different if Therese had come back? How might they have faced the trials of the years together?

"Of course I forgive you," Magdelaine said. "If you will forgive me."

She rose from the bed and Therese stood too, and they embraced. Suddenly a thought occurred to Magdelaine that made her laugh out loud. She pulled away and said, "I prefer you to Father Adler in every way. But now who will we get to marry Esmee and Jean-Henri?"

"Oh, dear," Therese said, sinking back down on the bed. "There isn't anyone else?"

"Well, we do have a priest on the island now, but he is less than ideal." Magdelaine's words made Jean-Henri groan.

Therese sighed and nodded. "I've heard some things

about him. I worried about trusting him, but he was always amenable, as long as he was paid on time. And he had enough secrets of his own to keep quiet about mine. . . . I apologize for involving him if it has caused trouble."

"You have no idea. Someday I will explain it all to you, but now I am too tired. And too happy." Magdelaine heard the dogs begin to bark and went to the window to look down.

A tall man in a rumpled coat stood in front of the house. He wore a dented hat and an uneven smattering of whiskers that marked a weary traveler. "Therese," she said. "Did you travel with a companion? Someone to see about your things?"

"No. I brought nothing other than my small case, and that is downstairs in the front hall. I didn't know if I would be staying for just a few days, or perhaps longer . . ."

Magdelaine smiled at her sister. The question hung between them. Susannah would stay, and Therese would stay. And perhaps Josette's happy ghost would return too, flitting from room to room and causing their candles to flicker. It was a pleasant thought.

"How strange—there is a man downstairs who appears to be waiting for something."

Therese looked at her in confusion. Then her eyes widened and she bolted to the window.

Chapter Twenty-three

S usannah, we have to get you out of sight." Therese rushed
over to her on the other side of the bed. "Where can we
put her, Magdelaine?"

Jean-Henri stood too. "The pantry." Magdelaine nodded
at him. "Come on," he said, taking her elbow.

Susannah felt a surge of fear. "Why? What is happening?"

"It's Edward," Therese said. "He is here."

Susannah shook her head in disbelief, her face blanching
white in terror. Magdelaine, Esmee—they had reassured her
so many times that she was safe here. How could Edward
be here?

They raced her down the stairs and through the kitchen,
where Esmee was feeding Raphael. Jean-Henri ushered her
and the baby out the kitchen door. They could cross through
the yard to the church without being seen, he whispered.
Magdelaine nodded. There was no telling what Edward

would do, and he wanted to get Esmee and Raphael as far away as possible from the target of Edward's search. His mother, he knew, could fend for herself.

"He must have followed me onto the boat," Therese said as Susannah backed into the pantry.

Magdelaine handed her a lamp. "Be very quiet," she said.

Susannah nodded, her heart racing.

"It will be all right," Magdelaine said. Therese wedged the door closed.

Susannah turned up the flame on the lamp, and a circle of light spread across the small space. She set it on one of the shelves. The inside of the pantry smelled of burlap and the dried herbs that hung suspended in bouquets tied with string, and Susannah sat down on a large sack of rice.

On the other side of the door she heard the sound of chair legs scraping the floor, then footsteps, the front door opening. Voices. Susannah couldn't make out what Edward was saying, but she didn't need to know. The familiar cadence of his voice felt like a cold hand reaching through her flesh to give her spine a good shake. She took hold of the shelf to steady herself, pressing her forehead against her knuckles.

Her eyes darted around the interior of the pantry, looking for something, some clue to her salvation. She tipped her head back and looked up at the flame of the lamp. The conversation in the front hall was growing more heated, Edward's insistence echoing as he bellowed. Hot tears welled up in Susannah's eyes, but she felt that if she let them fall, all was lost. She held very still, breathing through her nose.

Just then her eyes found the musket that hung upright on the wall beside the door, and she thought back to the day

Magdelaine had put down the rabid dog. Magdelaine *had* been afraid—anyone would have been—but she had acted in spite of her fears. Magdelaine had plenty of fears. She just didn't let them own her. Susannah saw that her own fear of Edward was like a reflex, something her body marshaled when it heard his voice, long before her mind had a chance to catch up. But it didn't have to be that way. She could do what Magdelaine had done. Despite her terror, Susannah knew she had to face Edward once and for all and end this madness.

Susannah nodded to herself and took a breath, her tongue clenched against her bottom teeth. She reached for the weapon. It was heavier than she expected, with most of the weight at the breech end. She remembered that after the dog had been shot, Jean-Henri had loaded it again before he put it away. Susannah doubted whether she could fire it, but perhaps the sight of the gun would be enough to scare him off. It was difficult to maneuver in the small space, but she stepped carefully and tipped the long weapon upright. When Susannah rested the butt on the floor next to her foot, the muzzle came up to her ear.

With her left hand she lifted the latch on the door and pushed it open about an inch. The voices in the front hall instantly grew louder.

"I won't leave," Susannah heard Edward say. She pressed her face to the crack of light, but they were still out of sight.

"Mr. Fraser, please," Therese said. "Be reasonable. Your wife is not here."

"You are lying." There was no anger in his voice. It was a simple statement of fact.

But Therese pressed on. "You have gotten an idea in your head, and it caused you to follow me here, and I regret that you had to make this long journey only to hear what I have already told you many times: Your wife lies at the bottom of the falls. I am so sorry for your loss, but there is nothing I can do in this world to help you. You must pray for her soul, and for your own."

More footsteps, and then she saw Edward come prowling into the kitchen, and the shock of seeing him made her step away from the door. Her shoulder blades made contact with the shelves behind her.

Gathering herself, she pressed her face to the sliver of light once more, still clutching the barrel of the musket. There he was, the man who had stalked her halfway across the continent, the man she had feared for so long. But he was much changed by the journey. His once-impeccable hair was overgrown, stringy, and hung down over his eyes and the collar of his filthy shirt. His trousers hung slack at his waist, the cuffs dragging on the ground. Whiskers, black with a dusting of gray, crawled unevenly around his jaw. Beneath the fringe of hair his eyes were wild.

Magdelaine and Therese rushed into the kitchen behind him. He wouldn't leave, Susannah knew. He would turn Magdelaine's house upside down until he found her, and who knew what he would do to the rest of them in his pursuit?

Susannah took a breath and stepped into the kitchen, holding the weapon with her right hand.

"Here I am, Edward," she said, her voice quiet and steady.

Behind him, Magdelaine and Therese stood frozen.

He stood absolutely still, staring at his wife. His eyes took in the musket, but Susannah could see him making a calculation about whether she would be able to heave it up to her shoulder, aim, and shoot it before he had the chance to swipe it away, whether she even had the nerve to try. His pale lips, chapped from the cold air that blew across the boat's hurricane deck, stretched into a smile. And he began to laugh.

"I knew it. I knew you were alive."

Susannah nodded and something came into her voice then, something as sure and sound as the hull of a steamboat. "I *am* alive." She was prepared, now, for whatever he would try to do. She planted her feet into the floor, felt her knees, her hips, holding her up. Her eyes were locked on his and she waited, bracing herself for him to lunge at her. She would step back and hoist the gun up to her shoulder, or if there wasn't time she would swing it like a club and knock him out. If he knocked her down and tried to take it, she would clutch the barrel with all the strength in her body. She would throw her legs around it. She would bite his fingers. She would spit in his face, kick at his stomach like he was a monster from a dream.

But then he did something for which she was unprepared. Edward Fraser fell down to his knees with a sob.

"Mrs. Fraser," he said, using that particular name to try to call her back to herself, she knew. He pressed his clenched fists to his eyes. "I have lost everything."

Susannah said nothing, just watched him as she had watched that dog in its pen: raving, unmaking itself, almost pleading for death. She felt fear, then pity, then fear again, fear of the pity itself, as if it were a trap Edward was setting for her. She pulled the cold iron barrel closer to her chest.

"I've done terrible things, Susannah. I cheated men out of money they earned with their own hard work. And I was caught. They took me to jail. I've been there for months."

She raised her eyebrows. She wasn't surprised to learn that Edward had broken the law to get what he wanted, but the idea that someone had confronted him and held him accountable for his crimes, that someone had been able to take him by the collar and put him in a jail cell, was a surprising piece of news indeed.

"I have nothing. No house, no land. But if you will come back to me, if you will forgive me, we could start again. Everything will be different, I swear to you. I will do anything you ask." He looked up at her, his wide brown eyes full of sorrow. The sight shocked her. She couldn't look away. Despite everything she knew about his cruelty, his eyes, his low state, plucked at her heart.

"Susannah," Magdelaine said, stepping forward.

Susannah wanted to look at her—she knew that if she could, the spell might be broken, but she could not tear her eyes away from Edward.

"You must not listen to him."

He would have to get an honest job, for the first time in his life, Susannah was thinking. He would have to change his name and move to a new city and write letters of inquiry and find someone willing to take on a clerk who came without any references, without any history of work. It would humble him. He would not be able to endure it unless he became a different sort of man. She squinted down at him.

Did he mean what he said? Why would he care for her now when he never had before?

"Please, Susannah," he whispered. "If you want me to beg you, I will." And he stooped down then and pressed his forehead to the toes of her boots.

The back of his neck was dark with grime. She eased the butt of the musket to the floor, then slowly set it down. Susannah looked at her husband, slumped on her boots. Since her parents had died and left her alone in the world she had longed for a family, and Edward had promised to be that for her. She reached down and touched the top of Edward's head with her left hand.

But as she saw the hand's shape, the mangled bones jutting strangely beneath the skin, something shifted in her, a crossbeam sliding into place across the door. Here was the man who had mangled that hand. Here was the man who had terrorized her each minute of the day until she feared sleep, until she feared breathing. And he thought she would forget what he had done?

She looked across the kitchen at Magdelaine and Therese. They watched her, waiting to see what she would do. When Susannah had been at her lowest point back in Buffalo, she had been alone in the world and had thought she would go on being alone forever. Instead, she had found Therese, and Therese had brought her to Magdelaine, to Mackinac. She had a home here on the island now, a new family. She wasn't alone anymore—and nothing could drag her back to her old life.

"Edward," she said calmly, and he lifted his head. "I want you to get up off the floor and get out of this house."

She took a breath and moved her foot to step away from him, but Edward slipped his fingers around her ankles and clenched them tight.

"Didn't you *hear* me?" he asked, the meekness in his voice slipping away like a mask. He gave her legs a shake, but she managed to stay on her feet. He let go and pushed himself to standing, stepped closer to her as she stepped away. He tried to make his voice gentle again, but it was too late. "You *will* come back to me. We will start again."

Susannah shook her head, her whole body trembling. Magdelaine and Therese rushed to her side, steadied her. He couldn't make her go, not with them here to help her. Her voice was a startled bird, beating its wings in her throat. "No," she said. "I am not going anywhere with you."

Edward laughed. "Who do you think you are?"

"No longer your wife—of *that* I am certain. This is my home now, and you are not welcome here."

"Aren't you sure of yourself," he said, looking from Magdelaine to Therese with disgust. "You and your motley crew. Well, I'll get a judge to declare you've deserted me. You'll have nothing from me."

"I want nothing." She nearly felt sorry for the way he clung to the old bluster, now meaningless. His life had become a farce.

His eyes flicked to the musket on the floor and he lunged for it, but Magdelaine anticipated his move and swept it up before he could get to it. He stared at the three women, assessing his options.

"Don't you see?" Susannah said, her voice still calm. She felt the truth of her words as she said them, like the satisfaction of a long-lost key opening a lock. "You have no hold over me anymore. I don't care for you. I don't fear you. You mean nothing at all to me."

Fear wasn't the thing that could do you in—loneliness did that all on its own. The difficulty of knowing someone else was nothing compared to the difficulty of letting yourself be known, be seen. But Susannah felt that she had done it, with Magdelaine, with Therese and Esmee and Jean-Henri. She had conquered her loneliness, and Edward couldn't use it to hold her anymore.

Susannah had never in her life seen Edward back down from any confrontation, but here he stood without another choice. He lowered his shoulders, shook his head, but still he did not move.

"Go," Susannah said, pointing at the front hall. "Get back on that boat if it is still in the port. If not, wait there for the next one." She could hardly believe that this moment had arrived. She would be free of him once and for all. "Go back home. Or to Chicago. Go to *hell*. But leave this place."

Edward stared at her, but she refused to break her gaze. He looked at Magdelaine, then Therese, who stood silent and steadfast by Susannah's side. They weren't going to budge either. His shoulders slumped and the broken man he had been when he arrived was back. Susannah was glad to see it, and glad to see him finally turn and leave the house.

Chapter Twenty-four

All the next day they braced themselves for Edward Fraser to come back to the house and make another attempt to reclaim his wife, but he did not. Jean-Henri went to Morin's store to ask about him and learned that the disheveled man had returned to the port in time to reboard the westbound boat.

So he would go on to Chicago, or New Orleans, Magdelaine thought. Of course, now that he knew where Susannah was he could always come back, but the prospect didn't seem to worry Susannah in the slightest. Magdelaine thought back to the trembling young woman Father Milani had brought to her front door less than a year ago. All she had wanted then was a place to hide. Now she was ready to claim more—a new home, a new family. A story that had a different ending.

The weather continued to warm as April turned to May, and Susannah's garden came alive. The crocuses and snowdrops emerged, along with the blossoms on the apple tree, and the yard hummed with bees. Susannah sketched a plan for the summer garden, with a larger plot of vegetables on one side and more transplanted thimbleberry bushes along the house.

Susannah put all of them to work. Therese and Esmee knelt in the established beds and pulled out anything that looked like a weed, then dug troughs as Raph sat on a blanket in the sun, shaking a jar of seeds. Magdelaine stared at her sister in awe, still fighting her own disbelief that she had found her way back home after all these years. Therese sat back on her heels to swat a bee away from her hair. Her eyes met Magdelaine's and she grinned. Life had given them something wonderful, Magdelaine saw: the chance to start a new family. They wouldn't waste it. They wouldn't take it for granted, not for a day.

Susannah interrupted her thoughts. "Now, Magdelaine, Jean-Henri," she said, handing both of them shovels, "you will be digging the new beds, over there." Susannah pointed to the meadow just beyond the apple tree.

"You're expanding, I see," Magdelaine said.

Susannah smiled. "That is where I will teach the botany lesson. Then you will take the girls over to Bois Blanc to hunt for specimens, and I will instruct them in making an herbarium—a catalog of all the plants these islands hold. After you finish with the beds, Jean-Henri, I want you to build me a bench."

Magdelaine feigned offense, then laughed as she nudged Jean-Henri. "Awfully domineering, isn't she?"

He smirked. "I wonder where she learned that."

They tromped through the tender spring grass to the site of the new beds. Just a few weeks earlier it would have been impossible to break the frozen ground, but now the thaw had crept into the soil, and it gave way to them.

They worked quietly, the *swish, chuff* of their shovels making a hypnotic rhythm. Magdelaine thought about how there were so many things in this life that humans could not accept, but how the earth accepted everything, every husk of a beetle, every spent blossom, every dead man and woman, with complete indifference. Then, if you waited a while, out came pink tulips on yellow-green stems, enough lettuce to send all the rabbits on the island into a frenzy. More than anything, it was patience a person needed.

"I suppose she wants the bench to go here," Jean-Henri said, gesturing with his arm alongside the beds. "The house will shade it in the morning."

She could see that he was already building the bench in his mind, imagining its lines, how to make it sturdy and beautiful. Just then she remembered the saw she had bought for him a year ago at Morin's store, but never gave him. Had she really been so hard-hearted that she would withhold even that small gesture of kindness?

"*Mon fils*, I have something for you," Magdelaine said. She hurried into the house and came back out a moment later with the saw. "I thought it looked like a good one."

Jean-Henri laid down his shovel and took the gift, turning it over in his hand, and looked at her in surprise. "Yes, it is. Thank you, Mother."

He took the saw inside and then joined her back at the beds. Taking up his shovel again, he worked quietly, almost as if he were afraid to disturb the rare moment of tranquillity between them. He absorbed himself in his work with a creased brow, and Magdelaine caught herself staring at him. She needed to do more than just give him the saw, she knew. She needed to tell him how she wanted things between them to change.

Finding a way to begin was difficult, but she knew she had to try. "Raphael has grown so much since he came to us. It is hard to believe."

Jean-Henri nodded, then paused in his shoveling. He jabbed the tip of the shovel into the pile of dirt and leaned on the handle. "Promise me, Mother, that you won't tell anyone else about where Raph came from. It is very important to Esmee, and to me. Sometimes I can almost make myself forget that he is not really ours. I feel about him just as I imagine I'd feel if he *were* my own son, and I would like to amend my memory to make it so."

He could be so serious. She wondered if he had gotten that from her. "Of course, *mon fils*. That is the way it should be."

He picked up the shovel again. "There is no good reason for him to know the truth, to go through life wondering about that piece of himself that is missing. Nothing good comes from that."

"I agree. A boy should not have questions about his parents."

Magdelaine glanced behind them, out at the water. The lake was always there. It had been there in every day of her girlhood, in every dream on every night that she slept. It was in her body, in her son's body, in the body of her grandson, who wasn't hers but *was*, in all the ways that mattered. If she could change the past she wouldn't change a thing except that: Let Raph have come through Esmee's body into the world. Let her son have seen the woman he loves heavy with his own child. But they had what they had and it could not be changed. They were taking this gift as it was, picking up the broken thing and loving its brokenness. Esmee and Jean-Henri were audacious to think they could rewrite that child's destiny, but they would probably succeed.

She left the shovel sticking up in the ground and touched Jean-Henri's elbow to get his attention. She tried to find the words. "You know, your father was twenty-five years old when he died."

He squinted against the sun and gave her a weary smile. "And look at all he had accomplished. I know. I should have known why you gave me that gift, so that you could broach the subject of my work once again."

Magdelaine shook her head. "No. You misunderstand me. What I mean is that he was very young. He was full of ambition and ideas, and who knows what he might have become had he not been killed on that riverbank. But he *was* killed, and now all we have left is what he intended to do. And it doesn't count for much. You, on the other hand, are in the midst of *doing* something, and it is a wonderful thing. It would be wrong to compare a man who is living an honorable life to one who might have, if he had been given the chance."

Jean-Henri stared at her as if he were sure he had misunderstood what sounded like an admission of fault. When she didn't say anything to correct that impression, he shook his head, then grinned and wiped his brow. "Yes, it *would* be wrong," he said, "were one to make that comparison. You are full of surprises today, Mother."

Magdelaine nodded. "Well, I have been wrong to do that. But what I am trying to say is that I will not do it anymore. I give you my word." It wasn't just pride that had made it so hard for Magdelaine to admit how she had failed him. She had been afraid to let her son know how much she loved him, as if denying it could protect her from the pain of losing him. But he wasn't lost. Susannah had helped her see that. None of them knew what the future held, but, today, he was here. And Magdelaine wasn't going to waste any more time.

"Mother, I know good and well that that is the closest thing to an apology I'll get from you. And I'll take it."

She pulled his face to hers and kissed his whiskered jaw. "I am proud of you, Jean."

He tried to hide his surprise at all of it—the admission, the affection—and kissed her back. "Thank you, Mother. Now we had better get back to work before we lose the light."

They worked until dusk, then went inside and ate a supper of cold meat and bread and cheese, washed down with wine. Magdelaine helped Esmee bathe Raph and put him to bed. Everyone settled in the sitting room for a while, and then one by one they began to yawn and find their way to bed. After everyone had gone upstairs and the house was quiet, Magdelaine took the lamp from the kitchen and slipped out the back door.

She crossed the yard in the darkness, the lamp casting an

orange glow on her feet. It was strangely warm for a spring night. The air was still, with no breeze to speak of, as if it were waiting to see what Magdelaine might say when she came to stand in front of Josette's grave. She had passed by this stone countless times over the years, and it never failed to remind her of what she had lost, what she needed to keep working to make right. But she had never let herself stop and speak aloud to her little sister, in case it might bring some unearned comfort. Magdelaine had long felt that she could say nothing to Josette until she could say that she had done something to amend the past. Tonight, finally, felt different.

Magdelaine cleared her throat. She set the lamp on top of the stone and fumbled with her hands. "Therese and I have done something, *petit lapin*, that I think you would like. Helped someone."

And in a halting hoarse whisper, Magdelaine told Josette about Susannah Dove. She explained about the other women—the other Misses Dove—whom they tried and failed to help, then how they arranged for Susannah to come to the island and what she went through in trying to get there. She explained that she had believed Susannah was saved when in fact her husband still searched for her, still intended to hurt her, but that he never had a chance of succeeding because Magdelaine had made her mind up that he would not, whatever the cost to herself. As she explained about Therese her throat ached and she felt her nose begin to run. They had wanted to bring this woman from Buffalo some kind of peace, but it was she who had fixed so many broken things. Susannah had helped Magdelaine see her son as he really was, helped her gain a daughter-in-law and a grandson. And Susannah had brought Therese back to her. The big unwieldy ship of her life had changed course, was headed for warmer waters, because Susannah had come to Mackinac.

"I think," Magdelaine said, wiping her nose on the sleeve of her dress, "that we will all be together now, really together, for as long as we can. Susannah is going to stay. Therese too. What do you think about that?"

Josette kept quiet on the matter, as she had on so many things. Magdelaine turned and walked past the graves and through the gate at the back of her yard. In their pen, the dogs slept in a warm heap on the straw, their chests rising and falling in unison. The big showy waste of a house stood in front of her, and beneath its roof was every person she loved in this world, sleeping and safe, at least for today. The past, all its wrongs, all its dead, were sleeping too now, finally, and it was quiet as she went in to lie down and rest.

Chapter Twenty-five

Susannah rose early the next morning. Downstairs she pulled on her cloak and boots, then stepped out onto the porch and felt the warm breeze off the lake. In the garden, she inhaled the scent of the overturned earth and admired the neat black rows in the beds, each mound holding the promise of a sprout. She felt pleased as she allowed herself to imagine the future. At the end of the summer they could have a real harvest celebration, with bouquets of wildflowers on the tables. Everyone on the island would be welcome.

Her gaze flicked to a cluster of birds chattering in the apple tree. She couldn't help looking for the dove each time she stepped outside the house. But the tree held only a flock of finches. Neither she nor Magdelaine had seen the dove again since the day they had released it. After spending so much time in a cage, it seemed unlikely that the creature even knew *how* to be free, but perhaps it had remembered some way, or learned the lessons anew.

She brushed off her hands and went inside for a drink of water. Magdelaine was sitting at the table with her sister. They seemed deep in conversation, and Susannah hated to interrupt them. But Magdelaine called her over.

"Jean-Henri went to Morin's this morning for rice and came back with this too."

Magdelaine handed an envelope to Susannah. The stationery was by now very familiar, and she opened it and unfolded the paper. As she had expected, it was another drawing of the potted peas, this time grown tall, the sprouts climbing a stake in the center of the pot. Susannah set the drawing on the table and crossed the kitchen to the cistern, dipping a cup into the water and drinking it down.

"He had better get them in the ground, don't you think?" Magdelaine said. "Now that spring is here?"

"Who is *he*?" Therese asked.

Susannah set her cup down and glanced at Therese, then stepped back over to the table and picked up the drawing again. She folded it back into the envelope and slipped it into her pocket. He would be teaching class now, finishing up the morning in just a few minutes. Perhaps she would call on him there later on, offer her help with the planting. "He is a friend," Susannah told Therese.

Magdelaine raised her eyebrows slightly but didn't say a word.

She left the sisters and went back outside. There was a boat in the port and a few families strolled down the gangway, the women carrying parasols, their children clutching their skirts. Each season seemed to bring more visitors to the island on pleasure trips. They wanted to see the way the natives lived, they said. They asked questions about the lives of the fur traders, a profession that was fast becoming a relic of history. A recent edition of a Detroit newspaper had informed them that the Michigan Territory was to become a state and there would be money from the federal government for roads and bridges and railroads. The island would not be a remote hideaway for much longer.

At the other end of the lane, the mission school stood already weatherworn after just a few winters. Ani, who had spent the morning making his rounds to all his friends, waited at the school's side entrance for the lessons to end. Just then, the door sprang open and a dozen children spilled out into the meadow. Susannah watched as three girls passed Ani, patting the top of his head. A boy of eight or nine years approached then and crouched down in front of the dog, giving him a vigorous rub on his neck and belly. Ani nuzzled him back. Susannah wondered if this was the younger, faster friend Magdelaine had joked was wooing Ani away from her. The boy clutched his book beneath his elbow and set off running across the meadow, the dog leaping joyfully through the mud ahead of him. Every few seconds, Ani glanced back to be sure his friend was still there. The sun was very bright and it shone on the boy's face. He closed his eyes but kept on running, despite his momentary blindness, because the world was a marvelous place and it had never hurt him, though it would someday. But not today.

She crossed through the garden, then out the front gate to the other side of the lane and down to the sand to walk along the water line. The waves arching in on the beach whispered something rhythmic that sounded like, "I am.

I am." Whatever that meant now, whatever it would mean, Susannah had the time, the space, to discover it. The thrust of the bracing wind off the lake pressed against her so fully that she had to lean into it to stay upright. She was heavier than the air all around her, heavier by far, but for a moment she felt a sensation like the force of lift beneath her arms, the impulse to rise.

ACKNOWLEDGMENTS

My gratitude goes to Claire Zion, Marly Rusoff, Julie Mosow, Michael Radulescu, Suzy Takacs, Brian Wilson, the marvelous team at Berkley, and the irreplaceable independent booksellers who have supported my novels. Thank you to Keith Widder at Michigan State University for correspondence on the history of Mackinac; to Ann McNees for her knowledge of heirloom jewelry and what sometimes happened to it in hard times; and to Stu Gruber, who not only understands but has shot every type of pistol and long gun made from King George III's time to the present, including Magdelaine's musket. Thank you to Jack and Kathy Mills for housing me on a research trip; to Brad and Susan Light for sharing their beautiful books about the island; to Amelia Musser and the Grand Hotel; to Ste. Anne Catholic Church on Mackinac Island; and to the Merchant's House Museum in New York City.

I could not have written this novel without the support of my family, especially my parents, Steve and Mary O'Connor; friends and fellow writers Eleanor Brown, Susan Gregg Gilmore, Kelly Harms, Lori Nelson Spielman, Renee Rosen, Tasha Alexander, Ellen F. Brown, Erin Blakemore, Claire Zulkey, Molly Backes, Kate Harding, Wendy McClure, Amy Sue Nathan, and Nicholas Demmy; and Christine Clark, whose love and attention to my daughter has made it possible for me to continue writing. Finally, thank you to my patient, brilliant, steadfast husband, Bob, who taught me about the physics of flight.

AUTHOR'S NOTE

The story and characters in *The Island of Doves* are fictional creations, but three of the characters were inspired in small ways by real historical figures.

Magdelaine LaFramboise (1780–1846) was one of the most successful fur traders, man or woman, in the Northwest Territory. Known as the "First Lady of Mackinac Island," LaFramboise took over her husband's business after he was murdered, and, after many successful years, sold it to John Jacob Astor's American Fur Company. This sale made her the wealthiest woman in Michigan at the time, a remarkable feat for a person of mixed Odawa and French-Canadian heritage. She is buried in the cemetery at Ste. Anne Catholic Church on Mackinac Island and her stately house now operates as the Harbor View Inn.

Benjamin Rathbun (1790-1873) was a prolific builder during the city of Buffalo's early years. In 1835 alone, he built ninety-nine buildings and employed nearly one-third of the city's workers. The following year he lost his fortune when he was convicted of forgery and sentenced to prison (after a brief stay in the jail he himself had constructed). Rathbun's fall may have been a catalyst for the Panic of 1837, America's worst financial crisis prior to the Great Depression.

Anna Brownell Jameson (1794-1860) was a British essayist and critic. Trapped in an unhappy marriage to a judge stationed in Toronto, Jameson used her wealth to arrange a long tour throughout the Great Lakes region, including to Mackinac Island, in 1837. Her travel journals detail the many intersecting cultures on the island and, in particular, record the stories and songs of its native people.

The following sources helped bring the settings and characters of this novel to life: *Magdelaine LaFramboise: The First Lady of Mackinac Island* by Keith Widder; *Reminiscences of Early Days on Mackinac Island* by Elizabeth Thérèse Baird; *The Living Great Lakes* by Jerry Dennis; "The Wildest and Tenderest Piece of Beauty That I Have Yet Seen on God's Earth" by Larry Massie in *Michigan History*; *Winter Studies and Summer Rambles in Canada* by Anna Brownell Jameson; *Wau-Bun* by Juliette Kinzie; *Summer on the Lakes, in 1843* by Margaret Fuller; *Mackinac Island* by Thomas and Pamela Piljac; *The Sound the Stars Make Rushing Through the Sky: The Writings of Jane Johnston Schoolcraft* by Robert Dale Parker; *The Literary Voyager* by Henry Schoolcraft; *West to Far Michigan* by Kenneth Lewis; *The Murder of Helen Jewett* by Patricia Cline Cowen; Chuck LaChiusa's "History of Buffalo"; "The Canal Boat" by Nathaniel Hawthorne; *From Lumber Hookers to The Hooligan Fleet* by the Chicago Maritime Society; *What Hath God Wrought* by Daniel

Walker Howe; *The Americans* by J. C. Furnas; *Our Own Snug Fireside* by Jane Nylander; *American Household Botany* by Judith Sumner; *An Introduction to Botany* by Priscilla Wakefield; *American Gardens of the Nineteenth Century* by Ann Leighton; and *The Douay Catechism of 1649.*

The Island of Doves

DISCUSSION QUESTIONS

1. In *The Island of Doves,* the past is anything but dead and gone. What aspects of their respective pasts are both Magdelaine and Susannah wrestling with? What events haunt them? How do they ultimately confront these ghosts and make peace with them?

2. How does Susannah's steamship journey and her sojourn in Detroit change her?

3. The island is a special place with a long history, but it is always in a state of change. How is the island changing as the story unfolds? What stays the same?

4. What kind of a mother is Magdelaine? In what ways is this role difficult for her? What kinds of things has she been able to teach her son that a more conventional mother could not?

5. What role does Susannah's love of botany play in her past, present, and future?

6. What is the source of Edward's anger and greed? Why can't he just accept that Susannah does not want to be with him, and let her go?

7. How are the lives of women in this novel (Magdelaine, Susannah, Therese, Esmee, and Noelle) controlled or limited

by men in positions of power? In what ways do they circumvent these limitations and claim autonomy or power of their own?

8. Why does Magdelaine teach the catechism to the young women, even though she isn't particularly devout in a conventional sense?

9. Why does Jean-Henri capture the dove for his mother? Why does she keep it even though she cannot stand to look at it?

10. Why is Jean-Henri so upset when Magdelaine steps in to shoot the rabid dog?

11. Why doesn't Magdelaine ever allow herself the comfort of lingering at Josette's grave and talking to her sister's spirit? What does that say about the kind of person Magdelaine is?

12. The obituary Edward submitted to the Buffalo newspaper after Susannah's "death" was probably formal and brief. What kinds of facts might Susannah have liked to see it include that Edward didn't know or value about her? If you were to write your own obituary now, today, what would you include? Do you think the people in your life who know you best see these aspects of your life in the same way you do?

13. What do you think about the Reveillon? Do you take the French outlook—revering life's blessings through joyful celebration—or embrace the Presbyterian missionary's view that people should show gratitude through sacrifice and self-denial? How are these competing philosophies still alive in our culture today?

14. Would you rather travel by steamship, dogsled, or canoe?

15. What does Alfred have to offer Susannah that Edward did not? What do you imagine might happen between them after the story ends?

16. What will life in the house be like now that Therese and Magdelaine are reunited at last?

NOTES

NOTES

NOTES